THE YELLOWSTONE CAMPAIGN

THE YELLOWSTONE CAMPAIGN

JUBILEE WALKER SERIES **BOOK 2**

TIM PIPER

Book design by The Book Designers
https://bookdesigners.com/

Maps by Jon Teegarden Artwork
https://www.facebook.com/jonteegardenartwork

ISBN 979-8-9884186-3-4 (hardback)
ISBN 979-8-9884186-4-1 (paperback)
ISBN 979-8-9884186-5-8 (ebook)

Library of Congress Number: 2023915186

Published by
Sunshine Parade Publishing
1907 Sinclair Ct.
Bloomington, IL 61704
https://www.sunshineparadepublishing.com

To Lee Piper

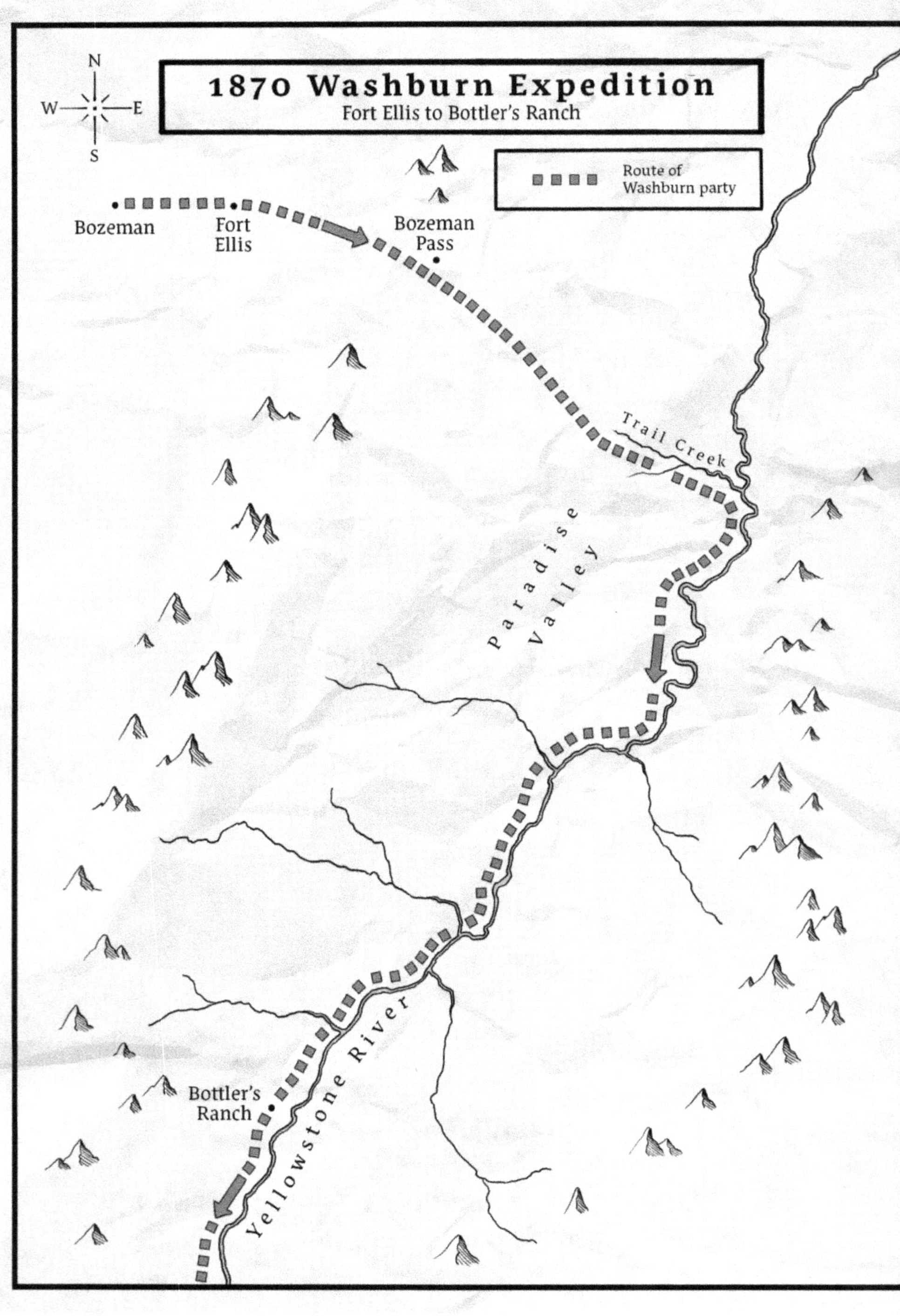

N
W E
S
1870 Washburn Expedition
Fort Ellis to Bottler's Ranch
Route of
Washburn party
Bozeman
Fort Ellis
Bozeman Pass
Trail Creek
Paradise Valley
Bottler's Ranch
Yellowstone River

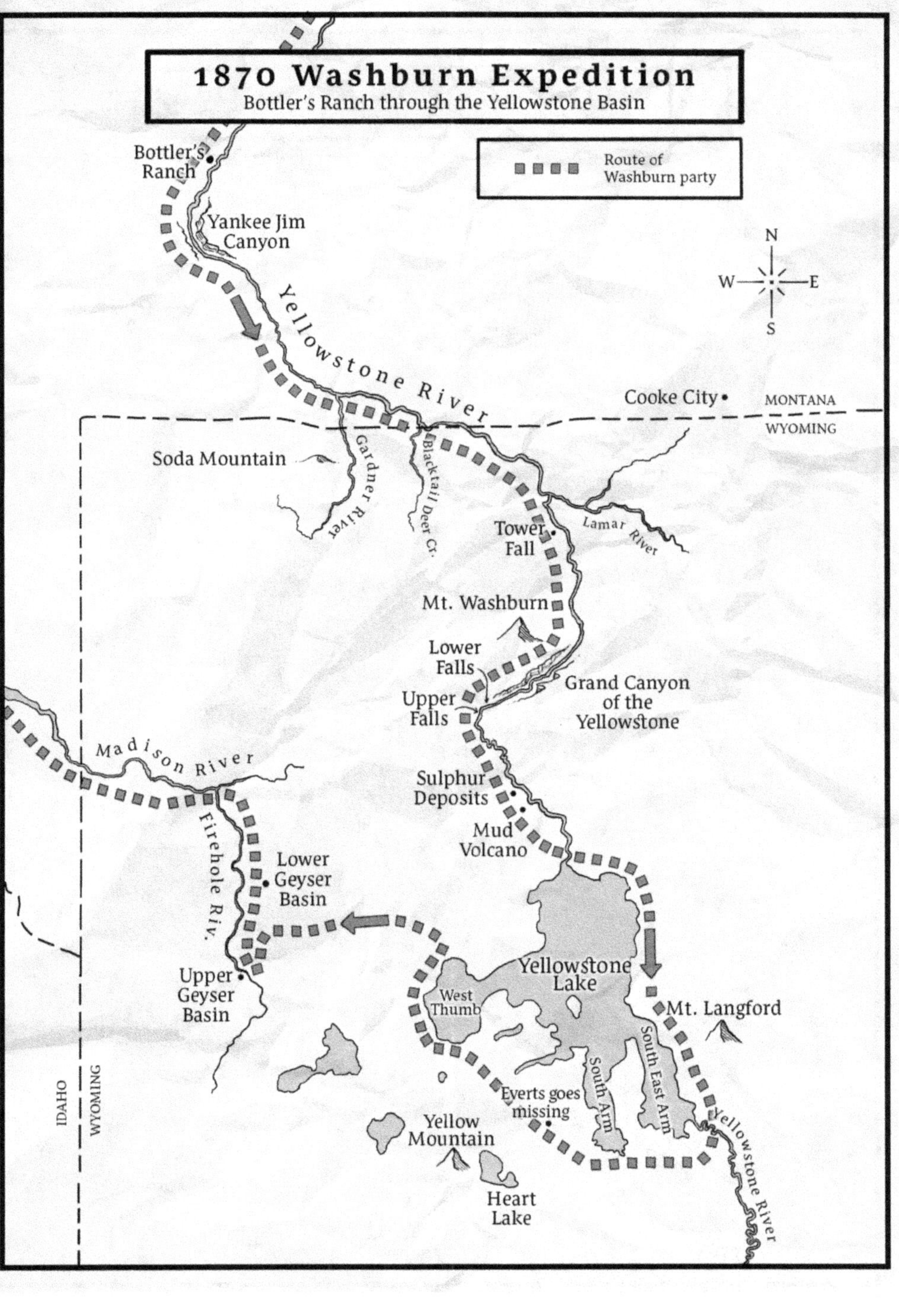

1870 Washburn Expedition
Bottler's Ranch through the Yellowstone Basin
Route of Washburn party
N
W E
S
Bottler's Ranch
Yankee Jim Canyon
Yellowstone River
Cooke City
MONTANA
WYOMING
Soda Mountain
Gardner River
Blacktail Deer Cr.
Lamar River
Tower Fall
Mt. Washburn
Lower Falls
Upper Falls
Grand Canyon of the Yellowstone
Madison River
Sulphur Deposits
Mud Volcano
Firehole Riv.
Lower Geyser Basin
Upper Geyser Basin
West Thumb
Yellowstone Lake
Mt. Langford
South Arm
South East Arm
Yellowstone River
IDAHO
WYOMING
Everts goes missing
Yellow Mountain
Heart Lake

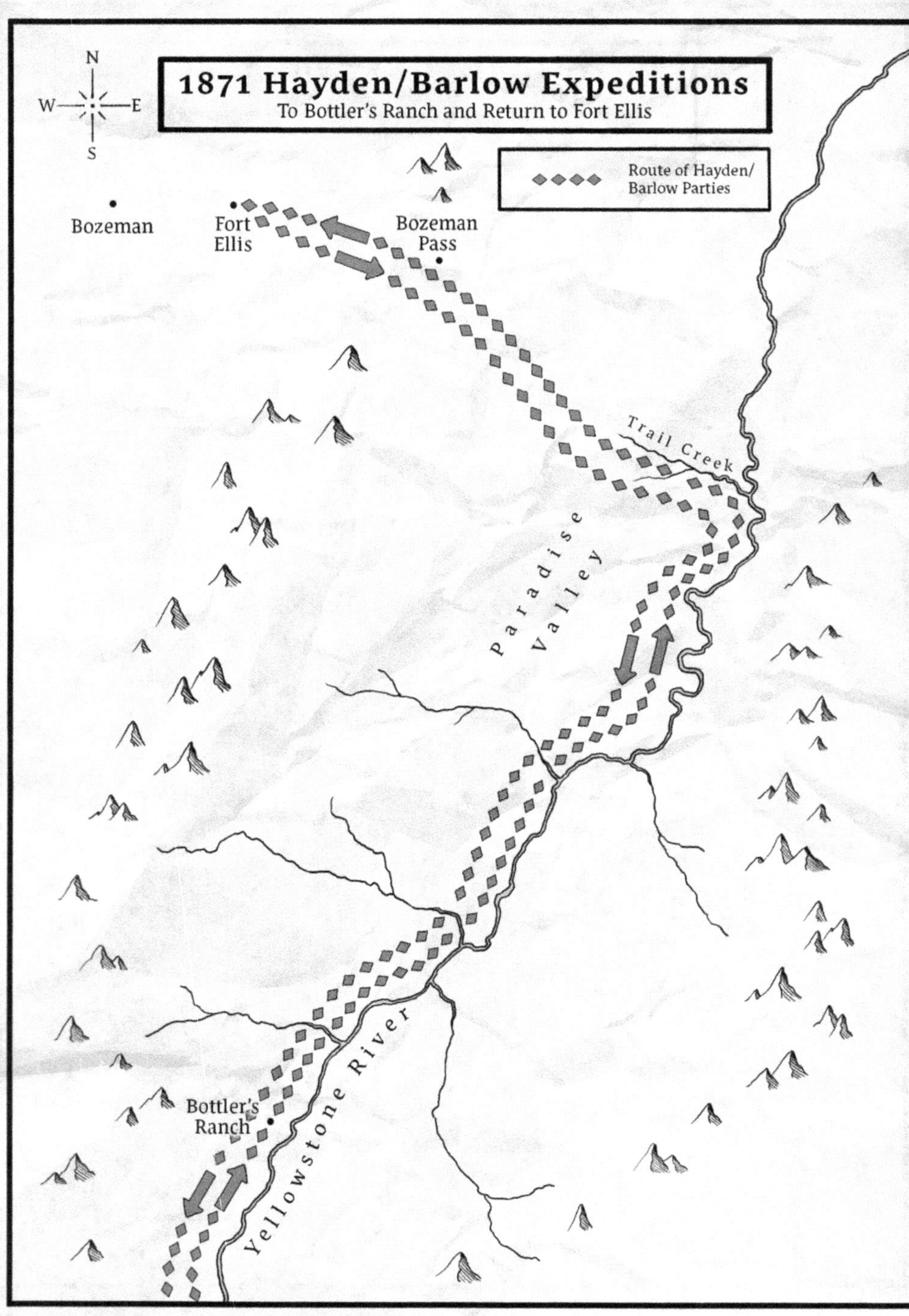

N
W E
S
1871 Hayden/Barlow Expeditions
To Bottler's Ranch and Return to Fort Ellis
Route of Hayden/
Barlow Parties
Bozeman
Fort Ellis
Bozeman Pass
Trail Creek
Paradise Valley
Bottler's Ranch
Yellowstone River

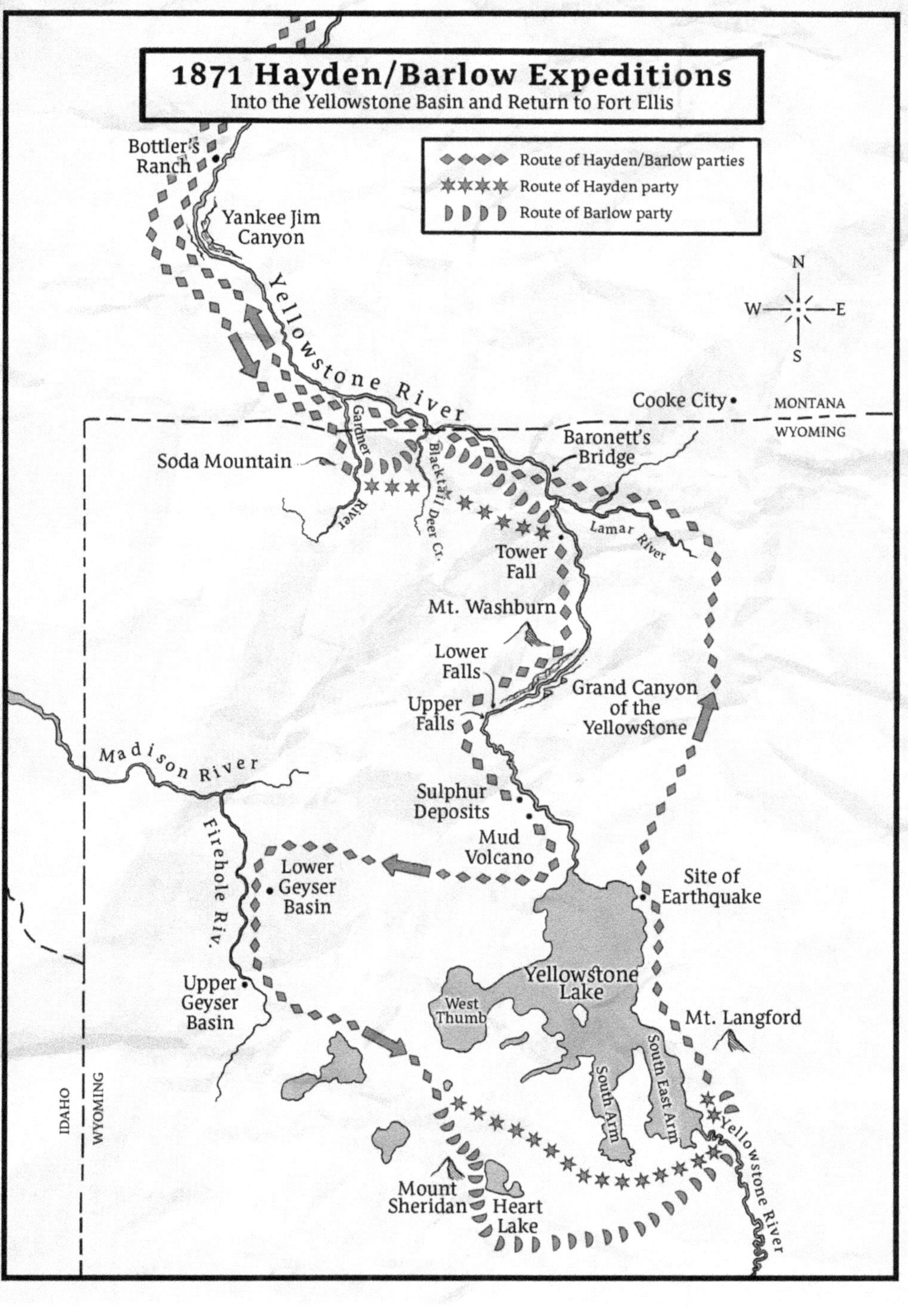

1871 Hayden/Barlow Expeditions
Into the Yellowstone Basin and Return to Fort Ellis
Route of Hayden/Barlow parties
Route of Hayden party
Route of Barlow party
Bottler's Ranch
Yankee Jim Canyon
Yellowstone River
N
W E
S
Cooke City
MONTANA
WYOMING
Baronett's Bridge
Soda Mountain
Gardner River
Blacktail Deer Cr.
Lamar River
Tower Fall
Mt. Washburn
Lower Falls
Upper Falls
Grand Canyon of the Yellowstone
Madison River
Sulphur Deposits
Mud Volcano
Firehole Riv.
Lower Geyser Basin
Site of Earthquake
Upper Geyser Basin
Yellowstone Lake
West Thumb
Mt. Langford
South Arm
South East Arm
Yellowstone River
IDAHO
WYOMING
Mount Sheridan
Heart Lake

CHAPTER 1

Jubilee Walker admired the way the spring sunshine created blue highlights in Nelly Boswell's black hair as they sat together on a blanket on the riverbank. He also admired the fried chicken she had packed in the picnic basket, which was crispy on the outside and juicy on the inside.

"This chicken is good," Jubil said, wiping his chin with a napkin. It was one of the many things he was looking forward to getting used to after they were married.

Nelly's blue eyes gleamed. "My mother made it," she said. "If you're counting on me to be the cook she is, you'd better rethink your marriage proposal."

Jubil laughed. "I don't care if we live on biscuits and beans. I'm just grateful you finally agreed to marry me."

"You became a much better marriage prospect, after you agreed not to risk your life every time you go outdoors," she said with a grin.

Jubil had spent three summers following Major John Wesley Powell on his Colorado exploring expeditions. This past summer he had accompanied Powell on the first expedition to navigate the Colorado River through the Grand Canyon. The experience had been so harrowing that Jubil swore he would not take such extreme risks in the future. He would focus on his adventure travel business, which, for his customers' sake, had to be relatively safe. It was only then that Nelly finally consented to marry him.

"I want to get on with it, before you change your mind," he said.

Nelly's bright smile faded.

"I'm sorry. I shouldn't tease about that," he said. Nelly had resisted marriage not only because of Jubil's dangerous lifestyle but also because of the impact it would have on her desire to have a career. She was currently enrolled at Illinois State Normal University, a teacher's college, but marriage would make her ineligible for that profession.

"You've applied to Wesleyan, then?" Jubil asked. Illinois Wesleyan University would admit female students for the first time this fall.

She shrugged. "Not yet. How many other women do you think will be there? I'm not anxious to be among the first few," she said glumly. "Besides, Wesleyan's stronger in the sciences than the arts. But I guess it's my only other option. They must have some writing classes there, don't you think?"

He nodded.

"It's Papa too," she continued. "In his opinion, since I can't be a teacher, I should give up university and start a family. I've told him I intend to find another career, but he disapproves. Here I am again, back at the beginning of the same battle with him."

Jubil could sympathize with Nelly's longing for freedom. He had dreamed of a life free from the routine of the family farm, but he had felt held there by his duty to his mother. He was now free to pursue whatever he wanted in life, but Nelly did not have that luxury. He had no ready advice. If his mother were still alive and disapproved of his plans, he was not sure how he would handle it. But it was difficult for him to understand Mr. Boswell's position. What was the harm in Nelly getting a college degree if she wanted one?

"Whatever you decide," he said, reaching for her hand, "I'm

with you."

"I know," she said, kissing him on the cheek. She smiled faintly. "Mama has been so excited about the wedding. She's done most of the planning."

He had noticed this and been somewhat uneasy about it, but had resisted the impulse to mention it.

They had chosen July 29—which was now only two months away—so that the weather would be warm on their honeymoon and fit for exploring the Colorado landscape Jubil had been so eager to share with Nelly.

"I'll wear the red satin she made for me last Christmas. Your mother's ruby ring will look beautiful with it. She'd be so proud of you, and I'll be proud to wear it. I know you reserved the church for the service, but if it's all right with you, Mama would like to have the reception at our house. She'll serve coffee and tea and have pieces of cake boxed up for the guests to take home."

"That sounds wonderful," Jubil said.

"But I'm still nervous. I'll be happier, I think, when all the fuss is over and we're setting out on our trip."

Jubil loved the way her eyes lit up when she mentioned the trip. He had arranged first-class accommodations on the new Denver Pacific Railway. They would take the train from Bloomington to Denver and spend August sightseeing in Colorado. This new rail line would open up the front range of the Rocky Mountains, just as the Union Pacific to Cheyenne had opened up the whole West to travelers.

"It will be such an adventure," Nelly said. She had never been so far from Bloomington, or been away so long. "I'm very much looking forward to seeing the mountains."

"And I'm looking forward to showing them to you," Jubil said. "Oh, Mr. Weed stopped by the store to tell me he knows of three houses we might want to rent until we make up our minds about something more permanent. If we decide on one soon, we could have it ready to move in before we leave on our honeymoon."

Nelly reached for his hand. "So many big changes to adjust to. I'm nervous."

"We'll be fine," Jubil said patting her hand.

"I'm sure we will be," she said with a weak smile. "It's getting late. We should go home. Do you want to look at the rental houses tomorrow?"

"I'd better not make any plans just yet," Jubil said. "Luke and I got a telegram this morning from his father saying he's coming for a visit. He'll be arriving tomorrow morning."

Since December 1867, for more than two years now, Jubil and his business partner, Luke Warner, had been proprietors of Warner and Walker Outfitters in Bloomington. Luke had grown up in Council Bluffs, where he and his father, Abe Warner, ran Warner and Company Outfitters. The Warners had changed Jubil's life when they had invested in the outfitting business in Bloomington.

"What a pleasant surprise," Nelly said. "It will be wonderful to see him again. Will Mrs. Warner be with him?"

"I don't think so," Jubil said. "His telegram didn't mention her."

"Too bad," Nelly said, as she began to pack away the remains of their picnic.

Jubil and Luke occasionally visited Council Bluffs to visit Luke's parents, but the Warners rarely visited Bloomington. The next morning, as Jubil sat down with Luke and his father in the dining room of the Ashley House hotel, he smiled noticing how Luke was a younger version of his father: They each had a full head of wavy hair, but Mr. Warner's was gray at the temples while Luke's was still dark. In spite of their matching potbellies, they were both in hearty condition.

Jubil's smile faded as he noticed that Mr. Warner was uncharacteristically somber. He found himself worrying as the waiter served them coffee.

"I got a letter from General Philip Sheridan," Mr. Warner began. "He has decided to establish his offices in Chicago rather than in Council Bluffs. Nevertheless, he thinks we are well situated to continue providing support for his western theater. He invited me to meet with him in Chicago, which I did yesterday."

General Philip Sheridan had replaced their friend General William T. Sherman as the commander of the Military Division of the Missouri. General Sherman had been a steady client of Warner and Company Outfitters during his command of all US Army forces in the western plains. Jubil's first trip out West had been riding with a Warner and Company wagon train from Council Bluffs to Fort McPherson, Nebraska, escorted by General Sherman and his soldiers. Sherman had been promoted to Commanding General of the Army earlier that year, when Grant had been elected President.

Mr. Warner sipped his coffee, and then looked pointedly at Jubil over the tops of his small square glasses, which he wore on the tip of his nose.

"General Sheridan made it plain that he would like to meet our partner, the celebrated explorer Jubilee Walker. He's familiar with the Powell expeditions, and he said General Sherman speaks highly of you."

Jubil sat up a bit straighter. "That is very flattering."

"But Sheridan's not asking you to pay him a social call," Mr. Warner said. "He has a proposition for you. An expedition is being organized to explore the Yellowstone River in Wyoming Territory, and he wonders if you would be interested in going along."

Jubil felt a jolt of excitement that caught him by surprise.

He thought his passion for adventure had been placated by his near-death experiences in the Grand Canyon last year, but his reaction to the news of a Yellowstone River expedition was instinctive. It would be a major adventure and a rare opportunity. He knew very little about the Yellowstone River beyond a comment Major Powell had once made about its unusual geography.

"When is the expedition planned?" Jubil asked.

"This summer," Mr. Warner replied.

Jubil's excitement was now competing with a sense of dread.

"Nelly and I have our wedding plans set," Jubil said. "Luke and I have been advertising our first guided adventure tour for this fall. We have paying customers already lined up . . ."

"Yes," Mr. Warner said sympathetically, "I knew this would be a dilemma. That's why I came to tell you in person."

Jubil nodded and studied the depths of his coffee cup. How was it that Mr. Warner had known that Jubil would find the prospect of such an adventure irresistible when this fact seemed hidden from Jubil himself? When the waiter came to their table to take their order, Jubil was too uneasy to eat.

"I should go see General Sheridan," Jubil said, "out of courtesy, if for no other reason. I'm going to go pack a bag and catch the train. I'll try to see him tomorrow." He turned to Luke. "If you see Nelly, just tell her I went to Chicago on business. Let me do my own explaining. After I talk to Sheridan, I may not even be interested in going."

"All right," Luke assured him. Mr. Warner nodded.

Packing a few things required only a stop at the tent Jubil kept behind the store, where he often camped rather than make the hour ride north to his farm. By early evening he was stepping out of Chicago's Great Central Station onto South Water Street, which followed the south bank of the Chicago River. To the east, the river flowed into Lake Michigan. As he walked toward Dearborn Street and the Tremont House, where he would stay for the night, he watched the boat traffic on the river and at the piers. Across the river was the workshop of Thomas Bagley, the craftsman who had built Major Powell's boats for the Grand Canyon expedition. The expedition had set out with four boats and concluded with two, one left behind in case the men who abandoned the expedition reconsidered, and the other smashed against the rocks, nearly drowning Jubil in the aftermath.

In the morning, he walked to the Court House Square. There, in the offices of the US Army Military Division of the Missouri he found a soldier at the desk in the waiting room. He introduced himself and asked if General Sheridan was available. While the soldier went into General Sheridan's office, Jubil reflected on his promise to Nelly. He would express his appreciation for the invitation to join the expedition, ask him to convey his thanks to General Sherman for the recommendation, and offer to assist with the outfitting, but he would not make any commitments that would upset his and Nelly's wedding plans.

The soldier came out of Sheridan's office and held the door open for Jubil. "Sir?" he said. "You can go right in."

Jubil entered a large open room with a long conference table along the left wall, a map table in the center of the room, and two small desks near the right wall. Straight ahead of him, General Sheridan was stepping out from behind a large desk that sat in front of a row of windows.

The general was modest in stature, perhaps six inches shorter than Jubil, who stood a lanky six feet. Major Powell was also of modest stature, but had an imposing presence that General Sheridan did not generate. Sheridan was imperfectly proportioned, with a long body, long arms, short legs, almost no neck, and a well-padded frame.

"Mr. Walker, how do you do?" Sheridan said, offering a

handshake and a half-smile.

"I'm well, thank you, General," replied Jubil, noting the strength of Sheridan's grip. He was softer-looking than Sherman or Powell, but based on his Civil War and Indian Wars reputation, Jubil knew he was anything but soft. "It's an honor to meet you, sir. Abe Warner suggested I make your acquaintance."

The general nodded and motioned toward the conference table, where he and Jubil sat down opposite one another.

"Warner is a good man," General Sheridan said. "He runs a solid business the army counts on for support. I understand you and his son have a store in Bloomington?"

"Yes sir," Jubil replied, "Mr. Warner's store handles mostly institutional business, our store in Bloomington is geared to business, leisure, and adventure travelers. Originally Warner supplied overland travelers trekking westward, but the railroad reduced that market, so we've diversified."

"It's good to see ambitious young men rewarded for their efforts. I understand you've also done some expedition travel. Did you come to your acquaintance with Major Powell through the outfitting business?"

Jubil explained his family's long relationship with Powell, how he met the Warners because of him and eventually came to join Powell's expeditions.

"Boldness and persistence," nodded Sheridan, "good signs of character. I imagine Mr. Warner told you that I am making plans for an expedition to explore the Yellowstone River area?"

"Yes sir."

"Are you familiar with the area?" Sheridan asked.

"I recall Major Powell once saying the geology sounded fascinating—if the tales about it were true."

Sheridan nodded. "This expedition's mission is, essentially, to determine whether those tales are true."

"Do you believe they are?"

"Some of them," Sheridan said, with a grin. "The frontiersman

Jim Bridger would have us believe we will find a petrified forest with petrified birds, singing petrified songs. And encounter places where you can shout 'time to wake up' before going to sleep, and the echo will return from the mountains six hours later to wake you." Sheridan paused good-humoredly for effect. "However, he also made reports of volcanic features that sound credible. Let me show you something," he said and then rose and led Jubil to the map table in the center of the room.

A large map of North America covered the surface. Beneath the table was a cabinet holding rolled-up maps. Sheridan pulled out four of them and unrolled two, weighting down their corners. Jubil thought fleetingly of the Grand Canyon expedition and how Oramel Howland, the mapmaker, had more than once lost his maps to the raging Colorado River. Oramel had not survived that trip.

Jubil leaned in to have a closer look at Sheridan's maps. One was primitively drawn, the other a more artful effort.

"The crudely drawn map was done by Jim Bridger," Sheridan explained, "renowned trapper, scout, explorer, businessman, and teller of tall tales. The other was done by a Jesuit priest named Father De Smet, in collaboration with Bridger. These maps were drawn in the early 1850s. As you can see, they illustrate and label a number of exotic geologic features."

Jubil studied the maps closely. Bridger's map was a simple set of scrawled lines, squiggles, and circles representing rivers, mountains, and lakes, some of which were labeled, some not. The Yellowstone River was a line that came in from the northwest, turned east for bit, and then went south, where it passed through an oval labeled Grand Canyon waterfalls, then on south into a circle representing a large lake. To the west of the lake, lines for the Firehole River and its confluence with the Madison were shown, and nearby was an area he had labeled *Volcanic Region*. In the northwest corner was a circle labeled *Sulphur Mountain*.

Father De Smet had redrawn Bridger's doodles and scrawls into a clearer, better proportioned picture of the area, with features artfully drawn and legibly labeled: rivers, lakes, mountains, and hot springs. The area in the west which Bridger had labeled *Volcanic Region,* was now labeled *Great Volcanic Region.* In the territory above and below the central geography, De Smet had added the names of two Indian tribes in large block letters: Blackfeet in the northwest, Crow in the southeast.

"Why was a priest drawing maps for Jim Bridger?" asked Jubil.

"He drew it for the army, not for Bridger," explained Sheridan. "In the mid-1840s Bridger established a trading post along the new Oregon Trail. He called it Fort Bridger. It was south of the Yellowstone area and east of the Great Salt Lake. By the early 1850s the Oregon Trail had split the buffalo plains in two, and the Indians were growing aggressive in retaliation. The government offered peace terms that allowed them to build forts along the trail, and in return the Indians would receive reserved lands. Father De Smet was a missionary administering salvation to the tribes around Fort Bridger, so the Army called on him to draw maps of these new Indian territories. While he was at it, he drew this one of the Yellowstone area."

"Then why is there still a question about what's actually there?" Jubil asked.

"De Smet never actually saw it," Sheridan answered. "He was just illustrating what Bridger told him was there. Now this one," Sheridan said, unrolling another map, "is of more recent origin."

The artistic quality of this map was far superior to that of the other two, but compared to De Smet's, it had fewer features. This map more clearly showed an irregular oval of mountains surrounding a massive, nearly empty basin, but inside the basin the only features labeled were the Yellowstone River, a peak called Sulfur Mountain, the Falls of the Yellowstone, and Yellowstone Lake. The volcanic areas and hot springs shown on the De Smet version were missing.

"In 1860," General Sheridan continued, "a military expedition was sent to explore the Yellowstone region led by Captain William Raynolds and the famous surveyor Ferdinand Hayden, with Bridger along as a guide. Raynolds set out late in the fall with a team of scientists and a military escort. They attempted to enter from the east, south, and west, but an early winter and deep snows blocked the routes through the mountains. Even though they did not enter the central area, they got views by climbing the peaks. They produced this map but omitted the geologic features Bridger claimed were there. Raynolds confirmed plumes of steam or smoke could be seen arising from the central basin, but he omitted them from the map because they were too far away to accurately observe."

While Jubil looked at this map, Sheridan unrolled another.

"Now this one," he said, "is the most recent yet. Last year, a group of local men organized an expedition, but fears over Indian problems reduced their ranks to only three—Folsom, Cook, and Peterson. They decided to try following the Yellowstone River in from the north and made their way down through Paradise Valley into the Yellowstone Basin, circumnavigated Yellowstone Lake, traveled through the volcanic region along the Firehole River, and then followed the Madison River out the west side of the basin."

This map was also professionally drawn, but the center was filled in with the features Sheridan had just described, and it also showed the route the Folsom–Cook–Peterson expedition had followed.

"The tales about the area are true then?" Jubil asked.

"Let's just say they are not entirely fictitious," Sheridan offered. "Folsom and friends were exploring, but they were not interested in personal notoriety, or inviting derision as propagators of tall tales. They did not publish their findings, but reported them to General Henry Washburn, surveyor general of the Montana Territory at the Government Land Office, who had his men update the maps."

Jubil studied this map closely and was drawn into imagining what it would be like to be in the midst of this landscape. He wondered whether the ring of mountains around the whole area would be obvious from within the basin, how the location labeled *Grand Canyon* on this map would compare to the Grand Canyon he was so intimately familiar with, how big the lake would look from its shoreline, and most of all, what exactly was in the area labeled *Volcanic Region*. He felt strongly drawn to see these sights for himself.

"If you're relatively sure what is in the area," Jubil asked, "what is the objective in sending another expedition?"

"This is the last *officially* uncharted part of our country," Sheridan replied. "The government is anxious to ensure safe settlement and learn what resources we have at our disposal. Commerce is anxious to put those resources to use. In order to do that, a scientific survey of the region must be conducted. A formal survey will define features and boundaries, evaluate habitability, and identify available resources, but a survey will be expensive. We need to make a preliminary reconnaissance to gather evidence to support Congressional funding of a survey. General Henry Washburn is organizing a mission comprised of prominent members of the community to serve as reliable witnesses to the extraordinary nature of the area. I am to provide them with a military escort."

Jubil felt a burst of pride at Sheridan's characterization of the membership of the upcoming expedition—prominent members of the community to serve as reliable witnesses. Being invited to join such a group was no small matter. He reminded himself to not let his pride overshadow his desire to marry Nelly and start their life together.

Glancing again at De Smet's map, Jubil's attention was drawn to the large block letters designating Crow territory to the southeast, Blackfeet to the northwest. "What's the Indian situation in the area?" Jubil asked.

Sheridan looked up from the maps for a moment. "I would like to say there is no unrest, but that is not the case. Most of the tribes, the Sioux, Shoshone, Flatheads, Crow, are reasonably calm, but the Piegan Blackfeet are stirring up trouble, particularly Mountain Chief and his band."

"They can't be convinced to maintain the peace?" Jubil asked.

"It seems not. I've seen no lasting acceptance of their defeat. Every pact, treaty, and land grant prove an exercise in futility." Sheridan said with an air of impatience. "But their distrust of anyone not of their own tribe is not the white man's doing. They've warred amongst themselves forever. It is their nature to roam the land, taking what they need to survive and killing anyone in their way. Ferocity constitutes an honorable life for them. We will never change them, and they will never live peacefully beside us. Our only option is to eliminate them." He shrugged, his mouth a hard line.

Two things ran through Jubil's mind during Sheridan's speech. First, from what he had read in magazines and newspapers, and gathered from conversations with Major Powell, the description of the Indian's nature—roaming the land taking what they need to survive and killing anyone in their way—seemed to apply equally well to the white people who were streaming into the Indians' native territories. In fact, the whites took more than they needed to survive—they took everything. Second, the Indians were not alone in failing to honor agreements. The US government had done more than its share of violating pacts and treaties.

However, he knew Sheridan was not alone in his thinking.

General Sherman had once made much the same point—the Indian's pride might lead them to extinction. But Sherman at least seemed to feel some remorse about it, where Sheridan seemed to have none. His coldness rubbed Jubil the wrong way.

"So that is your plan?" Jubil asked flatly. "Eliminate them?"

General Sheridan's eyes were hard as stone. "If the lives and property of the citizens of Montana can best be protected by striking, I will strike hard. This past January I ordered Colonel Baker at Fort Ellis to descend on Mountain Chief's winter camp and eliminate not only the people, but also the infrastructure of their survival: the teepees, clothing and blankets, food stores, horses. We will have an end to the unrest in this area."

Jubil could understand the use of violence to prevent or punish attacks made against innocent settlers and travelers, but the policy of eradication General Sheridan described was too much. If Sheridan was successful, the new maps drawn after his expedition to Yellowstone would make no mention of Indians. He would literally have wiped them from the map.

Sheridan watched Jubil's face, and Jubil clenched his jaw to keep from expressing his opinion of the general's policy.

"You understand this is not out of prejudice against the Indian race," Sheridan said. "We did the same thing to our own race during the Civil War. General Sherman left nothing behind but scorched earth on his march from Atlanta to Savannah. This is simply the nature of war."

Jubil knew there was some truth in this statement, but he did not believe Sherman's policy targeted the helpless as directly as Sheridan's. Helpless victims must have been caught up in Sherman's march to the sea, but there was a moral difference between the Civil War and what was happening in the Indian wars.

"It seems to me," Jubil said, "the Confederacy brought on their fate through their willingness to break up the union over enslaving another people. The Indians are just trying to protect what was theirs in the first place."

Sheridan leaned in and looked sternly at Jubil. "General Sherman told me you were something of an Indian sympathizer."

"General Sherman said that?"

"Not in those words," Sheridan admitted. "He told me you got attached to his Pawnee scout, White Man's Dog."

When Jubil had trekked across the plains with General Sherman, he and a few soldiers and the Indian scout, whose real name was White Dog, were out hunting when they were attacked by Chief Tall Bull's Dog Soldiers. White Dog was shot in the leg, and Jubil left his cover to help him to safety. In return the Indian gave Jubil his medicine bag, a powerful gesture of gratitude and friendship. When Jubil returned to Council Bluffs, White Dog insisted on accompanying him back across the plains to Fort Kearney, and, along the way, they became friends.

"His name is Taaka Asakis—White Dog," Jubil reported.

Sheridan shrugged, and Jubil could see that he cared nothing about the Indian's name.

He took a moment to calm his irritation before continuing. "I'll admit to some sympathy for the Indian's situation—for the peaceable ones at any rate. Which I suspect there would be more of, if we'd leave them alone."

Sheridan raised his eyebrows in surprise. "I have neither the time nor inclination," he said coldly, "to debate the plight of the Indian with you, Mr. Walker."

Jubil nodded, thinking his audience with Sheridan had come to an end. "I suppose I shouldn't take up any more of your time then, General," said Jubil.

Sheridan nodded, and as Jubil turned to leave the room, he asked flatly, "Will you be going on the Yellowstone expedition, then?"

Jubil turned back toward him. "I figured you had decided

against me," he replied.

"Your thoughts about Indians are of no consequence to me," Sheridan said. "I don't demand you fight them, unless it is necessary to protect the expedition."

"You needn't concern yourself there. I'll not be party to killing defenseless people, but if we face an attack, I'll do my part," Jubil vowed.

Sheridan nodded. "General Sherman said you handled yourself well."

Jubil ignored the compliment. "Will you lead the expedition yourself?"

"No," Sheridan replied. "The time commitment is more than I can afford. General Washburn is retired now. He will lead the expedition. If his reconnaissance finds justification, an official geological survey will be mounted next summer. I will travel to Fort Ellis soon, where I'll meet with General Washburn. If there has been no further trouble with the Piegan, I'll authorize the expedition. Washburn will select the expedition party, and Colonel Baker will assign an escort. I'll see you are included if you are interested. As an explorer and outfitter, you would be helpful with logistics—the moving and making of camp, handling of the animals, hunting and fishing. Some in the party do not have a great deal of wilderness experience."

"Thank you, sir," Jubil said. He could not bring himself to decline but cautioned himself not to accept. "I have some personal business to attend to this summer, and I will have to determine what flexibility I have with those plans. I will let you know my answer as soon as possible. I appreciate the invitation and the opportunity."

"I expect the expedition to set out in August," said Sheridan. "We'll set the exact date when I meet with General Washburn and Colonel Baker. I'll telegraph you for your confirmation." He shook Jubil's hand. "I'm pleased to have made your acquaintance, Mr. Walker."

Jubil walked back to Great Central Station to wait for the train to Bloomington. He had not warmed to General Sheridan as he had to General Sherman, who for all his prowess in war seemed sincerely sympathetic toward people and interested in them. Sherman had listened to Jubil's story about wanting to join Major Powell's expedition, and he had tried to help. Every evening, Sherman had spent time with his enlisted men, and he handled his relationship with White Dog respectfully. Jubil could not picture General Sheridan doing any of these things—but then Major Powell had not been perfect in that regard either.

On the train ride home, he thought about how he might explain his feelings to Nelly when he didn't yet fully understand them himself. Returning from his trip with Major Powell through the Grand Canyon, sunburned and nearly starved, he had been convinced that the desire for that kind of excitement had left him for good. But now he couldn't stop thinking about General Washburn's map of the Yellowstone area and what a thrilling experience it would be to explore it. He was also being invited to be in the company of some very interesting and accomplished men. If he earned their respect, it might be good for his outfitting business with the Warners. And he had to admit, it would be good for his reputation as an explorer. On his other expeditions he had been defined by his relationship to Major Powell, but on this one he would have to prove himself on his own. That challenge was appealing.

But he was concerned Nelly would be upset, as she had been years ago when he first announced he was going West. He had to assure her that this situation was different. Yes, he had made a commitment to avoid life-threatening expeditions, but after talking with General Sheridan, Jubil did not see this trip as especially hazardous. General Washburn would simply follow a trail blazed by others the previous year and do so under the protection of a military escort. Jubil brushed aside what Sheridan had said about the Indians in the area.

Jubil wanted to marry Nelly and dreaded threatening their plans, but he could not deny how drawn he was to this opportunity. What would happen if he refused it? What would happen if he accepted it? Before he made a decision, he had to talk to Nelly, with the hope that she would be amenable to changing the plans for their honeymoon. He hoped that once she had a chance to consider the situation, she might come to see it his way.

CHAPTER 2

Jubil arrived back in Bloomington early in the evening and set off for the store to drop off his bag. From there, he would go by the Boswells' to talk with Nelly. The store was closed for the day, so he let himself in through the back door with his key. Voices from upstairs told him that Mr. Warner was still visiting with Luke in his apartment.

The store was a two-story box, forty-five feet on each side, with four tall windows along each side on both floors. The building had previously been a residence, and when they'd remodeled it, they'd had the front quarter of the upper level made into an apartment for Luke.

Jubil joined the other two men upstairs and explained how he had left matters with Sheridan.

"The expedition is supposed to start in August," Jubil said, "so the honeymoon trip would have to be cut short. And I'm not sure when I'd be back, so our September guided tour to Colorado would have to be pushed off to next year."

"We can manage the situation with the adventure tour," Luke said. "We'll return their fees and put them on a waiting list. The Yellowstone expedition might even strengthen their desire to travel with you in the future—maybe even go there themselves one day."

"How do you feel about the expedition?" Mr. Warner asked

Jubil. "Did it sound appealing?"

Jubil knew what Mr. Warner was asking—*What is in your heart?*

"I'm surprised to say that it did, very much so. I feel drawn in, much more than I expected to. And going would be good for our business," Jubil said. "It's an honor to be invited. It would feel almost disrespectful to turn down the opportunity. But Nelly and I have plans for our trip, and I won't decide to change those plans without talking to her first."

"I don't know," Luke said, looking at him skeptically. "Don't you think she'll be upset that you didn't just dismiss the idea out of hand?"

"Her thinking has surprised me before," Jubil said. "When Powell denied me a spot on his first expedition, I got it into my head to go West alone. At first, she was upset I would even consider doing that, but after she calmed down, she was the one who came up with the idea for me to impress Powell by intercepting him along the way. If I hadn't listened to her, I never would have met you. She has a different outlook about my expeditions now too, thanks to your mother."

"My mother?" Luke said.

"Your mother told her a story about Nantucket," Jubil said, "about how the wives of sailors often lived independently of their husbands and how that helped them accept their husbands' dangerous way of life. She suggested Nelly view our relationship in the same light. Nelly loves the idea, and it's helped her feel less afraid of what might happen to me."

"Hmm. Well, I may be wrong," Luke said, without conviction.

Mr. Warner said, "I encourage you to think long and hard about your decision regarding the expedition. Very few people have opportunities such as this, and regret can be poisonous— it can kill your future happiness. You have to be honest with yourself before you can be truly honest with Nelly. Whatever decision you make, Luke and I will support you."

"Thank you," Jubil said.

He was grateful for Mr. Warner, who had become not only his business partner but his surrogate father. Jubil had been ten years old when his father was killed in an accident on the farm. His uncle Pete, his father's brother, took over the farm briefly, before enlisting in the Union Army. He had been killed at Shiloh. When Jubil's mother had died when he was seventeen, he was left an orphan. He felt lucky to have met the Warners and gained their support and friendship.

Jubil left Luke's apartment and walked to the Boswells' house, where he found Nelly sitting on the porch swing, reading a book.

"Good evening, Miss Boswell," Jubil said.

"Good evening, Mr. Walker," Nelly replied, closing her book.

She wore a white cotton dress with a blue pattern that matched her eyes, and a light blue shawl wrapped around her shoulders. Her long black hair hung down her back. She was wearing the beaded Indian moccasins Jubil had brought to her from his Longs Peak expedition. She looked so beautiful, and Jubil's conscience whispered to him, *It's not too late. . . . Just forget about the expedition.*

"Are you going to stand in the yard fidgeting with your hat or join me up here?" She patted the spot next to her on the swing.

"Sorry—I was admiring you," he said truthfully.

"You needn't do that from so far away," she said with a smile.

Jubil took the steps up to the porch with the dread of a man going to the gallows. He had a few more seconds in which to save himself, but an unstoppable force seemed to be pushing him forward. He sat down on the swing beside her.

"Did I interrupt your studies?" he asked, pointing to the book.

"Not really," she said. "I was just reviewing for my ancient history examination tomorrow morning. It's my last requirement for this term. I can recite the dates of nearly every war ever waged, if you are interested." She paused for effect. "No? Me either. Some of the things they have us learn I can't imagine ever finding useful."

"I agree," Jubil said. "It seems stories about the people who waged the wars and why they waged them would be the valuable lessons."

"I think it's just an easy way to see if students are paying attention," she said.

Jubil leaned against the porch railing facing Nelly. He stared at the hat in his hands.

"You're still fidgeting with your hat," she said. "What's wrong?"

"Mr. Warner came to visit Luke and me yesterday," he began.

"Yes, they stopped by last night to say hello," Nelly said. "They said you were called to Chicago to see a client. Did it go well?"

"Yes," Jubil paused to give himself one last chance to back out. "General Philip Sheridan is planning on sending an exploring expedition to the Yellowstone River area in Wyoming . . . And he invited me to go along."

Nelly sat up straighter in the swing. "It's a good thing you're no longer interested in such dangerous pastimes," she said.

"Well, this one doesn't sound so dangerous," Jubil said lightly, and not entirely honestly. "It's been pretty well mapped already, but it still remains an officially uncharted wilderness. This is just a reconnaissance mission to see if a scientific survey is warranted."

"The phrases 'doesn't sound so dangerous' and 'uncharted wilderness,' seem contradictory in my opinion," she said, looking at him skeptically. "What about Indians?"

"Sheridan believes it is safe," Jubil said, "but he's sending escort troops just in case."

"'Just in case'—another weakly reassuring phrase," she said.

"I guess I should have said 'relatively safe,'" Jubil admitted. "Certainly it sounds safer than my other expeditions."

"Hmmph," Nelly said in disgust. "You promised me you were finished with this kind of thing, that you would limit your adventures to guiding tours."

"I did say that...I'll admit it." Jubil sighed. "The strong appeal of this invitation is as much a surprise to me as it is to you. I can't necessarily explain it, but when General Sheridan described it to me, that feeling came back again, that I want to go along very badly. General Sherman himself recommended me. The expedition will be another historic effort, and it will be good for our business with the Warners. Mr. Warner gave me some good advice: that I have to be totally honest with myself before I can be honest with you. If I'm honest about it—I'd like to go on the expedition."

Nelly stared at Jubil. "Did you tell General Sheridan yes?"

"No, I said I would reply as soon as possible."

"When does the expedition party leave?" she asked.

"In August," he said.

"I see," she said. "So—our honeymoon trip?"

"We'd have to cut it short by a week or so," he admitted with trepidation.

Nelly narrowed her eyes at him. "You want to give up part of our honeymoon?"

"I'm not anxious to, but . . ."

"But what?" she challenged.

"I think I would regret it if I didn't accept this opportunity," Jubil said.

"*You* would regret it," Nelly replied with deepening anger. "I hear a lot of consideration for you—your reputation—your business. I don't hear much consideration for me—my feelings—my interests. You expect me to happily cut our honeymoon short?"

"No—not—not happily," he stammered, "but I thought perhaps . . . I don't know. I had to tell you the truth and get your reaction."

"My reaction?" she seethed. "I'll give you my reaction." She sprang up from the swing, lifted her textbook above her head, and slammed it to the porch floor with a bang. *That* is my reaction!"

Jubil's jaw dropped with shock. He had never seen her so angry.

Mrs. Boswell stepped out of the house onto the porch. "What on earth was that noise?" she asked, looking around. "Are you shouting, Nelly? Oh, hello, Jubil. I didn't know you were here."

"He was just leaving, Mama. I dropped my book," Nelly said, stooping to retrieve it. She glared at Jubil. "You can tell General Sheridan whatever you want. I'll make my decision about the wedding and forward it to you in due course." She turned sharply and strode past her mother into the house, leaving him stunned. Had she really said "the wedding," rather than "the honeymoon"?

Mrs. Boswell looked at Jubil, shock evident on her face.

"I—" Jubil started.

Mrs. Boswell held her palm out to silence him and followed her daughter into the house.

Jubil stood frozen on the porch. Nelly had been upset with him before, but nothing like this. He pondered what to do next—knock on the door and ask for an audience or just wait here for her to come back out. He decided, for the time being, not to risk irritating her further, if that was possible, and walked back to Warner and Walker Outfitters, where he went straight to the stable behind the store. His horse shook her head and whinnied.

"Hello, Star," he said, rubbing her nose while he patted her neck. Star was a sleek eighteen-year-old chestnut mare with a flaxen mane. She had been his father's horse and had belonged to Jubil since his father's death. "I've made a mess of things with Nelly," he said to Star as he saddled her. "Let's go up to the farm. Maybe I can think better up there."

Even though Jubil had never had an interest in farming, he loved his family's farm. More so because it was his family's property than because it was a farm. He enjoyed the feeling of closeness to them he had when he was there, particularly his uncle Pete. After his mother's death, Jubil had taken up residence in Pete's cabin rather than live among the ghosts in the farmhouse, and then those ghosts had been forced to relocate when the farmhouse and barn had burned down.

As Star took them out of town, the light of the moon cast a pall over the prairie. Jubil let Star walk as he pondered. Why hadn't he listened to Luke in the first place? *Don't you think she will be upset that you didn't just dismiss the invitation out of hand?* The question haunted him for the hour-long ride to the farm and late into the night. His truthful answer did not make him especially proud. He wanted to go on this expedition—he would forever regret it if he did not. And he wanted to marry Nelly and begin their life together. It wasn't the first time he had struggled with these two opposing impulses. He would try again to talk to Nelly, and find some way to make things right with her.

After a fitful night's sleep, he idled about the farm until midafternoon, then decided further pondering was accomplishing nothing and rode back to town. When he entered the store, Luke was there with Nelly's seventeen-year-old twin brothers, Ike and Eli Boswell, who had worked at the store without pay for two years as restitution for accidentally burning down Jubil's farmhouse and barn. Even after paying Jubil back, they had stayed on at the store, and for the past year they had been paid employees. Ike, usually quiet and shy, was

Luke's apprentice for all things involving finance and retail operation, while Eli, the more gregarious and boisterous of the two, unloaded and stocked merchandise and aspired to help Jubil with travel tours.

The twins stared at him coldly, with eyes the same crystal blue as Nelly's.

"Hello," Jubil said and waited in vain for a response. "Is something wrong?"

"The boys were just telling me about your talk with Nelly last night," Luke replied.

"Yes," Jubil said, "it went very badly."

"You can say that again," Eli offered unhelpfully.

Ike and Eli looked at one another for a long moment, having one of their silent conversations that Jubil found slightly eerie.

"After you left, she got in a big argument about the wedding with Papa, and she cried and cried. That made Mama upset, and she cried too," Ike said. "Then Papa said a man has got to do what he's got to do, but they weren't having that, and Papa went off in a huff. Eli went to talk to him, and I went to talk to Mama and Nelly, but they told the both of us to mind our own business. You've caused a fine mess at our house, Jubil."

Ike was usually reserved with his opinions, so his lecture hit Jubil like a punch in the stomach.

"I see it like Papa does, Jubil," Eli said. "You weren't the cause of the problem—Nelly is. You have to do this expedition; it's who you are. If Nelly can't see that, then you two shouldn't be married. Besides, she always has to have her way. You didn't ask to cancel the whole honeymoon, just end it early. You should do what you need to do, and just let her stew about it."

Jubil largely ignored Eli's opinions. He had always chafed under his older sister's dominance. "I've got to go talk to her," Jubil said. "We've got to get this straightened out."

"You'll have to wait a while," Ike said. "Eli and I just put her and Mama on the train to Council Bluffs. They're going out to stay with Luke's folks for a few days. Nelly wanted to talk to Mrs. Warner."

Over the next few days, Jubil searched for a reason Nelly would have gone off to visit Mrs. Warner, and the best one he could come up with was that Mrs. Warner had helped Nelly accept Jubil's dangerous adventuring before and might be able to help her adjust to this newest set of plans.

He was unloading a shipment of merchandise when Luke joined him in the stockroom. "There's a telegram for you," Luke said, handing him an envelope.

Jubil opened it hoping it was from Nelly, but it was from General Sheridan.

"The expedition will be underway in August. I'm to confirm my intentions to Colonel Baker by July 1. So I still have a week to reply," Jubil said. "I have to talk to Nelly."

That afternoon Ike and Eli went to meet Nelly and their mother at the depot, and returned to the store with a message for Jubil: he was welcome to visit Nelly at home. He left the store and walked to the Boswells', nervous but hopeful, and knocked on the door.

"Hello," Nelly said, giving him a weak smile. There was no anger in her eyes, a good sign. "Come in."

They went into the parlor. With none of the rest of the family milling about, it felt oddly funereal. Nelly sat on the sofa with her hands in her lap. He sat in one of the reading chairs facing her, his hat on his knee.

"I'm sorry to have upset you so," he began.

"I'm sorry I was so petulant," she said. "That was childish of me."

"I thought you'd be disappointed," he said, "but never that you'd be this upset."

"It's not entirely because of your expedition. You just invoked a landslide of feelings," she said. "Feelings I was already struggling with."

"Did Mrs. Warner help you come to terms with your feelings?" Jubil asked hopefully.

Nelly took a deep breath and exhaled. "When I talked to her last fall, she not only told me about the wives of the Nantucket seamen but about one of her sisters, Maria Mitchell, who is a prize-winning astronomer."

"All right," Jubil said, not understanding what the story had to do with their wedding.

"She also became the first American female professional in her field when she was appointed to the faculty of Vassar College in New York," Nelly continued. "Mrs. Warner told me her sister's story as an example of the way the Nantucket community encouraged not only strong, independent women but also intellectual equality between women and men. She told me as way of saying that marriage does not suit all women, that unmarried women are capable of finding their own respected place in society. Miss Mitchell is unmarried by choice."

Jubil's stomach knotted. He did not like the sound of this. He did not begrudge women finding their own respected place in society independent of marriage, but he did not want Nelly to be one of them. He thought better of saying this aloud.

"While you go on your exploring expedition," Nelly said, "I'm going on my own adventure. Mrs. Warner's sister, Miss Mitchell, has invited me to spend the summer with her in Poughkeepsie. Mrs. Warner will come to Bloomington to help me prepare for the trip, then travel with me to her sister's, and spend the summer there with us."

Jubil's eyes grew wide with surprise. These weren't ideas Nelly was pondering; these were plans that had already been made.

"What about the wedding?" Jubil said.

Nelly looked him square in the eye. "I'm not sure either of us is really ready to be married, Jubil." The weak smile returned to her face, and Jubil's heart sank. "You should go on your expedition, and we'll decide when you get back. I realize what an honor it is for you to be invited by General Sheridan and vouched for by General Sherman. I've never wanted to stand in your way. I'm proud of the person you are. I admire you."

"I appreciate that," Jubil said, "but I don't want to lose you over this."

"The truth is," Nelly said, sounding resigned, "this has made me realize . . . I actually want to be more like you."

"That sounds flattering, but I'm not so sure."

"One thing I've always admired about you," she said, "is that once you know what you want, you follow after it, no matter what. I want to have that courage myself."

"But I want to marry you," he said. "I want us to start a life together."

"And I do love you," she replied. "I'm not going to Poughkeepsie to get away from you, Jubil," Nelly said gently. "I'm leaving to learn more about what I want out of life myself."

A sense of despair came over Jubil like a wave. This was a far worse outcome than he had ever imagined. What would his life be like without Nelly? Incomplete, empty, lonely. He struggled to keep his wits about him and avoid looking into the abyss. A familiar feeling while mountain climbing, but one he never imagined he would feel with Nelly.

"You'll come back to Bloomington?" he asked when he was able to speak again.

"Yes," she said. "Classes begin at Wesleyan in September."

"When are you leaving?" Jubil asked.

"Miss Mitchell is expecting me July first," she replied. "When do you leave?"

"Late July."

Nelly looked toward the parlor door to make sure no one was listening to their conversation, and then she leaned toward Jubil conspiratorially. "My father is only allowing me to go because he believes Miss Mitchell is a spinster in need of assistance," she whispered. "It feels strange not to correct his assumptions about her, but my mother and Mrs. Warner and I all wonder if he would let me go if he understood what Miss Mitchell has made of her life without a husband. I'm certain he would see her as a bad influence."

Jubil nodded as she spoke, although he was only half listening. He left the Boswells' parlor shortly after that, feeling stunned and heartsick. But over the next two weeks, before Nelly left, he forced himself to adjust to the new situation. He wouldn't squander the time he had left with her, although his strongest impulse was to ride Star out to the farm and hole up in Uncle Pete's cabin. For the first time in his life, he felt an uncomfortable awkwardness in Nelly's company. Their conversations were overly polite and careful. What he found most heartbreaking was the physical distance that had opened between them. Ever since they had announced their engagement, they had felt freer to hold hands, hug, and kiss, but he resisted those impulses now, wondering if they were still engaged at all. He wanted to clarify the subject with Nelly, but he was afraid of what her answer might be.

When it was time for Nelly and Mrs. Warner to leave, Jubil followed the carriage to the train depot on Star. As Nelly prepared to board the train to Poughkeepsie, Jubil stood to the side, watching these people who were the closest thing he had to family. Mrs. Boswell, Ike, and Nelly cried openly. Eli claimed his watering eyes were from the coal smoke rolling out of the locomotive. Jubil was surprised to see Mr. Boswell wipe his eyes too, as he offered his daughter nuggets of advice for being helpful to her hostess around the house.

Mrs. Warner had taken command of getting their baggage

loaded, and her firm direction to the train conductor and baggage steward left Jubil with no doubt that Nelly was in safe hands for the trip. Nelly hugged her family before boarding and came to Jubil last.

"Will you write?" he asked, hoping their estrangement didn't extend to being entirely incommunicado for the summer.

"Yes," she promised. "I'll write before you leave. Be careful."

As she and Mrs. Warner boarded the train, Jubil and Luke stood with the Boswells, and they all waved as the train left the station.

Missing Nelly was nothing new to him. Over the past three summers he had spent most of his nights staring at the stars and dreaming of her. He would imagine being in her easy company, admiring her beauty, marveling at her sharp mind, laughing at her quick wit. But there was never a doubt she would be there when he finally made it home. Their separation this time was different. The longings were the same, but now there was no certainty that they would be fulfilled. His feelings were similar to those he'd experienced when his mother died—he had longed to see her, hear her laughter, share an embrace—but he knew it would never happen again. He told himself he was exaggerating his worries, and he recognized the irony of being the one left alone at home to wonder if Nelly would ever return.

In another ironic twist, while Jubil's love life seemed to be at risk of collapsing, Luke, for the first time, seemed to be developing one. Jubil had watched with amusement each time Miss Bateman, a seamstress in her mother's dress shop, had visited the store. Jubil and Nelly had gone to school with her, though she was slightly older. She was quiet, pleasant, and studious—maybe a good match for Luke. He had blushed when she'd said hello, and he had stammered out a response when she praised him for his taste and commitment to quality merchandise, but he regained his composure enough to accept her invitation to join her and her parents at church on Sunday. When Luke had invited Miss Bateman to attend a Saturday matinee at Schroeder's Opera House, and her parents had allowed it, Jubil was faced with the prospect of a new trajectory for Luke's future. He was happy for Luke and told him so. Luke insisted he and Miss Bateman were only friends, but Jubil could see that he was downplaying his happiness to spare Jubil's feelings. Watching Luke fall in love, Jubil remembered the euphoric days and weeks after Nelly had accepted his marriage proposal with a sick sense of regret.

It was a relief for Jubil to return his focus exclusively to business. First, the maiden Warner and Walker Outfitters adventure travel tour had to be rescheduled. Throughout late June and early July, Jubil went to visit each of the tour clients, to return their fee and explain the delay. They were all pleased to meet him and anxious to hear more about the Yellowstone campaign, perhaps even go there themselves one day. He hoped their interest would hold.

The postponement had also been a disappointment for Eli Boswell. He had been looking forward to going along as Jubil's assistant, and hoped to someday lead tours himself. Jubil assured Eli that the adventure tours would happen, but he was growing concerned that Eli might eventually lose patience and set out on his own, just as Jubil had.

Jubil's knowledge of geology was limited to what he could recall from school—how forces from the center of the earth push outward to create earthquakes, volcanos, mountains, islands, the whole surface of the planet. He would have liked to call on Major Powell to gain some insight into what he might expect or what he should be on the lookout for in the Yellowstone area, but Powell was away on another expedition to the Grand

Canyon. If his friend Lew Keplinger had still attended Illinois Wesleyan, Jubil could have gotten access to reference material on Yellowstone at the campus library. But Lew—with whom Jubil had climbed Longs Peak during Powell's second expedition—had passed the bar exam in December and moved to Humbolt, Kansas, to practice law. Other than Luke and Nelly, Lew was Jubil's closest friend. With Nelly and Lew both gone and Luke newly in love, Jubil had moments of feeling very much alone that summer.

On July 13, he celebrated his twenty-first birthday and was pleasantly surprised to receive a letter from Nelly. She wrote, *"Today I saw the Atlantic ocean—a vast, roaring, heaving, blue-green expanse teeming beneath its surface with exotic creatures, some of which we enjoyed in a delightfully hearty seafood chowder—a creamy broth filled with potatoes, carrots, whitefish, and tender clams."*

Jubil smiled while reading the letter, pleased Nelly was happy, but his generous feelings were shadowed by his selfish concern that she could be so happy apart from him. He recognized he was being petty and thought of the days out West when he hadn't thought of her at all. He reminded himself repeatedly that she was just as entitled to her adventure as he was to his. He just hoped her adventure would come to a natural end and she would come home.

That afternoon, Jubil received a telegram at the store.

Congratulations on Yellowstone expedition.
Interested in hearing your observations.
Please come to Washington upon your return.
General Sherman

Jubil did not know quite what to make of General Sherman's message. Of course, Sherman knew he was going to Yellowstone, but why he was interested enough in Jubil's observations to request his presence in Washington was beyond him, but he was pleased. He liked Sherman, and it would be exciting to visit Washington DC.

Luke invited him to have dinner that evening at the Ashley House to celebrate his birthday, and Jubil suggested he ask Miss Bateman to join them. Luke said he would feel awkward without Nelly there to make it a balanced foursome, and Jubil felt the pain of Nelly's absence even more acutely. Over dinner, he and Luke puzzled over the possibilities behind Sherman's invitation, but Jubil found none of their theories convincing.

The last two weeks of July dragged along until, finally, it was time to make his way to Fort Ellis, in the Montana Territory, the starting point for the expedition.

CHAPTER 3

Jubil studied the items spread out on the bed to make sure nothing was missing. Then he began loading them into his empty trapper's pack. He put a flint, a box of matches, and a tin pot in the bottom of the pack—in case he was caught out on his own and needed to make fire and boil water. Atop those he put a union suit, some fur-lined gloves, and heavy woolen clothes. He slid in a few sheets of paper, a pen, and a bottle of ink wrapped in a rag. He would write to Nelly once he reached Fort Ellis. He looked at the stack of dime novels on the shelf above the bed but decided against bringing any. Ironically, the novels that had once fueled his imagination for adventure lost their luster after he experienced the real thing.

On top of everything else he packed his Colt pistol and holster, and one hundred rounds of ammunition each for his pistol and rifle. In spite of Nelly's concerns about the dangers of an uncharted wilderness, he had no specific fears about this expedition. The greatest concern was not knowing what new dangers might lie ahead. But that was the appeal in exploring—braving his way through his fears to see what lay ahead. His greatest fear on the brink of this expedition was that he had done long-term damage to his relationship with Nelly because he had been so driven to go.

The last thing into the pack was White Dog's buckskin

medicine bag, which he would carry until he reached his destination and then wear. He didn't know if the remaining collection of spirit tokens—two animal teeth, a claw, a little rock, a few small bones, and an arrowhead—actually had the power to protect his life, but he was still proud to wear it. He closed the flap over the storage pouch and tied it down.

He cleaned and loaded his Henry rifle, and the pungent smell of gun oil and the smooth feel of the burnished wood of the stock brought back fond memories of hunting trips with his uncle Pete. Jubil wondered, not for the first time, if he had inherited Pete's need for adventure and if he too was destined to be driven by his own interests more than the needs of others. He would have said he lived more for others—the Warners, the Boswells, Major Powell, his family's legacy—yet here he was about to leave them all behind for the sake of another expedition. Uncle Pete had never had a wife or a family. Would that be Jubil's destiny too?

As he loaded the rifle and lashed it to his pack frame and sharpened his hunting knife and holstered it in a leather sheath that slid onto his belt, he remembered the advice he had gotten from Orville Gulley, who had returned to Bloomington after a stint out West: *keep your wits about you, keep your gun handy, and keep hold of your valuables.* That advice had saved Jubil's life more than once.

He strapped his money pouch, which contained eight hundred dollars, around his waist and pulled his shirt down over it. The money would cover his train fare, food, and lodging to and from the expedition, plus a fee to the army for his expedition provisions and other expenses. He also planned to buy a horse once he arrived at Corinne. The army would probably provide him with one, but he decided not to expect it. He would sell the horse again before he headed home.

Jubil met Luke, Ike, and Eli at the train depot. He hitched Star to the boot of the Boswell's carriage.

"I want to thank you boys," Jubil said, "for always taking such good care of Star for me while I'm away."

"She's a pleasure to have around," Eli said. "I sure wish I was going with you, Jubil."

"I'd enjoy having you along, Eli," he replied. "This will be my first trip where I don't know anyone I'm traveling with." Jubil turned to Luke. "I've decided not to stop in Council Bluffs on the way out, but I'll stop on the way back."

"All right," Luke said. "I'll tell my folks."

"I imagine the latest I'd be back would be sometime in October," Jubil said. "I'll send a telegram before I head home." Nelly would be home by then and well into her fall term at Wesleyan. Hopefully she would be ready by then to set a new wedding date.

As the train pulled out of the station, Jubil thought of the store's motto—The Journey Is the Destination—inspired by the way Uncle Pete had lived his life. He imagined Pete would be proud of him for embarking on this new adventure. He stared out the window and watched the prairie go by, the long grasses rippling in the wind.

After five days of train travel, he arrived at Corinne in the Utah Territory. The most ramshackle town he'd ever seen was Cheyenne, but that was before he stepped off the train at Corinne. The depot consisted of a twenty-foot-square wooden platform with a one-man shack housing the ticket agent. The main street was the only street, and it was lined with a few dozen mismatched structures. In Cheyenne the cobbled-together buildings at least had wooden or tin roofs. Here most were canvas or oilcloth, draped over rafters that were attached to a wooden storefront and walls. The town looked more like an encampment than a permanent settlement. From Corinne,

Jubil would take the stagecoach to Bozeman, in the Montana Territory. Finding the stagecoach depot was a simple matter, the ticket agent in the shack told him: he was already there.

Jubil had never ridden a stagecoach and was not looking forward to the experience. His summer-long trek on the supply wagon train with the Irish teamsters and General Sherman had provided him with all the bone-jarring wagon travel he would ever need. He considered forgoing the stagecoach and buying a horse in Corinne to ride to Bozeman, but traveling alone across the unfamiliar plains invited assault by Indians or highwaymen even more than riding the stage did. He resigned himself to the journey and found his worry about an uncomfortable ride was not only well founded, it was underestimated.

For four days he baked in the hot little box under the blazing sun, breathing through a handkerchief to filter the dusty air, bouncing along on a thinly padded wooden seat, and jostling against the three other sweaty and uncomfortable men with whom he was confined. The terrain they crossed was unchanging under an endless sky. The plains stretched to the horizon in every direction, occasionally crossed by rivers lined with stands of timber. Low rolling hills flowed by like swells over a vast lake, and purple mountains that never seemed to come any closer loomed in the distance. Overnight stops at depots along the way brought little comfort. The food was bland and the bunks were uncomfortable, but at least the travelers were indoors.

When they finally arrived in Bozeman, Jubil found it a decided improvement over Corinne. There were still a number of crudely built establishments, but most were wooden buildings. Some were even painted two-story affairs, with second story patios that provided shade to a sidewalk below. Midway down the main street was a large brick building. The stagecoach pulled to a stop in front of it, and Jubil was pleased to learn it was a hotel. He made a vigorous effort at brushing the dust off himself and his pack before entering the lobby.

"Good morning," said the desk clerk. "Welcome to the Metropolitan Hotel."

"Thank you," Jubil replied, "I'm in need of a room, a bath, a laundry, a decent meal, and a horse."

The clerk smiled. "You've come to the right place for all but the last one. No horses here, but I can point you to an honest trader."

As Jubil registered and paid for his room, he conversed with the clerk, who asked what business brought Jubil to Bozeman. The clerk was interested in his expedition, and gave him directions to Fort Ellis, where he would meet with General Washburn.

The hotel was simple but nicely appointed. It was new and clean, so much so that Jubil regretted sullying it with his dust-covered presence, but his bath would have to wait until he had found a horse. He locked his pack in his room and made his way to the livery stable recommended by the desk clerk. The horse trader there led Jubil out to the corral to review the stock available, and a handsome brown and white pinto stallion caught his eye.

"What kind of temperament does that pinto have?" Jubil asked.

"He's saddle broke. Not too feisty but spirited," the trader replied. "Maybe eight years old. The fellow who sold him said he didn't spook easily."

Jubil asked for a bridle and entered the corral. As he approached, the horse watched him warily and shied away, but he did not bolt or rear up. Jubil patted the horse and talked soothingly to him. "Would you like to do some traveling with me this summer, boy?"

The horse turned and looked at him and, to Jubil's surprise, nudged him in the chest with his nose and lifted his head, as if inviting Jubil to slip on the bridle, which he did.

"How much for this one?" Jubil asked. They haggled a bit

on the terms, with Jubil agreeing to a price of two hundred dollars for the horse and tack. The saddle was good quality for the price. It was unadorned leather but had a padded seat, saddlebags, and a scabbard for his rifle. He continued to talk to the horse as he saddled him.

"You're a hearty fellow," Jubil said, "and a fine-looking one to boot, a regular Apollo." The horse turned his head and looked Jubil in the eye. "You like that name? All right then, Apollo—let's go explore Yellowstone." Jubil paid the horse trader and took Apollo out for a get-acquainted ride. He would return to board him overnight and then pick him up the next morning.

Back at the hotel he enjoyed a bath, availed himself of the laundry, and stretched out on the bed for a decent nap before dinner. The desk clerk told him the hotel had the best chef and the freshest food around, so he looked no further for his evening meal. Once he had ordered, he saw a tall man in a dark suit with slicked-back hair and a well-groomed mustache speaking with the waiter, who pointed Jubil out. The mustached man approached his table.

"Mr. Walker?" the man inquired. He appeared to be at least a decade older than Jubil. "I'm Phineas Black. Sorry to interrupt your supper. I just wanted to meet you."

Jubil rose to shake hands. "How do you do, Mr. Black? Are you with the Yellowstone expedition?"

"Not directly, no," Mr. Black replied, "but I'm very interested in it." He had a deep voice and spoke softly, as if to keep their conversation just between the two of them. "I have various business interests, primarily mining operations, but I'm also part-owner of this hotel."

"Congratulations," Jubil said amiably. "It was quite a relief to reach your hotel after the stagecoach ride from Corinne."

Mr. Black bowed his head briefly to accept the compliment. "I also own the mercantile in town. I hear you're also in the outfitting business."

"Yes sir," Jubil said. "I've only just ordered my meal. Would you care to join me?"

"For a few minutes, thank you," Black replied, pulling out the chair opposite Jubil's. "Unfortunately, I have a previous supper engagement. I thought this might be my only chance to catch you before you set out."

Jubil regarded him with curiosity. "I'm not sure why you would bother," he said.

"I'm a businessman, Mr. Walker," Black said, "and I'm always interested in talking with other businessmen. I see great potential for this community and the Montana Territory. Your expedition may open up great business opportunities, don't you think?"

"To be honest, Mr. Black, I haven't thought much about that," Jubil said.

Phineas Black smiled, but the gesture seemed rusty to Jubil, and he wondered how often the man was used to smiling.

"I've seen Warner and Walker Outfitting ads in the *Chicago Times* and the *St. Louis Dispatch* offering a guided adventure tour to the Rocky Mountains led by Jubilee Walker, a veteran of the Powell expeditions."

Jubil nodded and shifted uneasily in his seat. He was sure many people had seen those ads, but he still wasn't used to being a person who was recognized in public by strangers.

Black leaned forward, his forearms on the table. "I'm curious about your intentions here, Mr. Walker. I'm wondering if you are considering expanding your operations into Montana. Maybe thinking of setting up a new store in Bozeman?"

"Like I said," Jubil insisted, "I haven't thought about it. I'm here as an explorer, not as a businessman. The Warners and I have had no conversations of that sort."

"Maybe not yet," Black replied crisply, and Jubil began to tire of the conversation.

"Once you've had a chance to see for yourself what the

business potential of the area is," Black said, "you'll have those conversations. If you are just guiding tourists to the Yellowstone River, I'm in favor of that. But if you and the Warners were to open an outfitting business here in Bozeman, that would detract from my mercantile operation, and I would be very much opposed to that."

Black's warning was of little concern. Bozeman was far too small and remote to be of any interest to the Warners. Besides, who would operate it? Jubil had no interest in moving to Bozeman, and Nelly certainly would not. Luke might, conceivably, as an adventure, but Jubil thought it highly unlikely. He kept these thoughts to himself, not wanting to appear intimidated. This man must have seen how young he was as an invitation to bully him, but Jubil had never been able to stand a bully. "I believe the Montana Territory has the same free enterprise system as the rest of the United States," Jubil said flatly.

"Yes," Black replied, "it does. But that's not my point. What I'm proposing is to save us both time, trouble, and money. As far as Bozeman goes, if you leave the outfitting to me, I'll leave the guided tours to you."

"Well, I suppose I should thank you for your candor," Jubil said.

Black ignored Jubil's sarcasm. "I also want to give you a word of caution," he said. "If Nathaniel Langford and Jay Cooke's plans are successful, they will corner the tourism market out here."

This warning caught Jubil's attention. Competition with the adventure tour business was a concern. That was part of the reason he was here—to familiarize himself with the area and gauge whether it was a viable site for a future tour. It had already occurred to him that delaying the start of their tours might open the door for someone else to do it.

"I haven't met Mr. Langford or Mr. Cooke," Jubil said.

"Well, you're about to meet Mr. Langford," Black said, sneering slightly when he said the other man's name. "He is one of your expedition leaders and an untrustworthy, arrogant scoundrel. I will admit that he has built up some credit as an explorer, but his feats are hardly as impressive as yours. Banking, lumber, politics—he's got his fingers in a dozen pies. He knows all the right people. He weaseled his way into an appointment as Collector of Internal Revenue and National Bank Examiner. He was even named governor of Montana, but Congress showed some rare good sense and refused to ratify his appointment.

"He's a dangerous man, Mr. Walker. He was one of the ringleaders of the Virginia City vigilantes, who killed more people around here than any criminal ever did. He's ingratiated himself with Jay Cooke, the financier, who plans to build a railroad from Minnesota to the Pacific Northwest. Langford is telling Cooke that the Yellowstone is going to draw flocks of tourists who will ride his railroad, and he wants Cooke to run it through Helena. He's talked Cooke into financing your expedition. If things go their way, they will likely shut everyone else out of the tourist business in Montana."

"You make Langford sound like quite a menace," Jubil said evenly, although this news about Jay Cooke did spark some apprehension in him. He supposed he had been naïve to believe he was the only one to think of making a business out of guiding travelers in the age of the transcontinental railroad. Who better to respond to that opportunity than the man who builds the railroads? "I'll consider myself warned."

Jubil was relieved to see the waiter appear with his meal. "Well, Mr. Black," he said, "I wouldn't want to keep you from your supper engagement."

"One more thing," Black said, as he stood to leave. "My mining operations are quite lucrative. If you discover any valuable deposits, it would be worth a cut of the operation for you to inform me of their location when you return. I'd take that as a gesture of goodwill."

Jubil considered the request. "I'll keep that in mind."

He reflected on their conversation as he ate his supper. Black's imperious attitude left Jubil feeling leery of him. He was skeptical about how much of Black's characterization of Langford and Cooke to believe, but he would have plenty of time to assess Langford's character for himself.

In his room after supper, he wrote Nelly a letter. He gave an unflattering description of stagecoach travel and a flattering one of his handsome new horse. He could not decide how to characterize his encounter with Phineas Black, so he made no mention of it, and instead spoke enthusiastically about the upcoming expedition. He closed by saying he looked forward to returning home to share his stories with her, to hear stories of her travels east, and to make new plans for their future together.

It was so odd to think of Nelly and not be able to picture where she was or what she might be doing. He had gotten used on his trips to imagining her going about her daily business, hanging laundry or sitting in a classroom at Normal University, but now his image of her in his daydreams was out of focus.

He put aside his worries as he got into the comfortable bed, grateful to enjoy a good night's sleep and have breakfast in the hotel dining room before setting out for several weeks of living rough. As he prepared to leave, he removed his revolver and White Dog's medicine bag from his pack and strapped them on. As he left the hotel, the desk clerk wished him luck and assured him a room would be waiting on his return. Jubil thought Phineas Black could take some lessons in hospitality from his clerk.

When he entered Apollo's stall at the livery stable, the horse took a step toward him and nudged him with his nose. "Good morning, Apollo. I'm glad to see you too," Jubil said patting the horse's neck. "I can already tell I'm going to hate to leave you behind at the end of this trip." Jubil saddled up, strapped his pack across Apollo's haunches, and set off for Fort Ellis, riding to the south end of town and following the well-worn trail that led east. It felt good to be on horseback again, close to the land rather than observing it from a train or stagecoach. The adventure was just beginning, and Jubil could feel his excitement build. He was anxious to see whether this landscape lived up to its reputation.

He rode across the wide plains surrounded by mountains on the north, east, and south. Fort Ellis first appeared in the distance less than an hour later as a group of white dots, which Jubil could see as he got closer were a collection of buildings scattered across about one hundred acres. The fort was a busy place. The first buildings he rode past were the livery stables and barn, which were attached to a large corral filled with horses. Jubil stopped to chat with a soldier, who pointed out the headquarters building, a whitewashed two-story rectangular structure. He rode over and introduced himself to a sentry on the front porch, who led him into a large room where four men were standing around a map table. Three were uniformed military officers and one was in civilian clothes. All appeared to be in their thirties, substantially older than Jubil. They stopped their conversation and regarded him.

"Excuse me, gentlemen," Jubil said. "My name is Jubilee Walker. I'm to report to Colonel Baker as a member of the Yellowstone expedition."

"I'm Colonel Baker," replied one of the officers, stepping forward. The colonel had a neatly trimmed beard and bore a slight resemblance to General Grant. He wore a Stetson hat and a frock coat, unbuttoned and open over a white shirt with a black cravat. His uniform was well-worn and dusty.

"Welcome to Fort Ellis," Colonel Baker said, studying Jubil carefully. "You're the last to arrive. Come meet the leaders of the expedition."

Jubil felt the men watching him as he stepped up and took a place at the map table. He felt nervous in the older men's company, but he hoped he appeared calm. He recalled the time his friend Lew Keplinger had introduced him to General Sherman. He had been so intimidated by the famous man he could hardly speak, but he had grown more accustomed to being in the company of accomplished men. It was important to him to comport himself well here and to be thought highly of by these men—as a matter of pride, certainly, but also because good relationships with them might attract them to his outfitting business and make him a stronger partner for the Warners.

"Gentlemen, Mr. Walker is General Sheridan's man on the expedition," Colonel Baker said matter-of-factly.

Jubil did not think of himself as "Sheridan's man" but felt awkward about denying the characterization.

Colonel Baker continued, "Walker's in the outfitting business and has done some exploring with Major Wes Powell. He's also acquainted with General Sherman." Baker turned to the officer standing next to him and said, "General, would you like to do the introductions?"

"How do you do, Mr. Walker, I am General Henry Washburn," the man said. He was as tall as Jubil but thinner. He had a receding hairline but a full head of hair, a moustache, and bushy chin whiskers. "I was recently appointed by Congress as surveyor general of Montana. In that capacity, I petitioned for military support for this expedition. Colonel Baker won't be traveling with us, but he has orders to provide us a security detail. He has put this gentleman in charge of our support detail," he said, pointing to the third military man. "This is Lieutenant Cheyney Doane."

Doane wore a kepi cap and a short jacket with a wide sash angled across his chest that held his sabre hook. He was a large man, three inches taller than Jubil and sturdily built, with black shoulder-length hair; sad, heavily lidded eyes; and a huge walrus mustache that covered his mouth and tapered into handlebar points that stood out horizontally from his face. Jubil wondered if the mustache would stay so finely groomed during the trip.

"Mr. Walker, I'm aware of your experiences in the Grand Canyon," Doane said, with a slightly bitter tone. "I made a proposal to conduct that survey myself, but Major Powell won the funding." Doane didn't offer a handshake, but Jubil noticed him absentmindedly massaging his right hand and saw that his thumb was bandaged.

Doane eyed the medicine bag Jubil wore.

With a friendly smile, Jubil said, "If you're wondering how I came by the medicine bag, it was given to me by a friend."

Doane frowned and nodded.

"And this gentleman," General Washburn said, referring to the man in civilian clothing, "is Nathaniel Pitt Langford. Mr. Langford is the primary organizer of our expedition and one of Montana's most energetic champions and prominent citizens."

Langford had neatly trimmed brown hair, a prominent brow, and deep-set eyes. He wore a full beard to chest length, and had a muscular build and a serious manner. Jubil took note of Langford's rugged but high-quality clothing. His coat was tanned buckskin that buttoned to the neck, with fur trimming at the collar and sleeves. A seam of short fringe ran down the sleeves, and the front had two large pouch pockets. Jubil thought Luke would be impressed by that coat, and he made a mental note to describe it to him. Langford carried a fringed tote bag slung across his torso that rode on his right hip, just as Jubil carried his medicine bag. His boots were knee-high oiled leather. All of his gear was in good condition but well worn.

"Mr. Walker," Langford said, fixing Jubil with his intent gaze. "I understand we share some interest in adventure tourism."

Jubil wasn't sure whether Langford's comment was a welcome or a warning. He nodded in what he hoped was an amiable manner. "Yes, so I've heard," he said. He would hold any mention of Phineas Black until he and Mr. Langford were better acquainted.

"There will be eleven members in our party," General Washburn explained, "plus two packers, two cooks, and five soldiers in Lieutenant Doane's detail. You'll meet them all soon. I was about to review our expedition plans. Step up and have a look at the map."

Jubil recognized the professionally drawn map showing the route beginning at the north and following the Yellowstone river. "Is this the Folsom, Cook, and Peterson route?" Jubil asked. "General Sheridan reviewed it with me."

General Washburn looked impressed. "Yes, and we will follow that same route. I expect the trip to take around four weeks. Starting as late as we are in the year, we'll have to be very cautious of the weather. If severe weather threatens to set in early, we'll have to make our way out quickly. We don't want to get trapped there for the winter."

Early winter snows had blocked the way into the region for the Raynolds expedition, but Jubil had not considered the possibility of snow blocking the way out. Fortunately, the general had.

"We'll make our way over the Bozeman Pass to the Yellowstone River and then follow it upriver south through Paradise Valley," Washburn continued. Jubil noted the anomaly of a major river flowing north, but such was the lay of the mountains in the region. "We'll encamp at the Bottler brothers' ranch at the head of the valley, then follow the Yellowstone River into the basin, making our way past the Grand Canyon and the falls, and on down to the lake. This is around one hundred twenty miles, which I expect will take us a little over a week. From there we will circumnavigate the lake, find the Firehole River, and follow it through the volcanic region to the Madison River. We'll follow the Madison west out of the basin through the Madison Range, then turn north for Bozeman.

We should be back by early October." The general looked at the men. "Any questions?"

Jubil could hardly wait to set out and see what these places looked like, and what challenges they would face along the way. He was so excited to be here that it almost overshadowed his concerns about his decision to come—almost.

Hearing no questions, the general turned to Jubil. "Tell me something, Mr. Walker. General Sheridan left the selection of the expedition party to me and Mr. Langford, except for you. How is it you come to us through him? And do you have a specific mission? I would have asked Sheridan himself, but he was reassigned before we had a chance to speak."

Jubil had expected members of the party to share stories of how they came to join the expedition, since that had been his experience on his adventures with Powell. But his role on this expedition was not as clearly defined as it had been with Powell. It was a fair question—why was he here?

"First off, I'd say Colonel Baker's reference to me as 'Sheridan's man' makes me sound far closer to the general than I am," Jubil began. He explained the business relationship he and the Warners had with the army and about Sheridan's awareness of Jubil's experiences with Powell. "He thought my expedition and outfitting experience would be useful, so I'm prepared to help make and move camp, tend the animals, hunt and fish. Just generally help with logistics. I'll also admit I'm here to satisfy my sense of adventure and curiosity about what we might find."

"Did Sheridan ask you to keep a journal, or deliver a report to him of any sort?"

At the mention of delivering a report, Jubil thought of General Sherman's telegram—*interested in hearing your observations / please come to Washington on your return*. He was concerned that declaring he was on an information-gathering mission for Sherman would arouse suspicion and alienate him from the other men. He had no idea why Sherman would ask this of him, so he had no explanation for it. He decided to answer the general's question narrowly.

"No sir, General Sheridan made no request of that sort," Jubil declared truthfully.

"Hmm," General Washburn said studying Jubil. "Well, Mr. Stickney has been in charge of logistics and supplies, but I suspect he'll welcome your experience. You need to see him first anyway, to settle up your contribution for expedition costs. Agreed?"

"Yes sir," Jubil said, as Washburn, Langford, and Doane continued to assess him.

General Washburn assigned a soldier to help Jubil board Apollo and settle into the barracks. On his way to meet the other members of the party, Jubil tried to sort out his quandary about keeping General Sherman's request a secret. He could see no benefit from revealing it, and it was important to him to be accepted and respected by these men—his own pride demanded it, and he wanted to make the Warners proud. It would be hard to achieve acceptance and respect if they started out viewing him with greater suspicion and polite reserve than he already felt from them.

Luke had theorized it might have been General Sherman who wanted him on the expedition in the first place, not General Sheridan. But even if that were true, it still did not answer his main question—why?

CHAPTER 4

The other members of the expedition welcomed Jubil with none of the suspicious skepticism he felt from the party's leaders. When Jubil offered his help with the details of the expedition, Benjamin Stickney gave Jubil the once-over and nodded thoughtfully.

"I'm happy to have your assistance, Mr. Walker," he said. He spoke with a high-pitched nasal twang that made Jubil smile. "And you can be sure I will avail myself of it."

Stickney was in his early thirties, short and wiry, with a large mustache that added a few years to his otherwise baby-faced appearance. When Stickney said he was the owner of a large dry-goods store in Helena, Jubil was tempted to ask if he knew Phineas Black, but decided to wait for a more private conversation.

Jubil felt a particular sense of comradeship with Walter Trumbull, who was twenty-four years old and had been the youngest member of the party until Jubil showed up. Walter was slightly taller and thinner than Jubil, with brown eyes, brown hair, a fair complexion, and a long clean-shaven face. Walter's family home was in Alton, Illinois, but he had also lived in Springfield, Illinois, and Washington, DC. His father, Lyman Trumbull, was a US Senator from Illinois, who counted among his accomplishments coauthoring the Thirteenth Amendment, outlawing slavery. Walter now called Helena home and had come west partly to escape his father's shadow but also out of a sense of adventure. This was his first expedition.

Walter had traveled to Fort Ellis with Mr. Truman Everts, who, at fifty-four years of age, was the oldest member of the party. He had been the federal tax assessor for the Territory of Montana, but recently President Grant had given that appointment to someone else. Walter had been Mr. Everts's assistant, and he still followed Everts as they sought out a new appointment. Mr. Everts wore a pair of oval glasses perched on his nose, which were attached to a loop of cord he wore around his neck. He had a tall forehead, thin brown hair, a full beard and a heavyset frame. To Jubil, he looked more like a tax assessor than an explorer, but he seemed like pleasant company.

The expedition was made up of a total of twenty people—eleven explorers, five soldiers, two packers, two cooks, the horses they all rode, and a fleet of nine mules. The mules were laden with a thirty-day supply of staples—flour, sugar, baking powder, coffee, rice, beans, dried beef, dried apples, bacon, carrots, potatoes, and onions. Some of the men's names and backgrounds registered with Jubil immediately; the rest he would sort out along the way.

The next morning, Stickney introduced Jubil to the packers, Charles and Elwun, brothers in their mid-twenties from south Texas. They seemed to be good-natured fellows as they went about loading the mules, and they appreciated Jubil's help in manhandling the cargo. When the job was finished, Jubil went to check on his new friend, Walter, and found him and Mr. Everts saddling their horses. As they made their final preparations, General Washburn, Mr. Langford, and Lieutenant Doane rode up and came to a halt in front of them.

"Are you gentlemen ready to travel?" Langford asked.

"Very nearly," Everts replied, struggling with the cinch of his saddle.

"Would you like a hand with that, Mr. Everts?" Jubil offered.

Mr. Langford spoke up. "Mr. Walker, I thought the general asked you to offer your services to Mr. Stickney, not Mr. Everts."

Jubil held his temper. Phineas Black had warned him about Mr. Langford. But he did not know yet if this rude, irritable manner was how Langford dealt with everyone, or if it was directed only at him. Langford's behavior toward others would soon become apparent, as would whether he was actually dangerous, as Black had suggested.

"I helped pack the mules this morning. Since Mr. Stickney asked me to help with the animals," Jubil replied evenly, "my offer to Mr. Everts seems reasonably related."

Langford continued to stare at Jubil, who held his gaze, squinting up from beneath the brim of his hat.

"I believe I have it now," Mr. Everts said, giving his saddle a final tug to make sure it was secure. "Lead on, Mr. Langford."

General Washburn stood in his stirrups to address the expedition party: "Gentlemen, we are ready to depart. Mr. Langford, Lieutenant Doane, and I will lead out. If you must fall behind for any reason, make sure someone is aware of your situation. We'll make our way over the Bozeman pass today, then find a place to camp."

Jubil, Walter Trumbull, and Mr. Everts fell in behind Washburn, Langford, and Doane. As Jubil settled into the saddle, he was moved by a sense of well-being. He had no doubt he belonged here. He tried to set his heartache about Nelly aside for a while—there was nothing to be done about it now. He would spend some time during the expedition pondering how to mend their relationship, if he could, but for now he would focus on his surroundings and his mission. He needed to prove himself to these men and leave here feeling the expedition had been worthwhile.

He turned his attention to the landscape and breathed in the pungent aroma of pine needles as the trail followed the East Gallatin River over hilly country with pine timber covering the northern slopes. The ravines and small valleys were filled with aspen and willow that quaked in the warm, fresh breeze, and the streams sparkled in the sun as they splashed toward lower ground. Six miles from Fort Ellis they crossed the Yellowstone divide, a ridge along the Gallatin Range forming the apex of two watersheds; one that sloped to the Gallatin River, the other to the Yellowstone. As the trail ascended, Jubil looked ahead to see a notch depressed several hundred feet below the ridge's usual altitude. This was Bozeman Pass, which allowed a tolerable wagon road across the Gallatin range. When the leaders reached the top of the pass, General Washburn paused to look at his map. Jubil and his companions rode up nearer the general.

"Paradise Valley," General Washburn said, looking at the map and then gazing out at the expanse before them, "and down there is the Yellowstone River."

All the way to the southern horizon the Yellowstone River meandered through a valley that was several miles wide and bounded by snow-capped mountains on either side. Spread across the floor of the valley were thousands of grassy acres dotted with the habitations of pioneers. Jubil had seen expansive landscapes before, the most dramatic being the view from the summit of Longs Peak in the northern Colorado Rockies, but the Yellowstone River and the verdant valley had a lusher appearance. It was not hard to see why it was named Paradise Valley.

They traveled down a gentle declivity until they came to Trail Creek, where they set up camp for the night, having traveled about fifteen miles from Fort Ellis. They would follow the creek to Yellowstone River. While Jubil, Walter, and Mr. Everts were hitching their horses, they noticed some serviceberry bushes nearby, of which Mr. Everts was particularly fond. The berries were ripe, so they filled their hats and shared them with the other men.

That evening Jubil had a chance to become more familiar with some of his fellow explorers—Samuel Hauser, Cornelius Hedges, Warren Gillette, and Jake Smith.

Nearly all of the men on the expedition seemed to be dignified, professional men. Samuel Hauser had once been a civil engineer, but was now partners with Langford in owning a bank in Helena. He had a receding hairline, wavy swept-back brown hair, a pointed nose, a pointed beard, and so far, a quiet manner. Cornelius Hedges was a lawyer and judge. He had dark hair, neatly cut and parted, and was clean shaven but for a full mustache. Hauser and Hedges were in their thirties, and the way they rode and handled their gear suggested to Jubil that they were not experienced outdoorsmen. He thought of how the inexperienced travelers on the Longs Peak expedition had complained and sometimes even hurt themselves due to their lack of knowledge or skill. He hoped that wouldn't be the case during this trip.

Warren Gillette looked somewhat older than the other men. He was bald on top with a ring of wispy straw-colored hair, a large brushy mustache, and a clean-shaven chin. He was distinguished by his sideburns and the whiskers from his cheeks, which, oddly, grew to chest length. Gillette had once operated a retail store but had sold it and was now in the shipping business. Stickney and Gillette both chewed tobacco, which gave them a rough edge the others lacked.

Then there was Jake Smith. Jubil noticed right away that Smith didn't fit in with the other travelers. He was in his late twenties, a former butcher and tannery owner. He was fit but had a big belly and was loud and boisterous. He seemed to consider himself lively entertainment. In camp that night, conversation came around to their defense in the event of an Indian encounter. Smith bellowed, "I'll wager twenty-five cents a shot there's not one of you fellers can hit my hat with a revolver at twenty yards!" He stepped off the distance and nestled his hat in a bush. Jubil watched as several of the men took Smith up on his wager and missed. Before Jubil could step up and have a try, four rapid-fire shots rang out as Smith looked around in surprise. "That was a mighty loud report for a revolver! Who was that?" he declared. As he went to retrieve his hat, Langford stepped out from behind a bush with his rifle. He caught Jubil's eye and winked. Smith came back frowning at the holes in his hat. Jubil wondered why Langford was treating him as an accomplice to the joke. He also wondered why Langford had invited Smith if he had so little respect for him.

In the morning, recalcitrant mules caused a delay in the expedition's departure. One of them had decided he was unwilling to stand for having a heavy load tied to his back, and his attitude encouraged two more similarly. Whichever direction Elwun the packer approached from, the problem animal would sidle away in the opposite. If the other packer, Charles, tried to block his escape route, the mule would spin and kick. As the packers fought a battle of wills with the mule, Lieutenant Doane announced that he and his soldiers would ride ahead to scout for Indians.

Jubil learned that Elwun's good nature had limits, as the packer struggled with the mule and shouted a stream of profanities into the poor animal's ear. Jubil stepped in to take over.

"Let me have a go at him," Jubil said to Elwun, reaching for the mule's lead rope. Elwun continued to curse the animal as he handed off the rope. Mr. Stickney stood watching.

"Step away from him a few feet," Jubil said to Elwun, as he slowly drew the rope in and talked reassuringly to the mule. As it began to calm, he patted the animal's neck and shoulder, as he did whenever he saddled Star or any horse he rode. In a short while, the mule calmed and Jubil signaled Stickney and the packers to try approaching again—and this time the mule stood still. By midmorning the party set out with all the mules having finally conceded to being loaded up.

"Thank you kindly, Mr. Walker," Stickney said once they were on their way again. "I guess I never thought of doing it that gentle, but it worked. Imagine that."

As they followed Trail Creek south down the mountain into Paradise Valley, the trail was bounded by immense piles of black rock in shards and columns that lay jutting out from the mountainside and jumbled in all directions. They appeared to have been snapped into gigantic pieces and strewn about by some immense force. Were they a sign of the volcanic history of the region?

"Do you know what kind of rock that is, Walter?" Jubil asked his friend.

"I think it's basalt, but I'm not sure," Walter replied. "You should ask Lieutenant Doane—he's very knowledgeable about the geology of the region."

Jubil was surprised. Doane did not strike him as an academic sort—though Jubil's friend, Lew Keplinger, had not at first either, and he was a wealth of knowledge on many subjects. But where Lew had been friendly from the outset, Jubil didn't feel comfortable yet approaching the lieutenant uninvited.

When they reached the foothills, Jubil found Benjamin Stickney and Samuel Hauser waiting for him beside the trail.

"Good day, Mr. Walker," Stickney said in his high-pitched nasal twang. "Mr. Hauser and I are riding out to hunt antelope, if you'd care to ride along."

"I'd enjoy that," Jubil said happily. He was pleased by the acceptance implicit in Stickney's invitation.

Jubil turned to Walter Trumbull, who was riding with him. "If you don't mind, I'll be along in a while."

"I don't mind," Walter said, turning to rejoin the expedition. "I'm not anxious to display what a poor shot I am."

As they rode into the foothills, Stickney suggested they

spread out, and he asked Jubil to ride toward a copse of pines ahead of them up the slope. Below them the expedition party was visible, winding along the river. Jubil rode high up toward the pines, following signs of antelope. When he crested a ridge, however, he was frozen by what he saw below: a band of Indians on horseback sitting on a flat plateau nestled among the hills that offered a view of the same valley and river along which the expedition party was traveling.

The Indians had not yet noticed Jubil. Two of them sat on their horses near the edge of the plateau. The rest, perhaps one hundred of them, sat further back from the edge. Jubil imagined the expedition party would see only two Indians observing them, but they gave no indication of knowing they were being watched. He held Apollo as still he could as he considered what to do. Mr. Gulley's advice came to him once more: *keep your wits about you.* Jubil motioned to Stickney, who was further down the hillside, to come up, and Stickney waved to Hauser. The two other men rode up and looked down on the scene below.

"That ain't good," Stickney said. "Crow . . .a mess of 'em."

Mr. Hauser, Langford's banking partner, remained silent.

One of the Indians at the edge of the plateau noticed them and pointed out their location to his companion, who turned and walked his horse toward Jubil a few steps, then stopped.

"Better fire a warning shot to show 'em we mean business," Stickney said, reaching to pull his rifle from its holster.

"Don't," Jubil said, holding out a hand to stop Stickney. "We don't want to provoke anything. Without the soldiers, there is no way we could outgun them."

"Well, then let's get out of here, before they come for our hair," Stickney declared.

"Just hold up a minute," Jubil urged. "I think if they wanted to take us, they would have just done it. I believe they're just curious." He looked down at the Indian that had ridden closer to him, then turned his attention to that Indian's companion.

Jubil had an odd but strong feeling of kinship toward the Indian. He could almost swear he was looking at White Dog, but his hair and clothing looked nothing like his friend's. Besides, that was impossible. White Dog lived hundreds of miles away, in Nebraska. What would he be doing here?

Jubil felt a sense of calm as he urged Apollo to take a couple of steps forward. He wondered fleetingly what General Sheridan would say—most likely that Jubil's Indian sympathizing was bound to get him killed. He raised his right arm, palm out, and signaled hello to the Indian looking up at him. The Indian sat staring at Jubil for several more seconds, then wheeled his horse around and rode away in the opposite direction, leading his band off the plateau and back into the hills.

"Well I'll be," Stickney said. "They just turned and high-tailed it out of here. You got some kind of Indian magic in that beaded pouch you're wearing?" He pointed at White Dog's medicine bag that Jubil wore at his hip.

"Yes sir, I do," Jubil said with a grin, patting the bag. After the initial shock of seeing the Indians below, he had seen no sign of threat, but he still felt relieved that they were gone and pleased that his instincts had this time proven right. "You want to ride back, or hunt?" Jubil asked his companions.

"I'm ready to get back with the others," Mr. Hauser said, wide-eyed.

As they set off to rejoin the expedition party, Stickney asked how Jubil came to own the medicine bag, and he gave a brief accounting. By the time they had rejoined the others, the party was well out of the foothills and riding south through the great expanse of the Yellowstone valley. They continued south along the river until they met Doane and the soldiers camped on the western bank of the Yellowstone, near Emigrant Mines. Across the river was Bottler's Ranch. The ranch was a collection of rough-built, single story structures—a house, bunkhouse, stable, sheds—owned by a German hunter, Fredrick Bottler, and his fellow-bachelor brothers, Philip and Henry. Though it was called a ranch, it served more as a rest and supply center for miners and hunters coming through Paradise Valley.

That evening at the campsite, Stickney recounted to the expedition party his version of the Indian encounter. General Washburn complimented Jubil on his presence of mind. Langford remained silent but nodded in agreement. Lieutenant Doane looked at him with suspicion.

General Washburn announced that beginning that evening, an all-night watch would be set. Four men would stand watch each night, two until 1:00 a.m. and two until dawn. Each man in the party would be on watch three times a week. Even if the Indians did not assault them, they might make sport of stealing their horses, mules, and supplies if given the opportunity. Wildlife predators were also in abundance in the area—bears, mountain lions, wolves, coyotes.

That evening it began to rain. The packers, cooks, and soldiers had their own fly tents, and Lieutenant Doane had brought a pavilion tent that allowed the explorers to stay dry, though the sleeping arrangements were cramped. Jubil was happy for the shelter but less than pleased to be woken before dawn by the force of Walter Trumbull's elbow striking his ear. He had not slept well, not so much because of the sleeping arrangement as his conscience.

General Washburn's public praise of him that evening had given him a significant measure of the acceptance and respect he had hoped for among these men. It would have been a good time for Jubil to inform the general that he had failed to mention General Sherman's invitation, and yet Jubil did not take the opportunity to mention it. He was embarrassed to admit, even to himself, that he had been so needful of the other men's acceptance. Now, he would have to admit to being both deceptive and self-doubting, which would surely cost him the respect he had only just gained. He had gotten himself into a corner.

The rain continued until noon the next day, so the party did not break camp and depart until early afternoon. Mr. Everts had developed an unpleasant bout of digestive distress—perhaps brought on by too many serviceberries. Rather than slow everyone down by having to dismount frequently, he insisted on remaining behind for a while. He said he would catch up in a day—two at the most. Walter would not leave Everts there alone, so Jubil offered to stay as well. General Washburn said he would send a man back for them if they had not caught up in two days. He also warned them to be careful of the tricky terrain through Yankee Jim Canyon. He cautioned them that if Mr. Everts was not fully recovered, there would be no stopping along that section of the trail.

While Mr. Everts recovered, Jubil and Walter spent the time in easy conversation. Walter was very interested in Jubil's travels with Powell, particularly the previous year's expedition through the Grand Canyon. In turn, Jubil asked about Walter's interests, and he confessed that he was a journalist of sorts, serving as a contributor for the *Helena Rocky Mountain Gazette* and the *Overland Monthly*. He also recounted some of his own family history, and how he had come to work with Mr. Everts. Jubil was surprised to learn that Mr. Gillette, of the long muttonchop whiskers, was soon to become Mr. Everts's son-in-law. Jubil wondered if Everts's daughter found the whiskers attractive, and he wondered what she might look like, but he did not ask. He considered unburdening himself to Walter about the invitation from Sherman but felt awkward making such an admission of poor judgment to his new friend.

By early that afternoon Mr. Everts announced that he was fit to travel, and they set off to catch the main party. Late in the afternoon, they found a likely camping spot near a stand of black cherry trees, but on closer inspection Jubil noticed claw marks and broken branches that were the work of bears, something he had learned to recognize from Lew Keplinger in

Colorado. He suggested they move a little further south before camping for the night.

In the morning, they set off again along the river. A few miles south, the mountains closed in and formed a narrow canyon. An Indian trail wound up the western canyon wall, which was steeply sloped but passable, until it reached a ledge that traversed the canyon wall, and then wound its way back down to the river as the canyon opened up again.

"This must be Yankee Jim Canyon," Jubil said. "You feeling all right now, Mr. Everts?"

"I'm fine, thank you," Everts replied. "Lead on, Mr. Walker."

They rode single-file up along the canyon wall. When the path leveled out, Jubil saw that the trail ahead followed a narrow rock ledge, just wide enough for a wagon, with the river several hundred feet below. There was plenty of room for a rider on horseback, but if a snake or lizard startled a horse, one step off the trail meant a long drop to the river. Jubil had experienced some hair-raising episodes in the Rockies and navigating the walls of the Grand Canyon, but this was the first time he had been exposed to such heights on horseback.

Apollo started surefootedly along the narrow trail, and Jubil gave him a loose rein and avoided looking down at the river. He kept his breathing as steady as he could and turned in the saddle occasionally to make sure Walter and Mr. Everts were close behind. It took about thirty minutes to traverse this narrow ledge, then Jubil felt his shoulders relax as the canyon opened up again and the trail began to wind its way back down to the river. They continued to follow the Yellowstone until they reached the mouth of the Gardner River, where they found General Washburn and the rest of the party camped near the confluence.

The general said that this point marked the border between the territories: they were now leaving Montana Territory and entering northwest Wyoming. As Jubil laid out his bedroll, he noticed that Lieutenant Doane had gone off to soak his sore right hand in the cold water of the river.

General Washburn pointed out Indian smoke signals rising from a nearby bluff and announced that caution was in order. That evening after supper he asked Mr. Langford to make assignments for guard duty.

"Mr. Trumbull and I will take first shift watch," Mr. Langford said. "Mr. Walker and Mr. Smith will take second."

Jake Smith spoke up. "I don't see this guard duty as worthwhile. If them Indians want our scalps, they'll just sneak in here and take 'em. The guards'll just be the first ones in line for a trim."

Even if Smith were right, Jubil did not see any sense in making it even easier for them.

"I doubt they'll have much interest in your paltry pelt, Mr. Smith," Mr. Langford said scornfully. "You'll either keep watch over us, our animals, and our supplies, or you'll mount up and ride home."

The camp fell silent during Mr. Langford's outburst. Jake Smith glared at him. "Fine," he said, "you'll have your way." Then he turned away with a look of disgust.

Jubil thought Langford was justified to insist that their situation be taken seriously and that Jake do his share, but he thought threatening to send him away was going too far. He also thought Langford could have made his point directly to Jake, without shaming him in front of the group.

Walter Trumbull looked at Jubil with raised eyebrows and a grin. "Looks like you have a sleepy ride ahead of you tomorrow," Walter teased.

"I haven't mastered sleeping on horseback," Jubil said, grinning. "I guess I'll get some practice. By the way, why do you suppose Langford invited Jake Smith? He doesn't seem to have much use for him."

"Mr. Everts told me, that Smith kind of invited himself," Walter said. "He heard about the expedition and told Langford he wanted to join up. General Washburn was too gentlemanly to turn him down. It looks like he might regret that decision though."

That night the disagreement between Langford and Smith went from bad to worse. During Jubil and Smith's watch, sometime between 1:00 a.m. and dawn, Langford found Jake Smith sleeping, and roundly and loudly berated him, waking everyone else. Langford did not repeat his threat to send Jake away, so the incident passed, but Jubil thought Jake deserved the scolding.

Walter Trumbull thought the episode was funny and at breakfast drew a cartoonish sketch of the scene titled "Jake Smith on guard." It showed Smith lying comfortably at the campfire, saddle for a pillow, rifle beside him, saying, "My lone watch I'm keeping—Indians don't bother me." Everyone but Smith got a laugh out of it, and when Jubil praised Walter's drawing, Walter signed the corner of the image in his neat handwriting and gave it to him.

That morning, some of the mules again resisted taking up their burdens, and Jubil had a private word with Stickney.

"I think the problem is more with Elwun than the mules," Jubil said. "I'd be glad to take over handling the animals."

Stickney looked Jubil in the eye, then nodded. "Thank you, Walker," he said and walked back to the struggling packers.

"I've come to an agreement with Mr. Walker," Stickney said. "He'll be responsible for the animals from here on, and you fellows will take your orders from him."

Neither Elwun or Charles had any objections, and Jubil again stepped in to calm the animals and convince them to carry on. Lieutenant Doane had no patience for these efforts, so he and Mr. Everts left to scout the trail ahead.

By late morning the party finally set off to the south. From this point, the Yellowstone River entered a canyon that offered no trail alongside it, which forced them up and over the mountains. The way here was rocky, and animals and Indians had left little or no trail. Mr. Langford led the party in the direction he thought Doane would have taken, but it led to an impassable dead end. As they retraced their steps, Jubil noticed a path leading up the hillside through a stand of trees they had passed earlier but ignored. He pointed it out to General Washburn, who agreed that Jubil should take a closer look.

On the hillside, Jubil discovered the drag marks of lodge poles and the hoofprints of unshod horses, but no signs of shod horses.

"It's possible they came this way," Jubil reported to General Washburn and Langford. "If the Indians came along after Lieutenant Doane passed, they probably covered his tracks. That would also mean these Indian tracks are fresh."

"And they are directly ahead," General Washburn said.

"Doane must have come this way," Langford said. "I think we should follow the trail."

General Washburn looked at his compass and map. "The river is in that general direction, so we can't go too wrong. We'll hope the Indians are peaceful, but I'll tell the soldiers to be prepared."

Jubil was not especially worried about the Indians, but he was troubled about having anyone separated from the main party. Trying to survive alone out here would be a daunting challenge, but Doane was surely capable—or would be with two good hands.

They followed the trail without incident, reaching a creek that ran down the mountainside to the Yellowstone. General Washburn decided to set up camp early on a flat open area where Doane and Everts might see their campfire. Jubil recalled the time he and Lew Keplinger had been making their way down from scouting Longs Peak in the dark—the campfire at the base of the couloir had most likely saved their lives.

As the packers set up camp, Jubil went with Langford to

look for some sign of Doane and Everts. They continued along the trail until they came to another Indian trail that crossed it. Jubil dismounted to have a look.

"Two sets of shod hoofprints here," Jubil said with excitement. "This must be the Lieutenant and Mr. Everts."

"Good," Langford replied, with relief. He looked at the sky, which was growing dark. "We'll follow on in the morning. They're probably camped along the Yellowstone, waiting for us."

Jubil and Langford returned to camp. The horses and mules were tethered on long lead ropes in a small stand of aspens near a little stream, where they could graze and drink.

As Jubil and Langford removed their horses' saddles, Jubil heard a screaming whinny. One of the mules was spooked, rearing and tugging on his lead rope in an effort to escape some perceived danger that Jubil could not locate. Langford dropped his saddle and went to settle the mule. The animal was thrashing wildly, requiring Langford to dance around to keep from being trampled. He was making a grab for the lead rope when the hitch knot came loose. The tension on the rope caused it to recoil toward the mule, and by chance it flew straight into Langford's grasp. He wrapped the lead rope around his wrist to get a firm grip and hold the mule under control. Still panicked, the mule resisted and reared up, pulling Langford off balance. When the mule's hooves touched the ground again, the animal bolted and pulled Langford off his feet, dragging him behind as he fought to right himself or free himself from the rope.

The mule ran left and then right, and Jubil ran to intercept him, but he changed direction again, cutting back abruptly to the left. Langford was swung in an arc behind the animal and thrown into a downed log. Jubil winced as Langford's head hit the log and he went limp.

The mule veered again and this time rushed straight toward Jubil, still dragging Langford, who was now unconscious. Jubil stood still, trying not to spook the mule, and as he ran past, Jubil ran alongside him for a few feet and then sprang toward the mule. He locked his arms around the animal's neck and lifted his feet off the ground, putting his full weight on the mule in an effort to slow him down. He then lowered his feet to the ground and dug his heels into the dirt to bring the mule to a halt, digging furrows in the ground for several yards before the mule finally stopped. Jubil was able then to grab the mule's halter.

The campfire and the other men were a hundred or so yards away. Jubil called to his friend, "Walter, come tend to Langford!"

Walter ran over, shouting for more help when he saw what had happened. He freed Langford from the lead, then helped Jubil control the mule. Mr. Stickney was next to arrive on the scene. He splashed some water from his canteen in Langford's face to revive him, and Langford sat up and reached for his sore head. Stickney inspected Langford for injuries and asked him to carefully move his arm and shoulder. He found a pronounced lump and a small cut on Langford's head, but he declared him free of any breaks, sprains, or other serious injuries. Stickney helped Langford to his feet, and the two men walked over to camp, where Langford could rest and recover.

Later that evening, as Jubil lay on his bedroll looking up at the stars and thinking of Nelly, Mr. Langford approached him. "Mr. Walker," Langford said, "I'd like to thank you for stopping that mule. I appreciate your quick thinking and your courage in apprehending him."

Jubil sat up and looped his arms around his knees. "You're welcome," he said. "I'm glad I was able to catch him."

"Yes," Langford said, studying Jubil. "I also appreciate how you handled that encounter with the Crow. That could have gone very badly."

"Yes sir," Jubil agreed. "They just seemed curious, not threatening."

Langford nodded. "Mind if I sit down?" he asked, gesturing at a nearby log.

"Not at all," Jubil replied. Langford took a seat.

"I believe General Sheridan was correct—your experience is proving to be an asset to our expedition," Langford said.

"I hope that's the case," Jubil replied.

"But I confess, I'm still puzzled about why you would come all this distance, at your own expense. The rest of us are residents of the area, driven by personal and civic pride to develop the region, and, quite frankly, looking for ways to economically benefit from that development. I'm still not sure I understand your motivation for being here."

Langford's question struck Jubil as reasonable and respectful, motivated by curiosity rather than suspicion. He answered accordingly. "I don't see my motivation as much different from your own. I'm not a resident, but I'm still proud to help develop the region. I've been fortunate to follow Major Powell into unexplored places on two occasions. When General Sheridan offered me this opportunity, my pride demanded I accept. But my business partners and I are also interested in how this region might fit with plans we have been pursuing."

"Adventure tourism?" Langford said.

"Yes," Jubil replied. "As you said when we met, we share a common interest in that area. I had already been informed of that, but wasn't sure of the reliability of the source."

"Informed by whom, if I may ask?" Langford said carefully.

"Phineas Black, in Bozeman," Jubil replied, watching for a reaction.

Langford looked surprised. "You are acquainted with Phineas Black?"

"He introduced himself to me at the hotel in Bozeman," Jubil explained. "He warned me he would be a fierce competitor if my partners and I decide to open an outfitting business in town. I didn't find him very congenial."

Langford grinned. "A great number of people would agree with you on that."

Jubil grinned as well, feeling a sense of connection with Langford for the first time. "He also said he was interested in the Yellowstone area for mining purposes," Jubil added. "He said it would be a gesture of goodwill if I would report to him before I leave the area."

"Do you intend to?" Langford asked.

"No," Jubil answered. "He may find me, but I won't seek him out."

"If you don't mind some unsolicited advice," Langford said, "you should be very cautious about Black. His enemies seem to fall victim to bad luck that coincidentally favors him. Are you considering opening a store there, in Bozeman?"

"No," Jubil said. "I'll discuss it with my partners when I return home, but I'm sure they'll agree Bozeman is too small and too remote for a store like ours."

"You should come have a look at Helena," Langford said. "It's far more civilized than Bozeman. The First National Bank of Helena can provide you financing, and my lumber operation can supply building materials at a good price."

Even though Phineas Black had warned him that Langford would try to partner with him for his own benefit, Jubil was not feeling ill at ease as he had in Mr. Black's company. After all, Langford was inviting him to do business in Helena, while Black was trying to chase him away from Bozeman.

"I appreciate the offer," Jubil said. "Of more immediate concern to me is the adventure travel business. You're aware of the tour I had planned this summer, so you know my interests, but I don't know your plans. Do you see me as competition?"

"I don't see us as competitors," Langford said. "My plans are not as specific as yours. If our expedition finds the folklore is true, people will come from far and wide to see the wonders of Yellowstone. There will be commerce of every sort that will spring up. I want my bank, my lumberyard, and my community involved in that growth. For that to happen, we have to get all those travelers out here, so my bank is working with the financier Jay Cooke to complete the Northern Pacific Railroad. My hope is that his railroad will bring people right to our door in Helena."

"Black said he thought you and Cooke would somehow corner the market on the tourist business and shut competitors out," Jubil said.

Langford shook his head. "Black exaggerates the power of his enemies. It justifies his overreaction to perceived threats," Langford said. "You'd best watch your back around him."

Jubil felt Langford's warning was out of sincere concern for his wellbeing.

Langford stood up. "If you'll excuse me, I'm going to go lay down my aching head. I just wanted to thank you for saving me from being dragged all over Wyoming."

"You're welcome," Jubil said, standing and shaking the hand Langford was offering him.

Jubil lay down again on his bedroll. It appeared Langford's brusque manner at the outset of the expedition did not represent his predominant nature. Since that episode, Langford had been even tempered toward everyone except Jake Smith, which Jubil had concluded was not unfounded. Their conversation had confirmed what he had suspected: it was not Nathaniel Langford he had to be cautious about, it was Phineas Black. Jubil was pleased to have gained Langford's acceptance, but he was troubled that he had allowed himself to miss another opportunity to set the record straight about General Sherman's invitation.

CHAPTER 5

Jubil was relieved when, by midday the following day, they found Doane and Everts already camped by Hot Spring Creek on the Yellowstone River. It was the first hot spring Jubil had ever seen and a sure sign they were entering a volcanic region—the Yellowstone Basin. The spring was a small flow of water too hot to touch but not boiling. It smelled like rotten eggs, which Doane said was because the water was laden with sulfur. They had now been on the trail for seven days, and for the first time, General Washburn decided to spend more than one night in the same place. Mr. Everts called it Camp Comfort.

Doane ordered some of his soldiers to remain in camp, to guard the pack animals and supplies, while he led Jubil and the others to see some features of the area he and Everts had located the previous day. At the mouth of Hot Springs Creek was a collection of five large springs and half a dozen smaller ones with many standing pools, the largest of which was about twenty feet in diameter. Its color was an ugly greenish yellow, and Jubil was stunned to see that it was boiling like a cauldron. It was one thing to read or hear about the mechanics of such things, and another thing altogether to see them with his own eyes. The water from the largest spring flowed nearly black, looking more like oil than water. The acrid odor of sulfur and alum burned his nose and throat, and made his eyes water. Everyone found the area disagreeable, and they soon moved on.

To the south of their camp, they followed Tower Creek, another tributary of the Yellowstone, to the most dramatic waterfall Jubil had ever seen. Mr. Stickney ventured to the edge and, with a stone attached to a strong cord, measured its height at one hundred and five feet. After some debate, the group decided on what Jubil thought was a decidedly lackluster name: Tower Falls. He wondered what his friend Andy Hall would have called it. In the Grand Canyon, Andy had named an intimidating section of the river Lodore Canyon, inspired by a poem he recalled—"The Cataract of Lodore." He wondered where Andy was these days.

It was an easy climb down to the base of the falls, but Jubil saw Doane wince as he reached for a handhold. The bandage had come off Doane's thumb, and the digit was a horrible sight, swollen and suppurating. When it was time to return to camp, Doane stayed behind to soak his hand in the cold creek water. Jubil, hiking behind Langford, heard him say that Doane had hardly slept for the past two nights because of the pain, and that he was concerned that the infection could get into Doane's bloodstream and kill him.

Jubil was alarmed by this information. They were a long way from a doctor or a sickbed. He wondered if Mr. Stickney could do anything about Doane's thumb. After all, he had looked after Langford capably after the incident with the mule. The only remedy Jubil knew for a wound was his mother's—coating the wound with honey—but they had no honey. Besides, that was more of a preventative measure to stave off infection than a cure for an infection that had already taken hold.

Back at camp, the party found that General Washburn and two soldiers had ridden out to a peak to the south. When they returned late in the day, the general was enthusiastic about what they had seen. "Tomorrow morning we'll all return together," he said. The general handed his reins to one of the soldiers. "The exertions of the day have worn me down a bit, so I believe I'll go lie down. But I'll be ready to ride in the morning." As he walked away, leaving the soldier to tend to his horse, Jubil could see the weariness in his slumped posture and slow steps.

"You don't you suppose the general is taking ill, do you?" Jubil asked Walter.

"I hope not," Walter replied. "His health has been frail for some time. He served two terms in Congress, but then he contracted tuberculosis and did not stand for reelection. He obtained an appointment as surveyor general of Montana and moved out here in the hopes the clear air would improve his constitution."

Jubil and Walter shared a look of concern. Jubil realized how miraculous it had been that no one on his previous expeditions had taken sick or been seriously injured. Of course, on the way to Fort McPherson with General Sherman, he had seen Lieutenant Jenkins shot in the head during an Indian raid. They had buried him and moved on, but he had dreams about the incident for several nights afterward, and he still tried to keep his mind from returning to that moment. He supposed if someone became too disabled to travel, they would have to somehow pack him out. He'd do his part if that became necessary.

That evening after supper, Jubil noticed Washburn, Langford, and Doane each at work updating their expedition journals. As he passed near Lieutenant Doane, he heard him grumbling and noticed that holding the pen was a struggle because of his infected thumb.

"I'd be glad to serve as your scribe, Lieutenant," Jubil offered.

Doane frowned up at him. "I'll manage, thank you," he said tersely.

Jubil wondered if Doane was just cranky—congenitally or from the pain in his thumb—or if he truly did not like Jubil because he had been a member of Powell's Grand Canyon expedition. Doane's insistence that he could tough the situation out reminded Jubil of his friend Lew Keplinger, who had more than once shown that his bravery could push him to recklessness.

"Well, good night then," he said to the lieutenant and went to bed.

He wasn't sleepy and found his thoughts wandering to Nelly. Thinking of her used to be a way to lull himself to sleep when he was away from home, but now thinking of her did not bring the sense of comfort it once had. She had said she was not leaving Bloomington to get away from him but to find what she wanted in life.

Nelly had always been more outspoken and more independent than other girls. She was whip-smart and saw right to the heart of matters. He knew that she was reluctant to be a wife and a mother, like the other women he knew, but in an ironic twist he had still not fully come to terms with, his own rejection of a quiet life on the farm in favor of a life of adventure had set her wanting the same for herself. He fell asleep hoping that when she returned home at the end of the summer there would still be a place for him in her life.

The next morning, as the expedition party rode along the river, the canyon narrowed again, and the only passable route south led up a long grassy slope and onto the great plateau, an immense undulating prairie that extended for miles. The plateau was dotted with groves of pine and aspen, and etched with lake-fed streams that flowed down the canyon to the river. Here Jubil got a lesson in the power of water and time as he studied the gash the Yellowstone River had carved through this plateau, creating a winding and impassable canyon reaching a depth of two thousand feet—the Grand Canyon of the Yellowstone.

The sun highlighted the canyon's walls, which had been stained yellow, red, white, and pink by the minerals percolating out of the hot springs. Steam rose from openings in the rock walls that Doane referred to as "vents." Although this canyon was indeed beautiful and colorful, it did not measure up to the Grand Canyon of the Colorado River. There, the river had carved a channel two to three times deeper through solid rock for nearly three hundred miles. In Jubil's mind, that would always be the grander of the two canyons.

They followed the course of the river south until they reached the base of the mountain General Washburn had climbed yesterday.

"We will leave the soldiers here to guard the packers, cooks, and mules," the general said. "The rest of us—and you, Lieutenant Doane—will ride to the summit. The route up is a gentle slope from this side, but, be warned, on the south face, it drops off precipitously."

The surface of the mountain slope was porous lava rock covered by a thin blanket of weeds and brush. Occasional out-croppings of granite protruded and lay scattered about.

When the general reached a point about halfway to the summit, he stopped and said, "Look to the east."

The mountain was just west of the canyon, and from this vantage point, they were able to see between ridges of the mountain into the Grand Canyon of the Yellowstone below them. Despite the altitude they had gained, they still could not see the river flowing along the bottom of the canyon.

"Now look over there," General Washburn said. "See that smoke?" On the other side of the canyon, the mountains were heavily wooded. Far in the distance, snowcapped peaks walled in the eastern side of the region. In the middle distance, rising from the woods, was a plume of smoke. "Watch and listen," the general said with a mysterious smile.

The men sat quietly watching the plume. Soon it rose to three or four times its previous height, and Jubil and the other men gasped audibly. A few seconds later, they heard a faint roar.

For the first time on the trip, Jubil saw Lieutenant Doane

smile. His cheeks rose, his eyes sparkled, and Jubil caught a flash of teeth under his mustache, the ends of which no longer stood out but instead drooped to his chin.

"That's a geyser," Doane said with obvious glee.

General Washburn returned Doane's joyous smile. "Yes."

A cheer arose from the explorers, and Jubil joined in with gusto, his heart pounding. As they continued their ride toward the summit, he realized he was smiling with joy at what they'd seen and in anticipation of what lay ahead. He looked at Walter and saw that he was smiling too.

When they reached the summit, a flat plateau with a rim on the southern edge that dropped off steeply into the vast Yellowstone Basin, Jubil dismounted, held Apollo's reins, and stared in amazement. It was as though he could see to the very edge of the Earth. Jubil had never felt so small in his life—like an ant on an anthill. He thought of the view from the window of Mr. Warner's office overlooking Council Bluffs and the Missouri valley, the view from the summit of Longs Peak in the Colorado Rockies, the view from the Colorado River looking up at the mile-high walls of the Grand Canyon—all sights that had expanded his view of the world—but this was more stunning than any of them. Lieutenant Doane took a barometer reading and found they were at slightly less than ten thousand feet.

"I'd venture to say we can see the whole layout of the area as clearly from this point as looking at my map," General Washburn said. He opened the map, and Langford and Doane came to stand on either side of him. Jubil, standing next to Langford, couldn't see the map very well, but he could still recall the image from General Sheridan's office. It was a strange sensation to picture the map in his mind and see what it was depicting spread out in reality before him.

"I'd say we're standing about here," the general said, "near the north rim of this vast basin. This whole thing is some thirty to forty miles in diameter." He swept his arm across the vista. "To the east the Absaroka Range, the Tetons to the south, the Madison Range to the west, and the Gallatins behind us to the north. You can see breaks have occurred in the circle over the ages, but there was obviously once a continuous ring of mountains surrounding the basin."

In the center of the basin was Yellowstone Lake, perhaps twenty miles long and fifteen miles wide. The lake's outline resembled a misshapen hand—the palm was the northern portion of the lake, and held a few islands; a large bay on the west formed the thumb; the fingers were ridges encroaching into the lake on the south end; the largest finger of the lake was in the pinkie position at the southeast, and beside it were two smaller misshapen fingers, while the index finger was missing altogether.

"The lake will be our next objective," the general said. "We'll follow the Yellowstone past the Upper Falls, which according to the map are just south of here, and then continue on to the lake."

Jubil traced the course of the river as it entered the south end of the lake, its source somewhere still further south, and then emptied out of the north end of the lake, beginning its atypical northward flow. To the west of the lake, he noticed dozens of plumes of steam extending in a northwesterly line for miles.

"Look there!" he shouted. He recalled Jim Bridger's crudely drawn map and the legend scrawled in the southwest corner: *Volcanic Region.*

"That has to be the geyser basin," General Washburn said. "We'll come around the lake with the goal of exploring it."

Doane, who had been drawing a map and taking notes in his journal, tucked the notebook under his arm and massaged his hand, which was apparently irritated by his efforts. "General," he said, "notice how all of the mountains surrounding the basin drop steeply in. Notice the thermal springs and geysers, which show that it all sits on top of a boiling caldron.

I believe this whole area we are looking at is the caldera of a huge ancient volcano, now extinct—or perhaps not?"

"That is a fearsome thought, Lieutenant," General Washburn said, "but I cannot argue with your conclusion."

Jubil stared at the almost delicate jets of steam issuing from the basin and imagined the force of an explosion that would create a caldera forty miles wide. He pictured what the view from this peak must have been eons ago—a sea of boiling lava. As he turned and looked around at the plateau, he reminded himself that they were already in the basin. He was not standing on the rim of the volcano but on a small island in the northern part of the crater. The idea was almost too big to comprehend, and more than a little unsettling. He thought the volcano must be active, otherwise there would not be hot springs and geysers visible. But how active was it? For the first time, Jubil's enthusiasm for exploring the mysteries of this place was tinged with a mild foreboding. How safe was it, really, to be riding around in the basin of an active volcano?

"Have you completed the sketch for your map, Lieutenant?" General Washburn asked, interrupting Jubil's reverie.

"Very nearly," Doane replied, "With your permission, sir, I'd like to label the peak we are standing on Mount Washburn."

"Here, here!" Judge Hedges cried, and Jubil joined in as the other men took up the cheer.

"I'm honored, gentlemen," General Washburn said. "Thank you."

As the men made their preparation to leave, Jubil took a final look at the Yellowstone Basin. The notion of a sea of boiling lava had put him in mind of the term having "the fear of God" put into him. It was impossible to be in the presence of powerful works of nature—whether on the summit of a mountain, in the depths of a canyon, or on the rim of a massive volcano—and not wonder what power created it all. The loss of his family had left Jubil less than accepting of God's will or plan, but his travels brought him closer to a God that he could love, a God who had made the wilderness. This was part of what drove him to seek these places out—to be reminded of and to appreciate the mysteries and the wonders of life.

They made camp that night near a small stream that ran to the Yellowstone, and Jubil went to sleep feeling that he was truly where he belonged—somewhere in the wilderness. Around 3:00 a.m. he woke with a start and sat up on his bedroll. He had dreamt he was standing on Mount Washburn when Yellowstone Lake suddenly collapsed into an abyss which then erupted in a fiery column of steam and lava a mile high. He chided himself for an overactive imagination, but he lay awake awhile before drifting back to sleep.

The party continued south along the rim of the Grand Canyon until they reached the Upper Falls, which immediately replaced Tower Falls as the most dramatic waterfall Jubil had ever seen. Both falls seemed to him about the same height, but the overall aspect of the Upper Falls was much more dramatic. As the river approached the falls, it was squeezed into a narrow spout about eighty feet wide that poured over a series of what Doane described as lava ledges—five of them, thick sheets of black rock with a drop of ten to fifteen feet between them. There, the force of the water pushing through the narrowed channel hurled the water clear of the rock with a hiss. It fell onto a rock ledge below and sprayed a fan of mist out some sixty feet before continuing in a sheer drop of over one hundred feet. Jubil had seen some small waterfalls in the Rockies, but nothing like this. He could not imagine one grander than this. The brink of the Lower Falls could be seen downriver about one-half mile, but it was too late in the day to view it.

That night, Jubil had the late watch with Warren Gillette, Mr. Everts's son-in-law to be. Gillette was not unfriendly, but he was very reserved. Jubil had hardly learned anything about him. Now, the two of them were posted on opposite sides of the camp, so they still had no opportunity for conversation. The moon was a waxing crescent but, thanks to a cloudless sky, gave off light adequate to see by. Jubil climbed atop a waist-high pile of boulders and sat cross-legged, his rifle in his lap, still sleepy from being roused from his bedroll.

All of his watches had passed without incident, and he found himself distracted by memories of navigating the often dangerous waters of the Colorado River. Not long into that expedition, he had nearly drowned after his boat had crashed into a boulder. And by the time the journey ended, he knew what it felt like to face day after day without enough to eat. So far, the relatively comfortable conditions of this expedition stood in sharp contrast to those of his last one.

He heard a rustling in the brush some fifty feet to his left and came to attention. He listened carefully for a few moments and heard it again . . . then again, followed by a chuffing sound. He stood up on the boulders and peered in the direction of the sound. He heard a horse whinny, and then another, where they were hobbled and hitched with the mules downstream a few yards from the camp. Then the bushes and saplings shook again, accompanied by the chuffing sound. He hoped it wasn't what he thought it was. He brought his rifle up and waited. The brush parted, and Jubil saw the rounded outline of a large bear, making its way toward the horses and mules. He couldn't let it reach them.

"Hey bear!" Jubil shouted. "Hey! Hey bear! Get out of here!"

His friend Lew Keplinger had prepared him to deal with bears during their expedition in the Colorado Rockies, but Jubil had been fortunate enough to never have encountered one. That good fortune had now run out. Lew had told him that many bears would run away from people, especially peo-ple who made a lot of noise. But the only thing Jubil's shouting accomplished now was to draw the animal's attention to him. It came toward him in a loping run, covering half the distance in a few bounds.

Jubil tried to draw a bead on it, but his aim on the moving target was poor in the low light near the ground. He fired anyway, but missed. When the bear was within ten feet of him, it reared up on its hind legs, spread its arms wide—each of its paws as big as Jubil's head—and gave a roar that caused him to recoil and almost lose his grip on his rifle. *Keep your wits about you*, he told himself. Chances were that he would only get one more shot before the bear reached him. The outline of the animal was clear against the moonlit sky. Jubil took aim at its head and fired, and the bear dropped in a heap.

Jubil's heart continued to race as he climbed down from the boulders.

Warren Gillette, also on guard duty, rushed to Jubil's side, his weapon at the ready.

"Are you all right, Walker?" he asked.

"I'm fine, Mr. Gillette," Jubil said. "Just a little spooked."

"You done good," Gillette said, spitting tobacco juice as he admired Jubil's kill.

Lieutenant Doane appeared. He looked at the bear and at Jubil, then walked over and poked the bear with the barrel of his rifle. When it did not move, he turned and walked back.

"Good shot," Doane said, as he walked past Jubil without stopping. "I'll send the cooks over to dress it."

The other men gathered around to see what had happened. Soon, they and the cooks who had butchered the bear returned to bed, but Jubil remained on full alert for the rest of his watch. This place might not be as life threatening as riding the rapids of the Colorado River, but there were still a variety of ways in which it could kill a person.

The next day, the explorers returned to the Upper Falls. Jubil watched as Mr. Hauser bravely ventured onto a rock outcropping and dropped a weighted rope over the edge, measuring the falls height at one hundred fifteen feet. Afterward, they all continued down the rim of the canyon to view the Lower Falls, which was a little over half a mile downriver.

The Lower Falls at its brink was about ninety feet across and without rapids, though the current was very swift. A rock ledge stood about one hundred feet above the brink and overhung the pool at the base of the falls. They climbed to the top of the ledge, and the view was grand. The heavy body of water poured over a wide slab of black rock and made a magnificent drop of three hundred and twenty feet, dissolving into foam as it poured into an immense circular cauldron. An eerie humming sound came from the depths, very different from the roar of the Upper Falls.

"I'd venture you didn't see a match for either of these falls along the Colorado River," Lieutenant Doane said, standing near Jubil as they peered into the abyss.

"Thankfully, no," Jubil said. "It would have been a fearsome portage if we had, or a spectacular end to us if we'd been caught unaware."

"Yes," Doane said, "I believe these cataracts are among the greatest waterfalls of the continent."

"I don't doubt that," Jubil said, pleased that Doane, for the first time on the trip, had spoken to him unprompted.

After examining the falls, General Washburn announced that he would return to camp for a rest. "I confess the rock climbing has winded me," he said.

The other men were split between exploring the falls and the rim of the canyon further or returning to camp with the general. Jake Smith, who seemed determined to develop his reputation as a contrarian, declared, "Well, boys, I have seen all there is to see of these waterfalls, and I am ready to break camp and move on."

Everyone ignored him, and Lieutenant Doane spoke up. "I'm going to go see if I can find a route to the bottom of the canyon."

"I'll go along," Jubil said, thinking the adventure might be a chance to get better acquainted with Doane. "If you don't mind."

Doane looked surprised, frowned slightly, and then shrugged. "Suit yourself," he said. "I plan to move along sprightly, though. You'll be on your own if you can't keep up."

"I'll do my best," Jubil said.

As they set out on horseback to look for a route down, Doane was silent, which Jubil did not mind. They rode back along the canyon rim a few miles. Doane recalled having passed a stream that ran down a reasonably gradual slope. He thought it might offer a passable route. When they reached the stream, they followed a game trail down to a point where it was too steep to continue on horseback. They hitched the horses and continued on foot. As they followed the stream down the canyon wall, Jubil stepped carefully across rocks in the stream bed, gauging the grip of his boot and the stability of the rock before committing his weight to a step. Falling and breaking a bone could be a death sentence out here. It wasn't just his feet he had to pay close attention to, it was also his hands. With almost every step down, he steadied himself against the rock outcroppings. He noticed Doane struggling to avoid putting weight on his right hand. This slowed Doane's pace, which Jubil easily matched. After four hours, they reached the bottom of the canyon and the Yellowstone River.

Doane went to the river, knelt down, scooped up some water and tasted it, then spit it out. "Sulfur . . .and warm," he said. He looked up and down the margins of the riverbed. "There are all kinds of chemical springs leeching into the main channel," he said.

Some of the springs deposited craters of calcareous rock, others oozed muddy black, blue, slaty, or reddish water. Jubil had no interest in tasting it.

Jubil knew from experience that canyon depths could bring oppressive heat, and this one certainly did, but the temperature here was made tolerable by a breeze drawing down the canyon. It was not enough, however, to eliminate the sickening purgatorial smells. The vents in the canyon wall emitted a strange frying sound that mingled with the rush of the current and created a continuous high level of background noise.

Doane looked up and down the canyon, "A desolate place," he said. "I suppose there's nothing much more to be found here—we might as well start back up." Doane looked up at the rim where they'd started. "I'd put the canyon's depth here at around seven hundred feet. What would you say?" he asked Jubil.

Jubil was surprised Doane would ask his opinion. He had spent weeks following Major Powell through the Grand Canyon, helping take measurements and keep records of the height of canyon walls, and he thought Doane's estimate was off by a wide margin. He wondered if Doane was testing him.

"I'd say closer to twice that," Jubil said, squinting up at the rim of the canyon.

"You may be right," Doane said with a hint of a smile, as he instinctively massaged his right forearm.

Jubil noticed that Doane's entire hand was now badly swollen and red. The pain must have been excruciating for him climbing down. What would happen if the infection got worse? Jubil couldn't bring himself to ask Doane about it.

"We'd best move out," Doane said.

It was well after dark by the time they made their way back to camp. Lieutenant Doane and Jubil unsaddled and tended to their horses, then Jubil went to find some supper. The cooks had prepared biscuits and a hearty stew of potatoes, carrots, onions, and bear meat. This was Jubil's first taste of bear, which he found slightly greasy but surprisingly tender and flavorful. As he finished eating by the light of the fire, he saw Doane once again struggling to hold the pen to update his journal. He decided to try again to be helpful.

"That hand must be troublesome after the climb today," Jubil said. "I'd be glad to handle the pen while you dictate your journal. My penmanship is nothing to brag about, but it's legible."

Doane looked up at Jubil and put down the journal and the pen.

"Langford thinks we should lance my thumb," Doane said, rubbing his hand. "I'm concerned that might take it from bad to worse."

Jubil sat down on the log next to the lieutenant.

Doane studied Jubil. "You and Major Powell are close?"

"After a fashion," Jubil said. "He was a friend to my uncle in their early years, and my uncle served under him in the war. The major and his wife came to my mother's funeral. We belong to the same church."

"Powell took you under his wing when you were orphaned?" Doane said.

"No." Jubil smiled. "It took some convincing before he let me join his expedition. I chased him all summer the year my mother died, trying to prove myself."

"That was when you rode with General Sherman?" Doane asked.

"Yes, but Powell still turned me away," Jubil explained. "Once I had my affairs in better order and had gone into the outfitting business, the major had more use for me."

After a moment Doane said, "My hand could use a rest." He passed the journal, pen, and inkwell to Jubil. "We'll go at your pace. Headline the entry as *Tenth Day—August 31*."

As Doane began to recite, Jubil focused on the mechanics of writing rather than the content. But soon he became so entranced by what Doane was saying that he had to ask him to repeat passages. He had expected Doane to dictate brief statements outlining the events of the day. Instead, he was recording a word picture of what the expedition party had seen and done. With brevity and clarity, he alternated between broad scenes and narrow details—dimensions of things, their makeup, colors and shadows, sounds and smells. His language was simple, but his imagery vivid. Jubil had to ask how to spell several of the geologic terms, but Doane was gracious about it.

"Every great cascade has a language and an idea peculiarly its own," Doane said, "embodied, as it were, in the flow of its waters. Thus, the impression on the mind conveyed by Niagara may be summed up as 'overwhelming power,' of the Yosemite as 'altitude,' of the Shoshone fall, in the midst of a desert, as 'going to waste.' So the upper fall of the Yellowstone may be said to embody the idea of 'momentum' and the lower fall of 'gravitation.' In scenic beauty, the upper cataract far excels the lower. It has life, animation, while the lower one simply follows its channel. Both, however, are eclipsed, as it were, by the singular wonders of the mighty canyon below."

Yes, Jubil found himself thinking as he wrote, *that's just how it is*. He had never seen the other cascades Doane mentioned, but he felt he knew something about them now. He also caught a glimpse of the wide experience Doane must have in the field.

When they were finished, Doane looked it over.

"That's a fine job," He said, "far better than the miserable scratch marks I've been making."

"I enjoyed doing it," Jubil said. "You're very good with words. How do you know all the names of rocks and their formations?"

"It was my specialty in college," Doane said. "I've been in the field a while too."

"I'll help again, any time," Jubil said as he rose to leave. Before he walked away, he stood thinking this would be a good time to reveal Sherman's invitation, to be free of this mess of his own making. But Doane's good opinion of him had come hard-earned, and he decided he would not risk dashing it so soon.

Doane's knowledge of geology gave Jubil cause to reflect,

as he lay on his bedroll, on his own education. He had considered looking into classes at Illinois Wesleyan once he and Nelly were married and settled into their life together, but he wondered now if he would ever follow through with that. That led him to wondering again if he and Nelly would ever be married, and he fell asleep with an uneasiness about his future hanging over him.

In the morning, the expedition followed the Yellowstone River south out of the Grand Canyon and across the basin toward the lake. Toward noon, Jubil saw yet another new type of wonder—a grouping of gray mounds surrounded by earth that smoked and steamed. Within a circular area some two thousand feet in diameter, a crusty surface was punctuated by dozens of bubbling hot springs and pools spewing colored mud—dark brown, pink, yellow—the consistency of wet plaster.

Jubil and Walter sat on their horses and stared at the mysterious landscape before them.

"Have you ever seen anything like that?" Walter asked.

"No, and I'd sooner ride around it than across it," Jubil said as they watched Doane and Langford go for a closer look. As they rode out onto the crust between the mud pools, their horse's hooves clopped across the material with an unsettlingly hollow ring.

Jubil watched with concern, then cautiously led Apollo out behind them. Suddenly, Apollo's right front hoof broke through the crust, and the horse lurched forward. Jubil instinctively leaned back in the saddle to keep his balance as Apollo staggered and then regained his footing. The foul odor of sulfur and a hot breeze arose from the hole created by Apollo's hoof. Jubil dismounted to lighten the horse's load. He held the reins close as he rubbed Apollo's neck to comfort him and keep him from spooking and breaking away. Langford's horse had the same experience, followed by Doane's. The men retreated from the crust and gathered nearby.

"That is an impressive deposit of sulphur," Doane said, gesturing toward the circular area. "The vapor issuing from the crevices condenses and leaves these deposits. There must be thousands of pounds lying here and being continuously built upon."

"What is forming the boiling mud in those pools?" Jubil asked Doane.

"Some combination of water, minerals, and heat," Doane replied. "It would take scientific analysis of the material to answer you properly."

Langford retrieved two small glass jars and went to take samples of the mud. He put on gloves, lay prone on the crust, and carefully dipped material into each jar. Jubil felt a strange anxiety, as if he were standing on a sheet of thin ice, but the lake below was a boiling cauldron.

They made their way around the circle of encrusted sulphur and began the search for a source of potable water. Good water sources had not been an issue so far, but this far into the interior of the basin, they approached several springs only to find they were heavily laced with dissolved minerals. Finally, five miles down the valley, they found a stream that was tolerable, though still slightly tainted with a mineral taste.

After they made camp next to the stream, Doane retreated to his bedroll without eating supper. Hauser, Judge Hedges, and Everts fell into a discussion of politics, while Stickney, Gillette, Walter, and Jake Smith played poker. General Washburn and Langford went off to work on their journals, so Jubil went to see if Doane felt like updating his. Doane accepted Jubil's help, and Jubil struggled to stay silent on the subject of Lieutenant Doane's health. His level of alarm was nearing a point where he would not be able to remain silent much longer.

As he took down Doane's observations, one in particular caught Jubil's attention.

"The amount of pure crystalline sulphur deposited in this

locality is very great," Doane said. "Probably one hundred tons could be gathered in sight on the surface. The continuous supply will one day be turned to account, in the manufacture of acids on a large scale."

Jubil thought of Phineas Black. This was exactly the kind of thing he would bring his miners in to exploit for the purpose of lining his own pockets. He pictured this wonder of nature being chipped away with pickaxes and the crusty surface being carried away in baskets. He would do nothing to help Black with any such effort.

"I've been lucky enough to see a few grand places," Jubil said, "but I've surely never seen anything like this place. Have you?"

"I've seen many of the elements—hot springs, rivers, waterfalls, and lakes," Doane said, "but never on so grand a scale. Some things I've never seen—like the boiling colorful mud pots—and I'd venture to say few have. I'm looking forward to a closer look at the geysers."

"It would seem a shame if anyone were to spoil any of it for a profit," Jubil said, "like you mentioned about the sulphur deposits."

Doane looked pensively at Jubil and stroked his long droopy mustache. "I would not disagree, but the wheels of commerce typically roll right over such concerns."

Jubil considered Doane's point and nodded. But he was wondering if that always had to be the case. Was there no way to keep the wheels of commerce at bay?

The following morning, they explored the area, setting off west, away from the river. When they stopped to examine a unique cavern in the side of a hill, the general dismounted to have a careful look. The opening in the rock was some five feet in diameter, and every few seconds, a horizontal jet of deep-green water spewed from it. There was no smell of sulphur or other mineral, yet the sides of the cave were covered with dark green deposits. Doane did not recognize the material, so Langford took a sample for later analysis.

As they examined the cavern, they heard a faint booming sound coming from somewhere in the distance.

"What do you make of that noise?" General Washburn asked.

"Sounds like cannon fire," Doane said.

They stood measuring the regularity of the explosions and discovered that they occurred every five seconds. Whatever it was, Jubil thought, it had to be dangerous.

"Let's go have a look," Langford said, leading out. Jubil's instincts told him not to approach the source of these explosions any closer, but his curiosity insisted.

They tethered their horses and walked south from the cavern, in the direction of the sound. As they moved along, the volume increased, but more disturbingly, Jubil began to feel the earth tremble with each report.

"Here we go again," Walter said, "heading straight toward danger instead of skirting it."

"I reckon that's what exploring is all about," Jubil said, presenting a brave face to cover his own anxiety. He once again had the feeling they were walking on a thin surface of earth floating above an inferno.

On the slope of a steep wooded ravine, they spotted the crater of a mud volcano some thirty feet in diameter, bounded on the upper side by the hill and an elevated rim on the lower side. Heavy volumes of steam rolled out of the crater and ascended three hundred feet. With each booming concussion from far down inside the Earth, a sound that shook the ground under Jubil's feet, mud flew from the crater. He struggled to understand the force that was belching out enough mud to crush flat the young pines nearby. In a wide circle around the crater, trees were broken, their branches festooned with dried mud.

"Have you noticed, sir," Jubil said to General Washburn,

who stood beside him on the barren earth near the crater, "that we're well within range of that crater?"

"Hmm," the general said, glancing at the fresh mud splatters at their feet and giving Jubil a smile. "Perhaps we should move downrange a bit."

In the morning they followed the Yellowstone over marshy ground for two miles, from which point they spotted a broad sheet of water in the distance. They skirted an estuary for three miles, passed over a sand levee grown up with sagebrush, and found they had arrived on the sandy beach of the great Yellowstone Lake. It was a windy day, and the water was marked with whitecaps. Good-sized waves lapped at the sand. Satisfied with their progress for the day, they camped in a grove on the lakeshore.

After supper, Jubil offered to help Doane with his journal, but Doane declined. He was in too much pain to concentrate. Finally, Langford spoke up.

"We're growing very concerned about that thumb, Lieutenant," Langford said calmly. "It's getting worse rather than better. If we don't open it up, I'm afraid it might kill you."

Doane looked at his thumb and massaged his forearm, then looked up at Langford.

"I have some chloroform in my pack," Langford offered.

"All right," Doane said reluctantly. "If you can put me out, we'll do it."

"Good," Langford said. He recruited Judge Hedges and Jubil to serve as assistants and went to make preparations for the surgery.

Doane lay down on a large flat boulder, and beside him they set a crate containing army cartridges—he would rest his hand on the crate during the surgery. Beside that crate, they set another crate with a lantern placed on it.

"I believe we are ready, Lieutenant," Langford said, as he approached the boulder with his knife in hand.

Doane eyed the three of them suspiciously. "Where is the chloroform?" he asked.

Langford frowned. "The fact is, I've never administered it. After thinking the matter over, I'm afraid to give it to you. I'd hate to be responsible for killing you with my good intentions."

Doane stared at Langford for a moment and then rolled his head back and stared up at the sky. He laid his hand out on the cartridge box—palm up with his thumb extended. Langford sterilized his knife over the lantern chimney and wiped it down with a handkerchief.

"Get it over with then," Doane said with resignation.

Jubil and Judge Hedges steadied Doane's arm and hand. Without hesitation, Langford inserted the point of his knife deep into the pad of Doane's thumb and then pulled it quickly out to the tip, near Doane's thumbnail, creating a deep incision. Doane gave a shriek as the released corruption flew out into Langford's handkerchief.

Much to Jubil's surprise, when he looked at Doane, the lieutenant was regarding Langford with a smile.

"That was elegant!" Doane exclaimed with a sigh and lay back with his eyes closed.

Langford directed the cooks in the making of a poultice of bread and water and applied that to Doane's thumb. Jubil and the judge helped Doane to his bedroll, and within a few minutes he dropped off into a seemingly peaceful sleep.

CHAPTER 6

Doane was still sleeping soundly long after the rest of the party finished breakfast the next morning. General Washburn decided they would remain camped until he awoke and could travel. While Doane slept, Washburn and Langford wrote in their journals, Judge Hedges and Mr. Hauser read, Stickney and Gillette went hunting, and Jake Smith went fishing with the packers and cooks. Jubil, Walter, and Mr. Everts went out reconnoitering along the north shore of the vast lake.

The northern point of the irregular shoreline was near their camp, which was along the west bank of the Yellowstone River, where the river left the lake. The wind had died down overnight, and today the waters of the lake were deep blue and as clear as crystal. Jubil squinted to make out the southern shore about twenty miles away, where timbered ridges projected far into the water, dividing it into large bays and channels—the fingers he had seen from atop Mount Washburn. The eastern side was a sand beach that extended all the way to the southern shore. It reminded him of the beach in Chicago along Lake Michigan. The western side featured a large bay, and the sandy shoreline ran under a low bluff of timbered ridges. There were several islands in the lake, a few of them of formidable size. After about an hour's walk they reached a small bay, but rather than round it to continue, they turned back for camp.

That evening Doane continued to sleep, his peaceful expression and loud snoring indicating that he was quite comfortable. After supper, General Washburn reviewed his original plan for the expedition: They would continue clockwise around the lake, visit the geyser basin, then go north to the Madison River and follow it west through the Madison Range before turning north for Fort Ellis.

Mr. Hauser's opinion was that the expedition had already seen enough to confirm the folklore and warrant a full government survey. He was ready to turn around and go back home, retracing their route in. His banking partner, Langford, did not agree. Langford pointed out that the expedition had prepared for a month-long trek, and they should avail themselves of this opportunity to explore. Their exchange brought to mind Jubil's relationship with Luke and how easy things were between them. He wondered how men of such different outlooks could operate a business together.

Stickney and Jake Smith agreed with Hauser. Mr. Gillette stroked his side whiskers thoughtfully and said that he felt circumnavigating the lake was likely to reveal very little of interest, and suggested instead that they head west, directly toward the geyser basin. Jubil agreed with General Washburn's plan, though he would have happily followed Gillette's suggestion. He certainly did not want to turn back and head for home, and he was uncertain why anyone would have joined the expedition in the first place with such a dismissive attitude.

Washburn put the matter to a vote and, with the support of Jubil, Walter, Everts, and Hedges, won a majority in favor of his proposal. The general then volunteered to part with provisions and mules if anyone wanted to take another route or go home, but he reminded them that Doane and the soldiers would stay with the main expedition party. A unanimous decision was reached to follow General Washburn's original plan.

Jubil was impressed by the way Washburn had turned

divided opinions into unanimous agreement without harsh feelings. On Jubil's last expedition, Major Powell had never asked for an opinion from the expedition party, and that had not served him or the party well. Dissention in the ranks led to three men leaving the expedition and climbing out of the Grand Canyon, only to be killed by Indians. Jubil shook his head thinking of how their deaths could have been avoided.

Midmorning the next day, Doane awoke in good spirits after thirty-six hours of rest, and General Washburn announced the expedition would set out again the following day.

The next morning after breakfast, Jubil, Elwun, and Charles completed packing the mules with relative ease. The animals and men seemed to have finally adjusted to one another and to the routine. In order to circumnavigate the lake clockwise, they would have to make their first river crossing, so it was important that the packing be done well. At the point the river left the lake, it was about one hundred yards wide with a slow but steady current. Jubil was proud of the job he and the packers had done as they made their way across without incident. He was also pleased with Apollo's performance. The horse entered the river gamely and swam confidently, giving Jubil another moment of gratitude for his equine companion.

The party trekked along the east side of the lake, where the smell of sulfur grew stronger and stronger. They paused on the brink of what Doane called a brimstone basin, an area where the ground was covered with blue clay and a yellow calcified deposit perforated by orifices that emitted sulfur vapor. As they started across the basin, the odor was so strong that it burned Jubil's nose and made his eyes water. Apollo and the other horses and mules flared their nostrils and jerked their heads up to try to escape the smell. Jubil spoke softly to Apollo and guided him carefully around patches where the crust of the basin appeared thin.

Beyond the basin, the area grew heavily forested, and the

route became obstructed by deadfall timber. They tried skirting it by moving to the lakeshore but found it miry and also often blocked by both driftwood and deadfall. As they weaved slowly through the timber, the going was often slowed further by swampy areas. This section of the trip tested Jubil's patience considerably, but he made his best effort to set a calm example for Elwun and Charles as he helped them deal with the mules. The mules' wide cargo loads, short legs, and temperamental natures made movement through the forest a tedious process. It took them all day to reach the southeastern tip of the lake where the Yellowstone River flowed in.

The river bank here was impassably muddy, making crossing impossible. The general decided to make camp and search for a route across the river the following day. Trout were abundant here, and Walter and Stickney set to work catching some of them. After Jubil helped unload and stake the mules, he and Gillette went out hunting and brought down a deer. While they field dressed their kill, Gillette, who was usually very quiet, asked Jubil about his other expeditions. Jubil gave a summary as he helped Gillette, who quickly and skillfully processed the deer. Gillette seemed most interested in Jubil's experiences in the Grand Canyon, but declared he was not anxious to experience it for himself.

The venison and trout added pleasant variety to the monotony of their staples. Jubil noticed that, in spite of the improved supper menu, General Washburn ate very little and retired early. His concern for General Washburn's health was growing. Ever since they had left the Falls, the general had been retiring early.

The pain in Doane's thumb had subsided, but it was still awkwardly wrapped in a poultice. Even though Jubil was scheduled for the late watch, rather than sleep for a couple of hours, he offered to help Doane with his journal. It was a joy to hear Doane's scientific, and occasionally poetic, description of the places and things they had seen. After their session, Jubil asked Doane if he would mind if he read some of the earlier entries. Doane did not mind, so before he went on watch and while Doane slept, Jubil read the journal with a growing sense of admiration.

The entry for their fifth day on the trail—the day that Doane and Everts had been separated from the rest of the party overnight—described a sight that Jubil and the others had not seen. On Doane and Everts route, they had come across a canyon that Doane described in almost mystical terms:

Standing on the brink of the chasm, the heavy roaring of the imprisoned river comes to the ear only in a sort of hollow, hungry growl, scarcely audible from the depths, and strongly suggestive of demons in torment below. Lofty pines on the bank of the stream "dwindle to shrubs in dizziness of distance." Everything beneath has a weird and deceptive appearance. The water does not look like water, but like oil. Numerous fish-hawks are seen busily plying their vocation, sailing high above the waters, and yet a thousand feet below the spectator. In the clefts of the rocks down, hundreds of feet down, bald eagles have their eyries, from which we can see them swooping still further into the depths to rob the ospreys of their hard-earned trout. It is grand, gloomy, and terrible; a solitude peopled with fantastic ideas; an empire of shadows and of turmoil.

At 1:00 a.m. Jubil took his position for the night watch. He was near the area where the horses were hobbled and hitched, and Jake Smith was in position to guard the opposite side of camp. Jubil passed the time thinking of how he might explain the wonders he had seen to Nelly. He wondered if Doane would allow him to copy his journal and share it with her.

A human scream rang out from the forest, bringing Jubil to his feet and sending a chill through him as he raised his rifle. The horses and mules, hitched close to camp, stirred uneasily. As Jubil waited to see if something or someone might emerge from the darkness, he wondered if someone had wandered away from camp and been attacked by an animal. Should he go into the forest after them? A nearly full moon lit the area with pale gray light, but visibility in among the trees was limited. Another scream, close by. Jubil eased forward a few steps and heard a rustle behind him. He spun around with his rifle at the ready.

"Hold your fire," Lieutenant Doane said. Seconds later Langford appeared.

Jubil pointed in the direction of the sound. "It came from that way. Is anyone missing from camp?"

"No," Langford said.

"It's a California lion—a mountain lion," Doane said, peering into the night. "And it's close by."

Jubil knew of mountain lions, but he had never encountered one. "Why do they scream like that?" he asked.

"It's either a female's mating call," Doane explained, "or a male warning off a rival."

The idea of large nocturnal predators in the trees, waiting to pounce, was unsettling, to say the least. Bears were to be feared, but they were not likely to sneak up on you. Cats were another matter. For the first time in his life, Jubil felt like a mouse.

"Fall back closer to the camp," Doane instructed. "I'll build up the fire some. It won't come near the fire."

"Keep a close eye on our animals," Langford cautioned. "If the cat gets hold of one, don't be afraid to shoot at it."

For the remainder of the night, Jubil kept a nervous watch and was relieved to reach sunrise without further evidence of the creature.

General Washburn and a few volunteers went on a scouting mission to find a route across the river, leaving the pack train and others in camp. Doane announced that he, in the meantime, intended to climb a nearby peak to get an improved view of the lake for his maps. Langford decided to join him, and Jubil, still full of nervous energy, went along. Their plan was to climb the peak, return to camp, and if they found the party had moved on, follow their trail to the next campsite. Jubil would not have attempted this by himself, but he was confident that Doane could find the others again if they were separated.

The peak they planned to summit looked no higher than Mount Washburn, but the slope was forested and at a steeper grade. It took them two hours to reach the tree line, where they hitched their horses to finish the climb on foot. The pitch was steep but nothing like the treacherous conditions Jubil had experienced on Longs Peak or on the walls of the Grand Canyon. Jubil climbed carefully anyway. The granite slopes were covered with loose talus, and he didn't want to risk sliding down the mountainside and breaking a bone.

Finally, they reached the summit. From their vantage point, they had a clear view of the southern part of the Yellowstone Basin. Below them, the Yellowstone River flowed in from its origin somewhere further south, possibly from a lake visible several miles distant. To the southwest were three large lakes, several small ones, and the Snake River and its tributaries. The centerpiece of the southern basin was a tall peak directly south of the thumb of Yellowstone lake. Doane struggled to hold the pen and sketch a detailed map.

As Jubil viewed the expanse from this new angle, he pictured his location against the image he held in his mind of the general's map. They had been traveling for seventeen days, come about one hundred twenty miles, and reached the southernmost point of their planned route. Rather than feeling daunted by the distance left to travel, Jubil felt slightly melancholy that the trip was already half over.

As Doane was finishing up his map, he addressed Langford.

"On my map, I propose to label the peak upon which we

are standing Mount Langford, in recognition of you having been first to make the summit."

"Well, Lieutenant," Langford said with a smile, "that is quite an honor. I proudly accept your nomination—with the caveat that of course General Washburn will have the final say."

"I'm sure he'll agree," Doane said.

"That big yellow mountain south of the lake," Jubil said, pointing southwest, "what are you labeling it—and why is it that color?"

"I labeled it just that—Yellow Mountain," Doane said. "It must have a high sulphur content. Given that, and its size and shape, I'd say it was once an active volcano within the larger Yellowstone caldera."

When they returned to the campsite, they found that the expedition party had indeed moved on. Doane spotted a trail that followed the bank of the Yellowstone upstream away from the lake, and they took it to a point where the trail crossed the river. Once again, Apollo swam with ease. They came up the bank on the opposite side and followed the trail through open forest and across a grassy valley. Suddenly Lieutenant Doane brought his horse to a halt.

"This doesn't seem right," Doane said, pointing at the trail ahead. "You can see this trail goes right up the valley wall onto the mountainside. They wouldn't do that."

"It's leading further away from the lake too," Langford added. "It's going to start getting dark soon. I think we should camp for the night and retrace our steps to the river crossing in the morning."

Doane reluctantly agreed, so they gathered wood and made a fire. As soon as the fire was set, Doane made a torch.

"As long as I still have some light," Doane said, "I can't let the fact rest that I missed their trail. I'll be back in a while."

With that, Doane hiked back along the trail toward the

river. Neither Langford nor Doane seemed worried in the least about being separated from the main party, so Jubil felt no real concern, although he did wonder what would happen if they somehow never found their traveling companions. At least he was in good company, he supposed. Jubil sat warming himself by the fire as Langford tended it.

Jubil was much more comfortable in Langford's presence than he had been at the outset of the expedition. Langford's character was similar to Major Powell's in some ways—often warm and friendly, sometimes stern and imperious. But he had no doubt Langford was more respectable and trustworthy than Phineas Black.

"If you don't mind my asking," Jubil said, "what originally brought you out West?"

"Gold…adventure, what else?" Langford said with a grin. "In 1862 I signed on with the Northern Overland Expedition to blaze a route to the Salmon River gold strike. I left St. Paul in the company of one hundred thirty men led by Captain James L. Fisk. We labored through dangerous territory for eighteen weeks, reaching Grasshopper Creek, near the head of the Missouri, with our supplies nearly exhausted and cattle too tired to continue. We wintered over there in that area, which was also the rendezvous for the Bannack Indians. I stayed on there and got involved in the settlement of the region."

"Did you strike gold?" Jubil asked.

"No, not technically," Langford said with a laugh. "I made my money off those out to strike it rich. Hauser and I opened a bank, and I opened a lumber mill."

"Wise move," Jubil said with a grin. Phineas Black had mentioned that Langford had done some exploring. Jubil was coming to like Langford. Their interests in adventure and business gave them a lot in common.

As the sunset faded, Doane returned wearing a disgruntled expression.

"It pains me to admit," Doane said, "but I missed the signs where our party turned off the trail and headed back toward the lake. I plead human fallibility." Doane stroked his giant mustache and grinned.

Langford and Jubil laughed.

"If you gentlemen don't mind, I'd like to rejoin them tonight," Doane said, "to spare them the worry."

They all took torches and walked their horses back along the trail to the point of their error, and turned in the direction of the lake. They hiked for about an hour and came in sight of a campfire about a mile distant. When they arrived within hailing distance, Langford gave a loud call, and a dozen relieved voices called out in return. By the time they rejoined their companions, it was nearly ten o'clock.

Jubil was exhausted from the rigors of the day and his lack of sleep the night before. He fell asleep quickly and was spared the unpleasantness of dwelling on being lost in the vast and unforgiving wilderness with few supplies.

In the morning, Doane showed General Washburn and the other explorers his newest map of the lake and pointed out their current location. They were now camped on the southwestern bank of the little finger of the misshapen hand, which was the largest arm of the lake. This was both the halfway point of circumnavigating the lake and the approximate halfway point of the expedition.

From there they would move west around the ring finger. The ridge that formed the finger rose a few hundred feet, then dropped back to the lake. The shoreline was swampy and blocked by deadfall, so the only way forward was up and over. The angle of ascent and descent were steep, and the whole thing was heavily timbered. Jubil had seen this section of their route clearly from the summit of Mount Langford. He dreaded the drudgery to come but was resigned to persevere through it. The same kind of perseverance had been necessary during the portaging of the boats and gear in the Grand Canyon, but on this trip, Jubil wasn't worried about starving to death. He had learned that not every moment of adventuring was exciting. Just like life in general, it was sometimes transcendent, sometimes terrifying, and sometimes tedious—you had to take the bad with the good.

Once they rounded these two fingers of the lake, they could angle northwest toward the thumb. The terrain in that area was flatter and more open. Knowing which way to go to reach that open ground was far easier than getting there. They set out single file up the heavily forested ridge and soon came across an impassable deadfall heap. Jubil and Stickney scouted out an alternative route and then returned to lead the group forward again. But they hadn't gone far through the dense forest when one of the packers called out for them to stop. Turning Apollo back, Jubil saw that one of the heavily laden mules had gotten stuck between two trees. Their pace from that point on was glacial as they found openings wide enough for the mules and their cargo.

General Washburn consulted with Langford and Doane, then called everyone to attention.

"We're going to try a different strategy in crossing this ridge," he said. "Rather than assault it in a single column, we're going to spread out in a row parallel to one another. This will allow each of you to find your own way around obstacles without being held up by others. But it is imperative that you keep in sight of the men on either side of you, and call out any warning or guidance to them. We'll cross the ridge and reconvene at the southern tip of the next finger. We'll camp there for the night, and whoever arrives first should build a fire as guidance. Any questions?"

Hearing none, Washburn signaled them to move out. Jubil guided Apollo up the ridge, glancing from side to side occasionally to make sure he could still see Langford and the other explorers on his right and Walter on his left. He was near the end of the row, with only Walter and Mr. Everts farther left. Sometimes it was easier to dismount and lead Apollo through a narrow gap between trees or through a snarl of dead branches. They took wide detours occasionally, but Walter was always in sight to his left, though he did occasionally lose sight of Langford and the others for brief periods. On the other side of the ridge, sweaty and exhausted, Jubil met with Walter and Mr. Everts, and they moved together along the shoreline toward the tip of the finger, where they spotted a campfire. By sundown, all the men had regrouped except Judge Hedges and Mr. Stickney. General Washburn thought it best to not go in search of them in the dark, so the men waited watchfully. Several hours later, they heard a call.

"Hello! Hello in the camp! Don't shoot us for a bear!"

Jubil recognized the high nasal twang of Stickney's voice and was relieved. Several of the men returned Stickney's call and rose to greet them as the men stumbled into camp, tired and happy to have found their way back.

"What happened to you?" General Washburn asked. "How did you come to be separated from everyone?"

"I saw the judge dismount to lead his horse around a difficult patch, but his horse spooked and broke away. I saw him chase after it and went to help. We chased the horse south, where the ridge flattened out to a plateau. We finally found the horse, but we had lost our bearings—it's hard to stay oriented in these blasted woods! We dropped down into a valley hoping it would lead back to the lake, and we were just lucky it was this valley."

General Washburn pondered Stickney's story and then spoke. "Gentlemen, we have had a few instances of being separated, and I feel somewhat remiss in not having set a clear policy in the event that anyone finds himself unable to locate the main party. I propose this: Should anyone go missing, we will search for one day in the vicinity where we are separated, and then we will move to set up camp on the shoreline of the west thumb of the lake. We will camp there and send search parties out. We'll set a signal fire on the shoreline and wait. If you become separated, make your way there. We will remain camped there as long as we can, but remember—we will not be able to remain indefinitely. Winter will close in, and we will run out of supplies. We will be forced to move on."

Jubil felt a sense of foreboding as the general spoke. He hoped it didn't come to that. But everyone understood that the whole party could not take the chance of being trapped here because of the misfortune of one individual.

As they moved northwest toward the thumb, the landscape was still hilly, but the ridges were not as steep. The forest was just as thick, however, and the going just as difficult. They continued to travel laterally rather than in single file, plodding forward in the same positions along the line—Langford and the other men to Jubil's right, Walter on his left, and Mr. Everts at the end of the row. As the day wore on, Jubil had the disconcerting feeling the woods were closing in around him. He was decidedly weary of this section of the trip. They were only making five miles a day. There was nothing to see but trees, and an overabundance of those. The general estimated they had one more day of this part of the trek before the terrain would open up. Based on the view from Mount Langford and Jubil's memory of the map, he could picture their location in the basin. He knew how wide this stretch of forest was, but there was nothing to do for it but push on. Moving forward became a mindless routine.

Midafternoon Jubil faintly heard someone shouting and stopped to listen. He realized he had drifted off into his own thoughts and allowed himself to lose track of his fellow explorers. He looked around to locate his partners in the row. At first, he was shocked to see no one, but then he spotted Langford further ahead to his right, and General Washburn further to Langford's right. To his left, Walter was nowhere to be seen. He realized it had been several minutes since he had last seen him. He heard the voice calling again, "Truman! Truman!" It was Walter. Jubil mounted Apollo and rode toward his voice.

"Truman's gone missing!" Walter said. "I let my attention lapse and lost sight of him—that was stupid of me." Walter looked around anxiously.

"Don't chastise yourself, Walter," Jubil said. "I had lost sight of you as well."

Walter thought he hadn't seen Mr. Everts for fifteen or twenty minutes. But he and Jubil agreed that time was slippery in this forest.

"He can't have gone far," Jubil said optimistically, even though he knew a person did not have to be more than a hundred yards away to be entirely out of sight and out of range of hearing a call—sound did not carry far in these woods. "Was he on horseback or on foot?" Jubil asked.

"He was on horseback," Walter said. "He was on my left maybe two hundred feet away, riding around a deadfall—his back was to me . . . He's not an experienced outdoorsman. I should have put him between you and me instead of leaving him on the end of the row."

"Chastising yourself won't help," Jubil said gently. "You didn't do anything wrong."

Walter looked away to hide the tears welling in his eyes.

"Stay here," Jubil said, "I'm going to go tell the general."

Walter nodded.

Jubil explained the situation to General Washburn and Langford.

"We'll make camp here and search until dark," Washburn said. "Notify the others, please, Mr. Langford."

Within the hour they had established camp, cleared an area and set a large signal fire, and organized search teams.

Jubil, Walter, and Gillette rode off together to search, taking care not to lose their bearings and add to the problem. They found the deadfall where Walter had last seen Mr. Everts, but by sunset they had found no sign of him and were forced to return to camp before dark.

The mood in camp that evening was somber. Jubil had little appetite, and Walter had skipped supper and gone off by himself. Jubil collected bowls of stew and cold biscuits for himself and Walter, and went to offer it to him.

"Want some supper?" Jubil asked.

Walter shook his head. "No thanks."

"Feel like some company?"

Walter shrugged. "I don't mind."

"Do you think Mr. Everts will remember the plan—to go to the thumb?" Jubil asked.

"He'll remember," Walter said, "but I'm concerned about his ability to execute it."

"It would be difficult for any of us to follow a trail through the heavy forest," Jubil said. Both Washburn and Doane had lost the trail over much easier ground. "But he should be able to find the lake, and from there he'll see how to make his way around to the thumb."

Walter nodded. "He is terribly nearsighted though. If his spectacles get lost or broken, he'd have to be right on top of things to see them. He wouldn't even be able to find his way by climbing a peak. All he would see is a vast blur."

Walter's observations altered Jubil's thinking about Mr. Everts's situation. On a broad scale, it would not be hard to find your way out of here: Climb a peak and find the lake, follow the lakeshore to the Yellowstone River, follow the river back to Montana and the Bozeman pass. Not hard to do, if you could see where you were going. Keeping bears, mountain lions, wolves, or Indians at bay, and hunting for food would also require the ability to see well enough to aim his rifle.

"We'll make a hard search," Jubil said. "We'll do our best to find him."

"Yes," Walter said pensively, "we'll do our best."

Jubil could see that his words were cold comfort, so he sat quietly with his friend for a while and then went to try to get some sleep. He lay trying to have optimistic thoughts, but the possibilities for the ills that could befall Everts were overwhelming. If his own feeling of helplessness was distressing, he imagined that Walter's, with the addition of guilt, was crushing. He had not fully considered the weighty responsibility he would be taking on by leading an adventure trip. What would it be like to lead a group of adventure travelers into the wilderness and have someone go missing?

Everts did not show up in camp that night, and in the morning, General Washburn ordered the cooks to put together a sack of rations to leave for him at the campsite. They put in a few handfuls of rice and beans, a couple of potatoes, and some dried beef, along with a note that Gillette wrote. It occurred to Jubil that he had some gear that might be of use to Everts, and from his trapper's pack removed the tin pot, matches, and flint he had packed in case he became separated from the party. He added these to Everts's supply sack, which they nailed to a tree.

While he had his pack open, he also retrieved his union suit and fur-lined gloves. The nights were turning cold, and he welcomed any comfort, no matter how small.

Having done all that they could for Everts at this location, they reluctantly set out to establish a rendezvous point at the thumb.

Along the way, Walter and Gillette used hand axes to mark blazes on trees, hoping Everts would find and follow them. Jubil hoped Everts had not lost his glasses so that he would be able to see them. By noon the terrain began to gradually slope upward, and the trees began to thin out. Jubil was greatly relieved as they topped a ridge to find below them an open plateau with grassy spaces and a network of small lakes. The plateau extended for miles, with the big lake visible to the north, and after an easy ride, they reached the thumb. Jubil would normally have felt an exhilarating sense of satisfaction after such a difficult trek, but his good feelings were muted by worry about Mr. Everts, out there somewhere alone.

The next day, General Washburn sent out three search parties. Jubil, Walter, and Jake Smith hiked along the lakeshore. Hauser and Gillette rode back through the forest, over the same route the party had taken the previous day. General Washburn and Langford rode off in a southwesterly direction to summit a peak and look for any signal fires Everts might have set. The others stayed behind to wait. By late afternoon, most of the party had regrouped at the rendezvous point.

Hauser and Gillette had not yet returned to camp, but they had taken their bedrolls and a small supply of rations in case they could not make the round trip in one day. When Langford and General Washburn returned, Langford told of yet another hazard he had encountered. His horse had broken through a surface of grass that concealed a hot spring beneath, scalding the poor animal's front legs badly and almost dumping Langford into the pit. This added yet another possibility to the list of what might have happened to Everts, though no one speculated aloud to that effect. For the first time, it occurred to Jubil that even if Everts were dead they might not find his body.

The following day, the sky was overcast and the air heavy and damp. Shortly after breakfast, Jubil retrieved the slicker he had rolled up and lashed to his trapper's pack and put it on before the skies opened and poured down an unpleasant mix of rain, hail, and light snow. General Washburn decided to remain in camp to avoid riding in such weather and to wait for Hauser and Gillette to return. By late afternoon the two men arrived after making a thorough search of the trail and finding no sign of Everts. Gillette's mood was low, and his long bushy mutton chops hung wet and bedraggled, the very picture of despondence.

In the evening, with an icy rain falling and the temperature dipping below freezing, Stickney gave a report inside the pavilion tent on the party's level of remaining provisions. The expedition had left Fort Ellis with supplies adequate for thirty days, and they had now been in the field for twenty-three. The coffee, sugar, and flour would last perhaps ten days longer, if rationed. The risk of starvation any time soon was negligible, as trout and other game had so far been plentiful, though there was no guarantee that would continue.

The greater concern was getting snowed in and trapped for the entire winter. The snow here would not be measured in inches but in feet. Any time now it might begin to fall and not stop again for days. Being caught in those conditions without shelter would mean certain death.

This was the first weather below freezing they had experienced, and Jubil donned all the cold-weather protection he had brought, including a union suit, a wool shirt, a hooded wool parka, a hooded oilcloth slicker, waterproof leather boots, and fur-lined oiled-leather gloves. These kept him tolerably warm for now, but they would not be enough to get him through the brutal winter cold.

Overnight the mixed precipitation changed to heavy snow. The men emerged from the pavilion tent in the morning to find it two feet deep on the ground and the water in their pail frozen. On the north side of the thumb, they could see that the ground was clear, so the whole region had not been hit by the storm, but if Everts had been caught by this weather unprotected, everyone knew what that would mean. Sending search parties out in these conditions was not reasonable, so the men were forced to stay in camp.

Doane had not only brought along the pavilion tent but a small camp stove. The stove had been used thus far by the cooks for baking, but was now a great comfort in the tent for keeping the men warm and drying out their wet gear. Jubil and Langford had the best all-weather gear in the party, so they volunteered for the chore of chopping a supply of firewood.

By the following day, half the snow had melted, but lingering at the campsite much longer was inadvisable. Feeding the men was one matter, but feeding the animals was another. The supply of grass in the area was wearing thin. The horses and mules were also an attractive food source for predators, though as yet none had been attacked. Still, every night the quiet had been broken by the unnerving screams of a mountain lion, triggering uneasy thoughts for Jubil that the sound might mean that Everts was being attacked.

In spite of the weather, a watch still had to be set, and Jubil volunteered to take the late watches. He enjoyed testing his gear against the elements. The Warners looked forward to his reports, and Luke had taken many of his suggestions and incorporated them into their merchandise. Also, while these men were easier to travel with than some he had known, being alone gave him time to sift through his thoughts.

He thought about the impact Mr. Everts's disappearance was having on those close to him—particularly Walter and Everts's soon to be son-in-law, Gillette. The previous summer, during the Grand Canyon expedition, erroneous newspaper reports had led Nelly and her family and the Warners to believe that Jubil and the rest of Powell's expedition party had drowned during the trip. He would hate to put Nelly and those he loved through such grief again. In truth, he had almost drowned, but he never admitted it to Nelly or the others. He felt sorrowful that his adventuring might one day bring them grief, but here he was—doing it again anyway. He could not escape the fact that, in spite of the dangers, he belonged here.

General Washburn called the men together the next morning. "Gentlemen," he said, "I believe we all agree we cannot remain here indefinitely, searching and waiting for Mr. Everts. Do I assume correctly?"

As the men began to nod reluctantly, one by one, Langford spoke. "I don't think we need to leave here believing the worst has happened. It's very possible that Everts has decided to retrace our route back home, rather than move deeper into unknown territory trying to catch up to us."

"I believe that is a real possibility," Doane said. "Retracing our route would be a sure way out of here and would account for why we've seen no sign he came this way."

Jubil looked over at Walter Trumbull, who was sitting with his hands clasped, elbows on his knees, staring at the ground.

Walter spoke up. "I know you're right, General. We can't stay here indefinitely. We've searched and searched and found no sign of him at all. This place is so huge we could never search it all. He has no shelter. He must not even have his rifle, or we would surely have heard it. How could he escape the predators? If he is still alive, it is by the grace of God alone. Whether he survives or not, as it is for all of us, is in God's hands. We have done all we can. I know Truman would agree."

Several of the men nodded in silent agreement as Walter provided the confirmation needed to accept the situation. Jubil hoped that if he ever brought grief to Nelly through his travels, that his fate be known without a doubt. It seemed to him that the effort of trying to keep hope alive was more of a struggle than accepting the loss and moving on.

"We'll break camp then," General Washburn said solemnly. "We'll move on northwest along the Firehole River, through the geyser basin, then up to the Madison, and homeward."

By late morning they were ready to move. They trekked up the beach for half a mile, detoured through the woods to avoid quicksand on the lakeshore, returned to the beach when the timber became impassable, and moved around to camp on the opposite side of the thumb.

At breakfast the next day, Mr. Gillette announced a change in his thinking. "General, I understand the position you and the men have taken, but I've concluded it won't set well with me to not make more of an effort. I'm going to stay on here for a while and search for Mr. Everts."

General Washburn sat quietly considering Gillette's decision. In those moments, Jubil decided that he, too, would stay behind, if Walter wanted to join Gillette in his search.

"I understand your concern, Mr. Gillette," General Washburn said. "The best we can do is provision you with rations adequate for a few days, and one pack mule. Lieutenant, I'd like you to assign two men to accompany Mr. Gillette."

Jubil turned to Walter Trumbull. "Do you want to stay with Gillette? I'll stay too, just say the word."

Walter was considering the question when Gillette interjected, "Let me spare you both the decision—I'd rather you didn't. Honestly, Walter, I'll do better if I don't have to worry about your safety too. I'm sure you and Mr. Walker are capable of looking out for yourselves, but I'd appreciate it if you just made your peace with the situation and went on with General Washburn. The soldiers and I will spend a few more days here and follow on soon, with Truman or without him."

Jubil had never heard Gillette string so many words together. He was impressed with Gillette's commitment and courage—perhaps these were the traits Miss Everts admired about him rather than his whiskers.

Walter shook his head. "You're a good man, Warren. Take care of yourself. Miss Everts needs you."

Everyone said their farewells to Gillette, and the cooks packaged up a share of rations for him and the soldiers.

Then General Washburn led the expedition party off on a northwesterly course. They traveled up a gradual rise through open timber then down into a deep, open valley that contained a tributary of the Firehole River. There they made camp at the riverside.

That evening as Jubil ate his supper at the fire, he was over-whelmed with regret. Would he—would any of the men who had moved on—ever be able to truly feel they had done all they could to find Mr. Everts? Logic told him that they had, but his heart had doubts. And Walter, he was sure, would be troubled by even more powerful regret than Jubil was feeling. He believed Truman Everts would not have expected anyone to sacrifice themselves for his sake. He would have appreciated the efforts they made to find him, and relied on God's will thereafter.

These thoughts of regret led Jubil to consider another situation that was likely to trouble him in the future—his mistake of not being open about Sherman's invitation to visit him after the expedition. If he did not break the hold this dilemma held over him soon, the expedition would be over—and he would regret having said nothing.

He considered what Nelly would think. She might understand his initial failure to mention Sherman's invitation but doubted she would support his continued concealment of it. It was time to unburden himself and let the men think what they would.

After supper, the general left the pavilion tent and Jubil followed along.

"Could I have a word with you, General?"

"You certainly may," the general said, then interrupted himself with a deep alarming cough. "Excuse me—I seem to have a touch of a chest cold. The damp weather I believe."

Jubil wondered if they would lose another traveler before the end of the expedition.

"I was going out for a short constitutional," the general said. "Will you join me?"

Jubil fell in beside the general as they strolled toward the area where the animals were hobbled and tethered.

"General, when we met, you asked me a question that I

answered truthfully, but I didn't answer it fully. You asked me whether General Sheridan wanted me to make any kind of report to him about the expedition. My answer was no, which is true. What I did not say is this—I did receive a telegram from General Sherman. He congratulated me on joining the expedition, and asked me to visit him in Washington after my return. He said he would be interested in hearing my observations."

General Washburn stopped and looked at Jubil with surprise. "I see," he said. Jubil felt uneasy as Washburn stared at him. He felt he had exposed himself as untrustworthy.

"Why didn't you just tell me that from the outset?" Washburn asked, resuming his walk.

"I was concerned it would jeopardize my standing with the other men. I thought you might see me as a spy. I'm not a spy—a spy has to know what he's looking for. I have no idea what Sherman wants, but hiding his invitation has been bothering me. I've decided it just isn't honorable to keep it to myself, so that's why I'm telling you now."

"I see," Washburn said. They reached the animals, and the general made a routine check of his horse for ticks, sores of any type, or hoof problems. "I'm sure General Sherman has his reasons for wanting to visit with you. I have no concerns about what you report to him. You needn't have troubled yourself as far as I'm concerned, but I appreciate your candor. Give my regards to General Sherman," Washburn said, his face breaking into a grin.

Jubil went to check on Apollo before he returned to the tent. His conscience was eased somewhat but not fully. He suspected that, like General Washburn, most of the men on the expedition would not care about the information Jubil shared regarding General Sherman, but he still felt he needed to come clean with those he'd grown closest to during the trip— Langford, Doane, and Walter Trumbull.

Jubil took a walk with Walter Trumbull that morning as

well. When he told Walter his story and apologized for his secrecy, Walter said he understood Jubil's concern but thought he was making too much of it. Even as Jubil spoke, he felt foolish for having distracted himself with the issue for so long. He decided to talk to Langford and Doane about it another time.

CHAPTER 7

As they were breaking camp the next morning, something startled the mules, and three of them, fully laden with gear, bolted into the woods. As the beasts fled, the cross-braced pack frames remained strapped to their backs until they hit a thick stand of trees. The gaps between the trees were too narrow for both mule and cargo, and the pack frames caught and shattered, scattering the gear.

Stickney and Langford helped Jubil and the packers corral the runaway mules one by one. While Elwun and Charles collected the gear, Jubil and Langford picked up the pieces of the broken pack frames. Jubil watched, impressed, when Langford brought out from his pack a kit rolled in a sheet of buckskin and tied with cord. Inside were a pair of pliers, a hammer, a small saw, a screwdriver, and a box of nails and screws.

Jubil held the crosspieces while Langford fastened them back together.

"I have to be honest with you, Mr. Langford," Jubil said lightheartedly, "I'm so impressed by your repair toolkit that I'm stealing the idea. I suspect my partner will have kits like this for sale in our store by Christmas."

"I should demand a royalty," Langford joked as he continued to work. "Selling kits is actually a very good idea."

"I'm serious," Jubil said. "I often tell my partner Luke

Warner how gear fares in the field and how it could be improved, and he works with our suppliers to manufacture custom goods for us."

Langford stopped working for a moment and looked up at Jubil. "I should very much like to see one of your stores."

"I do believe you would enjoy it," Jubil said. "You keep yourself better outfitted than anyone I've ever traveled with."

"I appreciate the compliment," Langford said. "Have you given any more thought to opening a store in our area?"

"I'll discuss it with my partners," Jubil said, "but I don't know who would operate it."

"I assumed you would," Langford said.

"I don't believe my fiancée would take to Montana," Jubil said. "No offense to Montana."

"We have a seasoned explorer marrying a city girl, then?" Langford teased.

"I'm hoping she goes through with it," Jubil said, forcing a lightheartedness about the subject he didn't really feel.

Jubil dreaded having to make his confession again, but he had to get this business with Sherman off his mind. "I have something I'd like to be honest with you about," he said.

"What would that be?" Langford said, as he examined the frame they had just mended. Satisfied it would hold, he handed Jubil the crosspieces for the next one. While they worked, Jubil explained about General Sherman's telegram and why he had not been open about it from the start.

"Knowing you will report to Sherman doesn't trouble me," Langford said. "I'm impressed he thinks so highly of you. Give him my regards."

Jubil thanked Langford and was quiet as they finished repairing the frames. He was embarrassed he had troubled himself over this for so long and shown himself to be such a worrier. He would clear it up with Doane soon enough, put it behind him, and not repeat the mistake.

Once the gear was reloaded onto the mules, the group set out in a northwesterly direction from the thumb of the lake toward the steaming geyser basin. They rode along the tops of ridges where possible to avoid the downed timber that clogged the forested areas, but the going was still slow. Midmorning, they came to a forty-foot-wide torrent, which Doane identified as the Firehole River, named by trappers during Jim Bridger's early days here. The plan was to follow the Firehole through the geyser basin to its confluence with the Madison River, which would lead them out of the Yellowstone Basin. They were all anxious to see the source of the columns of steam they had witnessed from atop Mount Washburn.

As they followed the course of the river through a narrow canyon, they passed two sets of beautiful waterfalls, one twenty feet high, the other fifty. In any other place, Jubil thought, these falls would be notable, but here they were humbled by their spectacular setting. As the canyon began to open up, they entered a valley that descended into a deep basin filled with rising plumes of steam—the Firehole Basin. They moved down to a central point of the valley and camped in a grove of pine timber near a small lake.

The rest of the day was spent exploring the area. In the valley, there were more than a thousand hot springs of various sizes and character. Over half of them were issuing forth steam—some occasionally belching out rolling billows while others emitted a steady flow like a chimney. The whole surface of the basin was a calcareous bed deposited by the water of the hot springs. Jubil watched carefully where he directed Apollo and silently urged the horse to step lightly, unable to avoid the thought that just below the surface of this entire region was a raging furnace. Near the head of the valley, one of the geysers was throwing water with a roaring hiss in a plume that reached over one hundred feet. Around its opening were walls eight feet high made of spherical nodules varying in size from a few inches to three feet in diameter, all encrusted with a shiny glaze that Doane said was silica. From a distance, the color of the walls was ashen, but on closer inspection they were a shiny metallic gray with delicate pink and yellow margins, the colors shining and brilliant. The sights and sounds of the hundreds of rising columns of steam confirmed for Jubil that he had finally arrived in the place Jim Bridger had labeled *Volcanic Region*.

"What makes some of the geysers sit quietly for a while and then erupt with such force?" Jubil asked Doane as they looked out over the steaming basin.

"They are formed by long tube-like holes that run deep into the Earth's surface," Doane explained. "The tube fills with water, which is heated by magma near the bottom of the tube. The water in the lower part of the tube comes to a boil and begins to steam, which builds up enough pressure to eject the column of water above it. The eruption will continue until all the water is forced out of the tube, or until the temperature inside the geyser drops below boiling. The tube then fills with water again, and the process starts over."

"Amazing," Jubil said, imagining the natural steam engine operating below the surface.

That night Jubil lay awake listening to the rush of steam and the hissing of the geysers as they erupted in the darkness, a constant rumble filling the warm, damp air. Just a few nights ago, and only six miles from here, he had been buried in two feet of snow. He had not been troubled by any more visions of the whole Yellowstone Basin erupting, but it was difficult to keep those images out of his mind here in the Firehole Basin. He finally drifted off into a dreamless sleep.

They spent the next morning exploring the basin and enjoying the delightful surprise of the eruptions. It was impossible to say how many of the hundreds of boiling springs were actually geysers, since the only way to distinguish the active ones was by watching them spray. General Washburn encouraged the men to suggest names for the geysers, and then he selected the most popular one—or sometimes the one he most favored. They displayed a remarkable variety of shapes, sizes, and power, and inspired such names as the Beehive, Giant, Giantess, Castle, and Grotto.

The cone of the Grotto formation was twenty feet high and forty feet in diameter. It made Jubil uneasy when one of the soldiers gleefully crawled into one of the cavelike openings on the sides of the cone and called to the other explorers to come see the interior cavern. Two other soldiers followed the first one in as Hauser and Judge Hedges shook their heads disapprovingly. Jubil looked around for Lieutenant Doane, who would surely advise the soldiers against such a foolhardy adventure. The soldiers finally crawled back out of the cave, and their jaws dropped when, minutes later, the Grotto erupted, throwing a column of water six feet in diameter to the height of sixty feet.

Jubil understood the urge that had drawn the men into the cave, but he was also reminded that curiosity should have its limits here and on any similar expedition. How would he stop travelers in his adventure travel groups from indulging such dangerous curiosity?

Several members of the expedition began timing the intervals between certain geysers' eruptions, but only one showed any consistency. Its mouth was a crevice of irregular form, about four feet long by three feet wide. Around the mouth of the crevice were accreted globules of calcium from six inches to two feet in diameter. Over the course of the day it shot columns of water to a height of eighty to one hundred feet at intervals of sixty to sixty-five minutes. It was so regular in its performance that General Washburn named it Old Faithful.

They moved out of the geyser basin that afternoon and continued to follow the Firehole River on its way north to join the Madison. Before dark they found a good spot to camp at the confluence of the Firehole River and one of its unnamed tributaries, and the next day they continued north and left the geyser basin.

About eight miles along they came to yet another wonder different from anything Jubil had ever seen. He and Walter sat on their horses and stared.

A cone had grown some thirty feet above the valley floor, and within the basin at its top sat a large round pond of dark blue spring-fed water. The water was forced up the inside of the cone and flowed down the outside, leaving the mineral deposits that had ever so slowly built up to bring the cone to its current height.

"Just when you think you've seen every oddity that nature can concoct," Walter said.

It was an idyllic sight—until Jubil saw that the water in the center of the pond was boiling gently. He watched a small flock of ducks sail down to land on the brilliant blue surface. At the last moment, they seemed to sense danger and rose into the air again—all but one. The unfortunate duck came down in the scalding water, made a frantic but futile effort to rise again, and, with a single squawk of distress, was dead.

Jubil and Walter exchanged a shocked glance, eyebrows raised.

"Whoa," Walter said. "Another reminder of the lethal beauty of this place."

"Yup," Jubil agreed. Walter dropped his eyes, and Jubil could tell he was wondering about Mr. Everts's fate.

General Washburn showed no interest in naming this feature. He steered his horse onward with a deep, ominous cough that curled his shoulders inward. Jubil winced at the sound, and wondered again what they would do if the general fell too sick to travel.

Following the Firehole River north was relatively easy until they neared the confluence with the Madison. There the river flowed through a narrow canyon that forced them up and over a timber-covered ridge before dropping them into the valley where the two rivers converged.

After they had established camp, Langford, Doane, Jubil, and a few others rode to a small peak in the southwest corner of the valley to gain a better view. The view was worth the ride, but nothing spectacular on the measure of things they had already seen, so they rode back to camp. There was nothing of great interest to explore in the river valley either, and, with a sinking feeling, Jubil realized their explorations had come to an end. After thirty days of making their way through this wonderland, tomorrow they would start for home. It was a bittersweet thought. Jubil wanted to go home, but he did not feel ready to leave this place behind—the vista from Mount Washburn; the beauty and power of the falls; the mystery of the mud volcano; the fearsome Firehole Basin—these places had been etched in his mind forever.

After supper, the men gathered around the campfire, sharing their thoughts on the expedition.

Mr. Stickney said, "Seems to me that a fellow would do well to hold a piece of property near some of the sights we've seen. I've seen some fine places to build a cabin or maybe even lay claim to a quarter-section and homestead it."

"Better yet," Hauser, the banker, said, "a man could lay claim to three quarter-sections along the Yellowstone between the Upper and Lower Falls and build some visitors' cabins. That could be very valuable property."

"What I'd do is take a stretch of land along the base of Mount Washburn and run me a fence along the bottom of the summit trail and put a toll gate on it—charge people six bits to ride to the top and see the Yellowstone Basin," Jake Smith proposed dramatically. "I'd retire in ten years—a rich man."

"Another good spot for visitors' cabins would be near the Firehole Basin," Walter Trumbull offered. "People would love to watch Old Faithful erupt, then wander around the basin looking at the other geysers and predicting when they would go off. You could probably build more than visitors' cabins there—you could probably build a sizeable hotel."

"You gentlemen are aware that Jay Cooke is helping support our expedition," Langford said. "He has begun construction on the Northern Pacific Railroad, and the route will come right through our area. Cooke is anxious to popularize Yellowstone to put riders on his trains. I imagine he'd gladly build a spur right to your hotel's doorstep in the Firehole Basin, Mr. Trumbull, but you'd better build it soon, or he'll do it himself. In fact, if any of you gentlemen actually want to act on these plans, I advise you to do it before Cooke gets a chance."

Jubil looked around to see the others' reactions. The conversation had caught him off guard. In the month they had been traveling, there had been no mention of anyone taking ownership over this place. It had never entered his mind that anyone could. He exchanged a glance with Doane, who seemed to be studying his reaction. General Washburn remained quiet, studying each man who spoke but with a slight frown, which Jubil read as either puzzlement or concern.

"Perhaps we should consider some form of corporation," Hauser proposed. "Rather than have these individual ideas for commerce in the area, we could all band together and own the whole operation. That would put us on a closer footing to the likes of Cooke."

"That's a much better plan than competing with one another," Langford agreed, then turned to Cornelius Hedges and asked, "What do you think, Judge? Care to offer any advice on how to approach the Territory of Montana with such a proposal?"

"Excuse me, Judge," Jubil interrupted, and turned to Langford. "I'm not ready to be part of any commercial enterprise here, Mr. Langford. I have the Warners to consider, and

I won't agree to any business deal without their opinion, but I'm willing to state my own. I'm not interested in owning this place. I don't think anyone should own it. I don't think anyone should be able to build cabins, or hotels, or railroads, or put up toll gates, or do anything else to try and own the wonders we've seen."

Jubil looked around at the other men. The hint of a smile showed beneath Doane's limp mustache. Walter Trumbull was nodding in agreement.

"You have stolen my thunder, Mr. Walker," Judge Hedges said good-naturedly. "I was going to answer Mr. Langford with the same opinion—ownership of this unique landscape should be held in the public interest, and commercialization should be prohibited or tightly controlled."

"I'm not aware the government has ever done such a thing," Langford said. "Am I wrong about that, Judge?"

"The Yosemite Land Grant of 1864 comes to mind," the judge replied. "President Lincoln deeded the Yosemite Valley and the Mariposa Grove of sequoias to the state of California. Over the years, the state's management practices have created something of a public furor. The state's leaders have been challenged by John Muir and others for valuing commerce over preservation. I would like to see today's government write a similar bill, but one that benefits from the lessons learned in California. Mr. Trumbull's father might be willing to help write such a bill. I think we should all dedicate our efforts to creating a great national park here, for the benefit and enjoyment of all the people."

"I'll be happy to discuss the idea with my father," Walter said.

"Even if the area is designated a national park, there will be decisions that must be made about how to manage it," Langford said. "Exactly how we allow people to benefit from it and enjoy it. We should be very diligent in making sure the spirit of the law is adhered to in practice."

"And you are just the man to see to it, Nathaniel," said Langford's partner, Hauser. "I hereby nominate you, Nathaniel Pitt Langford, as mayor of Yellowstone Park."

Langford shook his head as the men laughed.

"We are all agreed, then?" Judge Hedges asked. "We will recommend and encourage the creation of a national park here?"

"I wholeheartedly agree with your conclusion, gentlemen," General Washburn said. He seemed genuinely relieved the men had come to this decision. "There is not another place on Earth, that I'm aware of, with such unusual geologic features. It deserves protection."

Jubil too was pleased with how the conversation had turned out. His fellow explorers must not have been serious about all their business proposals, since they so easily fell into line with Judge Hedges's proposal.

As Jubil lay on his bedroll that evening, reflecting on the expedition, he felt deeply satisfied with the outcome. His mission had been to make himself useful, which he believed he had done, and to earn the respect of the other explorers, which he felt he had, in some measure, also accomplished. And while he had come here expecting to see an exotic landscape, he could never have imagined the wonders he would behold—sights that had inspired him to join in a pact to defend Yellowstone against mankind's baser impulses. This new commitment was as uplifting as it was unexpected, and he was proud to be part of it. He hoped this greater purpose would help convince Nelly that his decision to come had been worthwhile.

On the remaining leg of the journey, the travelers weren't exploring new wonders every day but were simply trekking through relatively dull geography. They followed the Madison River along its course through the Madison Range, which formed the western rim of the Yellowstone Basin. For the next four days they pushed westward, through canyons where possible and up and over ridges where not. Everyone was unusually quiet in camp in the evening, and Jubil wondered whether they were experiencing the same mixture of emotions that he was: exhaustion, preoccupation with returning home, and melancholy over leaving Yellowstone. And then there was Mr. Everts's disappearance casting its long shadow over them all.

On September 23, they exited the northwest corner of Wyoming and briefly entered Idaho Territory. Rounding the south end of the Madison Range, they turned north following the river up the Madison Valley and reentered Montana Territory. There, the party began to splinter. First to leave was Langford, who was going to Virginia City.

"It has been a pleasure to make your acquaintance, Mr. Walker," Langford said to Jubil. "Just as General Sheridan proposed, you were an asset to the expedition. Thank you for your help in making it a success. I hope you will stay in touch. I strongly recommend you and your business partners consider expanding into Montana. You should visit Helena."

"You make an appealing case," Jubil laughed. "I promise to stay in touch. I enjoyed traveling with you. I appreciated how you and the general worked together and treated the opinions and needs of the men with real consideration. If I'm ever in your position, I hope to do as well."

"Thank you," Langford said as they shook hands. Jubil and the rest of the party moved on a few miles and camped.

The next morning, Jubil, Lieutenant Doane, and the three remaining soldiers turned east toward Bozeman and Fort Ellis while the rest of the party continued north to Helena. Jubil shook hands with all the men and wished them well, and he and Walter Trumbull exchanged addresses and vowed to write. He entreated Walter to write immediately if there was any news of Mr. Everts.

Jubil, Doane, and the soldiers were now about twenty miles

from Fort Ellis and would arrive before dark. After thirty-four days of traveling through the most astonishing landscapes he had ever seen, Jubil was almost back where his journey had started—and he still had not told Doane his secret about General Sherman.

"I've got something on my mind that I've been meaning to tell you," Jubil began before explaining General Sherman's request.

Doane was, just as General Washburn and Mr. Langford had been, curious rather than upset.

"You have no idea why he wants to see you?" Doane asked.

"None at all," Jubil confessed.

"Well," Doane said, "I'm sure he has a plan."

"I think he encouraged Sheridan to invite me," Jubil said, "even though Sheridan was suspicious of me as an Indian sympathizer."

Doane turned his head to look Jubil in the eye. "Well, aren't you?"

"Measured against him I am," Jubil declared. "Against many others too, I suppose."

"If we're going to retain our fellowship," Doane said, his expression hard, "I'd suggest we let the subject go."

Jubil agreed, understanding that Doane must have dealt with Indians in his role in the army in ways that Jubil would find abhorrent. The men rode the remainder of the way lost in their own thoughts, Jubil's centered on reuniting with Nelly and making plans with the Warners. As they passed south of Bozeman, Jubil turned north and bid Lieutenant Doane and his soldiers farewell as they continued on east to Fort Ellis.

"Thank you for allowing me to help you with your journal, Lieutenant," Jubil said in parting. "I wish my friends at home could read it. Your words go far beyond my own ability to express what we've seen."

"Thank you. I appreciate your assistance in my time of

need," Doane said. "I'll be filing it as a report with the army." His mouth lifted in a smile, and he stroked his mustache. "I imagine General Sherman can get you a copy."

The two shook hands and parted ways.

When Jubil arrived in Bozeman he rode straight to the livery stable. He had not decided whether to take the stagecoach to Corinne or ride Apollo, but he would stable the horse until he decided. He was certain that he wanted to avoid Phineas Black, so he asked the liveryman to suggest a hotel other than the Metropolitan and was directed to the Guy House, which the liveryman said was comfortable and had good fare.

Jubil found the hotel modest, but, after several weeks of sleeping rough and eating camp cooking, it suited him fine. A decent meal—fried chicken would be the height of luxury—and a comfortable room for the night, each priced at seventy-five cents, was a bargain compared to the Metropolitan Hotel's rate of two dollars for the room and one dollar for the meal.

The next morning, he went to see if there was space available on the next stagecoach to Corinne. This required him to enter the lobby of the Metropolitan Hotel, which served as the ticket counter and depot for the stage line. Jubil was dismayed but not surprised to find Phineas Black standing at the hotel desk, but he was very surprised to see the stern looking man with the handlebar mustache and slicked back hair standing beside him. The face and mustache Jubil recognized immediately, though the man had traded well-worn, dusty clothes and boots for a tailored suit and polished boots. Since he could not avoid the situation, Jubil approached.

"Hello, Mr. Black," Jubil said, then turned to Black's companion. "Quite a surprise to see you here, Mr. Murphy."

Murphy eyed Jubil suspiciously for a moment before

nodding slowly. "Top of the morning to you, Mr. Walker," he replied with an Irish lilt.

"Welcome back," Phineas Black said. "What a coincidence that you two have met. Mr. Murphy has told me all about it."

Three years before, on Jubil's trek with General Sherman from Council Bluffs to Fort McPherson—across Nebraska and back—Murphy was one of the Irish teamsters handling a freight wagon for Warner and Company Outfitters. He was by far the most opinionated, profane, perpetually sullen person Jubil had ever met.

"Mr. Murphy handles security for me," Phineas Black explained. "My mining operations and the hotel require some vigilance beyond what our local law enforcement can provide."

Jubil glanced at Murphy, who was scowling at him. Jubil would normally have found this offensive, but he knew from experience that it was Murphy's normal expression.

"I heard you arrived yesterday," Black said. "I'm disappointed you didn't choose the Metropolitan Hotel for your stay."

"Just being frugal," Jubil offered with a shrug.

"Then be my guest here tonight. You can tell me all about your expedition over dinner," Black offered.

"Very generous of you to offer," Jubil said, "but I'm in a hurry to be on my way home. I've come in to see if I can catch the next stagecoach."

"I'm sorry to say Mr. Murphy just booked the last seat," Black said. "He's needed in Idaho Falls on mining business. Unfortunately, he can't give up his seat, as his schedule is inflexible. There will be another stage in two days. You can be my guest here, and we'll have time to discuss what you found on your explorations and agree on how we might profit from it."

"Thanks, but I'll just ride to Corinne," Jubil said. "I don't much like the stagecoach anyway. Too much like riding on a freight wagon."

Murphy's scowl deepened.

"How disappointing," Black said as he studied Jubil. "I very much wanted to hear about what you found on your expedition. It could be of great value to both of us."

"We don't need a lot of time for me to tell you what I saw," Jubil said. "I saw wonders of nature the likes of which I've never seen—things unlike anyplace else on Earth. Jim Bridger and the trappers weren't exaggerating—it's all there, and more. But in terms of making a profit from it, you'd be wise to look for your fortune elsewhere. General Washburn and the men agreed the Yellowstone should be set aside as a national treasure, a park perhaps, to keep people from tearing it up for a dollar."

As Jubil spoke, Phineas Black stiffened and drew his head back.

"General Washburn and the men agreed, did they?" Black said with a sneer. "If it's to be set aside, it should be by Montana for the benefit of its residents, not by Washington for the benefit of nobody."

"You'll have to take that position up with someone influential in Montana," Jubil said. "Perhaps Mr. Langford."

"Mr. Langford is no more influential than I am in Montana," Black spat, "and the only position he'll respond to is the one that best feathers his own nest."

"Unlike your own," Jubil said facetiously, "which is purely in the public interest."

"I'm trying to be civil, Mr. Walker," Black said, "but you are trying my patience. If there is a fortune to be made from the Yellowstone, whether it's by digging it up or charging people to see it, I intend to be in on the bounty. Neither Washburn nor Langford nor you can stop me."

Jubil knew he should just walk away, but he felt compelled to put Black in his place.

"That may be," Jubil said, "but I'm on my way to report to General Sherman—he could stop you. Walter Trumbull was on the expedition, and his father is a US senator—he could stop you."

"I don't take kindly to threats, Mr. Walker," Black said, his fists clenching. Murphy straightened his posture and dropped his hands to his sides, as if readying for a fight.

"Can't say I do either," Jubil replied, "and I recall that's exactly what I heard from you when we first met: a threat against competing with you by opening a store in Bozeman. Which, by the way, you can forget about. Bozeman is too small. But I might have a look at Helena."

"Then maybe you best clear out," Black snarled.

"I'm doing you a favor by bringing you news about Yellowstone—just like you asked me to," Jubil said flippantly. But as he said it, his temper began to cool, and he almost regretted causing the twisted expression that had taken over Black's face.

"You'll be doing me a favor by leaving Montana," Black said, "and staying away. I think even Helena is too close for comfort. I don't like your attitude, Walker. And I don't trust you and your high and mighty friend Langford—not for a minute. I won't warn you again not to interfere in my business interests."

The stagecoach rolled to a stop in front of the hotel, drawing their attention. Murphy and Black exchanged a glance, and Black nodded. Murphy straightened his lapels and walked out of the lobby without acknowledging Jubil.

Jubil turned to leave, and Black said, "Good riddance. I hope I don't have to deal with you again."

Jubil walked out of the hotel without responding. He had never felt such contempt for another person. He went to collect his pack and Apollo at the stable. He was glad to be on his way home and finished with Phineas Black.

CHAPTER 8

Before Jubil left Corinne on the train for Council Bluffs, he sent telegrams announcing his arrival to Mr. and Mrs. Warner, Luke, and Nelly. He did not expect a hero's welcome, as he had gotten when he returned from the Grand Canyon expedition—when everyone was celebrating his return after the expedition party had been given up for dead—but he daydreamed about seeing Nelly there to welcome him. By now her classes were in session at Illinois Wesleyan University, so it was unlikely she would be there in Council Bluffs, but he was looking forward to seeing her when he arrived in Bloomington.

The train let its passengers out on the far side of the Missouri River, as the railroad bridge into Council Bluffs was still under construction. Jubil collected his pack and made his way to the ferry, smiling to himself as he listened to some of the other passengers grumbling about the inconvenience of the transfer. There was no one at the ferry stop on the other side to meet him, so Jubil shouldered his pack and walked to Warner and Company Outfitters on Lower Broadway. Through the front window of the store he saw Mr. Warner and Luke talking by the cash register. Luke had come from Bloomington to greet him, and he suppressed an unreasonable sense of disappointment that Nelly had not come with him.

"Jubil!" Luke exclaimed when he came in, rushing to shake

his hand exuberantly. "Welcome back!"

Mr. Warner clapped Jubil on the shoulder. "You look in fine shape! None the worse for wear this year."

"Thank you," he said, "I was not damaged this year, though the trip did have its moments. I have so many stories to tell that I don't know where to begin."

"Lily is going to want to hear every word," Mr. Warner said, "so you might as well hold your tales."

As Mr. Warner went to lock the front door and put the till in the safe, Jubil asked Luke, "Everything all right at home?"

Was it Jubil's imagination, or did Luke hesitate before replying?

"Yes, of course, everything is all right. Ike and Eli are anxious to see you, especially Eli. He has tried to sell everyone in Bloomington and Normal on an expedition to Yellowstone with you—and him, of course."

Jubil smiled. "And how is Nelly?"

"Fine . . .as far as I know," Luke said. "I actually haven't seen her for a while."

"Why not?" Jubil asked, frowning. "Is something wrong?"

"Well . . . ," Luke said with obvious discomfort.

"All right boys," Mr. Warner said, and ushered them out into the Warner's carriage. After loading his pack, Jubil took a moment to greet the carriage horse, Rocky. Jubil had ridden Rocky on his trek from Council Bluffs to Fort McPherson and back. When the army did not need him back, Mr. Warner kept him to pull the family carriage. Rocky was the only horse from Jubil's adventures that was still with him, but not the only one he remembered fondly. He had spent the Longs Peak expedition with a black mare he'd named Diablo. By the end of the expedition, he had hated to give her up. The same was true this year with Apollo. On the ride back to Corinne, he had seriously considered keeping him, but in the end, he had said goodbye and sold him to the liveryman. Most of all, he missed his horse at home—Star, his longtime companion and his last link to his parents and their farm.

He rode in Mr. Warner's carriage toward the northern edge of town, where a huge two-story Victorian house with turrets at the front corners sat atop a tall bluff. When Jubil had first seen the Warners' home, it had looked imposing, but he now thought of it as a second home.

Mrs. Warner stepped out the front door of the house to greet them as Mr. Garcia, the groundskeeper and groomsman, led Rocky and the carriage away. Mrs. Warner was a regal matronly woman with graying hair who usually dressed formally, but today she wore a stained painter's smock and flat shoes. She threw her arms wide as she caught sight of Jubil.

"Jubilee Walker," she gushed, her New England accent flattening his last name. "I do believe you get more handsome with every expedition!"

Jubil laughed and accepted her hug. She had become like a mother to him. "Perhaps I should go away more often," he joked.

They stepped into the entryway with its dual curving staircases that Mrs. Warner decorated beautifully at Christmastime, and Jubil recalled the first night he had stayed in the Warners' home. It had felt like a hotel to him. Now Jubil had a bedroom of his own there, just down the hall from Luke's, and he felt at ease wandering into Mr. Warner's office in the turret on the west corner of the house or Mrs. Warner's studio in the east turret.

Mrs. Warner urged him to take his pack to his room and then come to her studio for a chat. She had a letter for him from Nelly, she said.

"A letter? I'll be home in two days," Jubil said.

"I know, I know," Mrs. Warner said. "Now run along."

Jubil stowed his belongings and nervously made his way to the east turret. Why was everyone acting so strangely when they spoke of Nelly?

Like Mr. Warner's office, Mrs. Warner's studio had a stunning view of Council Bluffs below, the town's namesake bluffs to the east, and the Missouri River valley to the west. He found her standing at an easel near the windows, working on a painting—a seascape in blue and white.

"It's beautiful," Jubil said as Mrs. Warner turned from the canvas, a paintbrush in one hand, a cleaning rag in the other. The room was perfumed with brush solvent and oil paint.

"Thank you, Jubil," Mrs. Warner said. "Rosie has poured us coffee." She gestured toward the circle of armchairs and low table in the center of the room.

Jubil took a seat and nervously sampled the coffee.

"I'm sure you missed Nelly while you were away," Mrs. Warner said.

Jubil nodded. "I surely did," he said. "I'm wondering what's happened to her that you are all acting so strangely whenever I mention her name."

Mrs. Warner laughed softly. "Nelly is safe and sound," she said. "You know, I've grown very fond of her. Her mother and I have grown close as well. During their visit here this summer, we formed a sisterhood that I cherish. In many ways, her mother and I are more alike than my natural sister and I, though I do love Maria."

"Nelly certainly values your insights, ma'am," Jubil said. "It was your story about the wives of Nantucket seamen that inspired her to accept my marriage proposal . . . which I seem to have upended."

"If you don't mind some advice," Mrs. Warner offered, "I suggest you focus less on the wedding for the time being and more on your friendship. Nelly may need a best friend right now more than she needs a husband."

"I thought I was her best friend," he said. It was difficult to get past the idea that Nelly no longer wanted to marry him.

"I believe you still are," Mrs. Warner said, "but right now

her feelings are confused. Most young girls are content to find a husband and have children, like the women they see around them. But some young women don't feel that calling. Nelly may want those things someday, but right now she wants some accomplishment of her own beyond caring for a husband, a house, and children."

Jubil was dismayed to think that in the context of what Mrs. Warner was saying, he would be *a husband*, which seemed to mean the same thing as *a burden*.

"I'll help her accomplish whatever she wants," he said. "I just want her in my life."

"Then that is exactly what you should tell her," Mrs. Warner said with a warm smile.

Jubil felt his spirits lift as a plan of action came into view. "I will," he said. "I'll tell her as soon as I get home."

"That's an excellent plan," Mrs. Warner said. She handed him the letter from Nelly. "I'll let her tell you the rest in her own words."

Jubil accepted the letter with a feeling of foreboding. "Thank you," he said, and went to his room to read it.

Dear Jubil,

I am writing to tell you that I am staying in Poughkeepsie for the time being, and have enrolled in classes at Vassar College. I am sorry for any hurt my decision to stay here may cause you. I want to reassure you I am not doing this to punish you, or avoid you. I am grateful for the opportunity to expand my world, and fortunate Miss Mitchell has offered to mentor me. I feel I am meant to do this. I'm sure you will understand that feeling.

My father, of course, does not approve of my decision, and I'm sorry to report that his displeasure now extends to the Warners and Miss Mitchell. He has refused to continue providing me with financial support, but Mrs. Warner has offered to pay my tuition and expenses. Miss Mitchell has invited me to live as her guest while I finish college. At first, I was embarrassed to accept such charity, but they see it as supporting women's rights. I have offered to repay them one day, but they won't hear of it. They say my success will be their reward. I am determined not to disappoint them.

On her way home, Mrs. Warner went to see my parents to answer for leaving me in her sister's care. Papa made it clear he did not appreciate her interference, and that he was surprised Mr. Warner did not support his position.

I suppose I should be grateful he is not coming to drag me home. My only regret is for Mama. She is doing her best to act as a peacemaker and still support me, but I know how troubled she is by all this. I am also sorry for any tension Papa's displeasure with the Warners creates between you, Luke, and my brothers.

I hope your expedition was successful, and that you have returned undamaged. I look forward to hearing of your adventures, and think an experienced explorer, such as yourself, should have no difficulty locating Poughkeepsie, New York. I will be there, and happy to see you.

Truly yours,
Nelly

Jubil was unable to fight back his tears as he read, and he was glad to be alone. He struggled against an overwhelming sense of loss—she was gone. She would not be in Bloomington when he returned, smiling and relieved he had made it home safely, which he had imagined would happen in spite of the conditions under which they had parted. He had never thought she would stay in Poughkeepsie. If not because of their rela-tionship, then because she would not want to be so far away from her family.

But he had underestimated her desire for adventure. She had said she wanted to be more like him—driven by a passion that would shape her life—and she was proving good to her word. He should be proud of her. He was proud of her. He just didn't want her to be so far away or drift further away over time.

Jubil recovered his composure enough to join the Warners for supper. He heard them laughing as he approached the din-ing room, but their laughter faded as he entered the room.

"Sorry if I'm late," he said, taking a seat. "I've read Nelly's letter. It breaks my heart she is staying in Poughkeepsie, but to some degree I understand it. It's bold of her to stand up to her father's disapproval, and I'm glad you're supporting her. I'm sorry to hear you've fallen out of favor with him."

"Yes," Mrs. Warner said, "that is unfortunate. He wrote Theodore a letter insisting he put an end to my 'meddling' in Boswell family affairs." She shrugged. "We do not share his philosophy on a woman's place in the social order."

Mr. Warner and Luke looked on in silent agreement.

"I'm going to go see her," Jubil said.

"That's good," Mrs. Warner said. "Your support will be very important to her." He remembered her advice—focus on their friendship, not their marriage.

As they ate, the mood lightened and he recounted his trav-els. He told them about the terrible loss of Mr. Everts and the agreement to campaign to make Yellowstone a national park. Mrs. Warner offered to help promote the national park idea through her civic societies, and suggested it would also appeal to her sister's scientific and academic circles.

"I'm sure we could arrange any number of opportunities for you to address different groups," Mrs. Warner said.

"I'm not the best speaker to send out on tour," Jubil

admitted. "But Mr. Langford will be filling halls soon enough. After I visit Nelly, I'm going to Washington. General Sherman has asked me to recount my Yellowstone experiences, so I'll get his advice on the park. Walter Trumbull's father is a senator from Illinois, so I may also visit with Senator Trumbull."

After supper, Jubil, Mr. Warner, and Luke adjourned to Mr. Warner's office to talk about the next steps in their outfitting business. On the way, Jubil stopped by his room to get something from his pack.

Mr. Warner and Luke were already seated in armchairs in front of the huge desk, and Mr. Warner had poured a whiskey for himself and Luke, but Jubil, never much interested in liquor, asked for water. The room was filled with the haze and aroma of Mr. Warner's cigar. Jubil looked around the room at Mr. Warner's extensive collection of books, art, models, and other souvenirs—gifts from clients or items collected by him and Luke. Among them were two chunks of granite Jubil had collected—one from the summit of Longs Peak, the other from the last rapids in the Grand Canyon.

"I brought you a souvenir," Jubil said, handing a sheet of paper to Mr. Warner. It was the sketch of Jake Smith keeping watch that Walter Trumbull had drawn. "I thought you might like it for your collection."

Mr. Warner laughed at the image. "This is marvelous, thank you. I must get a suitable frame for it," he said. "Now, what are your thoughts about the prospects for Yellowstone as a tour destination?"

"It undoubtedly will be," Jubil said, "and a great one, but it is very remote right now. That will change when Jay Cooke gets his railroad built, but that's a few years off. Right now, it's a four-day stage trip up to Bozeman through rough territory, and from Bozeman it takes a little over a week to reach Mount Washburn and the falls. Any expedition to Yellowstone in the meantime will be a much more rugged affair than the tours we had been planning to Colorado."

"You think we should table the idea for now?" Luke asked.

"Not necessarily," Jubil said. "I'm willing to offer a tour. But if we have any takers, I'll have to make very clear what it is they're signing up for. I do think the tour will be well worth their money. We also have to keep in mind that there are currently more people than us scrambling to capitalize on General Washburn's expedition."

He described his encounters with Phineas Black in Bozeman and seeing Murphy before his departure.

"Murphy's the security man for Black?" Mr. Warner said incredulously. "There's a case of the fox guarding the henhouse. That fellow is trouble."

"Black is counting on Bozeman becoming a boomtown," Jubil said, "which it may if the railroad goes through. But Mr. Langford encouraged me to consider Helena. It's already about the size of Bloomington and Normal. We might want to consider that idea."

Luke nodded enthusiastically.

"It hadn't entered my mind for us to have a store out there," Mr. Warner said, "but I imagine it would work. I imagine there would be a good market there for the products that you boys have developed. It would also be a good base of operations for your tours. If that's what you want to do, Jubil, I'm willing to have a go at it."

"The idea hadn't entered my mind before I went out there," Jubil said, "but everyone kept asking me if that was our plan, so you have to wonder if it isn't a pretty natural idea. My main question is, Who would operate it? I dismissed the idea myself, because I didn't think Nelly would want to be in such a remote place, and I'm sure of that now. I suppose if she decides to make our separation permanent . . . well, I don't know what I'll do with myself then."

"If it comes to that," Luke said, "and you want to open a

store in Montana, we'll do it together. I'll go with you."

"What about your friend, Miss Bateman?" Jubil asked. "You'd leave her behind?"

"I didn't say that," Luke answered with a grin. Mr. Warner beamed with joy.

Jubil smiled at Luke. He was fortunate to have such a friend. It was Luke he had to thank for much of the current satisfaction and happiness in his life. Luke had befriended him and asked Mr. Warner to put him to work in the stockroom, a situation which had enabled Jubil to meet Lew Keplinger and take the next step in his plan to join Powell's expedition. The store in Bloomington had been Luke's idea, and its success was largely thanks to him. Without this solid base, Jubil would probably be aimlessly moving from one adventure to another, with no good prospects for the future.

"If it comes to that," Jubil replied, "I'll take you up on it, but let's see what Nelly has to say. It would be a shame to have to close the store in Bloomington."

"We could let Ike and Eli run it," Luke said.

"Are you serious?" Jubil said. "Those boys burned down my farm."

Luke shook his head and fixed Jubil with a stern look. "Will you ever let that go? They were just kids. They're already running your store—while you're out running around in the wilderness."

"All right," Jubil said with a rueful smile. "I take your point. You would trust them with our store?"

"I would," Luke said. "I already do. I know Ike could do it alone if he had to. Eli wants to be where the real adventure is. You should start taking him more seriously."

"Nelly's mother would have my hide," Jubil said. "First I inspire her daughter to move a thousand miles away, and then one of her sons follows me a thousand in the other direction."

Luke and Mr. Warner chuckled.

They finished their drinks and talked of smaller business matters. Jubil told the story of Langford's tool kit saving the day, and just as he expected, Luke immediately saw the possibility of creating a branded kit for their stores. He said he would stay over a day or two in Chicago on his way back to Bloomington, find a supplier, and have some in stock before Christmas.

Jubil retired for the night, but sleep was slow in coming as he made plans to visit Nelly. Luke had agreed to take Jubil's pack to Bloomington for him, and the only clothes Jubil had with him were those he had worn or packed for his expedition. He needed to do some shopping before getting on the train. He would purchase what he needed, check the train schedule, and be on his way to New York tomorrow, if possible. He had little hope now that Nelly would agree to reschedule the wedding date. At this point, he would be satisfied if she just agreed that someday they would be married.

CHAPTER 9

It was Jubil's first trip east, and it had a strange effect on his nervous system. Traveling west, watching the landscape flatten out and open up as the population density dropped from crowded to sparse, he always felt himself relaxing into a sense of well-being. Going east, he found his body tensing up as the forested landscape closed in and the number of people per square mile rose to levels he had never experienced. He was intimidated by the crush of people in the station when he changed trains in New York City, and he already dreaded doing it again, on his way to Washington to see General Sherman.

He felt more at home when he arrived in Poughkeepsie, which was only slightly larger than Bloomington. The agent at the ticket window recommended the Morgan House as a good place to stay and gave him directions. Jubil stepped out of the station and admired the bustling landing along the Hudson River, then walked away from the river, east on Main Street through the business district.

The Morgan House was a stately affair, similar to the Ashley House in Bloomington. What distinguished Poughkeepsie from Bloomington was how long it had existed. The town had been settled long before the American Revolution, and the streets and the buildings had a feeling of being solidly established, well organized, and well maintained.

The hotel desk clerk told Jubil that the distance to Miss Mitchell's house and Vassar College was a walk of a mile and a half, but he also pointed out that coaches for hire were readily available. Jubil decided to walk. The mid-October weather was mild, the sun was bright and the air crisp, and the leaves on the trees were in full fall display—yellow, orange, red, and rusty brown.

He also wanted to walk because he was nervous about seeing Nelly. Before leaving Council Bluffs, he had sent a telegram telling her he was coming, so she would not be shocked at his arrival. So much had changed since he'd left at the end of the summer that he didn't quite know what to expect from her. Was she still the same person she'd always been? He remembered how awkward their last days together in Bloomington had been and wondered if they would ever get back to the easy company they had always been for each other.

Miss Mitchell's house on College Avenue was a Victorian two-story that looked to Jubil like a miniature version of the Warners' house, without turrets. He collected his thoughts, took a deep breath, and knocked on the door, only to be told by Miss Mitchell's silver-haired housekeeper, Miss LeVault, that Nelly was not at home. She was most likely at the college, Miss LeVault said, but she was expected home within an hour.

The college was nearby, so Jubil decided to have a look at it. Miss LeVault pointed him in the right direction, and he set out for the southeast corner of town, where a great four-story building of gray stone sprawled majestically across a huge groomed lawn. Behind it lay miles of rolling tree-covered hills. The grounds around the building were landscaped with ornamental birch, ash, and oak trees, holly, juniper, and privet bushes, and planting beds divided by a network of walking paths and roundabouts. Jubil thought the place looked more like a grand palace than a college.

He would never find Nelly in a building that size, so he

found a bench beside a path he thought she might follow home and waited. After a few minutes, his patience was rewarded. Although she was wearing a hooded cape, he picked her out at a distance. She seemed lost in thought as she walked along carrying her books, focused on the path in front of her. Jubil rose from the bench as she neared him, but she remained unaware of his presence. When she was a few feet away, he stepped into the center of the path. She stopped abruptly and looked up.

"A penny for your thoughts, Miss Boswell," he said.

She hurried to greet him with a one-armed embrace, still holding her books in the other arm. Jubil could not resist wrapping his arms around her, and he was thrilled when she kissed him on the cheek.

She stepped back, her blue eyes shining. "I'm very glad to see you, Jubil."

"I'm glad to see you too, Nelly," he said. As they spoke, her books slipped from her arm and Jubil caught them. "May I carry your books?"

"Yes, you may," she said. "Just like when we were children."

"No pesky boys to bother you at this school," he teased, but he was secretly happy about that arrangement.

"Yes, that is an advantage," she said with a grin. Then her grin faded. "Were you angry with me when you learned I had stayed here and enrolled?"

"No, not angry," he said, "more like . . . concerned. I was afraid—I still am—that I might be losing you."

She put her hand on his chest. "I'm not lost. I'm right here. Thank you for coming."

Looking into her face, he saw that she was the same old Nelly. "I thought you might be more . . . conflicted about seeing me," he said, grinning with relief.

"Oh," Nelly said, rolling her eyes, "I'm conflicted aplenty, but not about seeing you."

Jubil pondered this for a moment. "I think that's good," he

said, "but I'm not sure. Maybe you can explain while we walk?"

Nelly glanced toward College Street. "If you don't mind, let's just sit here on the bench for a while. Miss LeVault is a darling person, but nothing much escapes her attention. Let's just keep her guessing about us for a bit," she said conspiratorially.

Jubil smiled as they took a seat. He was tempted to cut to the heart of his concern and ask how she felt about them getting married someday, but then he reminded himself of Mrs. Warner's advice—*focus less on the wedding for the time being and more on your friendship.*

"I guess what I'm most curious about is . . . what changed?" he asked. "I mean, what made you decide to stay here rather than come back to Bloomington? I realize I'm always running off somewhere for weeks or months at a time, but this move seems so permanent."

Nelly sighed and looked out across the campus. "Shortly after I arrived this summer, Miss Mitchell took me on a tour of the college. It was the most impressive place I had ever seen, but also one of the most intimidating. At first, I could not imagine having the courage to finish my education here. I worried my previous schooling might not have been rigorous enough, or I might not be intelligent enough to keep up, or I would be too homespun to fit in with the other students, or any number of other fears of weakness and inadequacy." She stared at her hands, folded in her lap.

"What changed your thinking?" he prompted.

"It was such a relief to be away from Papa's disapproval. The feeling of freedom I found here was so compelling, but I was still afraid. Then I thought about you," she said, looking over at him. "What did you do when Powell rejected you and you faced the prospect of going West alone? What did you and Lew Keplinger do when you stood at the base of Longs Peak, looking up at a summit no one had ever reached? What did you do when you could hear the roar of the rapids in the Grand

Canyon, when you couldn't see a way around them? You faced your fears and moved forward, rather than turning around and returning to safety. That's what I decided to do . . . face my fears."

Jubil loved Nelly even more at that moment than he had before. At the same time, he selfishly wished she could face her challenges somewhere closer to him. He reminded himself to focus not on what he wanted but on what she wanted. He reached for her hand and she clasped his in both of hers.

"I'm proud of you," he said.

"Thank you," she said, gripping his hand tightly. "That means a great deal to me."

"How are you doing with your studies?" he asked.

"Well enough, I think," she replied. "It's early yet in the term, but my fears of being unprepared or incapable seem unfounded. That's not to say the program isn't challenging, but I seem to be staying abreast of it. My English teacher, Professor Backus, has been very complimentary of the essays I have written. He thinks I should focus on a career as a journalist or an editor, maybe even as a novelist. I'm very encouraged that he thinks I have some talent."

"That is very impressive," he said. "Could I read something you've written lately?"

"You certainly may," Nelly said, sounding pleasantly surprised. "I'll pick something out for you."

Jubil sat wondering whether a career for her as a writer would lead them closer together or further apart. Nelly was lost in thought too, still staring at their clasped hands.

"Are you happy here? Have you made friends," he asked, "or do they find you homespun?"

Nelly pursed her lips and raised her eyebrows. "I have made some acquaintances at the college but none yet that I would call a friend. Though no one has been rude, no one has gone out of her way to befriend me. Social standing is a more complicated affair here than we are accustomed to. Many of the students come from prominent families and either already know one another or know *of* one another. It's not easy to break into those circles, but I won't put on airs to try. Being Miss Mitchell's ward gives me a sense of mystery and a certain status, and I'm fine with that. I am very grateful for Ruthie—Miss LeVault. She has been so considerate and helpful that I now consider her a friend."

"What about Miss Mitchell?" he asked. "She must be very supportive."

"She is, but she is very busy with school and professional activities. It's not unusual for me to go days without seeing her, or to see her only for a short time, especially since the fall term began. I'm sorry to say she's away this week, so you won't get to meet her. Did you know she is the first woman to be elected a Fellow of the American Academy of Arts and Sciences? She's also the first to be elected to . . . oh, some other organization whose name escapes me." Nelly shrugged sheepishly. "So, I don't see her much, and when I do, she's often . . . preoccupied."

Jubil smiled. "Sounds like you're coping fairly well with the rarified social air. Turns out our experiences have been similar in that regard. My associates on the expedition were more prominent businessmen and politicians than explorers."

"Where are my manners?" Nelly exclaimed. "All this talk about me, and I haven't even asked about your expedition."

"That's all right," he assured her. "It went well. Yellowstone is a marvelously unique place."

"I'm anxious to hear about it," she said. "I'm sure Ruthie won't mind if I invite you for supper. She'll love your stories. How long are you planning to stay?"

"A couple of days," he replied. "I don't want to distract you from your studies, and I have business in Washington. General Sherman asked me to report to him on the expedition."

"My word," Nelly said, "you are traveling in lofty company

—summoned to the nation's capital by the general of the army."

"I'm as surprised as you are," he said.

At supper that evening, Nelly and Miss LeVault encouraged Jubil to spare no detail in his narrative about the expedition, and they expressed wonder at the sights he described. During the story of Mr. Everts's disappearance and their futile efforts to find him, Nelly's eyes narrowed as she listened intently.

"What a terrible fate for that poor man," Nelly said. "Perhaps you'll understand my skepticism the next time you tell me an expedition will be 'relatively safe'?"

Jubil considered a rebuttal, then conceded with a nod and continued his story. Nelly was especially interested in Jubil's description of Lieutenant Doane's journal, and he promised to obtain a copy and share it with her. If she was going to be a writer, he could think of no better tutorial. Nelly and Miss LeVault were excited by the idea of a campaign to declare Yellowstone a national park, and Jubil was deeply gratified when Nelly told him she was proud of him.

Nelly had no classes the next day, so Jubil hired a carriage and they went sightseeing around Poughkeepsie. Miss LeVault packed them a picnic basket, which they enjoyed from a spot overlooking the Hudson River and the surrounding hills, which at this time of year were a lively patchwork of colored leaves. In the afternoon, Jubil left Nelly to her studies, and she sent him along with one of her essays to read, a personal narrative about standing up for oneself.

She had written about William Brown teasing her at school. Jubil remembered the culminating event well. Brown had found he could cause Nelly great aggravation by calling her Cornelia, her Christian name, which he then shortened to Corny. She demanded that he respect her preference of Nelly, which he eventually did—but only after Jubil pounded some sense into him. Jubil and Nelly had been best friends ever since.

That night they had dinner together at the Morgan House.

Jubil had also invited Miss LeVault, but she had politely declined.

"I enjoyed your essay very much," Jubil said. "I think your professor is correct—you are a gifted writer."

"Thank you," Nelly said.

"I think even Brown would agree, you captured the moment well," Jubil said, with a smile. "I appreciate being portrayed as part of the solution, rather than part of the problem. And your talent really showed as you described how the whole affair made you feel."

"I'm truly glad you liked it," Nelly said sincerely.

The conversation lapsed into silence as Jubil looked for another topic in order to avoid asking what was constantly on his mind—Did Nelly still want to marry him? He was hoping she might volunteer the answer, but he was running out of time.

"One of the things I enjoy here," Nelly began, breaking the silence, "is how common and accepted it is to be anonymous. Back home, everyone knows everyone else's business. Here, no one much cares. Isn't it relaxing to be here at dinner together, unconcerned over what people are thinking about who we are to each other?"

Jubil looked around the room. "I suppose that's true," he agreed. "Though I'm not sure what to think about that myself these days."

Nelly frowned and lowered her eyes.

"What I'm trying to say is," he said. "I know you're glad to see me and that you care about me, but . . . do you still love me . . . and do you still want to marry me?"

Nelly sagged in her chair. She looked defeated. "Those are two different questions," she said.

"I was unsure where we stood when you left in the spring," he said, "and I thought about it all summer, but it's a question I can't answer myself. I can't go away tomorrow unsure where we stand."

"You're right," Nelly said, nodding. "I should tell you what is clear to me: I do love you. There is no doubt of that."

Jubil couldn't help but grin at these words that made his heart feel whole again.

"You've always been my best friend," she said, "and I can't bear the thought of losing that. Your adventures that once frightened me, I now see as accomplishments I admire greatly. I'm glad you did not let my timidity stop you from being who you are, and I'm glad I'm no longer letting my timidity keep me from finding the person I want to be. The problem is I'm not that person yet, and until I am, I don't feel ready to be married. I'm sorry if that sounds selfish, but I'm glad we didn't marry only to have us both surprised to learn how unhappy I was with myself."

"You should never feel unhappy with yourself," he said. "What you are doing is very brave. I just wish we didn't have to be so far apart."

Nelly narrowed her gaze at Jubil—a sure sign she was growing irritated.

"Yes, being apart is difficult," she said flatly. "How many times have I experienced that difficulty while you were off in the wilderness?" she asked. "Living here a thousand miles from the people I love, trying to excel at one of the best colleges in the country—this is my mountain to climb . . . it's the river I have to ride to my fate. I have to prove myself here. I can't do it at home. I've been given this opportunity, and if I don't meet the challenge, I'll regret it the rest of my life."

Jubil was moved by Nelly's determination and spirit but still concerned about the distance growing between them. "I understand being motivated by regret. It was my fear of regret that triggered this whole thing—if I had been able, without regret, to decline the opportunity to join the Yellowstone expedition, none of this would have happened. We would have been happily married by now."

"We would have been married . . . but I don't think I would have been happy," she corrected. "I was already fighting regret over not living up to my potential. That regret might well have grown to consume our happiness."

Jubil had no rebuttal.

"I would never want to see you unhappy," he said. "But I also don't want to lose you. I'll wait for you to find your path. We can be married then and go wherever you like. I can live anywhere and still lead tours. I'll work something out with the Warners about the store."

"That means a great deal to me, thank you," she said, reaching across the table for his hand. "But I don't think we should make promises right now that we aren't sure we can keep."

"I'm sure I can keep that promise," Jubil declared, as he looked into her eyes. "Are you saying you no longer want to marry me?"

"I'm saying I'm not I sure I'll ever want to be married . . . to anyone," she confessed. "This college is exclusively for women, and independence is the standard. Watching Miss Mitchell function independently as a successful professional woman has opened my eyes to what is expected of women and how these expectations are a trap for the human spirit. She has introduced me to other independent women too, both here and on Nantucket. I agree with their view of the world very much."

Somewhere in the back of Jubil's mind, he wanted to know what she meant about her new view of the world. But this thought was lost in the consuming pain of the moment. Nelly might never marry him. The thought made him feel lost—more lost even than when his mother had died. He went through the motions of paying the bill without consciously knowing what he was doing.

"I'm sorry to have upset you," Nelly said as they prepared to leave the restaurant.

Jubil nodded and shrugged. "I love you, Nelly," he said, struggling to control the emotion in his voice. "I always have, and I believe I always will."

"You may meet someone who is a better marriage prospect," she said. "I don't expect you to wait for me forever."

Jubil did not reply as he helped her on with her cape.

The carriage ride to Miss Mitchell's house was short, which made their silence tolerable. When they arrived, he helped Nelly down from the carriage and walked her to the door.

"Thank you for coming to see me," she said. "I hope you'll come again."

"It has been my pleasure," he said sincerely, although his heart was breaking. He struggled to find some of the good humor they had always shared. "I'll tell everyone at home how impressively you have set yourself up and how you are thriving here."

"You may be teasing," she said, "but thank you anyway."

He raised his right hand. "I speak nothing but the truth."

She stepped closer, and they kissed. Jubil could feel her love for him in the gesture, and a great sense of joy swelled in him and mingled with the sense of loss he was feeling. It was a bittersweet moment. The fact that they loved each other did not mean what he had always assumed it would mean—that they would be married and that their everyday lives would be bound together forever. They held their embrace until Jubil felt tears begin to well in his eyes. He would not stand there and cry. He stepped back, still holding her hands.

"Goodbye, Nelly," he said. "Good luck. I know you'll do well. I'll be back again as soon as I can. I love you."

"I love you too, Jubil," she said, wiping tears from her own eyes. "Give everyone at home my love."

He waved to her as he drove away in the carriage, unable to keep the tears from spilling down his cheeks. Seeing Nelly had satisfied some basic need in him, but he could not have been more disappointed with the outcome of his visit. He wondered if they would grow further apart, until they barely knew each other anymore. Perhaps he was destined to live like White Dog, roaming from place to place with little connection to anyone.

CHAPTER 10

Jubil awoke disoriented after a restless night at the National Hotel in Washington, DC. He had spent the previous evening in the hotel, having dinner, relaxing in his room with the newspaper, and trying to avoid thoughts of a future without Nelly.

General Sherman's offices were in the War Department Building, which was located on the northwest corner of the White House grounds, straight up Pennsylvania Avenue, about a mile from the hotel. Jubil had seen photographs in the newspaper of the White House and the Capitol Building, but never of Pennsylvania Avenue. It was an impressively wide street, paved with gray blocks, lined on both sides by poplars, and bustling with carriage traffic. The White House, however, did not meet his expectations. It was not small, but it was also not as imposing as pictures had led him to imagine. He also thought it gave no impression of being a house; it looked more like a small museum. The War Department building looked in keeping with its function—a utilitarian brick four-story building.

When Jubil arrived at the War Department, he showed General Sherman's aide the telegram he had sent to make sure the general would be available that day. The aide informed him the general was currently meeting with President Grant and suggested he come back in the afternoon.

Jubil agreed and decided to take his chances and see if Walter

Trumbull's father, Senator Lyman Trumbull, could meet with him in the meantime. Since the senator did not know him, Jubil had not wired ahead. He set off south across the White House lawn for the Capitol, noticing as he walked a white tower under construction a few hundred yards in the distance. He went to investigate. The tower was made of smooth marble blocks that rose to a height of about one hundred fifty feet, and it was capped by a rig for hoisting materials to the top. A few thrown-together wooden buildings sat around the base of the tower, but there were no workmen on the job. Jubil asked a passerby about the structure, and he explained it was to be a monument to George Washington. The man then went on a rant about the construction impasse caused by squabbles between the Know-Nothing political party, the Washington National Monument Society, and the US Congress. Apparently, this bickering had slowed the construction, and the Civil War had brought it to a halt. Since then, no plans had been made or funding allocated to complete it. The man shook his head in disgust and went on his way, and Jubil continued toward the Capitol.

The Capitol building was beautiful but severe, a barred fortress with huge columns that reminded Jubil of his insignificance. He couldn't help compare the Capitol grounds, which looked to have been recently stripped of trees and bushes, with the palatial grounds around Vassar College. He wondered if the long delay in tending to the grounds was also due, like Washington's monument, to bureaucratic bungling. He wondered if there was any chance that he and the other members of Washburn's expedition could move the members of Congress to act in a timely way to protect Yellowstone before it was ransacked by self-interested businessmen like Phineas Black.

When he found Senator Trumbull's antechamber, he introduced himself to the secretary as a fellow Illinoian and a friend of the senator's son. The secretary then went into the office and returned with the senator himself. He was fiftyish, tall and thin, with a long, thin clean-shaven face etched with deep lines of age and worry, and a prominent brow with sunken but bright eyes. He reminded Jubil of President Lincoln. Jubil looked for a resemblance between Walter and his father, and found it in their physical build and the shape of their faces.

"Mr. Walker," the senator said as they shook hands, "I'm Lyman Trumbull. I understand you know Walter."

"Yes sir, Senator," Jubil said. "I've recently returned from an expedition to the Yellowstone, and Walter was in the party."

"I knew it was planned," the senator replied, "but I've not heard from him since his return. I'd love to hear about your experiences. Come in." As they went into his office, Senator Trumbull's secretary reminded him he was due on the floor soon for a vote.

"Walter has always had an adventurous spirit," the senator said as he sat down behind his huge mahogany desk. "I'm glad he got this opportunity. Did he acquit himself well?" the senator asked wryly.

"He did," Jubil said, smiling. Sobering, he continued, "I'm sorry to say, however, that his partner, Mr. Everts, went missing. We searched for him for as long as we could, but found no sign. Walter took it hard."

"What a tragedy," the senator said, shaking his head. "Poor Truman. He was a good man and a good mentor for Walter." They sat silently for a moment, and then the senator asked, "Was this your first expedition as well?"

Jubil mentioned his trips with Major Powell and described his outfitting business and his invitation by General Sheridan to join the expedition, and then explained he was in Washington at the request of General Sherman.

"I am pleased that Walter was able to travel in your company," the senator said. "Did General Washburn consider the expedition a success?"

"I believe he did," Jubil said. "We confirmed that stories

about the area are not just tall tales. It is an astonishing place, probably unlike any other on Earth. We believe the place is so unique that it deserves protection from infringement. We agreed to campaign for the US government to declare the Yellowstone region a national park."

"That is an ambitious notion," the senator said, furrowing his heavy brow, "seeing as how the government is not presently in the park-operating business."

"Yes sir," Jubil acknowledged, "but if you saw the place, I think you would agree. It's too grand to allow people to come in and have their way with it. If we don't protect it, a few people will exploit it for themselves, or worse, all kinds of people will move in and ruin it."

"You realize, of course, there will be a sizeable faction," the senator said, "that believe that is exactly what should happen. That the government should keep its nose out of it and allow commerce and settlement to take their course."

"Yes," Jubil agreed, "we agreed to do what we could to build a case. Walter said he would introduce the idea to you. I hope he doesn't mind that I've already done so."

"Who would you imagine would provide the protection you are seeking for the area?" the senator asked.

"I suppose it would have to come from the army," Jubil said, realizing he had not given enforcement much thought.

"You should ask General Sherman what he thinks of that plan," the senator said, with an air of skepticism. "He still has Indian problems in that area. Bringing tourists in would likely increase efforts to clear the Indians out. Lord knows, we don't need another Marias Massacre on our hands."

"I'm sorry, I don't know what you're referring to," Jubil said.

"It was a travesty. In January, Colonel Baker led a detail out of Fort Ellis intended to punish a band of Piegan Blackfeet that had been rising up. Rather than hunt out the true perpetrators, Baker set Lieutenant Cheyney Doane and his men on a winter encampment, where they slaughtered some two hundred people, mostly women, children, and the elderly, then burned everything they owned. A dreadful shame."

Jubil was stunned. He recalled General Sheridan describing the "scorched earth" attack he had ordered. Stunningly, it had been Lieutenant Doane who carried it out.

The senator's secretary knocked on the door and stood in the open doorway. "Excuse me, sir, but you're due on the floor for a roll-call vote."

The senator rose from his chair, and Jubil did the same.

"It was a pleasure making your acquaintance, Mr. Walker. I'm indeed sorry to have to rush away. When I hear from Walter, I'll mention that we met. By the way, if you do pursue your national park campaign, remember it will require writing a bill, getting it reported by committee, garnering enough votes for passage, and bringing it to a vote. These things rarely move quickly in Washington."

Jubil walked back up Pennsylvania Avenue lost in thought. It was hard to accept that the same Lieutenant Doane he had grown to like and admire could be responsible for such slaughter of defenseless people, even if Doane was only obeying orders from Colonel Baker, General Sheridan, and General Sherman. They all supported this policy as necessary, but Jubil could not agree with it. He could not state exactly what the alternative should be, but there had to be one more humane.

It was still too early to return to General Sherman's office, so he stopped for lunch and passed the time admiring Lafayette Square. As he sat at the base of the statue of Andrew Jackson, he saw three uniformed military officers leave the White House and enter the War Department Building. The officer in the center had a reddish-brown beard—it was General Sherman. Jubil made his way back to the general's office and the aide escorted him in.

"Jubilee Walker," General Sherman said, coming around

his desk to shake Jubil's hand, "it is good to see you again. Welcome to Washington."

"My pleasure, sir," Jubil replied, "thank you for inviting me."

Sherman offered Jubil a seat and then sat in one of the guest chairs himself rather than talk to Jubil across his desk. "You are freshly back from the Yellowstone, I take it," the general said enthusiastically. "I'm sorry to say, I can't offer you dinner tonight, I have a previous engagement. But I have the afternoon, and I'm very anxious to hear about your experiences."

Jubil began with an abbreviated version of events, but the general soon slowed him down with a barrage of questions. He was interested in every detail—the terrain, the availability of fresh water, fish and game, predators, weather, natural hazards, Indians. Jubil did his best to provide the clearest picture possible but advised the general that Doane's journal would provide a far sharper assessment. When Jubil described the loss of Mr. Everts, Sherman was sympathetic, but he did not dwell long on the subject. Finally, Jubil summarized the discussion the men had had the night before leaving the Yellowstone Basin.

"A national park?" the general said skeptically. "That seems a stretch to me. Without the public pushing them, why would the government do it? If there's money to be made from exploiting the Yellowstone, the politicians are more likely to follow the money."

"I think if you saw the Yellowstone Basin, General, you'd agree," Jubil said. "That place is one of a kind, filled with marvels seen nowhere else on Earth. It should not be owned by anyone at the expense of others."

"That is a noble sentiment," the general said sympathetically, "but even if the Yellowstone deserves protection, the government already has too many irons in the fire and leaves more than a few unattended, to everyone's detriment."

Jubil thought of the unfinished monument to George Washington on the White House lawn, and the barren grounds of the Capitol Building. If the government was literally unable to tend to its own backyard, how likely was it to be a good steward over nearly inaccessible land, some two thousand miles away?

"It may be hardheaded of me, sir," Jubil admitted, "but I want to find a way to prevent that place from being torn up or walled in by anyone. Who besides the government can do that?"

"What part of the government do you think would protect it?" Sherman asked. "Do you think they would they create a new law enforcement group for it? Or ask federal marshals to do the job? Probably not. It would most likely fall to the army—and we've already got plenty to do."

Jubil nodded to acknowledge Sherman's point. "I stopped in this morning to meet Senator Trumbull," he said. "His son Walter was on the expedition with me. The senator said you probably wouldn't think much of the idea. He said there were still Indian problems out there. He was concerned the idea of a national park might lead to another Marias Massacre."

"That was an unfortunate event," Sherman said, frowning.

"Are there still problems in the area?" Jubil asked.

"Raiding parties still act up now and then," Sherman said. "It's a shame the Indians can't assimilate successfully. They have been granted large reservations, but they don't adjust to them very well. Speaking of Indians adjusting to change, did you encounter your old friend, White Dog, while you were out there?"

"I beg your pardon?" Jubil said, sure he must have misheard. "How would I have encountered White Dog?"

"He's there," Sherman said with a grin. "He scouts for Colonel Baker . . . well, I gather he does, whenever he feels so inclined."

Jubil was lightheaded with disbelief. Had it been White Dog he had seen riding beside the leader of the group of Crow on the plateau early on in the expedition? Had he recognized Jubil and advised the Crow leaders against attacking the expedition party? It was possible, although it was also possible that the Crow hadn't meant to attack anyway.

"What's he doing clear out there?"

"He stayed with General Sheridan after I got my current assignment," Sherman explained. "He rode to Fort Ellis once with Sheridan and decided to stay. He said Nebraska was getting too crowded. I understand his English has improved considerably. He's a sly dog, that one. Sets his own path."

"I would surely like to see him again," Jubil said, trying to absorb the idea. "Maybe I will. My partners and I discussed opening a store in Helena. I also plan to lead some tours out there, one of these days." White Dog's presence in the area added an interesting new appeal to the idea.

"You may get the chance to see him sooner than you thought," Sherman said pointedly. "I'm planning to mount another expedition to Yellowstone next summer. That's why I asked you here—to invite you to go along, if you're interested."

Jubil felt the rise of excitement and then hesitated. Would accepting the general's offer drive him and Nelly further apart? How would she interpret his actions if she returned home next summer for a rare visit and he was, once again, far away on an expedition? Then again, given her thinking lately, she might be more upset with him now if he turned down this opportunity. He recalled his sense of melancholy as he rode out of the Yellowstone Basin; he had been both anxious to return home and already longing to see that wonderland again. His hopes with Nelly might be wishful thinking, but if he turned this offer down, his regret would be real.

"Yes sir," Jubil said. "I'm interested."

"Good," the general replied. "I believe the US Army is overdue in making an assessment of the Yellowstone region. Now that you and your companions have confirmed the area is ripe for public viewing, it's going to open up. The army has never made our own reconnaissance of the area, and it's time we did."

"Yes sir, that makes sense," Jubil said tentatively, "but you keep referring to this being something the army needs to do. Are you asking me to join the army?"

Sherman threw his head back and laughed. "No, no," he said. "I've been working with General Sheridan on a plan, and we've agreed to send Captain John Barlow, the chief engineer of the Military Division of the Missouri, and Captain David Heap, a topographer. They are military men with scientific skills. Their mission will be to survey and map the area. They'll be accompanied by a support detail, and that's where you come in. Barlow and Heap are first-time explorers, so an experienced guide would be useful to them. You would be paid as an army scout. Do you want the job?"

"It would be an honor, General," Jubil said.

"Excellent," Sherman said. "There is something else you should be aware of. It's very likely there will be another expedition taking place concurrent with Captain Barlow's. Are you familiar with Dr. Ferdinand Hayden?"

"I know he's a famous surveyor," Jubil said. "General Sheridan showed me a map done after Hayden and Captain Raynolds visited the Yellowstone area, or made an attempt anyway." Theirs was the expedition that was snowed out of the basin and as a result left the entire basin almost featureless on their map.

"Yes, that was in 1860," Sherman said. "The Civil War prevented Hayden from having another go, and after the war he was appointed geologist-in-charge of the US Geological Survey of the Territories for the Interior Department. He's been off doing surveys of Nebraska and the Colorado front range, but he's got his eye on Yellowstone again. He's looking for Congressional funding, and if he gets it, he could very well be out there next summer also. That's fine if he is, but I believe the army needs its own intelligence about the area. I want Captain Barlow to be independent, even if they travel together for efficiency. You will take your orders from Captain Barlow. Do you still want the job?"

"Yes sir," Jubil said. "Would you be able to get me a copy of the Yellowstone map? Captain Barlow or Heap may bring one, but in case not, I'd like to."

"Yes, I'll have one sent to you," Sherman said.

Jubil left General Sherman's office considering all the time he had wasted during the Yellowstone expedition worrying about why the general had invited him to Washington. He had been foolish to think the expedition leaders would believe Sherman was using him to spy on them. If he had known the real reason, he would have been proud to tell them.

Jubil made plans as he walked back down Pennsylvania Avenue to the hotel. He intended to ask Colonel Baker at Fort Ellis about White Dog, who, Sherman had said, could be found if he was still in the vicinity and wanted to be found. If White Dog's English had indeed improved, it would be remarkable to have a real conversation with him—if he wanted a conversation, that is.

He had agreed to the upcoming expedition without consulting with Mr. Warner or Luke, but he was confident they would not object. However, these new plans meant another setback for their adventure tour business. Any tours would have to be planned around this expedition or delayed again. Jubil wondered how Eli Boswell would take the news. Luke had urged Jubil to take Eli more seriously. Maybe there was some way, between now and next summer, to start training Eli as a field representative.

Jubil went into the telegraph station on the corner of the block where his hotel was located and sent a telegram to Luke saying he was starting home the following morning. Thinking about riding the train home brought to mind the long trip from Bloomington to Fort Ellis, especially the interminable stagecoach ride from Corinne to Bozeman. If he'd known that he would be in Yellowstone again the next summer, he never would have sold Apollo to the liveryman in Corinne.

On a whim, he turned and went back into the telegraph station and sent a message to the liveryman, asking if Apollo was still available and directing him to reply to the hotel. Jubil was relaxing in his room after a pleasant dinner when a telegram arrived. The liveryman still had Apollo and would hold him if Jubil paid up front. Jubil immediately sent another message telling the liveryman to hold Apollo and that he would receive his money as soon as Jubil returned home.

Ike and Eli Boswell were waiting on the platform for Jubil as his train pulled into the station in Bloomington. He was relieved to be home, and the boys' endless questions about the expedition made him smile. In spite of the prospect of exploring the Yellowstone again, he had been struggling during his trip home to remain enthusiastic about the future, considering the disappointing outcome of his visit with Nelly and the lack of enthusiasm he had encountered in Washington for the idea of protecting the wonders he had seen in the Wyoming Territory.

It was too late in the afternoon to collect Star from the Boswells' stable and ride up to the farm, so he asked the boys to take him to the store. He would have supper at the Ashley House later and sleep at his campsite behind the store that night.

At the store, Luke handed Jubil a letter that had come while he was away. The return address indicated that it was from Walter Trumbull.

"Thanks," Jubil said. "How about the three of you join me for supper at the Ashley House? If you can tolerate hearing my stories again, Luke?"

"I'm sorry, Jubil," Luke said, "but I have dinner plans with Miss Bateman this evening."

"All the better for you," Jubil said. "Give her my regards.

How about you two?"

The boys were practically hopping with excitement at the prospect.

Jubil went into the storeroom to read the letter, in which Walter Trumbull shared the best possible news—Truman Everts was alive. Judge Hedges had, upon his return to Helena, offered a reward of six hundred dollars to anyone who found Everts. An adventurer named "Yellowstone Jack" Baronett had taken them up on it. He and his travel partner, George Pritchett, enlisted the help of two Crow scouts and set out to earn their reward. They had found Everts on foot, famished and delirious. His horse had gotten away, taking his gun and all his gear, and, just as Walter had feared, he had also lost his glasses. He was trying to return to Fort Ellis by following the Yellowstone back the way the expedition had come in but had lost his way. He had been removed to Bozeman to recover.

Walter's letter also said that Nathaniel Langford would soon be launching a speaking tour, sponsored by Jay Cooke. His intention was twofold: to put passengers on Cooke's railroad by drumming up tourists' interest in visiting the Yellowstone Basin and to try to build popular and political support for the idea that the Yellowstone area should be designated as a national park. Major Powell had always made a speaking tour after each expedition, but Jubil was never comfortable with the showmanship and salesmanship of such presentations. He replied to Walter by first rejoicing that Mr. Everts had been found alive and asking Walter to pass along Jubil's best wishes for his recovery. He then told Walter of General Sherman's invitation to return to the Yellowstone Basin the following summer with Captain Barlow.

Walter's letter brightened Jubil's spirit's considerably. He would be sure to tell Nelly this news—that no lives had been lost on the expedition.

At supper, the version of the expedition he told Ike and Eli focused more on the hardships, dangers, and narrow escapes than the version Luke and his parents had heard. They laughed at Jubil's melodramatic description of Mr. Everts digestive distress and the ride through Yankee Jim Canyon, high above the Yellowstone River valley.

When he told of his trip to visit Nelly, he described the town, the college, and Miss Mitchell's house. But Ike seemed to see right through him.

"Are you and Nelly still planning to be married?"

Jubil looked down at his plate and then forced himself to look Ike in the eye as he said, "As of right now, there are no definite plans. Your sister has the chance to follow her own interests and challenge herself, and I want that for her too," Jubil said around a lump in his throat. "I want her to be happy."

He then changed the subject with the revelation that General Sherman had hired him to guide another Yellowstone expedition.

"Can I go?" Eli asked.

"No, I'm sorry, Eli. I'm going because General Sherman hired me as a guide. And I'm sorry about delaying the adventure tour again," Jubil said, "but we'll get to it eventually."

Eli dropped his gaze to the table for a moment, then looked up at Jubil. "I won't pretend I'm not disappointed—maybe even a little angry," Eli said quietly. "You know—I don't plan to work at a store in Bloomington for the rest of my days." Eli looked away from Jubil to exchange a glance with his twin. Ike nodded.

"I know, Eli," Jubil said sincerely. "I understand completely, but I hope you'll bear with us a while longer." Jubil paused and considered how much to say with Luke absent, then decided to proceed. "We have a new idea that could interest you—both of you. The Warners and I have discussed opening another store near Yellowstone."

"Another store?" Ike asked.

"Near Yellowstone?" Eli asked.

"It's just an idea," Jubil said.

The twins looked at each other questioningly. "Who would run it?" Ike asked.

"We don't have all the details worked out yet," Jubil replied. "Luke and I would probably get it started, and then we'd decide how to manage things after that."

"What about the store here in Bloomington?" Ike asked.

"We thought you and Eli could take it over," Luke said.

Ike's eyebrows flew up. "Really?" Ike said. Jubil was not sure whether Ike was surprised they trusted him and his brother to run the store or surprised that he and the Warners had reached such a wise decision.

"What if I'd rather go to Montana?" Eli asked.

"That might be possible, but let's not get too far ahead of ourselves," Jubil interjected. "We've got plenty of time to think this through. Nothing will happen until next spring at the earliest. We've got the holiday season coming, and a trip to Montana isn't practical until at least March. As soon as we can travel, we'll plan a trip to visit Helena. Over the winter I'll be corresponding with a banker I met on the expedition, Mr. Langford. He'll be helpful to us in many ways. We'll figure out a way to make the whole operation suit us all."

The boys again looked at each other questioningly, then turned to Jubil and nodded simultaneously. Jubil wondered what silent message had passed between them.

In his tent that night, by lamplight, Jubil wrote Nelly a letter, telling her about his visit to Washington and Sherman's invitation. It would do him no good to avoid telling her—better to get it out in the open. He closed by telling her the idea of a new store in Helena and her brothers' new role in the business.

As he wrote, he realized how good his life was—his business was thriving, his reputation as an explorer was growing, he had the support and love of the Warners and the Boswells, but one vital aspect was missing: he had always imagined that Nelly would be at the heart of it all.

CHAPTER 11

The holiday season kept them busy at Warner and Walker Outfitting. Each year since they had opened, their holiday sales had increased, and this year was no exception. At the front of the store, they displayed the toolkit Luke had modeled after Langford's, and it became a popular gift item. Women bought them not only for their husbands and fathers but also for themselves, finding the smaller tool size and the tidy packaging appealing. Luke had a knack for knowing what would sell.

The rush of the season kept Jubil from dwelling on how much he missed Nelly, but the holidays themselves were difficult. He and Luke joined the Boswells for Thanksgiving dinner, but it was an awkward day. It was most difficult on Mrs. Boswell, who struggled to keep her spirits up under the melancholy of Nelly's first holiday away from home. Jubil and Luke did their best to help her through the day, and struggled to not be argumentative with Mr. Boswell when he expressed his displeasure about Nelly's situation. On Christmas Eve, he and Luke closed the store and went to Council Bluffs to spend Christmas through New Year's Day with Luke's parents.

After the holidays, Mrs. Boswell insisted on going to see her daughter, and Ike agreed to accompany her. Jubil was invited to go with them, but felt he would infringe on their time with Nelly, so he declined.

January through March was spent operating the store and enduring the midwestern winter. He and Luke made plans to save enough to replace the roof on the store that summer, and Luke ordered a shipment of roofing tar paper, which Jubil and Eli unloaded from the wagon and piled along the back wall of the storeroom.

During the dark and snowy late winter afternoons Jubil and Luke talked about their plans for the new store in Helena. Jubil wrote to Nathaniel Pitt Langford, and Langford replied that his Helena business contacts welcomed the prospect of a new outfitters store in their town. He would be back from his lecture tour by late spring. He assured Jubil that if he and Luke visited Helena then, he would see that they were introduced to people who could be helpful to them.

In late February, Jubil was sad to learn through Walter Trumbull that General Washburn had passed away. The Yellowstone expedition had stressed his frail constitution to its limit. Jubil wrote a letter to his widow expressing his admiration for the general's leadership and fellowship on the expedition. Walter also shared the news that he had attended Mr. Langford's lecture in the nation's capital, at the invitation of the Speaker of the House. Ferdinand Hayden had been in attendance as well, confirming Sherman's prediction that Hayden was interested in surveying Yellowstone.

On the last day of April, Jubil received a thick envelope from the War Department containing two copies of a document submitted by the Secretary of War to the forty-first Congress entitled *The report of Lieutenant Gustavus C. Doane upon the so-called Yellowstone Expedition of 1870*. Lieutenant Doane's journal! One copy for him and one for Nelly. Jubil wrote Nelly a note and put it in the envelope along with Doane's report, then went to mail the package. That night, at his campsite behind the store, he lit the lantern and lay down on his cot to read his copy.

It was even more compelling than he remembered. Doane had edited his daily journal entries into a tight, elegant report just under fifty pages long. It was filled with scientific and natural history observations of the awesome strange beauty of Yellowstone, and reading it was like reliving the expedition, except for one factor. For all the detail about the place, there was very little mention of the people. In Doane's defense, his report was supposed to be about the place, not the people. In any case, Jubil knew Nelly would enjoy it both as his friend and as an aspiring writer.

He read the report twice, then blew out his lantern and, with images of boiling mud pools in his mind, fell asleep.

Sometime during the night, Jubil came half awake. He had been dreaming of an episode from one of his expeditions—embers from his campfire had blown into the bushes around camp, and the whole area had gone up in smoke and flames—but the smell of smoke was no dream. He rolled over and sat up, now fully awake. Fire. He heard the crackle of burning wood and saw a dull glow through the wall of his tent. He threw open the tent flap and was stunned by the scene before him. The store was on fire. Flames were climbing up the left side of the back wall and had almost reached the eaves.

A man was standing there in the firelight. The light was too dim to make out his face, but the flickering light revealed he was of average height and weight, and wearing a wide brimmed hat, long coat, and boots. He stood about twenty feet from the store looking up at the flames, holding a burning torch in his right hand. When he saw Jubil, the man threw the torch into the burning building and ran.

"Hey!" Jubil called after him, but there was a more pressing problem at hand—Luke was in there. As far as Jubil could tell, the flames had not yet reached the front-right quarter of the building, where Luke's apartment was located on the second floor.

"Luke! Luke!" Jubil shouted as he ran to the back door. It was locked, and the doorknob was hot to the touch. He threw himself at the door and it flew open. Acrid black smoke billowed through the doorway, and the intense heat and flames inside pushed him back, burning his eyes and lungs and provoking a fit of coughing. He could see the fire had spread through the storeroom to the staircase, which meant he would not be able to go up the stairs to get to Luke. He looked up at the closed windows, then ran to Luke's side of the building and saw his windows were also closed. Maybe he had already gotten out of the building. Jubil turned in a circle, looking everywhere to see if Luke had collapsed somewhere in the yard, but he saw no one. He pounded his fists against the side of the store and called out again. "Luke! Luke!"

He heard someone call his name, and turned to see Mr. Humphrey, the neighbor across the alley, and his son Oscar. "Go for the fire department!" Jubil shouted. "And tell the Boswells!" Oscar sprinted off in the direction of the fire station, which was only two blocks away.

Jubil had to do something. Every business was required by the fire department to have a ladder and a bucket. Their ladder was on the opposite side of the building. He ran and hauled it over to Luke's window. He called to Luke again as he propped the ladder under the window and started to climb, only to realize he was barefoot and bare chested. He had run out of his tent with only his pants on. He ran back to his tent, pulled on his boots and grabbed his shirt and two blankets.

He had survived a wildfire in the Grand Canyon when brush around their camp had ignited and blazed out of control. The cook had doused a blanket in the river, thrown it over himself, and gone back into the campsite to salvage what he could. Now Jubil ran to the well and frantically levered the handle. He soaked both of the blankets and his shirt and ran back to the ladder. He tied his wet shirt around his nose and mouth and threw one blanket over his shoulders and tied it under his chin like a soggy cape. He draped the other blanket over his head and shoulders and started up the ladder. When he raised Luke's window, he nearly fell backward to the ground as black smoke and intense heat billowed out. He screamed for Luke but got no response.

Jubil stepped into the oven that was Luke's apartment and dropped to the floor, where he knew the smoke would be thinner. His wet blankets steamed. He held the wet shirt close to his face and took small breaths to avoid choking, but the smoke still burned his nose and throat, and his eyes watered, making the scene shimmer like a bad dream. He crawled across the room in the direction of Luke's bed. Halfway there, he ran into something—Luke, unconscious on the floor. Jubil shook him and called his name, but Luke's body remained limp. To get Luke and himself clear of the burning building, he would have to carry him back down the ladder. It had been adequate for Jubil, but carrying Luke—who outweighed him by thirty pounds—over his shoulder and backing down the ladder might be the death of them both. Frantic, he took the blanket from his head and laid it over Luke. There were two windows at the front of the apartment, over the porch roof. If he could get Luke out one of those windows onto the roof, they could wait there for help.

He pulled the other wet blanket from around his neck, rolled Luke onto it, and began to tow him toward the window. Jubil was surprised when the front window opened and in stepped a strange apparition: a man wearing a heavy leather hood with glass eye holes covered by a metal grid. A hose ran from his mouth to a leather pack he wore on his back. He was dressed in a long rubber slicker and heavy leather boots.

The firefighter reached under his hood, pulled the breathing tube out of his mouth, and plugged it with his index finger. "You all right, Jubil?" he shouted. "It's me—Chief Chuse.

Here—take a pull on this." Mr. Chuse, Chief of the Prairie Bird Fire Company, was a good customer of their store. The chief pushed the mouthpiece toward Jubil, who stuck it under the shirt he had tied around his face and drew in a couple of breaths of clean air, then motioned with the tube toward Luke.

"Let's get him out," the chief said.

They each picked up two corners of the blanket and carried Luke to the window. Jubil stepped out onto the roof, and then helped the chief move Luke through. There was a ladder there, propped against the porch roof. The chief shouted down to two firefighters on the ground, then he bent, lifted Luke, and draped him over his shoulder like a large bag of oats. He pulled out his breathing hose and yanked the leather hood off his head.

"Stand aside," the chief said. "I've got him. Can you climb down on your own?"

"Yes," Jubil said, pulling the fresh air into his lungs and beginning to cough.

The chief started down the ladder, carrying Luke with no apparent effort. Jubil watched as two firefighters stood at the base of the ladder, waiting to help break any fall. A group of four more moved the fire coach into place beside the store. The horse-drawn coach carried a steam boiler that pumped water from the coach's reservoir through a firehose. One firefighter controlled the hose as others drew water from the store's well to refill the reservoir. Jubil watched as the chief reached the bottom of the ladder and laid Luke on the ground.

Behind him, Jubil could hear the crackle and whoosh of the fire as it approached the front of the store. He needed to get off the roof. He stepped toward the ladder as Ike and Eli came tearing around the corner of the building, followed by their parents.

"Jubil!" shouted Eli, "Are you all right? Is Luke all right?"

Jubil still had his wet shirt wrapped around his face, so

he just raised his hand to acknowledge the Boswell family. He had no reply anyway. He clambered down the ladder and Mrs. Boswell rushed over and threw her arms around him.

"Oh, Jubil, Jubil!" she said through her tears.

He hardly heard her. He was coughing violently now, and his eyes, nose, and lungs burned. He was staring at Luke's slack face, which was streaked with soot.

Ike and Eli stood silently beside him.

Jubil moved closer to the chief, who hovered over Luke's prone form, forcing air into Luke's lungs by his own breath then pressing on Luke's abdomen to push the air out again. After doing this for a short while, the chief laid his head on Luke's chest, listening for a heartbeat, and pressed his fingers to the side of Luke's neck, searching for a pulse. Jubil waited for the movement of Luke's eyelids, the sound of his gasping breaths.

But there were no sounds, no movements. The chief resumed his efforts to revive Luke, but after a while he looked up and shook his head. "I'm sorry," he said. "We did our best, Jubil, but . . . Luke's gone."

Jubil felt as if he were being crushed by an invisible force, his heart nothing more than a searing pain inside him. He heard his own wheezing sobs as he fell to his knees next to Luke's body. When his tears were spent for the time being, he stood and found the Boswells there in a tight circle behind him, their faces contorted with grief.

The chief removed his jacket and laid it over Luke's chest and head.

"I'm sorry we didn't get here in time," the chief said. "Was he still in his bed when you found him?" he asked Jubil.

"No, he was on the floor, near the window," Jubil replied. If only Luke had been able to get to the window. If only Jubil had woken up sooner.

"I imagine the smoke was thick by the time he woke up," the chief said. "He was dealt a bad hand by this fire. Something is spewing out a whole lot of nasty smoke."

"Probably the roofing tar paper," Jubil said flatly. "It was stored in the corner where the fire started."

"I'm sorry," the chief said sincerely. "I want you to understand how quickly this happened. Later, you may tell yourself you didn't do enough, and I want you to know you couldn't have gotten to him in time. I've seen people blame themselves, and it can eat at you. You did a brave thing going in there. Don't ever let yourself believe otherwise."

"Thank you for your help," Jubil said, without fully meaning it. In spite of what the chief had just told him, Jubil could not help feeling they had all failed. If they had gotten to him more quickly, Luke would still be alive.

"We can take him to the undertaker, Mr. Woolcot, at the corner of Main and Grove," the chief said.

Jubil stared blankly at the chief and then at the Boswells. What occupied his mind was Luke's parents—he had to go to Council Bluffs and tell Mr. and Mrs. Warner what had happened. The thought of telling them that Luke was dead brought back that crushing feeling, as if the weight of the sky had fallen on him.

Mr. Boswell put a strong hand on Jubil's shoulder and said to the chief, "Yes, please do that, Chief. I'll be in touch with Mr. Woolcot first thing in the morning."

"Jubil, come home with us," Mrs. Boswell said as she came to his other side.

Jubil stared at the store, at everything he and Luke had planned and built together, as it was destroyed. Flames now shot out of the front window where Jubil and the chief had come out only a few minutes ago. The back wall, where the fire had started, was completely gone, and the front wall was now ablaze. The firefighters were hosing down nearby houses, and Jubil's tent, in an effort to keep the fire from spreading, but the store was gone. Jubil suddenly recalled the man he had seen in the firelight behind the store.

"Somebody set this fire, Chief," Jubil said. "I saw a man standing near the back wall with a torch in his hand. The fire was already up to the eaves. When he saw me, he tossed the torch into the fire and ran. I couldn't chase after him . . . I had to get to Luke."

"Did you recognize anything about him?" the chief asked urgently. "Anything at all?"

Jubil shook his head and described what he could remember of the man.

"Why would he still be standing there," Mr. Boswell asked, "if the building was already burning?"

"Maybe he was just making sure it was fully ablaze," the chief said. "I'll tell the police chief. He'll want to talk to you tomorrow."

"Jubil will be at our house," Mr. Boswell said to the chief.

Jubil stared vacantly at the burning building as two firefighters came to lift Luke's body and place him in the back of a wagon. He watched as the front wall of the store collapsed and the porch roof dropped into the burning remains of the store, sending aloft a shower of sparks, fire, and smoke.

Jubil and the Boswells walked in silence back to their house. When they arrived, Mrs. Boswell insisted Jubil have a hot bath, and she began heating water. He looked down at himself and realized he was covered in black soot. He thought of the black streaks on Luke's face and shuddered. Once the tub was filled, Mrs. Boswell gave him a basket in which to dump his ruined clothing. She left him a towel and a change of clothes, borrowed from the boys. Jubil went through the motions of his bath, his mind not fully connected to his body. His personal grief was overshadowed by the dreadful task before him.

When he went downstairs, the Boswell family was sitting in the parlor, talking quietly. They stopped when he came into the room and turned their attention to him.

"I've got to tell the Warners," Jubil stated. "I have to go to Council Bluffs."

Mr. and Mrs. Boswell nodded in tandem.

"We were thinking you could take the next train out," Mrs. Boswell said, "and we will bring Luke as soon as the undertaker is ready."

"We?" said Jubil.

"We're all coming," she replied. "Lily and Abe will need us."

Jubil nodded. He was so grateful to them that new tears sprang to his burning eyes.

"We have to tell Nelly," he said.

"I'll tell her," Mr. Boswell said. "I'll send her a telegram in the morning."

"We should tell Luke's friend Miss Bateman too," Jubil said.

"I'll take care of that," Mrs. Boswell said.

"Thank you," Jubil said wearily. "One more thing. If the police come looking for me, please explain why I had to leave. I wouldn't be much help to them anyway. I don't have any idea who that man was, or why he did this. Who would do this to Luke?"

He went upstairs to the guest bedroom and lay awake until the sun came up. When he went downstairs again, he found the Boswells had given up trying to sleep as well. The boys were fixing breakfast while their parents sat drinking coffee. Jubil had a cup as they made plans for the next few days.

Midmorning, Jubil went to pay the undertaker and talked about the plan for getting Luke back to Council Bluffs. The Boswells would pick up Luke's casket the following afternoon. Jubil went to purchase some clothing at a competitor's store rather than ride to the farm, and he accepted the salesman's condolences for the loss of his friend. In the early afternoon he caught the train, dreading this journey more than any he had ever made.

It was 6:00 a.m. when he arrived in Council Bluffs. Mr. Warner would just be opening the store. Jubil had not telegraphed ahead, and, worst case, he might find the Warners had gone out of town, but they always notified Luke before they traveled, and Luke always told Jubil.

He had eaten nothing since the previous evening and had slept only fitfully on the train. Grief was all-consuming, and all his effort went into trying to move his body forward, one step at a time. He had felt the same way when his mother had died. He credited Luke for helping him find new purpose after losing her, and together he and Luke had built a foundation that had given him hope for the future. Now that future was gone, and he had to tell the Warners their son was dead.

As he walked up Lower Broadway toward Warner and Company Outfitters, he thought about the first time he had stepped off the train in Council Bluffs three years ago. From the day they met, Luke had made Jubil's life better. First, he had befriended him and offered him a job as a part-time stock clerk, and from that point forward, Jubil had begun to find a direction in life. The outfitting business was unlike any job he had ever imagined. Without Luke, he would probably be an itinerant adventurer, scraping up a living between expeditions, much like Uncle Pete.

Mr. Warner was standing at the counter in the store, looking at some papers and sipping coffee. He looked up as Jubil closed the door.

At first, Mr. Warner smiled at the surprise of seeing Jubil there, but his smile vanished as he took in Jubil's grim countenance.

"Jubil?" he said. "Why are you here? You look terrible, son—what's wrong?"

Jubil felt sick as he looked Mr. Warner in the eye and tried to remember the words he had rehearsed countless times on his way there.

"There's been an accident," Jubil began in a voice raspy from the fire, and tears began to stream down his face. "Luke was in a terrible accident."

Mr. Warner began to sway on his feet, and Jubil stepped forward to help him sit down in a chair behind the counter. Mr. Warner gripped the arms of the chair tightly.

"There was a fire, in the middle of the night, at the store," Jubil continued, kneeling next to Mr. Warner's chair. "Luke was overcome by smoke. We got him out, but it was too late. He didn't survive. We've lost him, Mr. Warner . . . Luke's gone."

There they were—the words he had borne here that carried the weight of the world.

Mr. Warner shook his head. He looked as if he were about to say something but had forgotten how to speak. His gaze shifted aimlessly around the room. He focused on Jubil again, shaking his head and raising his hands, as if in question.

"That can't be," Mr. Warner said, looking down at his hands, which had fallen into his lap. "That can't be . . ."

"I'm so sorry," Jubil said. "He tried to make it to the window, but the smoke overtook him. I tried to get him out in time." Jubil felt as if he would choke on the words. "But I was too late."

Mr. Warner began to cry as he looked at Jubil, then he put his head in his hands and sobbed. Jubil placed his hand on Mr. Warner's shoulder. After a few moments Mr. Warner searched his pockets for his handkerchief. He wiped his eyes and blew his nose, then sat staring into space.

"How did the fire start?" he asked.

Jubil thought about the man behind the building, and

decided to spare Mr. Warner the upset of this mystery, at least for the moment. "It started along the back wall of the building," Jubil said truthfully. "That set ablaze some roofing tar paper we had stored, and the smoke from that was especially harsh. The fire chief didn't think Luke could have lasted more than a minute or two."

Mr. Warner sighed deeply and wiped his eyes. "But you got him out of the building?"

"Yes, sir," Jubil said, "with the help of a fireman. They took him to the undertaker. The Boswell family is leaving today to bring him home. They'll be here tomorrow."

"Oh, thank God," Mr. Warner said, closing his eyes. "At least we can have a proper funeral and burial."

"Yes, sir," Jubil said.

Mr. Warner sat with his eyes closed. He seemed composed enough to handle the rest of the story.

"There's something else you should know," Jubil said. "I don't believe the fire was an accident." He explained about the man he had seen, how he had gotten away, and that the police had been informed.

"Good Lord," Mr. Warner said in disbelief. "Who would want to hurt Luke—or you?"

"I have no idea," Jubil said. He had only one enemy— Phineas Black—but the idea that Black had traveled more than a thousand miles to Bloomington to set fire to the store seemed far-fetched. In spite of Black's angry rhetoric, Jubil could not imagine he presented enough of a threat to warrant such vengeance. Even if he were to make such an allegation against Black, what proof would he have to offer?

Mr. Warner sat back and closed his eyes again. Jubil waited for him to speak.

"I'm very concerned about Lily," he said, opening his eyes and looking at Jubil. "This may be more than she can bear. Did you know Luke had a brother?"

"Yes," Jubil said, "but he only spoke about him once. He said his mother struggled terribly after he died. He asked me to never mention it to anyone."

"His name was Samuel. He was three years younger than Luke, the same age as you. When Sam was six years old, he came down with chickenpox. The disease was toxic to his system, and he died. Lily was bedridden with grief for months, and she remained depressed for years. She finally managed to find herself again, but this news . . ." Mr. Warner looked at Jubil with tears in his eyes.

"I'll help you both in any way I can," Jubil said.

Mr. Warner reached up and patted Jubil's hand where it still rested on his shoulder.

"Thank you. I'm grateful to have you here with us."

Mr. Warner collected himself to take the necessary next steps. He and Jubil discussed the Boswells' arrival and the funeral arrangements. Mr. Warner insisted the Boswells stay at their home.

"We have plenty of room," he said. "Lily would insist."

"Would you like me to go with you to talk to Mrs. Warner, to tell her what happened?"

"It's kind of you to ask, but I think it would be best for me to tell her myself. Are you willing to call on the undertaker to explain the situation to him? Mr. D. M. Connell on Broadway. We already have a family cemetery plot. Our church is First Methodist, on Broadway. The minister is the Reverend Jack Frick. I'd like him to do the service tomorrow, if possible. We'll have the burial immediately afterward, and no event following. I want to get Lily past this quickly, so she doesn't dwell on the details."

"Yes sir," Jubil said reaching for a pencil and paper to make some notes.

"Then go to the newspaper office and tell them what has happened," Mr. Warner said. "They'll put a story in the paper, so folks will know. My surrey is behind the store, with Rocky hitched up. You can take it, and I'll have the stock clerk, take me home. If I've forgotten anything, just do what you think is best. Thank you. It's a great relief to have your help."

Jubil stood and offered Mr. Warner his hand to help him up from the chair.

After he had taken care of all the arrangements, Jubil returned to the Warners' house. In the kitchen, Mrs. Garcia prepared a meal for him while tears ran down her face. Mr. Warner came downstairs as Jubil ate, and the sight of his pale face and his red-rimmed eyes and nose took away what little appetite Jubil had.

"Were you able to get arrangements made for tomorrow?" Mr. Warner asked, as he absentmindedly wrung his hands.

"Yes sir, the service is scheduled for ten o'clock, but we can sit with Luke in private earlier if you want to. How is Mrs. Warner?"

"She is resting comfortably now," Mr. Warner said, his grief and exhaustion clearly written in every gesture. He sat down at the table across from Jubil and stared blankly at its surface. "I had to send for the doctor. She was . . . distraught . . . understandably. He gave her something to calm her nerves." He looked up at Jubil. "I hope she'll be able to get through the services tomorrow. If not—we're going through with it anyway."

"Yes sir," Jubil said.

Tomorrow he would bury yet another person he loved.

CHAPTER 12

When the Boswells arrived in Council Bluffs, they and Jubil watched in pained silence as the undertaker and his helpers unloaded Luke's casket from the train and placed it into the shiny black hearse.

Mr. Boswell had elected to attend the funeral, and even agreed to spend the night in the Warner's home so his wife could comfort Mrs. Warner. This was more considerate of him than Jubil had expected, and he hoped that comportment would continue. If Mr. Boswell was disrespectful to the Warners, Jubil would not be silent.

He explained to the Boswells that the funeral and burial services would take place at ten o'clock that morning. When Mrs. Boswell appeared startled, he explained, "Mr. Warner wants to get Mrs. Warner past it as soon as possible."

"Nelly will miss the services, then," Mrs. Boswell mused.

"Nelly's coming?" Jubil said.

"Yes," Mrs. Boswell said. "She answered our telegram and said she was on her way. She'll be here tomorrow. I know she'll be disappointed to miss the services, but she'll want to see Lily anyway."

"Oh . . . good," Jubil said. He knew she would have been very upset at the news of Luke's death, but he had not imagined she would make the trip back alone. Apparently, he had once again misjudged her determination.

Jubil drove the Boswells to the Warners' house in the surrey. As he turned up the Warners' lane, Eli spoke. "Is that their house?" he marveled. "I knew they were rich, but not *that* rich."

"Elijah Boswell," his mother snapped, "you mind your mouth and your manners when we get in that house."

Mr. Garcia was waiting at the door. He took the surrey while Jubil helped the Boswells unload their luggage. Mrs. Garcia showed the Boswells to their bedrooms upstairs, and then led them back down to the dining room for breakfast. They had not yet been seated when Mr. Warner joined them.

"Welcome, and thank you all for coming," Mr. Warner said, greeting them with handshakes while the Boswells offered tearful condolences.

"How is she doing?" Mrs. Boswell asked.

"Not well I'm afraid, Mattie," Mr. Warner replied. "She's not herself right now. The doctor gave her laudanum last night, and she's just waking up now."

"I understand, Abe," Mrs. Boswell said. "She told me about Sam."

Mr. Warner wiped his eyes with his handkerchief and nodded. "Yes . . . well, I'm sorry I won't be joining you for breakfast. I hated to leave her, even to come down to greet you, so I'll only be with you a moment. Go on to the church whenever you are ready. Mr. Garcia will drive Lily and me."

Mr. Warner left the room.

"Did you know that Luke had a younger brother?" Mrs. Boswell asked Jubil.

"Yes, he told me. But he asked me to never mention it."

Mrs. Boswell nodded. "When Lily told Nelly and me, she made it clear we were not to repeat it."

"I guess I just don't understand why anyone would choose to pretend someone so significant to them never existed," Jubil said. "I could never do that with the memory of my parents or

Uncle Pete."

"Don't be too quick to judge, Jubil," Mrs. Boswell said. "You've managed your grief, but not everyone is so fortunate. If every mention of your parents threw you back into the same despair and emptiness you felt the day you lost them, you might find the only way forward was to avoid any mention of them. I'm not sure there is such a thing as a right or wrong reaction when it comes to grief. Everyone finds their own way of coping."

This rang true to Jubil. "Yes, ma'am," he said.

When he and the Boswells arrived at the church, he was surprised at the number of people who had gathered on such short notice. The Warner family was widely respected, and the news must have traveled quickly. The casket was open for viewing, and Jubil steeled himself to walk past it and say good-bye to his friend. Luke looked like he was sleeping. Looking at him, Jubil felt nothing . . . no sadness . . . no guilt . . . only a silent numbness. As if this moment were not really happening, as if it were only a bad dream.

He stepped aside to make room for the Boswells, who were all weeping. After a moment, he showed Mrs. Boswell to the empty pew in the front row, and Mr. Boswell and the boys followed. Just then, Mr. and Mrs. Warner entered the church. Mrs. Warner wore a black floor-length dress, black gloves, and a black hat with a veil that covered her face. As they started down the aisle, they stopped abruptly and Mrs. Warner pointed toward the front of the church. Jubil felt a chill—she looked like death itself, pointing toward the casket with a black-gloved hand. He prepared himself for her to faint or cry out, but instead Mr. Warner spoke to one of the ushers, who then walked down the aisle to the casket and closed the lid. Only then did the Warners continue to their seats in the front pew. Mrs. Warner sat between Mr. Warner and Jubil, and he could feel her body trembling as she wept silently.

As the Reverend Frick began the eulogy, Mrs. Warner

reached for Mr. Warner's hand with her left hand and Jubil's with her right. The moment she touched Jubil, the numbness he had been feeling disappeared, replaced by a clenching pain in the center of his body. His eyes welled with tears.

"Brothers and sisters," the pastor began, "we gather today to honor the life of Lucas Abraham Warner, taken too soon, in his twenty-third year. Luke Warner lived his life as a shining example of how to follow God's commandment to honor thy father and mother, but Luke's devotion to his parents was not his only virtue. I call your attention to First Corinthians, chapter thirteen, verses four through seven: *Love is patient, love is kind. It does not envy, it does not boast, it is not proud. It does not dishonor others, it is not self-seeking, it is not easily angered, it keeps no record of wrongs. Love does not delight in evil but rejoices with the truth. It always protects, always trusts, always hopes, always perseveres.* Those who Luke loved knew this was the kind of love he had for them. Luke himself embodied these virtues."

Jubil remembered how Luke had only laughed when, after the Grand Canyon expedition, a newspaper reporter mistakenly credited Jubil with the idea of creating an outfitting business geared for adventure travelers, when the idea had clearly been Luke's. Luke never corrected anyone who, as a result, complimented Jubil on his foresight. As Jubil began receiving some notoriety as an explorer, Luke had never been jealous of the attention or used their relationship in any self-serving way.

"And I believe it is safe to say," the pastor continued, "that a kinder, gentler soul will have never passed through the pearly gates than Luke Warner. Let us pray."

Jubil bowed his head, trying unsuccessfully to block out the images of Luke lying on the ground, his soot-streaked face so terribly still.

At the cemetery, Jubil, Mr. Warner, Mr. Boswell, Ike and Eli, and Mr. Garcia carried Luke's casket to his grave, as the women looked on. The pastor commended Luke's spirit to heaven, and as soon as he had finished the benediction, Mr. Warner guided Mrs. Warner away toward the carriage.

That afternoon Jubil and the Boswells sat in the gazebo on the Warners' manicured lawn. Mr. Warner joined them briefly to ask Mrs. Boswell to sit with his wife, who had requested her company. Then Mr. Warner sat down to address Jubil and the Boswell men.

"It's a blessing to have you here with us," he said.

Mr. Boswell and Jubil nodded, while Ike and Eli sat quietly.

"We must now talk about the future," he said, in a weary tone. "I won't beat around the bush. Under the circumstances, Lily and I feel it's time for us to make some changes. She very much wants to move back to Nantucket, to be nearer her remaining family and in the place of her childhood, and my heart is with her, not in the business world, so I'm planning to retire very soon. Lily wants to move as soon as possible. I'll be taking her east to find a new home as soon she is able to travel. Once we are settled, and if I'm able to leave her, I'll come back to sell the house and the store. I'll help you in any way I can, Jubil, if you want to rebuild your store, but I'll be closing up Warner and Company Outfitters as soon as I find a buyer."

Jubil was overwhelmed at being forced to face what his future would be without Luke.

"I understand," Jubil said, as the odd numb sensation returned. "I haven't even begun to think about what I'm going to do yet. I could stay here and help you for a little while, but I'm committed to returning to Yellowstone the first of July. I'll have plenty of time to ponder then." He turned to Ike and Eli. "Sorry, boys. I suppose you're going to have to find your own way now."

Without Luke, there was no center. Without Luke, everything they had built together would fall apart.

Ike looked at Eli, sending one of their unspoken messages, then turned his attention to Mr. Warner. "We'll stay and help run the store until you find a buyer, if you'd like."

Eli nodded.

"That's very good of you boys," Mr. Warner said. "Would that be all right with you, Theodore?"

"Yes," Mr. Boswell replied proudly. "The boys are old enough to be making their own decisions."

Jubil was shocked to realize it was true. The boys who had burned down his farm had somehow grown into responsible young men. It also struck him how differently Mr. Boswell treated the boys compared to Nelly, who was older and whose actions had always shown how responsible she was. Yet her father was still treating her like a child.

The following morning he went to pick Nelly up at the train station, fighting a peculiar feeling of dread. His longing for her in addition to his grief for Luke seemed almost too much to bear.

Nelly stepped off the train looking beautiful, as always, although Jubil could tell she'd been crying. He met her on the platform and held out his hands to greet her, but she walked into his arms and held him—and he wanted to hold on to her that way forever.

"Oh, I can't believe he's gone!" she said, still holding him. "Luke was such a good friend, and a good person."

"Yes," he said, enjoying her touch while it lasted.

Nelly stepped back and looked him in the eye. "How are you doing?"

"About as you'd expect, I suppose." He shrugged. "Sometimes it hits me . . . other times . . . I'm just numb."

Nelly reached in her bag and retrieved a hanky to blot her tears.

As they drove to the Warner's house, Jubil retold the story of the fire, hoping this might be the last time he had to relive the experience. He warned Nelly of Mrs. Warner's condition and broke the news to her about the Warners' plans to close the store and move back to Nantucket.

"Oh, my goodness," Nelly said, shocked by the news. "What are you going to do?"

"I'm not sure yet," Jubil admitted. "I'll be leaving for Yellowstone again in a few weeks. When I get home . . . I'll figure something out."

Nelly glanced at him with concern, but she offered no advice or opinion. There had been a time when she had cared enough about him to share her observations of a situation, but Jubil supposed those times were gone. The remainder of the ride to the Warner house passed in heavy silence.

When they arrived, Nelly had a tearful reunion with her family. Mrs. Warner remained confined to her room, attended by Mr. Warner and Mrs. Boswell. Once Nelly arrived, she was also invited to sit with Mrs. Warner.

By early afternoon, Jubil was feeling unneeded and was growing ready to be alone with his own thoughts. He found Mr. Warner sitting in his office with Mr. Boswell.

"I don't want to seem to be running out on you," Jubil said to Mr. Warner, "but at this point, I don't know that I'm much help around here. I'm thinking of going on home. I've got some things I could be doing before I leave for Yellowstone. Whether we rebuild the store or not, the building site needs to be cleaned up. I could at least get that done and prepare the lot to be sold, if it comes to that."

"I understand," Mr. Warner said. "Speaking of the lot, that is all yours. You and Luke paid it off together, and there is no doubt he would want you to have his share."

"Thank you," Jubil said. "I won't sell it right away. If I don't reopen the store, I might sell my farm and build a house in town. I don't know. I've got a lot of decisions to make."

"Wait here for just a minute," Mr. Warner said, patting Jubil on the shoulder as he walked past him. "I'm going to tell Lily that you are leaving."

When he returned, he said, "She'd like to see you."

Jubil collected himself, then walked upstairs to the Warner's bedroom and knocked. Mrs. Boswell opened the door. As he stepped inside, Mrs. Boswell and Nelly left the room.

"Please don't leave without saying goodbye," Nelly said, as she walked past.

"I won't," he replied.

Mrs. Warner was sitting up in her bed with pillows behind her back. Her silver hair lay loosely on her shoulders, and he realized he had never seen it unpinned. She was pale, and her cheeks were hollow, her eyes red and watery, evoking a terrible memory of his mother on her deathbed. The memory was reinforced when Mrs. Warner weakly waved him over to her and patted the bed beside her—the same motion his mother had made during her illness when he came to check on her. He sat on the bed, and Mrs. Warner reached for his hand. Her grip at the funeral had felt like cold steel, but today it was weak, her grip feather-light. Was it possible that Luke's death would kill her? He pushed the thought out of his mind.

"Abe told me you went into the burning building to try to save him," she said shakily, making an effort to keep from breaking down.

He nodded. "It was too late." He could barely get the words out through his constricted throat. "I'm . . . so . . . sorry."

She patted his hand softly.

"You were the best friend he ever had," she said, as her tears welled.

He nodded. "And he was that for me." He took her hand in both of his, and they both fought back tears.

"I don't know if I can bear it, Jubil," she said through her tears. "He was all we had."

Jubil's heart was full of sympathy for her pain. "When my mother died, I felt like I had been left all alone in the world—like everything and everyone I loved had been taken away. I couldn't see any joy in anything, and I didn't have any desire to do anything. But then I realized I still had Nelly and her family, and Major Powell, and they led me to you and Mr. Warner and Luke—and you all changed my life and made it whole again. Don't give up, Mrs. Warner. There are still a lot of us that love you and want to see you happy again. You know Luke would agree."

She sobbed and opened her frail arms, and Jubil leaned in and held her close for a moment, thinking of his mother's embrace. Then she leaned back against her pillows and wiped her eyes. She sighed heavily, and Jubil could see she was struggling to compose herself. He didn't want to risk upsetting her again, so he rose to leave.

"Mr. Warner tells me you are moving back to Nantucket," he said. "I'll be going to Yellowstone again soon. But on my way back, I'll stop here in Council Bluffs to see you. If you're not here, I'll come see you on Nantucket, and you can show me the ocean."

Mrs. Warner nodded. "I'd like that very much."

Jubil left the room and found Nelly and her mother waiting in the hall. Mrs. Boswell returned to sit with Mrs. Warner.

"We've hardly had a chance to talk," Nelly said.

"Oh, well, I don't know what else there is to say. I'm not feeling very talkative anyway," Jubil confessed.

"I'm worried about you," she said. "I know you are heartbroken, but don't give up. You still have people who love you."

"Thanks," he said, noting how her words echoed his own to Mrs. Warner. "I'll be all right."

"Come and see me again," she said, "after you get back from your expedition."

He nodded. They hugged, and he went to his room to pack.

The afternoon train was on time, and Jubil began his journey home. He watched the scenery roll past, slept, ate, and tried in vain to care about his future.

Jubil spent the rest of May riding Star back and forth between the farm and the burned-out site of the store. Mr. Boswell had allowed him the use of his sturdy carriage horse, Moses, to help remove burned timbers. Star was capable of it, but Jubil was happy to spare her the effort. With Ike and Eli still in Council Bluffs, Nelly in Poughkeepsie, and Luke gone, he was more alone than he had been since his mother died. He had grown up treating Star as a friend rather than an animal, and he was already regretting having to leave her again so soon.

The business of pondering his future was not producing any solid ideas, much less a plan. It had been generous of Mr. Warner to grant Luke's share of the building site to Jubil, and Jubil appreciated his offer to help finance a new store, but he had not yet found it in his heart to rebuild. No matter how successful a new store might be, it would never be the same as what he had had with Luke. As Nelly had often reminded him, he thought more with his heart than his head.

There was another reason he was reluctant to open a new store—without Luke, he was afraid he would fail. It was no secret that it was Luke and his father, not Jubil, who had the business expertise and the temperament necessary to make their outfitting enterprises successful. Jubil's contribution had begun as a reliable and enthusiastic manual laborer, but it had grown as he became a respected explorer and authority on their store's products. Though he had come to value his own contribution to the business, he harbored no illusions about who actually operated it—Luke. Jubil had never paid much attention to their relationships with suppliers, he had never decided which products to stock, and he had never done any of the bookkeeping. Ike Boswell had seen Luke as a mentor and paid far more attention to those things than Jubil. And yet, Luke had never given any indication he expected Jubil to attend to those things, or expressed any disappointment that he did not. Jubil had not entirely ruled out the possibility of opening another Bloomington store with the Boswell twins, if they were interested, but he was not currently driven to make it happen, and he could not make much headway on the idea anyway, until he returned from Yellowstone in the fall, and Ike and Eli had returned to Bloomington.

A letter from Ike informed him that the Warners had gone east to find a new home on Nantucket. Once they were settled, Mr. Warner would return to Council Bluffs to deal with his store and house. Ike was proud of the confidence Mr. Warner had shown in him by allowing him to manage the store while he was away, and he was pleased that Eli and Mr. Warner's clerk, Caleb, had been very accepting of the arrangement.

A brief letter from Nelly told him that she had returned to Poughkeepsie. She said that by the time she and her mother had left Council Bluffs, Mrs. Warner had shown some improvement in her spirits, spending less time abed and taking her meals in the dining room, but her normally energetic personality and artistic nature had not yet reemerged.

In late May, Jubil received a letter from General Sherman informing him that Ferdinand Hayden had indeed received funding from Congress to conduct a survey of Yellowstone and that Hayden and his party would be in the area over the same period as Jubil and Captain Barlow. Sherman asked Jubil to serve both parties but to take his orders from Captain Barlow. He was to meet Barlow's party on July 1 at General Sheridan's office in Chicago, and proceed from there to Fort Ellis and then on to Yellowstone.

Jubil was anxious for the expedition to begin, primarily as a distraction from all his fruitless pondering, but he was also looking forward to seeing the wonders of Yellowstone again. He was certain the landscape there would act as a balm to his grief.

By early June, the store site had been cleaned up and made ready for use. Even though his regular income had been interrupted by the loss of the store, Jubil was largely unconcerned about money. He still had money in the bank inherited from his parents, there was no mortgage on the farm, and his living expenses had always been minimal. Even so, he decided to consult a real estate agent about the value of the store site, in case he decided not to rebuild, and the value of his farm, in case he decided to settle elsewhere. Now that Luke was gone and Nelly had left Bloomington, Jubil felt little holding him there. He learned that he could gather a respectable amount of capital by selling, but decided he would not do so unless he had a sound purpose for the money. Until then, he would draw lightly on his savings and rely on his army salary that summer.

He wrote his friend Walter Trumbull and told him of Luke's death and the loss of the store. He also reminded Walter that he was spending the summer in Yellowstone and could be reached by mail through Fort Ellis.

In late June, a lengthy letter from Nelly arrived. She had read Lieutenant Doane's journal and was effusive in her praise of his skills as a journalist. She had been so impressed that she had shared it with her English professor, who was also complimentary. He was surprised and impressed by her connection to a member of the exploration party and informed her of a recent article in *Scribner's Monthly* magazine, written by Nathaniel Pitt Langford. It was to be the first in a series of articles on his Yellowstone expedition. She had read Langford's article and was thrilled by the sense of adventure imparted by his story, the imagery in his descriptions, and the bonus of the woodcut illustrations.

Jubil experienced a moment of jealousy that he hadn't seen Langford's journal or the magazine article Nelly described. He would find a copy of the magazine.

Nelly went on to apologize for her past worry over Jubil's

safety and claimed to have reached a deeper appreciation for his passion and drive. She lightheartedly thanked him for raising her on the ladder of social standing among her class-mates—she was now known not only as Miss Mitchell's ward but also as the friend of an accomplished explorer. He appreciated the compliment but was disappointed that she had referred to him as her friend, not her fiancé. Was it time, he asked himself, to let go of the illusion that Nelly ever meant to marry him?

Other news she shared left him with conflicting emotions. She enthused about meeting two prominent members of society recently, at a dinner hosted by Maria Mitchell in her home. In attendance were Matthew Vassar, founder of the college, along with Elizabeth Cady Stanton, a prominent women's rights advocate and close personal friend of Miss Mitchell. Much of her letter went into describing Stanton and her accomplishments. Nelly greatly admired her strength of conviction, fearlessness in word and deed, determination and iron will, and found it delightful that all this issued from a petite white-haired grandmotherly woman. Nelly was very taken with her.

She had been pleasantly surprised when Stanton offered to recommend her for a position over the summer at a newspaper, as an editorial assistant. Stanton and her partner in activism Susan B. Anthony had co-founded *The Revolution*, a newspaper focusing on women's rights. They had recently sold the newspaper, but Stanton was still very involved with the publication. Nelly had enthusiastically accepted the recommendation, and, if all went as planned, she would be living and working in New York this summer rather than returning to Bloomington. She would resume classes at Vassar in the fall, to complete her final year of college.

As Jubil read Nelly's letter, he felt both proud of her and sad to see her slipping further away. While he did not begrudge her any of her successes, it was now clear that she was just as drawn in her own direction as he was in his, and the trajectories of their interests did not intersect. This was not just a phase Nelly was going through—this was who she was and who she always would be. The passion she felt for learning and writing was opening doors for her, just as Jubil's passion for exploring had done for him. In spite of his happiness for her, her news deepened his sense of melancholy. His future had come untethered from everything that was familiar to him, as though he'd lost his home. Was he now fated to travel from place to place, never settling anywhere?

He put Nelly's letter away and chastised himself for being morose and self-pitying. In a few days he would be in Chicago meeting Captain Barlow, and then he would be on his way to Yellowstone again. Maybe this expedition would reveal a new path into the future.

CHAPTER 13

Jubil entered General Sheridan's office to find two military men standing at attention beside the map table. Their formal pose struck him as odd. He wasn't certain how to react. Was he supposed to salute?

One of the men stepped forward and announced himself. "I'm Captain John Barlow. Thank you for coming." General Sheridan's chief engineer was in his thirties, about Jubil's height and build, and had a full mustache. "This is my second in command, Captain David Heap —our topographer."

Captain Heap was clean shaven, at least six inches shorter than Jubil, and about the same age as he was, though without the uniform, he could have easily passed for younger. They all shook hands.

"We've been briefed on your background," Captain Barlow said to Jubil, "so I'll move on to the matter of the expedition. There will be three other men traveling with us: a photographer and his assistant, and a draftsman to assist Captain Heap. At Fort Ellis, I plan to collect provisions, hire five packers and a cook, and requisition eleven mules and riding horses for the men. We will also be assigned a six-man military escort. We'll have several cases of equipment to be moved from Corinne to Fort Ellis. What are your thoughts about transportation from Corinne to the fort?"

"There's a good livery there. We can hire a teamster to haul your gear to the fort," Jubil explained. "I have a horse stabled there that I intend to ride, but you and your men can take the stage if you want. It's a little faster, so you'd arrive in Bozeman first. I'd be along in a day or two, followed by your gear a few days after that, depending on the weather."

Barlow and Heap exchanged a glance and nodded.

"Do you have any questions or concerns?" Barlow asked Jubil.

"Do your men have wilderness experience?" Jubil asked.

"Captain Heap and I have done surveying work," Barlow said.

"How about the other men?" Jubil asked, deciding to not question whether surveying constituted wilderness experience.

"Captain Heap and I will be responsible for the well-being of our men, Mr. Walker. Your job is to keep us on the route General Washburn followed last year, though frankly, that looks fairly obvious, but General Sherman was set on providing us a guide, so here we are."

Jubil heard Barlow's implication that he wasn't really needed, but at the moment he did not have the emotional energy to be offended. Sherman thought he was needed, or he would not have troubled to invite him.

"Well, Yellowstone is a hard place to travel," Jubil said, "Everyone has to be prepared to look out for themselves."

"We are fully capable of looking out for ourselves," Captain Heap said, pridefully.

"Good . . . that's good," Jubil said calmly. "I'm sure we'll all do fine. I'll meet you at the train station at 8:00 a.m."

With this short, uninspiring meeting behind him, Jubil returned to the Tremont House for the night. He was anxious to see Apollo and to return to Yellowstone, and General Sherman had hired him to do a job, but he was not especially looking forward to Barlow and Heap's company. However, at the moment, the only people he longed to see were those he could not. He hoped his mood would improve once the expedition got underway.

It did not. He met the other members of the party at the train station but spent most of the trip from Chicago to Corinne alone. Captain Barlow had purchased second-class seating for the men, but Jubil had opted to pay his own way and taken a compartment in a Palace Car. Captain Heap raised his eyebrows when Jubil shared that information, but the photographer, Thomas Hines, said Jubil was just showing good sense to appreciate comfort when it was available. When Jubil saw any members of his party in the dining room, he joined them. He enjoyed the company of Hines and his assistant, Henry Prout, but the draftsman in the party, William Wood, hardly spoke. Hines had asked for the story behind the beaded medicine bag that Jubil wore, and he had shared the story. Hines was impressed, but no one else commented. Captain Heap spoke very little as well. Jubil wondered if that was because his voice sounded as young as he looked. Jubil figured Heap must be a very capable topographer to have reached the rank of captain without having a more authoritative bearing.

Jubil passed the time by rereading his copy of Doane's journal from last year's expedition. He had also purchased, at a newsstand in Chicago, the issue of *Scribner's Monthly* in which Nathaniel Langford's account of the Yellowstone expedition appeared. Though Doane was the better journalist, Langford's description contained more stories about people and events. The only shortcomings Jubil found in the magazine article were the woodcut illustrations, which gave some impression of the landscape, but conveyed none of its grandeur—but then, how could they? Nevertheless, he enjoyed reading both versions and reminiscing about the trip.

In Corinne, Jubil found a ray of sunshine to brighten his gloomy outlook when he went to retrieve Apollo from the livery. The brown and white pinto stallion was as beautiful and strong as Jubil remembered. The horse did not immediately recognize him but quickly warmed to him as they saddled up, nudging him with his nose. The liveryman had taken excellent care of the horse and his tack. Even though Jubil had wired money to him the previous fall for Apollo's keep, he was so pleased with the man's reliability that he paid him a bonus. He also arranged, through this same liveryman, a teamster to haul Barlow and Heap's gear to Fort Ellis by wagon. Jubil helped Barlow and the other men book passage on the stage to Bozeman, then he rode out of town on Apollo.

Jubil's ride was unmarred by highwaymen or Indian raiders, and he arrived at Fort Ellis late in the day on July 13, his twenty-second birthday. The previous year, the fort had been a busy place, but nothing like what he saw as he rode in this time. In addition to all the soldiers going about their work, about two dozen civilians were laboring at loading and arranging gear on a row of seven wagons, while another dozen worked on the construction of a wooden framework of some sort. He rode to the headquarters building to verify that Captain Barlow had already arrived, and to pay his respects to Colonel Baker. He found the colonel had gone out on escort to the Northern Pacific Railroad survey party operating nearby, and Captain Edward Ball was currently in command.

Jubil introduced himself and explained his involvement in last year's expedition. Captain Ball was cordial, and Jubil learned that the multitude outside was Hayden's party. Not only would this crowd be going, their number would be doubled by a military escort of forty soldiers. Jubil was disappointed to learn that Lieutenant Doane would not be leading Hayden's military escort. That duty would fall to Captain George Tyler. Combined with Barlow's party, the expedition force would be about ninety men, a staggeringly large number to move through the Yellowstone terrain, he thought. He could not imagine why Hayden would burden himself with so many men. The quantity of supplies they would need to carry would be prodigious, and their numbers would make movement beyond difficult.

Finally, he was able to ask the question that had been on his mind for weeks. "Would you happen to know the whereabouts of an Indian scout named White Dog?" Jubil asked Captain Ball.

The captain shook his head. "No, I don't know of him, but I'm not normally stationed here."

"Excuse me, sir," the aide in the captain's office spoke up. "I know him. He may have met up with Colonel Baker and be riding with him, but I don't know for sure. I haven't seen him around the fort for a while."

"Thanks," Jubil said. "If he turns up, I'd appreciate it if you'd tell him I'm in the area."

"Yes, sir," the aide replied.

Captain Ball directed Jubil to the bunkhouse where Captain Barlow and company were awaiting his arrival. As Jubil left the headquarters building, he noticed the men in Hayden's party were winding down their workday and making their way to the mess hall. Jubil went to the bunkhouse to see if his party was there. He found it empty, except for one young man just leaving.

"Excuse me," Jubil said, "do you know where I might find Captain Barlow? I'm Jubilee Walker. I'm with his party."

"Hello, Mr. Walker," the man replied. He was about the same build as Jubil and had blue eyes, like the Boswells, and an easygoing manner. "I'm Albert Peale. I'm with Dr. Hayden. I believe Captain Barlow went to the officer's mess."

"Pleased to meet you. Just call me Jubil."

"And I'm Albert, or just Peale," he said, offering Jubil a handshake. "I was on my way to the enlisted men's mess. Would you like to join me?"

Over supper, Jubil learned that he and Peale were the same age and that Peale had recently graduated with a medical degree from the University of Pennsylvania but planned on a career in natural sciences. He had studied under Hayden at the university and been invited by him to join the expedition. Jubil found Peale easy to like. He took an interest in Jubil's expeditions with Major Powell, his outfitting business, his Yellowstone experiences, and how he had come to join the expedition this year.

"I'm kind of relieved to learn you don't know Barlow and Heap all that well," Peale said. "I find them a bit odd—especially 'the Buckskin Kid.'"

"Who?" Jubil asked.

"Captain Heap, in that fancy fringed set of buckskins he's sporting—brand spanking new . . . clean as a whistle."

Jubil looked at Peale skeptically. "Are you pulling my leg?"

"No!" Peale said, in mock indignation. "I'll swear—he looks like a hero on the cover of a dime novel!"

Jubil laughed out loud. It felt good to laugh. He hadn't done so for weeks. Not since Luke died.

"And Barlow has brought his umbrella along," Peale added incredulously. "Who carries an umbrella into the wilderness?"

"Oh . . . now you *are* joking," Jubil said.

"Nope," Peale shook his head. "A canopy fit for a London lawyer."

Jubil laughed again. "What have I gotten myself into?" he said, shaking his head.

"I take it they were disguised as normal people when you last saw them," Peale proposed.

Jubil laughed again. "Well, the uniforms make them all look alike," he said and was rewarded when Peale laughed. Still, he was leery that Peale might be good-naturedly testing his gullibility.

But when they returned to the bunkhouse, there was Heap,

dressed in new buckskins with long fringe down the arms and legs, trying to look the intrepid explorer and failing spectacularly. Jubil went to say hello to Captain Barlow, but returned soon to settle in on a bunk near Peale, purposely avoiding the other man's eye so as not to laugh aloud.

The next day, Jubil watched as Hayden's party completed their preparations to leave. The wooden framework turned out to be for a boat. They would carry the frame along with them and assemble it once they arrived at the lake, then cover it with tarred canvas. It appeared Hayden would be taking no half-measures on his expedition. The wagons were filled not only with supplies and shelter, but an abundance of scientific measuring devices.

In contrast, his own party's gear had not yet arrived from Corinne, including all of Hines's photographic equipment, a couple of crates of Heap's scientific gear—barometers, compasses, clinometers, steel tape measures, tools, and some amount of personal baggage.

Since Jubil had no other duties until Barlow's gear arrived, he helped Albert Peale with his preparations to leave. Midafternoon, a distinguished looking man walked up to chat with Peale. As they spoke, Peale signaled Jubil to join them. The man was in his early forties, tall, thin-faced with a pointed beard and deep-set dark eyes. He seemed to Jubil a very studious sort.

"Jubilee Walker," Peale said, "this is Dr. Ferdinand Hayden. Jubil was with General Washburn's party last year, sir, and General Sherman asked him to guide Captain Barlow this year."

Hayden studied Jubil as they shook hands. "Mr. Walker, how do you come to know General Sherman?"

Jubil explained that he knew General Sherman through his expeditions with Major Powell.

"Ah, very good," Hayden said politely, and Jubil realized

abashedly that he was used to people being more impressed by his association with General Sherman and Major Powell.

"Major Powell has done some excellent work, for an amateur," Hayden said.

Jubil was slightly shocked, but he let the comment pass and wondered how Powell would characterize Hayden—probably, Jubil guessed, as being a bit full of himself.

"General Sherman asked me to be of service to you if I can be, sir," Jubil said, "but I'm to take my orders from Captain Barlow."

"I will bear that in mind, thank you," Hayden replied. "I have the services of a guide—a Mexican named José. We should be fine, but it's good that Barlow has your help. He'll need all he can get."

Hayden made his last comment without emphasis or sounding overly critical, but the implication was obvious. Jubil's initial impression was that Hayden was, indeed, studious, also thorough, calm, and imperious—a lot like Major Powell.

"Captain Barlow plans to follow the same route as General Washburn last year," Jubil said. "General Sherman provided me with a map updated from last year's expedition. Will that be your route as well?"

"Possibly," Hayden replied. "We'll make our way to the lake first, and then assess the situation. Barlow's party is welcome to follow along, or he may go his own way, it matters not to me. Frankly, I'm not sure why General Sherman saw Barlow's efforts as necessary, but that's of no consequence to me. I'll not hinder him, but I can't be worrying about him—you'll need to be the one to see to that."

"Yes, sir," Jubil said. He did not find Hayden unpleasant in his frankness. He was simply being clear about his mission, and his dedication to that mission alone—just like Major Powell.

The next day he watched as Hayden's small army set

off—forty civilians, forty soldiers, five freight wagons pulled by four-mule teams, two ambulance wagons pulled by two-horse teams, twenty mules, and thirty horses. Jubil watched them parade away from the fort and thought about the difficulties they would face moving through the Yellowstone Basin. In some areas it would be impossible. The timber around the east and south sides of Yellowstone Lake would be impassable for all of those wagons. He assumed Hayden must know that, so it confounded him why the doctor would be traveling with all that gear.

Barlow's gear arrived late in the afternoon but too late for them to set out from the fort. Barlow ordered his men to move the materials from the freight wagon onto the one they would use for the expedition, and as the men moved to do so, Jubil approached Barlow.

"Captain," he said quietly, "I'd like to make a suggestion, if you'll humor me."

The captain nodded, regarding Jubil coolly.

"Well, the timber gets mighty thick down there around the lake. We'd be better off using pack animals instead of a wagon."

"Hayden's party just left here with a fleet of wagons," Barlow said. "Are you suggesting that the doctor doesn't know what he's doing?"

"Not at all, sir," Jubil said. "I'm sure Dr. Hayden has his reasons, but I'm just telling you that in my experience—"

"Thank you, Mr. Walker. If Dr. Hayden took wagons, so will we," Barlow said and turned away.

Barlow changed his mind about the wagon the next day. Their party had been on the trail about four hours when a driver going up a ridge put the wagon at too steep an angle and tipped it over, spilling its load, which included food supplies. Jubil watched with dismay as the flour and rice barrels were smashed and their contents dumped onto the hillside. He thought of his Grand Canyon expedition, when, half-starved, they would have been grateful for this food, even in its present condition. Fortunately, since they were still close to the fort, it would not be necessary to try and save it. Barlow sent the packers back for replacement supplies, instructing them to leave the wagon behind and return with mules. Jubil rode back with them, and when they reached the fort and began to pack the mules, he learned the packers, Wilbur and Mack, were inexperienced at the job. They were unemployed cowhands, a little younger than Jubil, quiet and good natured, and paid attention as Jubil showed them how to load the mules and tie a proper diamond hitch. When they were packed, he led them back to meet up with Barlow and the rest of the party, camped at Trail Creek.

By the end of the following day, Barlow's party caught up with Hayden's, who were camped at the Bottler brothers' ranch in the Yellowstone Canyon. It was there that Jubil learned Hayden's plan. The wagons had only been intended to haul in the large quantity of supplies and gear to this point. Hayden would use Bottler's Ranch as a base camp, from which they would haul supplies in to the expeditionary teams and haul out injured explorers if necessary. He would also establish a mail exchange, bringing mail in along with supplies and allowing the expeditionary teams to send outgoing mail. Jubil was impressed by Hayden's foresight and his sense of organization. Now he understood the need for all these people, and he looked forward to sending letters to Nelly, the Warners, and the Boswells, if he could find the time.

At Bottler's Ranch, Jubil met up again with Albert Peale, who introduced him to William Henry Jackson, one of the photographers with Hayden's party. Jackson was twenty-eight, Jubil's height but a stockier build, bearded, a mischievous grin, and spark in his eye. Just as with Peale, Jubil took an immediate liking to him. Jackson had been born in New York, but five years ago had ridden the railroad to the end of the line, which at the time was Council Bluffs, then moved across the river to Omaha and set up shop as a photographer. He felt a deep sympathy for the Indian tribes and extensively photographed the tribes of the area. He had won a commission from the Union Pacific to document the scenery along the new westward route, and from that work had been noticed by Hayden and invited to join this expedition.

When Jackson showed Jubil some of the photos he had taken of Paradise Valley on the way to Bottler's Ranch, Jubil was impressed he had been able to capture the huge landscape. He could imagine how powerful Jackson's photographs would be of the wonders yet to come. He wondered why neither Washburn nor Langford had thought to bring along a photographer last year. Hayden had also brought a painter, Thomas Moran, who, when introduced to Jubil, shook his hand politely and then absentmindedly walked away. Peale looked at Jubil and shrugged.

The party that Hayden led out the next morning was smaller by half, with half the military detail left to guard the people and supplies remaining at the base camp. Hayden's packers had their work cut out for them, loading and securing their animals with food supplies, scientific and photographic equipment, camp gear, and even the boat frame and canvas, but they went about their work skillfully. Jubil checked Barlow's packers and, once again, found their work lacking.

"Wilbur, look here," Jubil said, "you too Mack. Is this the method I showed you for lashing the load so it doesn't rock? No—it isn't. What you've got here will chafe the animal and work its way loose completely pretty soon. Now pay attention this time."

As he helped them reload the mules, he felt some responsibility for the situation. Even though Barlow had hired the packers, Jubil felt he should have verified their competence. His grief and other preoccupations had left him with a melancholy detachment that was affecting his focus on the job. He could not disappoint General Sherman by letting that happen. As Hayden's party began to move out, Barlow came to check on his men's progress.

"What is the delay here?" Barlow asked impatiently. "Hayden has far more gear than we do, and he's underway."

Jubil spoke up. "Sorry sir, some of the work needed adjustment. We'll get the hang of working together soon. We'll be ready shortly."

Barlow frowned. "Well, see that we are."

Within an hour, they were packed and ready to go. They caught up with Hayden's party before nightfall, where they were camped at the junction of the Gardner River and the Yellowstone River. Last year at this location, the Washburn expedition had continued to follow the course of the Yellowstone as it turned east and then south. In that direction were Tower Falls, Mount Washburn, the Upper and Lower Falls, and Yellowstone Lake.

Jubil was helping the packers prepare to travel the next morning when he saw Barlow emerge from the wall tent that Hayden used as both his sleeping quarters and expedition headquarters. Barlow was heading his way.

"I've just learned that Dr. Hayden intends to follow a different route than we had planned," he said. "His guide, José, has suggested Hayden follow the Gardner River south to a set of hot springs called the Soda Mountain, and then cut back east to the Yellowstone River."

"You want to follow him rather than stick to General Washburn's route?" Jubil asked.

"I don't want to miss an area of significance," Barlow said. "I'm counting on you to show us those."

"We didn't go that way last year, so I'm not sure what dangers we might run into," Jubil said, "but we'll follow Hayden if you want to."

"We'll follow Hayden," he said. "Be ready to leave within the hour."

Jubil was growing weary of Barlow's imperious manner, but he knew his grief over Luke was largely responsible for his lack of enthusiasm and patience. Again, he cautioned himself not to let these emotions get the best of him.

Both parties set out south along the Gardner River, and that afternoon Jubil was surprised at what they found upon arriving at the hot springs. Soda Mountain was another wonder as astonishing in its own way as any of the unique geological formations he had seen last year throughout the Yellowstone Basin. Issuing from the top of a hillside some two hundred feet high, the six-foot-wide hot springs emitted a steady flow of water about a foot deep. As the water cascaded down the hillside, it formed terraces and plateaus of colorful mineral deposits—mostly white, but also shades of brown, orange, green, and red—spread over an area of several hundred acres. In some areas the terraces held pools of hot water—some a foot or two in diameter, others ten to twenty feet across. Jubil sat on his horse marveling, the beauty of the colors lifting his spirits a bit. But he also marveled at how General Washburn's expedition had missed this sight last year. As if he had spoken this thought out loud, Captain Heap, still proudly dressed in his fringed buckskins, rode up beside him.

"I thought General Sherman sent you along with us because you were an experienced guide and had been here before. How could you have missed this?" Heap asked.

"We followed the Yellowstone River," Jubil said simply, refusing to react to the open disregard in Heap's expression. Heap turned his horse and moved on. Washburn's aim had been to follow the general route taken by Folsom and Cook in

1869, who had also missed these springs, so Jubil did not feel alone. But he did feel irritated by Heap's arrogant incivility.

As Jubil scanned the landscape, he noticed an unsettling sight: Perched on one of the steaming terraces of the hot spring was a small shed, and two men with towels were just entering it. A few hundred yards east of Soda Mountain, on a hillside near a stand of pines, was a cabin with a small corral that overlooked the terraces and the shed, and outside it was a man chopping wood.

Dr. Hayden and Captain Barlow rode up to join Jubil as he surveyed the scene.

"What do you make of that, Walker?" Hayden said.

"We didn't see this, or anything like it on our route last year," Jubil said.

"Of course not," Hayden said matter-of-factly. "Washburn followed the Yellowstone."

Jubil was grateful for Hayden's observation. In his peripheral vision, he could see Captain Barlow shift on his horse.

"It is a mammoth hot springs, that's a certainty," Hayden continued. "But I was referring to the inhabitants here. I don't recall learning that Washburn's expedition had encountered any people on its route."

"We saw a band of Crow," Jubil replied, "but no one else."

"Looks like someone is running a bath house here," Hayden said.

"That's what I was thinking too," Jubil said. "You know, last year as we were leaving, we got into quite a discussion about the commercial opportunities of this place. After some debate, Judge Hedges suggested we dedicate ourselves to the preservation of the area, rather than its exploitation. He proposed a campaign to establish Yellowstone as a national park, and we all agreed to do our part. With that in mind, I'm not in favor of what this fellow is up to here."

Hayden studied Jubil's face closely. "Yes, I heard Nathaniel

Langford say as much, in his lecture in Washington. I share your sentiment, but until Congress makes such a declaration, the proprietor here is within his rights, as long as he has filed a legal claim."

Jubil nodded as he recalled General Sherman's skepticism about the ability of Congress to act swiftly and effectively at much of anything, let alone the protection of a region as far removed as Yellowstone. If they did not, this place might soon be overrun with homesteaders like this one and beyond preserving.

"Perhaps we should explain our presence to the proprietor," Hayden said, urging his horse forward toward the cabin. Jubil and Barlow fell in beside him. As they neared the cabin, the man chopping wood stopped and mopped his brow, then waited as they approached.

"Good day, sir," Hayden said. "My name is Dr. Ferdinand Hayden. I'm making a survey of the area on behalf of the US Interior Department. This is Captain John Barlow, who is doing the same on behalf of the US Army, and this is one of our guides, Jubilee Walker. We'll only be passing through, but we would like to spend a short time here studying and surveying the area."

"Howdy do, gents," the man replied. "I thought I'd hit the motherlode of visitors! Sure, make yourselves to home anywhere you like. My name's James McCartney. I operate a bunkhouse and bathhouse here, along with my partner, Henry Hore. Henry ain't here at the moment though."

Jubil noticed a man with a well-groomed handlebar mustache emerge from the bunkhouse cabin, and a chill ran up his spine. As the man approached, Jubil could see the sneer of recognition on his face.

"Well, may the saints preserve us . . . if it isn't Jubilee Walker. You've brought along a fair army to protect you this time, eh?"

"What are you doing here, Murphy?" Jubil asked, unable to

keep the disgust out of his voice. He had no idea what business Phineas Black's security manager and henchman, Murphy the Irishman, had out here, but he was certain it wasn't good.

"I could ask the same of you, Walker," Murphy replied snidely. "It so happens I'm a business associate of Mr. McCartney's."

McCartney appeared quite nervous in Murphy's presence, looking anywhere but at Murphy and shifting his weight from foot to foot.

"I was just paying Mr. McCartney a visit to discuss Mr. Phineas Black's plans for building a fine new hotel here," Murphy said. "Not as elegant as the Metropolitan in Bozeman perhaps, but a considerable step up from McCartney's bunkhouse. Isn't that right, Mr. McCartney?"

McCartney nodded obediently.

Murphy looked past Jubil toward the expedition gathered on the hill with apparent curiosity.

"Looks to be getting a bit crowded around here for me," Murphy said. "I believe I'll just be on my way." He mounted up and faced Jubil again. "I'll be sure to give Mr. Black your regards, Walker. Do stop in and visit on your way out of town. I'm sure he'd like to have a word with you."

Jubil watched McCartney mop his brow as Murphy rode away. Hayden and Barlow looked at Jubil expectantly, but he remained silent.

"We should get the men settled," Hayden said, and Barlow followed as he turned his horse and rode away.

Jubil dismounted and stood face-to-face with McCartney. "I can't say I admire your taste in business partners," he said.

McCartney chewed his lip, and his eyes darted around as if looking for an escape route.

"If you know Black," McCartney said, "then you know it ain't wise to run afoul of him—though it appears you already done it."

"Well, you can be sure nothing you say will get back to him

through me," Jubil said.

McCartney studied Jubil carefully. "I'll say this then—Black and his boys think they're the biggest toads in the puddle. I own me a gentlemen's club in Bozeman that Black frequents—called the Golden Slipper. I believe he learnt of my doings here and sent Murphy to offer me a proposition. If I'd cut him in on my take, Black would have Murphy guard against any unfortunate happenings—like my bunkhouse or bathhouse burning down, or someone raiding and killing me in the night, or some such. And, as a bonus, Black would build a hotel here and cut me in on his operation—as payoff for my land claim. Murphy and his rabble don't make it healthy for a man to decline Black's proposals."

"I see your dilemma," Jubil said.

"Whatever quarrel you and Black have," McCartney said, "I'd be much obliged if you'd leave me out of it. I'm just trying to get along peaceful-like and make a living. That's easier to do if I stay out of Murphy's line of fire."

"I take your point," Jubil said. "I won't make matters worse for you with Black."

Jubil swung himself back into the saddle and turned Apollo toward the expedition teams. "Good luck, Mr. McCartney. Perhaps we'll meet again."

The expeditions remained camped at Soda Mountain for three days as Jubil received a lesson in patience and in the difference between exploring and surveying. On his past expeditions, Major Powell had taken some scientific measurements, but they were always done while the party was on the move—the focus was to see what was ahead. On this expedition, it appeared the focus would be to measure and document every aspect of an area before moving on. The reason Hayden had brought so many people became evident as the teams of specialists spread out and examined and documented the area. Heap and Stevenson took exact longitude and latitude readings for the Soda Mountain area, and measured and mapped its various dimensions in great detail. Peale and the other geologists collected and labeled samples of the various mineral deposits and measured and recorded the temperature of each of the pools of water. The photographers and artists captured the scene from every angle. And the botanists and zoologists scoured the nearby area for samples of interest. Jubil, having no particular responsibility during this period, made himself available as general labor—someone always needed something moved, carried, or held.

The night before they left the area, Jubil lay on his bedroll and found sleep hard to come by. He had hoped the expedition would deliver him from the melancholy he was in, but it had not. If anything, it had deepened it. He was enjoying the beauty of the Yellowstone wilderness again but struggling to enjoy the company of his fellow travelers. With the exceptions of Peale and the photographer, Jackson, he had hardly spoken to anyone. In spite of his mixed feelings about Doane, he had still hoped to travel with him again. He had even allowed himself a glimmer of hope he might have a reunion with White Dog, but now it seemed very unlikely.

It was tempting to bid Hayden and Barlow farewell and ride to Helena to talk with Langford about what Phineas Black was up to at the hot springs. He was not sure what he expected Langford to do about Black, but the trip sounded more productive than just riding around the Yellowstone Basin, sightseeing. What kept him from giving in to that impulse was his sense of responsibility to General Sherman and the shame he would feel in explaining to him why he had abandoned the expedition.

CHAPTER 14

The next morning Jubil chastised himself for losing sleep to self-pity and committed himself to a more positive outlook. He was not going to abandon the expedition, so he might as well make the best of it. If he could find nothing about it to enjoy, he would have no one to blame but himself.

His time at Soda Mountain, seeing the enterprise that McCartney was operating, had begun to change his thinking about leading tourists into the region. He did not like the idea of it being Phineas Black who profited from a hotel here, especially through his extortion of McCartney, but it had begun to seem inevitable that a hotel would one day be built. Perhaps it would even be for the best. When the Northern Pacific Railroad opened the area to tourists, there would probably be a steady flow of them into Yellowstone. They would have to stay somewhere. Expecting them all to make rough camp was unrealistic and might even be more destructive to the area than building roads to get them there and a place to house them. The idea of a park was not flawed, but his notion of what that would entail had perhaps been naïve. He would talk to Langford about how to factor these issues into the campaign. Thinking of the national park campaign helped him see a way into a new future, and he was grateful for that.

Hayden was now ready to head toward the Yellowstone River, where they would reconnect with the route Jubil had followed last year. Barlow had initially planned to remain in camp to finish some correspondence, so his party had not yet broken camp. Idling about while Barlow finished his writing had not been Jubil's preference, but he reminded himself of his commitment to a more positive outlook and went to groom Apollo. When Hayden was ready to leave, Barlow changed his mind and decided to ride on with Hayden, taking Captain Heap and Thomas Hines, the photographer, along with him, and leaving Jubil and the rest of Barlow's party to break camp, pack, and follow along when they were ready. This change of mind struck Jubil as inconsiderate, but he tried to accept it calmly. What difference would a few hours make? Still, he groused to himself as he went about packing up, and avoided any further conversation with Barlow before he rode off with Hayden.

An hour or so later, Jubil had the rest of the party—Wood, Prout, the packers, the cook, six soldiers, and the mule train—packed up and ready to move eastward toward the Yellowstone River. Hayden's trail was not easy to follow even before the terrain changed, but around noon the terrain turned rocky, and their trail disappeared completely.

Losing the trail highlighted a problem—Jubil's angry reaction to Barlow had distracted him from asking where Hayden was planning to make camp. He knew they were making for the Yellowstone River, but where exactly? At its nearest point, the Yellowstone was to the north, but Hayden might have wanted to move further east to Tower Creek Junction. Jubil consulted his map and found that to reach the Yellowstone at its nearest point, he should follow Blacktail Deer Creek to the north. When they reached the creek, Jubil still saw no clear sign which way Hayden had gone and decided to take the shortest route. He headed his group north, and by mid-afternoon they reached the Yellowstone River, but there was no sign of Hayden's party. It was too late in the day now to set off to retrace their steps. He told the men to make camp and they would catch up with Hayden the next day.

At sunset, Captain Barlow, Captain Heap, and Hines rode into camp.

"Apparently," Barlow said as he dismounted, "we had a failure to communicate our intentions regarding camp. Captain Tyler suggested this might be the route you would take."

"Yes, sorry about that," Jubil said. "I should have made a point of clarifying it."

"No harm done," Barlow said. "I should have spoken up about it myself. Hayden is at Tower Creek Junction. We'll catch up tomorrow."

Jubil appreciated Barlow sharing the blame for the miscommunication, but he still felt responsible. On this trip, he was not just an explorer, he was the guide. He had a responsibility to General Sherman to keep these people safe. His general malaise over Luke's death, the Warners' departure from Council Bluffs, and his estrangement from Nelly was upsetting his focus on the job, and he could not allow that.

"This might be a good time to discuss another thing," Jubil said. "I'd suggest we have a plan in case anyone is separated from the expedition. General Washburn set a policy that the expedition would remain camped for a full day and send men back to their last campsite to look for missing men before moving on to the next agreed upon campsite."

"That's a sound suggestion," Barlow said. "I'll tell the other men in the morning."

Late that night, Jubil lay on his bedroll trying to reflect on the lessons of the day. He told himself to stay in the moment and focus on the trail ahead, but he kept drifting into reminiscences of what he had once had. Finally he gave up trying to avoid the melancholy and let his mind replay whatever happy moments it stumbled across, until he finally slept.

The next day they caught up with Hayden, and the route turned south following the Yellowstone. The first stop was Mount Washburn, which Jubil had been looking forward to climbing again. The view was as spectacular as ever, but the wind was so strong that it was difficult to stand up on the summit, and it was impossible for the photographers to set up their equipment.

Disappointed, they made their way down the mountain and moved south to explore the Upper and Lower Falls. Here, the wind was not as strong, but as Jubil stood holding onto his hat, watching Barlow's photographer Thomas Hines set up his equipment to photograph the Upper Falls, a gust came up that blew Hines's camera into the Grand Canyon of the Yellowstone. Hines, perilously near to being blown into the canyon himself, staggered backward away from the rim of the canyon and sat down heavily on firm ground.

"My whole rig—gone a'flunking into the canyon," Hines said in disbelief, and Jubil was reminded of the indifference of nature to human concerns.

After one day at the falls, Hayden was satisfied with his survey and ready to move on, but Barlow wanted another day. Hines borrowed a camera from Hayden's photographer, William Henry Jackson, and captured photographs of the area, while Barlow, Heap, and Prout labored over longitude and latitude readings and measurements of the falls and canyon. Jubil applied himself as an assistant to whoever needed one.

The next day he led them to the mud volcano, where they found Hayden had already moved on toward the lake. After a day of Barlow and Heap taking their readings and gathering samples around the area, they moved on to catch up with Hayden.

Barlow's party arrived in the early afternoon at Hayden's campsite at the north end of Yellowstone Lake, and Jubil reunited with his friend Peale. They set out to take a walk along the lakeshore, where Jubil was impressed to see the boat frame had been assembled and covered with tarred canvas. A small mast was set in its bow, and a name was painted on the prow—*Anna*. Two men were preparing to launch the skiff along the shoreline to test it out. Peale waved and called out to one of them, "Chester!" Jubil followed Peale over to them.

"I'd like you fellows to meet Jubilee Walker. He's guiding Barlow's party," Peale said. "Jubil has some experience with boats. He ran the length of the Colorado River through the Grand Canyon with Major John Wesley Powell in 1869."

The younger boatman was Chester Dawes, a general assistant on Hayden's expedition and the son of Congressman Dawes from Massachusetts. The boat was named after his sister. The other man was James Stevenson, Hayden's general manager.

"How do you do, Walker?" Stevenson said. "Chester and I were about to see how our craft handles. Care to go with me to see how she compares to Powell's boats?"

"I would gladly," Jubil said, "if Chester doesn't mind."

"Be my guest," Chester said with a smile. "I imagine I'll have had my fill of it before the trip is over."

Jubil and Stevenson pushed the boat out onto the lake. It was small, only seating two comfortably, but very stable. The wind was light, and the waves on the lake were gentle as Stevenson rowed them away from shore. Then he hoisted a tent-fly rigged as a sail. The canvas caught the breeze, and the boat sailed briskly down the shoreline, spurring in Jubil a feeling of exhilarating freedom similar to what he had felt at times riding the Colorado River. The shoreline sped past, the little prow cutting through the waves and splashing him with cold water as he held on to his hat to keep it from blowing into the lake. This was the lightest his heart had felt in weeks. Stevenson ran down the shoreline then brought the boat around and tacked back toward the spot where Peale and Dawes waited on the sandy beach. Stevenson dropped the sail, and rowed for shore.

Talking to Stevenson and Dawes that afternoon about their plans for the boat, Jubil gained some further appreciation for what surveying entailed. The *Anna* would allow Hayden to measure the depths of the lake, map its shoreline accurately, and explore its islands. It was obvious now why Hayden needed more people in his party—in order to accomplish greater things.

The expedition's supplies were just beginning to run low when the first resupply mission from the base camp at Bottler's Ranch arrived with a load of staples, mail, and the news that two people had been killed in an Indian raid at a ranch near Fort Ellis.

"I was surprised to hear Captain Tyler has been put on notice that he might be recalled to the fort," Jubil said to Peale. "Seems that will leave our escort a little short."

"I imagine they'll send a replacement," Peale said. "They probably just need an officer of his rank for some reason."

Hayden wanted to circumnavigate the lake and asked his guide, José, whether it would be best to go in a clockwise, or counterclockwise fashion.

"It does not matter," José replied, shrugging. "You will see the same things going either way."

Jubil found José's answer amusing, but from the frown on Dr. Hayden's face, he did not.

"Mr. Walker," Hayden said, "do you have an opinion on the matter?"

Jubil described how General Washburn's expedition party had struggled through the timber on the east and south sides of the lake, and he noted the absence of any unique geological features there. Based on his answer, Hayden decided to proceed counterclockwise—the opposite of General Washburn's route. He would go to the geyser basins first, both Upper and Lower, then down to the West Thumb of the lake. From there they would move counterclockwise around the lake, return to the spot where they were currently camped, and then go out by the same route they had followed coming in.

There was much about this plan that Jubil liked. The fact that they were going to the geyser basins straightaway was exciting. If fighting their way around the lake had to be done, then putting it off until later was fine with him. He also preferred leaving by the route they had come in, rather than following the Madison River west and then turning north, which he had found last year to be dull travel.

That evening Jubil wrote letters to Nelly, Ike and Eli, and the Warners. The soldiers who had come with supplies would be returning to Bottler's Ranch in the morning and would relay the letters to the fort. His letters focused on the pleasures of seeing Yellowstone's wonders again, but revealed nothing of the melancholy he felt. Though the letters were perhaps not his best effort, at least everyone would know he was alive and well, and thinking of them. Writing to Nelly brought to mind how much he missed her and the idea he had clung to for so long that they would spend their lives together. But that was more in her hands than his, and he tried to keep it from possessing his every thought.

The move to the Upper Geyser Basin was uneventful, and the men settled in to spend several days surveying the area. While Peale was off collecting rock, mineral, and water samples, Jubil helped William Henry Jackson photograph the geyser basins. He rode with Jackson as he eyed locations, and Jubil carefully unpacked the photographic equipment from the mule's back and then packed it up again. Watching Jackson choose vantage points and set up his camera for different shots, Jubil saw that composing and capturing the images was an art, and developing the prints was a science. Jackson seemed to be adept at both.

Jackson was not pleased with the results of his geyser photographs. The pictures of the mineral cones around the geyser tubes were impressive, but he bemoaned the absence of their colorful hues in his black and white images. Further, the plumes of steam that arose from the geysers were often indistinguishable in his prints from clouds in the sky, and the columns of steaming water that gushed upward were so vigorously in motion that the plume on the photograph appeared as a large blur. Jubil assured Jackson that a layman would still find them impressive.

The artist in Hayden's party, Thomas Moran, was at work nearby painting a landscape that featured a geyser. Jubil had to admit, if only to himself, that Moran's painting presented a truer image of the wondrous landscape than Jackson's blurry black-and-white photographs. Moran used subtle shades of gray and white to clearly depict the stream of water issuing from a geyser's cone. He even captured the spray of mist against the cloudy sky. In the foreground was a pool of deep blue water surrounded by a red-rimmed crater of mineral deposits. It put Jubil in mind of Mrs. Warner's landscape paintings. Though he was admittedly not much of a judge of paintings, he believed Mrs. Warner's work would stand up in comparison to Moran's, and he thought she would like his work. Thoughts of Mrs. Warner led him back to Luke, and he rode out another wave of melancholy.

It was now early August, and they had been camped in the geyser basin for nearly a week. The previous night the temperature had for the first time dropped below freezing, and Jubil had donned his union suit and gotten out his lined gloves. That evening, as he sat warming himself by the campfire, he saw a soldier ride into camp sitting tall and straight in the saddle. He wore a kepi cap and had a bushy walrus mustache. As the man rode closer, Jubil smiled as he recognized Lieutenant Doane. When Doane noticed him, he gave him a grin and an informal salute and then rode on to Hayden's headquarters tent. While Doane was inside the tent, Hayden sent a man to fetch Barlow and Captain Tyler. It was nearly time to turn in for the night when Doane finally made his way over to the fire.

"Hello, Walker," Doane said. "I understand you've been sent out with Captain Barlow."

"It's good to see you, Lieutenant," Jubil said, standing and shaking Doane's hand. "That was why Sherman wanted to see me last year—mystery solved. I thought you might be along this year, but Captain Ball said you were away." *Likely somewhere punishing Indians*, Jubil thought but did not say.

"Yes," Doane said, "I got called as a witness in a court martial trial against a bad apple in the army. I'd rather be shot at than do that again. How goes the expedition?"

"All right, I suppose," Jubil said. "Successful for Hayden and Barlow, I believe. I set out to lead Barlow along the route we took last year, but Barlow seems to prefer following Hayden, who has had other ideas. But that's all right by me. I'll admit, they've tried my patience at times, but I imagine they'd say the same of me. Are you staying with us?"

"I am, but there's Indian trouble up around the fort, and Captain Tyler and some of the soldiers are returning to help out up there. I'll lead the military escort that stays here."

"Good," Jubil said.

"No Indians problems along the way so far then?" Doane asked.

"Nope," Jubil said, deciding he had carried his ambivalence about Doane long enough. "I thought you wiped out the Indian problem this spring at the Marias affair." Jubil could not bring himself to call it what Sherman had—a massacre— to Doane's face.

"It would appear I did not," Doane began, frowning at Jubil, "since I'm here to send Captain Tyler off to chastise them for once again killing innocent ranchers. What would you have us do, Walker?"

"I don't think killing women and children, and burning all

of their possessions is right," Jubil replied.

"I don't know that it's right," Doane replied, "but it appears to be necessary. I'm a soldier, and soldiers follow orders. I'm not hiding behind that—I'm proud of it. These people will not submit to defeat and integrate with our society. We have run out of options."

"Seems to me we haven't been all that honest in our efforts to integrate them," Jubil said.

Doane studied Jubil for a few seconds with what seemed like honest curiosity. "What exactly have you done to help with the problem?" he asked. "Seems to me you've done little more than aggravate it—adventuring through Indian territory and helping people like Barlow survey it, which means drawing more people this direction."

Jubil had felt his live-and-let-live philosophy was his contribution to peace, but he could see that Doane was right: he was being hypocritical.

"I probably should do more," he said, "but I still don't think it's necessary to be killing women and children. Sheridan told me he ordered it done, and I told him what I thought of it. He didn't seem to like me much, but the feeling was mutual. I've talked to General Sherman about it too. At least Sherman is remorseful. But from what I've learned about our treaties and Indian agencies, if the dishonesty and corruption were corrected, the military might not even be necessary."

"Maybe you should get busy straightening that out then," Doane said, shaking his head bemusedly and poking at the campfire.

Doane was right about that too, Jubil thought. He should make more of an effort on behalf of Indian relations. He thought about his friend.

"General Sherman told me White Dog is out here now," Jubil said.

"He is," Doane said. "He spends some time on the Crow

reservation, but he's not cut out for that life. He scouts for the army when he's in the mood; sometimes he just rides off on his own for a while. Captain Ball told the other scouts to pass the word along that you were around."

"I appreciate that," Jubil said. "I'd sure like to see him."

"You saw him last year, you know," Doane said.

Jubil nodded. "When I heard he was out here, I wondered if that was him."

"I didn't know then," Doane explained. "I saw him after we got back. He said he was riding with a band of Crows who encountered three white men, and he thought he recognized you. He asked me if that could possibly be, and I said yes. I don't imagine the circumstances were good for a reunion at that moment," he said wryly, stroking his walrus mustache.

Both expedition parties remained in the geyser basin for a few days before moving to the West Thumb. Two of Hayden's men, Elliot and Carrington, set out in the boat to make a survey of the lake. The plan was to meet them on the eastern or northern shore as the expeditions made a counterclockwise tour. Midway around the southern end of the lake, Captain Barlow caught Jubil by surprise with a proposed change of plans.

"I believe this would be a good point for us to move into the southern part of the basin to have a look around," Barlow said at breakfast one morning.

"Why would we want to do that?" Jubil asked. "I don't think we're likely to find much of anything in that direction but more trees and the Tetons."

"That area has not been mapped," Barlow said. "I'm here to do that."

"It's very difficult country," Jubil insisted. "That's where Mr. Everts got lost last year. It's easy to do." Jubil caught his tone rising and paused. Barlow stared at him, unmoved. "Look," Jubil continued in a calmer voice, "I'm just questioning whether we should separate from Hayden's party and attempt to meet up again with them several days later. If we lose them, it will be a struggle to make it back to Fort Ellis on our own."

"I intend to have a look at the southern basin," Barlow said with a frown, "but you can do as you wish." He walked away.

Doane sat finishing his breakfast of bacon and biscuits, and listening to the conversation with an air of amusement. He was pouring himself coffee and, as Jubil sat down beside him, he offered him a cup.

"You seem a mite touchy," Doane said.

Jubil, his temper already on edge, looked at Doane to see if he was being made fun of, but Doane's grin felt friendly.

"I'm a little surprised you don't seem very concerned about upsetting the army chain of command," Doane said, sipping his coffee and studying Jubil. "I thought your outfitting business did a fair amount of trade with them."

Jubil stared into his coffee mug, wondering how much to share with Doane.

"We do . . . or . . . we did," Jubil said, "but we've had a setback." Jubil told Doane the painful story of Luke's death, their burned-out store, and the Warner's decision to retire.

"That's a streak of bad fortune," Doane said sympathetically. "What do you plan to do now?"

"I'm not sure yet," Jubil admitted. "I came out here to think about it."

"Sounds like you have a clean slate," Doane said. "Move out here and start a new store—wait for the railroad to bring in the business."

"Langford says I should come to Helena," Jubil said.

"Langford wants your money in his bank," Doane said wryly. "The railroad will go through Bozeman—it's the most amenable geographic route."

"You say that like it's a fact," Jubil said, surprised.

"It is," Doane said, "The survey team has been working since we were here last year. The crew coming from the west is headed toward Bozeman as we speak. They may even be there by the time we get back. A detail was being sent to escort them as I was coming here. The crew coming from Duluth has reached Bismarck. They've still got about six hundred miles in between to survey. They left the most troublesome Indian territory for last."

This was big news. It would appear Langford's hopes that the railroad would come to his door had been dashed. The news also eliminated Helena as the best place for Jubil and the Warners to open a store—if they were to want one out here. If the railroad was coming through Bozeman, he would want his store there. Helena was a two-day ride from Bozeman. Why would he put his store there? Doane's comment about troublesome Indian territory also begged further explanation.

"I'd have to contend with Phineas Black if we were to open a store in Bozeman," Jubil said. "He's made it clear he would not welcome competition for his mercantile."

"The army has had its dealings with Black. He is a shady character all right," Doane said. "You wouldn't let him stop you though, would you?"

"Not if I truly had my mind made up to open a store," Jubil said. He described meeting Murphy at the bathhouse at the hot springs on the Gardner River.

"Murphy and his lot are trouble," Doane said.

"We need to get this area declared a national park," Jubil said, "to keep the likes of him from profiting off of it and destroying it in the process."

"Have you done anything to make this park idea happen?" Doane challenged.

He told Doane about his trip to Washington to visit Senator Trumbull. "The senator says that public sentiment is important to propel the cause, so I mention it every chance I get. I told my fiancée, who attends Vassar College, about the idea. I sent her a copy of your journal, and she shared it with her English class. Her professor also assigned reading Langford's magazine article about our expedition. Langford is promoting the park idea in his speeches, and I'm trying to help him get people's ear." The only exaggeration in Jubil's statement was in referring to Nelly as his fiancée.

"They read my journal in a class at Vassar College?"

"Yes," Jubil said, amused by how pleased Doane seemed. "I understand they thought very highly of your skills as a journalist and Langford's as a storyteller."

"Huh," Doane said, looking amused. "What's stopping you from getting on with opening a store, here or wherever?"

"My heart hasn't been in it," Jubil admitted. "I thought coming out here might help me find my path."

"Paths wander off in every which direction and often lead nowhere," Doane said. "Better to set your destination and then carve your own path straight for it."

"I'm not having much luck settling on a destination," Jubil said, as he stared into the fire. "My fiancée says I think more with my heart than my head, and that's not been working in my favor lately."

"You'll be married once she finishes college?" Doane asked.

"No," Jubil said. "That's a long story. We were planning to be married last summer, but I was invited to come to Yellowstone, and I asked to cut short the honeymoon trip. That didn't go well. At this point, it's postponed indefinitely."

"Well, no wonder that heart of yours is not much use—it's broken," Doane said kindly. "Time will mend it. You don't seem the sort to wallow in misery. Something will fire you up."

Jubil looked at Doane to see if he was teasing him, but he seemed sincere. It felt odd to be confiding such things to Doane, the hard-edged soldier and Indian fighter, but Jubil knew from Doane's writing that he also had a soul.

"A word of advice if I may," Doane said, rising to leave. "Consider going along with Barlow. If his party wanders off and gets themselves lost or killed, you'll feel bad about it later. I'm sure that's why Sherman sent you along—to look out for Barlow and the Buckskin Kid."

Jubil could see Doane grinning broadly beneath his mustache. He knew Doane was right about staying with Barlow.

"At least his buckskins are dirty now," Jubil said, shaking his head.

The next morning as Jubil and the packers were rechecking their loads, Doane and Barlow walked up.

"Good morning, Walker," Doane said. "I'd like to be sure our plans are clear, before you set out." Jubil appreciated Doane's involving him in the planning.

Barlow greeted Jubil with a nod and accepted without comment his change of heart about accompanying Barlow's group on the side trip to the southern basin.

"As I understand, you'll be surveying this area," Doane said, pointing to his map and circling an area of mountains and lakes some five to ten miles south of Yellowstone Lake and fifteen to twenty miles wide. "Dr. Hayden intends to move along the southern end of the lake and make camp here," Doane said, pointing to the southeast arm of the lake—the little finger—where the Yellowstone River flowed in. "I'm not sure which side of the river we will be camped on, but watch for signal fires as you approach the lake, and you'll find us. When it comes time to cross the Yellowstone," Doane said, looking at Barlow, "Walker knows where the best point is to ford." Jubil greatly appreciated Doane's vote of confidence. "If you have not reached us within a week, we will remain encamped there for as long as the weather allows, but that may not be very long." Jubil recalled this same conversation during last year's expedition, and the terrible feeling of having left Everts behind. Doane shook hands with them and left.

"I'm ready whenever you are," Jubil said to Barlow.

"We're ready," Barlow said, "except for Hines. His camera tripod has gone missing, and he insists on going back over yesterday's trail to find it. He says he will not abide having lost Jackson's borrowed equipment. I sent one of the soldiers with him. They will catch up to us at Heart Lake."

Jubil was uneasy about setting off with the party already split up, but he did not want to argue and risk spoiling the accord he and Barlow had reached.

They set out in a southeasterly direction for Heart Lake at the foot of Yellow Mountain, the tallest peak in the southern basin, some fifteen miles away. After a long day of making their way through the forested terrain, they reached the lake and made camp. By nightfall Thomas Hines and the soldier accompanying him had not made it into camp. This was of some concern but not yet alarming. They might not have been able to make the full distance of retracing the previous day's trail and also make it to Heart Lake.

In the morning, Barlow sent two soldiers back to the previous campsite to look for Hines and the soldier, Private Lemans. In the meantime, Captain Heap and William Wood, the draftsman, set out to begin their survey, and Barlow announced his intent to gain a look at the whole southern basin by climbing the mountain they were camped beside. Barlow asked Heap's assistant, Henry Prout, to accompany him and take readings, which would require a barometer and chronometer. Jubil told Barlow he would be happy to go along and carry the gear, and Barlow was agreeable. Jubil emptied his trapper's pack, loaded it with Prout's gear along with Barlow's map, compass, and journal, and off they went.

They were able to ride up the forested side of the mountain to about sixteen hundred feet before they reached the tree line and the terrain became too steep for the horses. They hitched them along a grassy stream and continued on foot up the rocky slope. The weather was cold and clear, and Jubil began to feel an exhilaration that he had only felt briefly on this trip, while riding in the *Anna* on Yellowstone Lake. The effort and monotony of the climb seemed to clear his mind as the goal of reaching the summit drove him thoughtlessly forward, one step at a time. He felt his sense of adventure returning, and imagined that with every step he was climbing above and beyond the gray cloud that had covered him since Luke's death. This was the feeling he had been missing, the reason he came on these adventures—the sense of freedom he had in the middle of the wilderness and the excitement he felt as he pushed himself beyond natural boundaries into the unknown.

He saw now that he had been wrong to urge Barlow to stick to the known route and not explore the southern basin. He remembered his own words—*I don't think we're likely to find much of anything in that direction but more trees and the Tetons.* Up to this point, his heart had not been fully in this expedition, and that had left him distracted and impatient. But climbing this mountain had rekindled his spirit—and he was grateful.

The climb was strenuous but not overly dangerous. Similar to the climb up Longs Peak, the route up was a forty-five-degree slope over talus fields, with the final few hundred feet requiring hand- and footholds to reach the summit, but this mountain was not nearly as tall as Longs Peak. Both Barlow and Prout managed the climb well, which impressed Jubil, since he imagined it was their first such experience. When they reached the summit, they were rewarded with a magnificent view.

Five miles to the north, Yellowstone Lake spread out below them, the thumb due north of where they stood. Some twenty miles beyond the thumb stood Mount Washburn. The mountain ranges surrounding the entire basin were visible. To the west, in the southwestern corner of the basin, were three medium-sized lakes, and to the east of them another one, all draining into the Snake and Yellowstone Rivers. Prout measured the summit at ten thousand three hundred feet, almost the same as Mount Washburn, but nearly four thousand feet short of Longs Peak.

The renewed sense of exhilaration Jubil felt inspired him to review his feelings toward Barlow and Heap. He suspected that much of his impatience and frustration on the trip so far had come from within him, rather than from them.

"I have to admit, you were right about exploring this part of the basin, Captain," Jubil said to Barlow. "We came out here to explore and map this whole thing, and not just ride over the same ground as last year. I was being overly cautious in my desire to avoid it."

Barlow studied Jubil for a moment, seemingly surprised by his admission. "I appreciate that," Barlow said. "I believe you meant well."

"Thank you. The loss of Mr. Everts in this area last year was a dreadful experience, and I let that cloud my judgment," Jubil said. "I'm still concerned about Mr. Hines and the soldier with him though. I hope they've come in by the time we return to camp."

"Yes," Barlow said pensively, "I do too."

Jubil said, "This is why anyone who comes out here has to be able to look out for himself."

"Yes," Barlow agreed, and then he surprised Jubil by doing something Jubil had not seen him do since they'd met—he smiled. "This summit is a new record for me," Barlow said, "but I suppose it's modest in comparison to Longs Peak." Jubil could see that their relationship had changed, and he felt his heart lighten.

"What it lacks in height," Jubil said, returning Barlow's smile, "it makes up for in grandeur."

"It is an astonishing place," Barlow said. "It must be a pleasure to see it a second time."

"It is," Jubil agreed. "Just last year I stood on one of those peaks over there," he said, pointing to a group of peaks near the southeastern corner of the lake. "and looked out at this very peak we're standing on. Lieutenant Doane, Mr. Langford, and I speculated that the view from here would be spectacular. Doane labeled this Yellow Mountain on his map."

"Yes, you were standing on Mount Langford at the time," Barlow said. "That would be it, third from the left of that group of seven on the southeast side of the lake. With all due respect to the lieutenant, I intend to label this peak as Mount Sheridan on my map. I believe the general deserves some recognition for his efforts to support the exploration of Yellowstone."

"I would not disagree," Jubil said.

Barlow studied Jubil. "I understand Mr. Langford and the other Washburn expedition members are on a campaign to have the Yellowstone Basin declared a national park. Are you involved in that effort?"

"I support the mission in my own circle," Jubil said, "but I'm not the public promoter that Langford is."

"Still an admirable endeavor," Barlow said. "I hope you prevail."

"Thank you," Jubil said.

When Barlow was ready, Jubil placed Prout's gear back in his pack, along with several pounds of rock specimens that Barlow had collected, and they set off down the mountain. When they reached the stream where they had left their horses, Jubil was pleased to see Apollo resting comfortably on a bed of pine needles in the shade of a tree. He wished Jackson could photograph the scene for him. He had grown very fond of Apollo. He was strong, uncomplaining, healthy, good natured, brave, and very handsome to boot— the same description he would give for his horse at home, Star. He missed her and wondered if she missed him.

When they returned to camp, they found Hines and the soldier still had not come in. Barlow was worried.

"Hines has had plenty of time to retrace his previous day's trail and return to our last camp," Barlow said, addressing the whole party. "It is very possible that he decided to catch up to Hayden, rather than come deeper into the southern basin to try and find us. We should remain here at least another day and search for them. In the morning we will separate into teams and make a search. But be careful—we don't want more people going missing."

In the morning, as Barlow began assigning search teams, Jubil made a request.

"If you don't mind, Captain," Jubil said, "I'd like to have one more look along the trail back to our last camp. I know we did that yesterday, but I have a feeling we should look again."

Barlow considered this for a moment, then turned to Captain Heap. "I think it's worth a try. I'd like you to ride with Mr. Walker, and see what you find." Jubil thought it was strange that Barlow would send Heap with him, rather than one of the soldiers, and from the expression on Heap's face, he thought so too.

The two set off northwest for their previous camp near the thumb of the lake, about fifteen miles away. The round trip would take them most of the day. They rode quietly for a while, but soon Jubil began asking Heap about himself, and Heap began sharing the details of his life. He had graduated from West Point in 1864 and served in the Army of the Potomac as an engineer, building fortifications and improving harbors before moving to the Division of the Missouri. He had also served with the US Lighthouse Service in various capacities and knew Nantucket well. He was not acquainted with but knew of Mrs. Warner's parents on Nantucket, and he was also aware of Maria Mitchell's accomplishments.

Jubil's connection to Nantucket triggered Heap's interest in his history, so Jubil explained his family connection to Major Powell and his expeditions, and his business relationship with General Sherman and Sheridan. Heap was very interested in the Powell expeditions and Jubil's outfitting business.

"I am aware that some of the men mock my appearance," Heap said plainly. "I hear I'm known as the Buckskin Kid."

Jubil was embarrassed and uncomfortable. "I've heard that said," he admitted. He considered defending himself by pointing out he had never called Heap that, but he knew his confession would be hollow. He had found it funny when he'd heard it from others.

"It's of no consequence to me," Heap said with a shrug. "I've been mocked for my stature and youthful appearance my whole life." Jubil heard the pain in his words and regretted his initial judgment of Heap. It was so easy to be hurtful, so difficult to be thoughtful and fair. Jubil vowed to do better.

"I don't think it was you they were mocking, so much as your clothes," Jubil said earnestly. "My advice is, the next time you buy new buckskins, put them on and roll around in the dirt for a while, maybe leave them out in the rain a time or two." He grinned over at Heap. "When folks see you in those, they'll figure you're a seasoned mountain man."

Heap laughed.

It was just before noon, as Jubil and Heap neared the thumb of the lake, that Jubil smelled smoke and spotted it rising from a point near the shoreline. They were greatly relieved to find Thomas Hines and Private Lemans along with their horses, gear, and the errant camera tripod, all healthy and camped comfortably by the lake. They had lost their bearings and wandered off the trail but had found their way back to the lake last night. Their plan was to wait one more day, then set out along the south shore of the lake to catch Hayden rather than chase Barlow through unknown territory.

The group rode back to Heart Lake, where Barlow and the others greeted them with relief. They spent three more days in the area, taking position readings of the lakes and other features, getting their measurements, and mapping the route of the rivers feeding into and out of the smaller lakes there. They then moved back north to Yellowstone Lake and made their way to the point where the Yellowstone River entered it. Along the eastern shore, the signal fires of Hayden's party were clearly visible. Jubil led Barlow's party to the ford across the Yellowstone River, and a few hours later the two parties were reunited. They remained camped one more day there until Elliot and Carrington arrived after surveying the lake in the *Anna* for a week. For the first time in almost two weeks, all the members of both expeditions were together again.

After three more days of effort, pushing north through the dense timber Jubil remembered so well, they reached the northeast corner of the lake and made camp. Jubil was setting up his bedroll when a sudden dizziness overcame him, and he swayed on his feet. Was he ill? He put a hand against his cheek, feeling for fever, and then he noticed the others around him similarly halted in their tracks. Flocks of birds rose into the sky as the trees began to sway and the ground began to roll under his feet—it was an earthquake. Terror struck him as he spread his arms wide to hold his balance. He had no idea what to do. There was nowhere to run, nowhere to hide. They were in the basin of a giant volcano—an extinct volcano if they were lucky. But what if their luck had run out? Waves passed beneath his feet—the most disconcerting sensation he had ever experienced—as he fought to balance on what had only moments ago been level, solid ground. The dreamlike feeling continued for several seconds, and then the earth was still once more. Jubil looked around, his body still tense as he awaited another round of waves. The others were similarly poised and looking at each other with anxiety plain in their faces.

"That was a helluva a ride, wasn't it?" said Albert Peale, who had been setting up his camping spot near Jubil's. "I've never been in an earthquake before. Now that was really something."

Jubil breathed a sigh of relief.

"All I could think about," Peale confessed, "was the ground cracking open and dropping us into the boiling cauldron we've been riding around on top of."

Jubil did not welcome Peale's imagery—it was too accurate. A few hours later, the ground shook again, and Jubil was plagued again by Peale's vision.

By afternoon the aftershocks had subsided. Jubil was filled with nervous energy and told Barlow and Hayden he was going out hunting. He left on Apollo, leading one of the pack animals to bring back any game. As he rode northeast from the lake, the going became easier as the timber thinned out. He didn't see any game and was about to declare the hunt unsuccessful and return to camp when Apollo pranced a step, raised his head, and snickered nervously.

Jubil scanned the path ahead, looking for what was making the horse uneasy; perhaps a bear or a mountain lion was nearby. He dismounted, hitching Apollo to a small tree, quietly chambered a round in his Henry rifle, and slowly walked forward with the rifle cradled in the crook of his left arm. He had taken a few steps when, twenty feet ahead of him, an Indian stepped out from behind a tree. He was not holding a weapon, so Jubil did not raise his rifle. The Indian raised his right hand and spoke. "Jubilee Walker," he said.

"White Dog," Jubil answered, not because the Indian looked like White Dog but because no other Indian would know his name.

As they approached each other, Jubil saw that the Indian's face was indeed familiar, a little fuller, perhaps. But his hair and clothing were very different. Gone was the shaven head with a topknot of braids and feathers, replaced by a full head of long, loose black hair with a single braid down the right side, from which a large black feather hung. Jubil remembered him as shirtless most of the time, but he was now clad in a light shirt and a well-worn army jacket, worn unbuttoned over the familiar deerskin trousers and moccasins. Jubil understood now why he had not recognized his friend last year.

At the center of the clearing, they met by grasping one another by the forearm.

"It's good to see you," Jubil said.

"I see you last summer," White Dog said. "Think my eyes lie. Doane says my eyes are true. Jubilee Walker is here."

This was more than Jubil had heard White Dog say during the whole summer he had ridden across Nebraska and back with him, four years before. Perhaps his English really had improved considerably or perhaps his friend just felt more talkative these days.

"When Doane told me that story," Jubil said, "I could hardly believe it was possible. You live with the Crow now?"

"Sometimes, yes," White Dog said, "sometimes soldiers, sometimes ride alone. Medicine strong for Jubilee Walker," White Dog said, pointing to the rawhide pouch riding on Jubil's hip.

"It is," Jubil said with a grin. "I lost the little pinecone token to the Colorado River a couple of years ago, but the rest of the spirits have pulled me through some tight spots. Doane told me you thought Nebraska was getting too crowded."

"Railroad . . . too much people," White Dog replied. "Buffalo gone."

Jubil couldn't argue with him. "You know they're going to run a railroad through the Montana Territory soon?"

"Yes . . . not good," White Dog said.

"Where will you go next," Jubil asked, "if it gets too crowded here?"

"Maybe north," White Dog said, with a shrug, "maybe south."

Jubil thought about the life that White Dog led, seemingly untethered to anything or anyone. He wondered whether his friend ever felt loneliness or concern over what he should do with himself.

"I'm riding with an army expedition," Jubil explained. "General Sherman hired me to guide for them. Next time I see him, I'll tell him I saw you."

"Sherman," White Dog said, "my friend . . . the devil."

Jubil nodded. He had to admit he felt somewhat similarly about Sherman.

"You could ride along with us for a while through the Yellowstone—if you want to," Jubil said.

"Too much people," White Dog said, shaking his head. "They don't need scout. They have you."

Jubil took that characterization as a compliment, whether it was intended as one or not.

"You live here now?" White Dog asked.

"No, after the expedition I'm going . . . back," Jubil said, trailing off as he realized he hadn't decided where he was going next—Council Bluffs, Bloomington, Poughkeepsie, Washington, Helena.

"You can ride with me," White Dog said.

Jubil stared at White Dog in unfettered surprise as he considered the offer. Never in all his flights of fantasy as a boy, when he lay in his loft bedroom reading dime westerns and dreaming of being somewhere other than the farm, had he imagined anything like this. He was acutely aware that he could actually do it if he wanted to—ride off with White Dog to wherever the spirit moved them. No one was waiting for him, no one was expecting him back at any particular time. He could stay a few days, or weeks, or as long as he wanted.

"It's getting too late to start back," Jubil said. "I'm going to camp here for the night. You want to join me?"

White Dog agreed, and they went about the business of making a camp. Jubil took the saddle off Apollo and tended to him, then collected firewood and built a fire, while White Dog went to a nearby stream and brought back two trout and a few bunches of cattail root.

As the evening wore on, Jubil learned that he and White Dog shared another kinship—they were both without any living family. White Dog had lived with his parents on the Pawnee Reservation in Nebraska until they died of an illness ravaging their tribe. Orphaned and without other family to take him in, he fell under the authority of missionaries who tried to put him in school, which lasted only a matter of hours, as he escaped the first night, stole a horse, and rode off. He had ridden to Fort Kearney and gotten work as a scout, and that's where he eventually met General Sherman, whom he followed so faithfully that the soldiers called him White Man's Dog. He followed Sherman until Sheridan took his place and then followed Sheridan to Fort Ellis in Montana. There, White Dog met some Crow scouts who welcomed him, and he loved the wide-open space, so he had stayed.

Jubil enjoyed hearing this part of White Dog's story, but when he asked about life on the reservations, the details of the story began to aggravate him. The year that Jubil met White Dog, 1867, Nebraska had been admitted to the union. The newly formed state government had promptly voided the treaty granting the Pawnee a reservation near the Loup River, sold off a large portion of their land, and informed them they would be moving, yet to be determined where or when. The Indians at the Crow reservation had, so far, not been deprived of their land, but Montana was still a territory. It also helped that settlement there was still sparse, but that was changing fast.

The federal Indian Agency was purportedly there to help enforce the treaty, but according to White Dog, food staples and other supplies promised to the Crow were almost always delivered short in quantity and usually of poor quality—even rotten. Cattle delivered to make up for their shortage of bison were likewise fewer in number than promised and often sickly and poorly fed. Adding insult to injury, the animal feed supplied to make up for the shortage of grazing was also of poor quality.

Hearing White Dog's account, Jubil was upset with his government and with the people of low character who would carry out such policies clearly intended to do harm. He thought again of Doane's challenge—What was he doing about the problem?

"I'm not sure if I can help," Jubil said, "but I'm going to try and get something done about the Indian Agency. There are some men on the expedition who might be able to help." Jubil felt his offer was weak, but at least was a start. White Dog nodded.

Jubil told White Dog an abbreviated version of his own life story, and White Dog listened, eyes intent on Jubil's face. He nodded once, when Jubil told him in a choked voice of Luke's death, but he offered no opinions or advice.

When they had talked themselves out, White Dog went to make a bed of fir boughs in a spot near the horses, but Jubil was not sleepy. He sat tending the fire and thinking about what life would be like riding with White Dog. He knew in his heart that he would not permanently want White Dog's way of life. He could ride with him for a while, and enjoy it for a few weeks, but civilization would call him back. It was still tempting, even if he would only be going along as a tourist. But why would he go in the first place, outside fulfilling some boyhood fantasy? Finally, he could not avoid the truth—he would be riding with White Dog as a way to run from the feeling of emptiness that had paralyzed him since Luke's death.

He thought about the people he loved and wondered what

advice each of them would give him. His father would tell him to go back to the farm, to settle down and quit wasting his time chasing adventure. His mother would tell him lovingly to do whatever made him happiest. His Uncle Pete and Eli Boswell would tell him to ride off into the unknown with White Dog. Luke Warner would tell him to get on with their business plans. Mr. and Mrs. Warner would wish him well, but they were too grief stricken to have much concern over his plans. Ike would say he was in no position to offer advice, but wish him well. Nelly's parents would disagree on the matter, and Nelly herself would tell him to follow his heart, even when it forced him into one challenging situation after another.

What his heart was telling him right now—what he wanted more than anything—was to have what he had had before he ever came to Yellowstone. He and Nelly were committed to each other and happy, and he had found a new family and a purpose with the Warners. Though he knew things could never be exactly the same, he needed to rebuild his life to regain as much of what he once had as he could, while remaining true to the spirit of adventure that lived in him.

Jubil awoke in the dim light of dawn to see White Dog sitting cross-legged on the ground, watching the dying embers of their campfire.

"Morning," said Jubil. "You on your way then?"

"Yes," White Dog said.

"It was good to see you," Jubil said. "I'll be riding back to the expedition. I expect to be in the area from time to time. I'll try to find you."

They stood and clasped arms.

"Jubilee Walker," White Dog said, "good friend."

Jubil remembered the sense of pride he had felt the first time

White Dog had called him *friend*, but this moment was even more special, because he was now a *good* friend. He watched as White Dog mounted up and silently rode through the timber.

Jubil had made his decision. Now he had to get to work.

CHAPTER 15

When Jubil returned to the expedition campsite, he learned that Hayden had decided to take a side trip before exiting the Yellowstone Basin, and Barlow had decided to follow him. The plan was to head northeast to find the Lamar River, which was the east fork of the Yellowstone River. They would survey the Lamar to its confluence with the Yellowstone and then follow the Yellowstone northward to Fort Ellis, the same way they had come in. As long as they were on their way out of the basin, Jubil was satisfied with the arrangements. He was ready to move on.

As the expedition set out, Jubil caught up to ride beside Lieutenant Doane.

"I went out hunting yesterday," Jubil said, "and ran into an old friend."

"Did you now?" Doane said, with a smile. "I take it you had a little powwow."

"Yes, we camped and had a good visit," Jubil said. "He's doing fine himself, but he mentioned the Indian Agency is doing the Crow reservation a terrible disservice."

"I believe you'll find Phineas Black has a hand in that," Doane said.

Not surprised, Jubil asked, "How so?"

"The local Indian agent met an untimely demise," Doane explained, "and was replaced by one of Murphy's crew named

"

Flynn."

"Oh, no," Jubil said. "A red-headed kid, docile as a sheep?"

Doane nodded.

"Good lord, I know him too. He was one of the teamsters on the trip with Sherman to Fort McPherson. The Irishmen—Murphy, Flynn, and O'Brien. O'Brien's probably somewhere around here too. Flynn was harmless. Did whatever Murphy told him."

"Well," Doane said, "Black is his boss now."

Jubil and Doane rode along in silence for a while as Jubil thought about how to deal with Phineas Black. After a while, Jubil asked Doane, "Do you suppose I'd have any success trying to talk to someone at the Bureau of Indian Affairs in Washington? I have a few contacts now."

"I wouldn't give you good odds on that," Doane said. "You know the head of that lot is a full-blooded Seneca?"

"Yes," Jubil said. "His name's Ely Parker. I've read about him in the papers."

"Well," Doane said, leaning over to spit, "not only has he not been able to straighten out the mess—the hounds are trying to force him out for not handling bidding on contracts properly—meaning not to their benefit. But if you think talking to him is the way to go, best of luck to you."

It took a full day to reach the Lamar River and then another to follow it westward to the Yellowstone. About two hundred yards past the confluence, they came across a well-worn trail and followed it as it switchbacked down a ridge. As they came to the bottom of the ridge and rounded a corner, they were surprised to find a bridge spanning the Yellowstone River.

The bridge was constructed of heavy timbers, set in two spans each about fifty feet long. These rested on an impressively engineered diamond-shaped log pylon set in the center of the swiftly flowing river. Support timbers for the deck ran from the pylon to each bank. The effort required to transport materials this far into the wilderness and the skill required to construct such a thing made its existence a small wonder. Across the bridge and partway up the trail leading away were a small cabin and a shed. Standing outside the cabin were two men who appeared to be in an argument. One was a burly bald-headed fellow, who was animatedly pointing up the trail and speaking his mind. The other man stood holding his horse's reins, staring sullenly at the man who was shouting in his face. This fellow, who had a mustache and dark hair, wore a pistol low on his hip, and though Jubil was too far away to tell for sure, he looked unpleasantly familiar.

As Lieutenant Doane and Jubil sat surveying the situation, Hayden and Barlow rode up beside them.

"Did you know this was here, Lieutenant?" Hayden asked.

"I heard someone had built a bridge over the Yellowstone," Doane said, "but I didn't know exactly where it was. It's nicely done. I believe a fellow named Jack Baronett built it as a toll bridge to get to the gold mines up around Cooke City."

"There are gold mines around here now?" Jubil said, dismayed. The bridge builder's name sounded familiar, but he could not recall where he would have heard it.

Doane nodded.

"Is one of those fellows Baronett?" Hayden asked.

Doane removed his field glasses from his saddlebag and studied the two men across the river. "The bald fellow might be Baronett," Doane said. "The other one . . ." Doane said, as he handed the field glasses to Jubil, "is named Murphy. He works for a man in Bozeman named Phineas Black."

Hayden looked at Jubil. "Is that the same fellow you had words with back at the Soda Mountain?"

"Yes, sir," Jubil said, as he handed the field glasses back to Doane.

"I'll ride over," Doane said, "and see if anyone takes issue with us crossing the bridge."

"I'll ride with you," Jubil said.

The men outside the cabin continued their debate until Doane and Jubil approached. The bald man waved the other one off and walked toward Doane and Jubil.

"Howdy," the bald man said. "Jack Baronett is the name."

Jubil saw that Murphy had only just now recognized him. Murphy stood facing them with a sneer, his hand resting on the butt of his revolver.

"Sorry to interrupt you, Mr. Baronett," Doane said, looking pointedly from Baronett to Murphy and back again. "I'm Lieutenant Cheyney Doane out of Fort Ellis. I'm escorting a US Interior Department survey of the region. That's Dr. Ferdinand Hayden over there," Doane said, pointing back across the bridge. "Any toll for us to cross your bridge?"

"Nah," Baronett said. "Bring 'em across."

"Thanks," Doane replied. Turning to Jubil he asked, "Care to ride back over and bring the others?"

"Sure," Jubil said. Before he turned Apollo, he called out to Murphy. "What are you doing here, Murphy? Got another one-sided business partnership going?"

"Now that is an unfriendly greeting," Murphy replied. "Mr. Baronett here is one of Mr. Black's most valued associates. Isn't that so, Jack?"

Baronett said nothing, but Jubil saw his jaw clench. Murphy mounted up and moved his horse a step or two forward.

"It must be about time for you to be leaving these parts, Walker," he said. "Good day, Jack. I'll tell Mr. Black you agreed to our deal—happily." Murphy kicked his horse and rode off up the trail.

Baronett turned to Jubil. "You know that weasel?"

"Yes sir," Jubil said. "Is Black pushing you for security money too?"

Baronett swore under his breath and looked away.

"It's a temptation to just plug Murphy and be done with

him," Baronett confessed, "but Black would just send another one. Folks are mining gold up around Cooke City, and Black is one of them. I hired some of his miners to build this bridge to make working the gold claims easier. I charge a toll to make my living, but Black comes along and tells me what a shame it would be for my bridge to get burned down . . . and how he'll see that don't happen—for a fee."

"Why don't you just call the law in on him?" Jubil asked. "He's doing the same thing to McCartney over at Soda Mountain."

"Pfft," Baronett puffed. "Try finding a jury that wouldn't be afraid for their own hide."

Jubil looked to Doane for his reaction, and Doane raised his eyebrows and shrugged.

"Somebody ought to stand up to him," Jubil said.

"Bozeman ain't a very big town, mister," Baronett said. "Black's got deep pockets for a place that size, and money talks loud. Those mines of his make money, that hotel does too. The mercantile is the only one in town, and he's got any number of—what did you call them—one-sided partnerships? He's rolling in government money too—got himself a sweet setup with the Indian Agency. They liberally overpay him for underdelivering. He's in everybody's pocket around here. Ain't nobody going to stand up to him in court with Murphy and his pack roaming about."

Jubil and Doane exchanged a glance. "You agree the law won't come down on him?" Jubil asked. He felt an anger growing in him that was made worse by people continuing to tell him there was no solution to the problem of Phineas Black.

"I think Baronett's got it pegged on that score," Doane agreed. "Local law might bring him to court, but if a jury is involved, it's going to be hard to convict him. There might be some federal or territory level of law enforcement that would act. If you want an authoritative word on that, ride up to Helena and talk to Langford and Judge Hedges. If anyone could bring Black to heel, it would be the likes of them."

"That's good advice," Jubil said, surprised he had not thought of it himself. Stopping Phineas Black would not only help preserve Yellowstone but improve the situation for White Dog and his people.

"And speaking of our companions from last year's expedition," Doane said, "you'll be interested to know that Jack Baronett here was the man who found Truman Everts last year and saved his life."

"You don't say!" Jubil said. Now he remembered where he had heard the name—in Walter Trumbull's letter. He dismounted and strode over to shake Baronett's hand. "Congratulations, Mr. Baronett! You saved a good man in Mr. Everts. There's a lot of people that appreciate your efforts, and that includes me."

"Thank you, son," Baronett said, smiling sheepishly. "It was no hardship for me to go out looking for him—I spend so much time in these parts, they call me 'Yellowstone Jack.' When I heard about the reward on your friend, I just gathered up a crew and went out for a look around. It was more luck than effort."

By this time, Hayden and Barlow had run out of patience and had ridden over the bridge themselves.

"What is the situation, Lieutenant?" Hayden asked.

"Sorry sir," Doane said. "We had to clear up a matter, but we're good to come on across now, courtesy of Mr. Jack Baronett."

Jubil mounted up again and went to fetch everyone. The trip from there on was easy: They followed the Yellowstone back north into Montana, rode up through Paradise Valley, then cut over Bozeman Pass to Fort Ellis.

On the last day of August, the expedition pulled in to the fort, and Jubil began to say his goodbyes. Hayden was already heading off to his next survey, and Barlow and Heap were taking the next stage toward home. Jubil's time with Albert Peale had been enjoyable, but like many of the friendships he made during his travels, he imagined this one would be fleeting. He hoped he might run into William Henry Jackson again someday, and he was sure he would hear of him. The photographs he had taken of Yellowstone were stunning, and would remove any doubt that the wonders of Yellowstone were real, and people would flock to see them.

Doane arranged for Jubil to lodge in the officer's quarters at the fort, which he enjoyed, especially meeting Mrs. Doane. He had known she existed but knew nothing of her beyond that. He was surprised at how such an attractive and genteel woman could be married to Doane, but he imagined that in her company he was the heroic poet rather than the massacring warrior.

"I've enjoyed riding with you, Lieutenant," Jubil said as he prepared to leave the fort. "I'll very likely be back one day. I've decided to have another go at the outfitting business, but not out here—not any time soon anyway. But while I'm out here, on your good advice, I've decided to ride up to Helena and have a talk with Langford and Judge Hedges. I want to tell them what I've seen going on in Yellowstone and talk about the prospects for the park designation. I'd also like to get Judge Hedges's thoughts on setting the law on Phineas Black."

"Be careful," Doane said. "Black and his boys are not just dishonest, they're dangerous."

"Thanks," Jubil said. "I'll be careful."

Jubil went to headquarters to collect his pay for guiding the expedition and added the money to the supply he carried in his money belt, then went to collect Apollo, who had been enjoying the luxury of the stable and being reshod. He filled his saddlebag with supplies procured from the mess hall, strapped his pack to his saddle, and rode off from Fort Ellis toward Helena. It would be an easy ride over mostly wide-open terrain. He was looking forward to the solitude.

When he came to Bozeman, he gave it a wide berth and rode around the town's perimeter to turn northwest. As he crossed Bridger Creek, he felt eyes on his back and turned in the saddle to see three men riding up behind him at a canter. His rifle was loaded and ready in its scabbard on the saddle, but he did not draw it. His revolver was covered by his slicker, so he tucked the coat behind it to clear his reach and turned Apollo to face the riders. As they approached, he was dismayed to recognize Murphy.

"Top of the morning to you, Walker," Murphy said. "And where would you be off to on such a fine day as this?"

"I'm riding up to Helena, to have a look around," Jubil replied. "Though I don't see how that's any of your concern." He wondered with growing alarm if he had underestimated the extent to which he had become a thorn in Phineas Black's side.

"Well now, it's not so much my concern, as it is my employer's, you see," Murphy said snidely. "Myself, I'd be glad to see you gone from these parts, but Mr. Black is disappointed he missed the opportunity to have a word with you."

"A word about what?" Jubil asked, sizing up the other men riding with Murphy. They did not look bright, but he guessed they could probably shoot straight.

"You'll need to talk to him to learn that, won't you?" Murphy said. "Now if you'll just ride along with us, we'll deliver you."

"And if I'm not of a mind to do that?" Jubil asked, turning Apollo so he could get a clear shot, if it came to that. Murphy didn't budge, but the other two riders reached for their weapons. Murphy held out his hand to steady them.

"Don't get too testy here, Walker," Murphy said. "It would be fine by me to just shoot you down, but Mr. Black wants to talk. Are you coming? Or would you rather shoot it out?"

Disgustedly, Jubil moved Apollo back across the creek and rode alongside Murphy with the other two flanking them a few steps back. The ride into Bozeman was short and silent. Jubil tried to think of some way to get free but came up blank, short of taking his chances with a showdown. The unsettling thought occurred to him that no one other than Doane knew his plans. Doane would have no reason to follow up to see if he had arrived in Helena. He would not be missed for weeks or months, and no one he cared about would ever know what had become of him. Mr. Gulley's advice came to him once more: *keep your wits about you*. These words had saved him more than once, and he tried to calm himself now and look for opportunities to escape.

At the edge of town, Murphy pulled up in front of a square two-story wooden building with a second-story balcony that covered a ground-floor boardwalk. Across the front of the storefront, on either side of a double door that stood open, were two large plate glass windows. Heavy red velvet curtains hung inside the windows, providing a picture frame effect. Painted on each window in ornate gold lettering was the establishment's name, The Golden Slipper Gentleman's Club, along with an image of a woman's slipper. This was James McCartney's establishment, which he had spoken of when they'd met at his bathhouse at Soda Mountain.

Murphy hitched his horse as the other two men waited for Jubil to dismount.

"Keep an eye on him," Murphy said to his men. He entered the building, and soon a stream of men strolled out, some looking Jubil over as they left, others talking and laughing and paying him no mind. As the last of them left, Murphy gave Jubil a mock bow and a sweep of his arm. "All right then, Mr. Walker, step right in. You two keep any visitors away for a bit," Murphy said to his men.

Jubil stepped inside and immediately began scanning the room for escape routes. Because of the windows, the interior was brightly lit. To his left there was a piano between the front window and a bar that ran the length of the room. An aproned man stood behind the bar polishing a glass, minding his own business. At the far end of the bar was a staircase that led to a catwalk along a row of closed doors. Beyond the staircase was another door to a back room. Jubil wondered if he could get out through the back room in time to avoid being shot. He still had his sidearm, and he wondered why. Maybe Murphy and Black figured he was outnumbered and therefore no threat to them.

To his right were two round gaming tables. Sitting alone at the table in the back corner was Phineas Black. Jubil stood in the middle of the open floor space in front of the piano. Out the window he could see Murphy's men, smoking and loitering near the horses. Murphy stood blocking the doorway.

"Mr. Walker," Black said, remaining seated, elbows on the arms of his chair, hands clasped at his chest. "Have a seat. Would you like a drink?"

"I'll stand, thanks," Jubil said. "I don't plan to stay long enough to finish a drink."

Black raised his eyebrows and nodded. "Suit yourself," he said and waved the bartender away to the back room.

"I'm here against my will, Black," Jubil said calmly. "That's against the law."

Black looked around the room. "Do you see any law handy at the moment?"

"What do you want?" Jubil asked.

"I want to know what you've been up to," Black said, leaning forward, elbows on the table, fingers steepled, "nosing around in my business—and why you're riding off for Helena now, rather than catching the train back to Illinois where you belong."

"First off," Jubil said, "I've not been 'nosing around your business.' I've been serving as a guide for the army and help-ing conduct a government survey. I just happened to come across a couple of places you are plundering. Who knows how many I missed?"

Black ignored the insult. "What exactly did you say to McCartney and Baronett?"

"I can't recall word for word," Jubil said, "but the gist of it was that they seem more like hostages than business partners."

"I'm doing those men a service," Black said, "providing security from anyone who might threaten their business operations."

"The biggest threat either of them faces is you and Murphy," Jubil said.

"Spreading opinions like that can cause trouble," Black said.

Jubil remained silent.

"I have legitimate business interests in Yellowstone," Black said, "whether you approve or not."

"You should do your business elsewhere," Jubil said. "When Yellowstone becomes a national park, the government will toss you out."

"This park notion of yours is a fantasy," Black said dismissively, "and it's not helpful to have you going around promoting the idea."

"Stopping me won't stop the idea," Jubil said. "There are more powerful people than me promoting it."

"Is that why you're headed to Helena, to see Langford?" Black said.

"As I said, it's no concern of yours," Jubil said.

"You've got a notion to see whether Langford can use this park idea to convince his political friends to run me out of business. Well, if he does, I guarantee you things won't wind up like you think. You just watch—if he puts me out of business, he'll turn around and do exactly what I was doing, and he'll keep all the profit. And you are naïve if you don't believe that. That's the way the West, and the US government, works."

"Yes, you would know about shady government dealings," Jubil blurted out, his anger rising. "Putting that poor dumb kid, Flynn, in charge of the local Indian agency must have required some political tomfoolery. I hear there've been some irregularities with vendors being overpaid and underdelivering. But I'm sure you know nothing about that."

Black seethed with anger, and Jubil realized that he should have stuck to Langford, the park, and business profiteering in Yellowstone. Why expand the scope of Black's concern? He glanced at Murphy, who was watching Black, not Jubil. Jubil glanced out the front window and saw Black's other two men, still loitering at the horse rail.

"I see it now," Black said, standing up, as he slowly tucked his coat behind his holster. "You and Langford have made some kind of deal, haven't you? You're in this together, aren't you? He's probably going to get his friends to give that Indian agency post to you. And then he'll be helping you set up your own outfitter's store as a vendor. Yes . . . it's all making sense now."

Was there any use arguing with Black, whose hold on reality was tenuous, at best? "I have no interest in the Indian agency post or opening a store in Bozeman," Jubil said.

"I had a bad feeling when we met," Black said, as if Jubil hadn't spoken, "that you were going to be a problem. I tried to warn you, one gentleman to another, but you're too thick or high-minded to listen to reason. Now here you are again, back in my territory, stirring up trouble for me on every front. I thought that burning your store to the ground would have sent a clear message that you should mind your own business."

It took a moment for what Black said to register. Jubil stared blindly at the floor, his heart racing, his head swimming. "It *was* you, then," Jubil said, almost to himself.

"Not me, personally, of course," Black said coldly. "My influence spreads far and wide. I telegraphed a fellow in Chicago who got the job done. Too bad about your partner. No one knew he lived in the building."

Rage and pain overtook Jubil's judgment. It was all he

could do to keep from drawing his revolver and opening fire on Black. If he could be sure of killing him, it would be worth dying for. But then he heard the voice in his head again saying, *Keep your wits about you.* Black and Murphy stared at him, expecting a reaction.

"When I was asked if there was anyone who would want to hurt Luke or me, the only person that came to mind was you. I didn't say anything, because I had no proof. And I also thought it was highly unlikely you'd be so vindictive over the small threat or aggravation I might present. But I appear to have underestimated how petty and vile you are. I'm finished talking, Black," Jubil said wearily. "I'm walking out of here and going for the sheriff."

"We both know," Black said, "that is not going to happen. I'll tell you what *is* going to happen. Murphy is going to escort you to your horse and ride with you back out to where he found you, and then he's going to shoot you down like he wanted to do in the first place. Mr. Murphy, please see Mr. Walker out of town."

Out the front window, Jubil saw a man with deerskin britches and long black hair drop down from the roof over the front porch and land atop the two men standing at the horse rail—it was White Dog. Jubil turned his attention to Black and Murphy. Black could not see the men outside from his position. Murphy heard the commotion and turned to see what was going on outside, presenting his back to Jubil.

In that moment, Jubil began to experience the world in slow motion, a feeling he had had before in perilous situations. Black began to draw his revolver, and as Murphy recognized his error, he too began to draw his gun and turn around to face Jubil. Before Murphy had his pistol clear of his holster, a shot rang out from White Dog's rifle that sent Murphy flying forward into the middle of the room, where he landed face down on the floor. As Jubil got his own weapon clear, he saw Black's gun already pointed at him. Jubil dove right, but a bullet slammed into his left shoulder. As he fell, he raised his own pistol and fired at Black before he hit the floor. He saw Black thrown backward into the wall by the force of the shot, and then the world went black.

Jubil opened his eyes. He was lying on a bed in a small bedroom. His left shoulder throbbed. If he was dead, or dreaming, it certainly hurt like reality. His mouth was dry, and he needed to relieve himself. He started to sit up, and a bolt of pain knocked him flat. He lay collecting himself before trying again. This time he rolled to his right side and managed to sit up in spite of the pain. He sat catching his breath, looking for the chamber pot, and found it at the foot of the bed, near the window. He started to stand but felt light-headed and sat back down. As he sat on the bed, steadying his head in his hand, a short teenage girl with braided pigtails appeared in the doorway.

"Oh," she said, "you're awake. Sorry, I only stepped out for a minute. Can you stand on your own? I can get help."

"I think I'll be all right, in a minute. . . . Who are you?" Jubil asked.

"Molly Jones," she said, pulling herself up to nearly five feet tall. "I'm Doc Jones's daughter. Papa asked me to keep an eye on you until you came around."

"Oh, hello, Molly Jones," Jubil said groggily. "Where am I?"

"You're laid up in the Guy House Hotel. Mr. Dodson, the proprietor, remembered you from last year," Molly explained. "He heard what happened and volunteered to put you up until you mend."

"I appreciate you folks looking out for me," Jubil said. "How bad am I shot?"

"From what I understand," Molly said, "the bullet just missed your collarbone and went clean through. Nothing is broken. If it doesn't fester, you should mend up fine. A little lower though, and it would have likely done for you. Papa will be by later to check on you."

"Hmm . . . thank you. Now if you'll excuse me for a minute . . . ," Jubil said, standing up to test his footing. "Close that door please?"

Molly closed the door and Jubil used the chamber pot. Then he stepped over to the wash basin, had a drink of water, and looked in the mirror. His left shoulder was wrapped in clean bandages. There was an armchair in the corner of his room with a book on it that Molly must have been reading. He opened the door to his room, but Molly was gone. He couldn't imagine having to get up from a prone position again any time soon, so he avoided the bed, moved the book, and sat down in the chair gingerly. He thought about how close he had come to dying and how strange it was to wake up and find himself alive. The thought of death took him back to the night he had stood waiting for Luke to show some sign of life and the emptiness and defeat he felt when he did not. He was grateful his loved ones would not know this had happened until he told them himself. A man appeared at his door.

"Mr. Walker," the man said, "I don't know if you recall meeting me, but I'm Phillip Dodson, the proprietor here at the Guy House. Good to see you awake."

"Thank you for your hospitality," Jubil said. "Forgive me if I don't get up."

"Just wanted to see if there was anything that we could bring you from the kitchen?" Dodson asked.

"Maybe soon, thanks," Jubil replied. "What about Black and Murphy, are they . . . ?"

"Dead," Dodson said. "The other two are in jail."

Jubil nodded and studied the floor. "Where's White Dog?"

"Camped out by Bridger Creek," Dodson said. "He's minding your horse and gear."

Jubil was somewhat surprised by this. He had half-expected to hear he was in jail.

"Are we in trouble with the law?" Jubil asked.

Dodson laughed. "Hardly! If you don't get out of here soon, you'll be elected mayor."

Jubil studied Dodson as he tried to decide what to make of this.

"Mr. Walker," Dodson continued, "if you had just shot those two down on general principles, half the town would still see you and your friend as heroes. The bartender was in the back room listening, and he and the girls upstairs heard the whole thing. Folks think they got what they had coming. Black didn't have many friends around here."

Jubil sat pondering the oddity of being on the delivering end of the swift and harsh frontier justice he had read about in so many yarns in his youth.

"I'm free to leave then?" Jubil asked.

"Whenever you're up to it," Dodson said. "Doc will talk to you about it, but my guess is it'll be at least a couple of weeks before you can travel."

Jubil imagined being on horseback with this injury and winced.

"Thanks for the information," he said. "I think I'll take you up on the offer of some supper. I'm not particular about what it is. And if I could ask one more thing—could you send somebody up to tell White Dog I'm alive?"

"Surely will," Dodson said, "I'll send a boy with your supper shortly."

"Thanks again for your help," Jubil said.

He sat resting quietly, searching his soul, looking for remorse over having killed a man, but he found none. Black had killed Luke, perhaps not by his own hand, but just as well as. It did not bother Jubil in the least he had been the one to administer justice for that. But it was White Dog he had to thank for being alive to tell about it.

A boy came with a tray of elk steak, mashed potatoes with gravy, buttered biscuits, and coffee, which Jubil wolfed down, and then he fell asleep sitting in the armchair. He awoke to find Molly Jones taking the empty tray away.

"You've got a visitor," Molly said nervously.

In the doorway stood White Dog. Jubil brought himself to his feet as his friend entered the room.

"You weren't hurt?" Jubil asked, looking him over for injuries.

"No," White Dog said.

"I reckon we're even now," Jubil said. "Thanks for saving my hide. I believe I can return your medicine bag." As he spoke, Jubil saw something in White Dog's face he had never seen there before—the hint of a smile.

"Medicine still strong for you," White Dog said, his eyes laughing now. "You keep."

"You must have been tailing me," Jubil said. "Why?"

"You want to ride alone. White Dog follow, to see you safe."

"Well, it's a darn good thing you did," Jubil said. "Thank you."

"Your horse and gear with liveryman now," White Dog said.

"You're leaving?" Jubil asked.

"Yes," White Dog said.

"I'll be back . . . sometime," Jubil said. They clasped arms, and White Dog left.

Jubil fought through the pain to ease his way back onto the bed, and soon he was asleep.

Over the next few days, he regained his strength and collected his thoughts. A telegram to Warner and Company in Council Bluffs confirmed that Ike and Eli were still operating Mr. Warner's store, and the Warners were on Nantucket Island. It was tempting to follow his original plan to go to

Helena to talk to Langford and Judge Hedges, but he decided the business of Yellowstone and the Indian Agency would have to be done through the mail. He was ready to go home for a while. He would stop in Council Bluffs to assess the situation there and then go back to Bloomington.

Jubil was pleased when Lieutenant and Mrs. Doane came to visit him at the Guy House, and brought with them mail addressed to him in care of the fort. His spirits were lifted by letters from Nelly, General Sherman, and Walter Trumbull.

While Jubil had been trekking through Yellowstone for the second time, Walter Trumbull had gotten deeply involved in a political campaign. Through his connections, he had joined on as an aide to William H. Clagett, Republican candidate for delegate to the US House of Representatives for the Montana Territory, who was running against James Cavanaugh, the Democrat incumbent. Walter's description of the hectic pace of travel around the territory, the bitterness of the rhetoric, and the rancor stirred up amongst citizens sounded unpleasant to Jubil, but Walter seemed to revel in the intrigue. Walter had been sending out dispatches to the *Helena Herald*, which he encouraged Jubil to read for further detail. Walter had encouraged Clagett to support the national park idea for Yellowstone, and while Clagett did not disagree, he did not see it as a campaign issue. Walter was still hopeful the idea would take root in action, as Clagett had been successful in his bid for office, and they would soon be moving to Washington.

Jubil wrote to Walter congratulating him and encouraging his efforts on the Yellowstone bill. He also asked for his politically astute friend's advice on to how to go about involving himself with the Indian Agency system, and Indian affairs in general. Walter would know who to talk to, as well as who to avoid, and possibly even arrange introductions.

The letter from General Sherman was a pleasant surprise. Barlow had reported Jubil's efforts as satisfactory, which Jubil appreciated, and Sherman had asked him to come visit whenever he was in Washington again. Jubil wrote back thanking him, and agreeing to visit. Sherman's advice on Indian affairs would also be helpful, but before he talked to him, Jubil felt he needed to better educate himself on the situation.

The letter from Nelly was only the second one he had received from her that summer. He could not complain—he had only written to her once during the expedition, and that was early on when he did not have much to say. It was now September, and she was back to finish her final year at Vassar College. Her summer employment at the newspaper in New York had been a success. She had gotten valuable experience and made other business contacts. The offices of *The Revolution* were in Printing House Square on Park Row in New York, one floor above *Scientific American*. Miss Mitchell authored the astronomical column for *Scientific American* and had written a letter of introduction for Nelly to the editor, Rufus Porter, who had encouraged Nelly about her prospects for employment in the future. Jubil wished she would have mentioned him in that future, but she had not.

Having time on his hands, he wrote Nelly a long letter explaining what had occurred. He also told her he had decided to open a new store but said no more about the particulars, because at this point there were none. He also wrote to the Boswells, the Warners, and Ike and Eli—who were staying at the Warner's house while they ran the store in Council Bluffs— to bring them all up to date. Black had been responsible for the fire that had killed Luke, he explained, and expressed his remorse for having brought Black into their lives. He also admitted he felt no remorse or guilt over the deaths of Black and Murphy. He closed each letter by expressing how grateful he was to be alive and how much he looked forward to seeing each of them again.

He might have been able to leave Bozeman sooner if he

had been willing to ride the stage to Corinne, but he was not. Going on horseback and tending to saddling and unsaddling Apollo, and managing his own food and campfire required him to be fit again, and by the end of September he was still sore but capable of these tasks. He had made many new friends during his weeks in Bozeman, and he made the rounds thanking people and saying goodbye before riding south toward Corinne. More than one person encouraged him to stay and open a store, which, with Black out of the way and the railroad headed this way, might not have been a bad idea. But right now, he had business to attend to in Council Bluffs.

CHAPTER 16

When Jubil reached Corinne, he realized he couldn't bear to leave Apollo behind, so he decided to take him home, to keep Star company in her final years. He was concerned that the long, noisy, shaky trip would upset Apollo, but when he visited him in the stock car, the stallion did not seem to mind the accommodations, which eased Jubil's conscience considerably.

When Jubil arrived at Warner and Company Outfitters, Ike and Eli were ecstatic to see him, and he had to keep them from affectionately thumping his sore shoulder.

"We got a telegram from Mr. Warner a couple of days ago," Ike said, "he'll be here tomorrow. He's meeting with a potential buyer for the store."

This news did not sit well with Jubil. He looked at the familiar surroundings of the store, and thought about his history there. It was where he had met the best friend he had ever had and where he had found his direction in life. This store, and the Warners who ran it, had enabled him to be not only an adventurer but a useful ally to important men—Powell, Sheridan, Sherman, Barlow, Hayden.

"I'd like to talk to you boys about that," Jubil said. "I'm going to ride on up to the Warners' house. We'll talk when you get home. Has Mr. Warner made a move to sell the house?"

"No, he said he would deal with that once the store was

sold," Ike said. "It looks just like it did when they left. He pays the Garcias to care for everything. They must have started afresh out East. All the furniture and things are still here, just like before they moved."

"Sometimes it feels a little strange," Eli added.

Jubil rode to the Warner's house, and the Garcias were pleasantly surprised to see him. Mr. Garcia praised his new horse and took Apollo to the stable for some pampering, while Mrs. Garcia did essentially the same for Jubil, helping ready his room and asking what he would like for supper. He had a few hours before the boys would be back, so he went to Mr. Warner's office to collect his thoughts. As soon as he stepped into the room, he was moved by how much he missed him, and of course Luke. The lingering aroma of cigar smoke brought to mind the many meetings they had held in this room.

When Mr. Warner had mentioned rebuilding the store in Bloomington, Jubil had been noncommittal, at the time mired in grief over losing Luke. The grief was still there, but he no longer felt so bogged down by it. Luke would want him to go on, to do some of the things they had planned together. While he had been recuperating in Bozeman, he had formed an idea. Now that he was here and could feel the presence of the Warners around him, he knew his idea was a good one—he could feel it in his heart. He would need to have his proposal ready by tomorrow, or he might miss his chance.

Sitting at Mr. Warner's desk, working on his proposal and looking out at the magnificent view, he felt another wave of appreciation for the Warners and this unique and wonderful place. He had been having moments of appreciation like this, sometimes over the smallest things, ever since he had woken up in the bed at the Guy House Hotel.

After supper—during which Jubil regaled the boys and Mr. and Mrs. Garcia with tales of the Yellowstone expedition— Jubil, Ike, and Eli retired to Mr. Warner's office to talk.

"Have you boys been making plans," Jubil asked, "for what to do when Mr. Warner closes the store?"

"We've talked some about it," Eli said, "but we're waiting to see what you do before we decide—at least I am."

"I am too," Ike added, with somewhat less commitment.

"I've got to be honest with you," Jubil said, "after Luke died, I was reluctant to rebuild the store. I relied on Luke so much, I wasn't sure I could do it without him. Ike, you know more about some parts of running the business than I do."

"That may be," Ike agreed.

"Since then, I've decided that I do want to own and operate an outfitting business," Jubil said, "but what I truly want is for our partnership to continue—you boys and me, and the Warners too. I want us to have as much as possible of what we once did. We can't bring Luke back, but his spirit can still keep us all together."

"I don't have to think about that for one second," Eli said. "You can count on me for whatever needs to be done."

Ike studied Jubil for a moment before he replied. "I can agree, generally speaking," he said cautiously. "But what exactly are we talking about doing? Rebuilding the store in Bloomington or building one out in Montana?"

Jubil laughed. This was exactly what Luke would have asked. He held up the notes he had been preparing. "I have an idea I'd like to go over with you."

The boys were excited by Jubil's idea, and they dove into the work of turning it into a plan. Jubil could see Ike was destined to be a successful businessman, with or without him, and he felt a gratitude for him akin to what he had felt for Luke. Eli's strength and adventurous spirit would be as important in the execution of the plan.

"One thing," Ike said, raising his index finger for emphasis. "Eli and I would like your word that we'll have some chance to travel as well. After all, you're not the only one with a taste for adventure."

Jubil laughed. "You have my word."

Mr. Warner arrived on the train the following morning, and Jubil went to fetch him from the station. His heart warmed at the look of surprise and joy on Mr. Warner's face when he spotted Jubil there in the surrey.

"We were so relieved to hear you are all right," Mr. Warner said. "I believe Lily would have completely lost hope if we had lost you too."

He said that Mrs. Warner was doing considerably better than when Jubil had last seen her. The change of scenery and being closer to her family had done wonders.

"She speaks of you often," Mr. Warner said. "She would love to see you."

"I'm looking forward to visiting you on Nantucket," Jubil said. "I've never seen the ocean."

After breakfast, Jubil and the boys presented their plan to Mr. Warner.

"We want to have a store, and I want to lead adventure tours," Jubil said to him, "just like Luke and I had planned, but we don't think Bloomington is the best place to do that."

"You're going to move to the Montana Territory?" Mr. Warner asked.

"No sir, we want to do it right here in Council Bluffs," Jubil said. "I'd like to buy you out of Warner and Company Outfitters, upgrade the store's presentation and offer the more stylish yet rugged products that Luke made so popular in Bloomington. It would be a whole new store. We would reopen it as Warner and Walker Outfitters. The boys have agreed to stay on and run it with me. But there is a catch: You can't retire completely. We need you as our advisor. I'll run back and forth to Nantucket, send you letters and reports, and burn up the telegraph lines staying in touch. But we need your help. We want to do this, but only if we can all do it together."

Mr. Warner studied the three of them. He reached into his jacket, removed his handkerchief, took off his glasses, and dabbed his eyes.

"I've got a buyer coming today who is going to be sorely disappointed," Mr. Warner said with a sad smile, "but if you're sure this is what you want, then the store is yours—and you don't have to buy it from me."

"We'll figure out the finances," Jubil said, "but I plan to sell the lot in Bloomington, and put that money into remodeling here."

Mr. Warner stayed for three days, helping Jubil and the boys refine their plans and order new merchandise. When Mr. Warner left Council Bluffs, Jubil rode the train with him as far as Chicago, then went on to Bloomington. The boys had welcomed Jubil's offer to explain the plan to their parents, and he was relieved at how positively the Boswells received the news. He had an emotional reunion with Star and apologized for what he was about to put her through—she would be riding the train with him back to Council Bluffs. He knew she would be very happy once the trip was behind her.

Jubil easily sold the parcel on which the store had once sat, and he made arrangements for the money to be transferred to a Council Bluffs bank. The proceeds were enough to cover the costs of starting up the new store, so he did not draw down any of the inheritance from his parents. He and Star rode up to have a look at the farm before returning to Council Bluffs. He decided not to sell it. He did not need the money, and his heart was just not ready to let it go.

Not long after Ike and Eli's nineteenth birthday in mid-October, the remodeled store in Council Bluffs was ready for its grand opening. It was an immediate success. Just as the case had been in Bloomington, there was nothing in town quite like it. The population of Council Bluffs was slightly smaller than Bloomington's, but its status as a key waypoint along the transcontinental railroad meant a considerably higher number of travelers passed through. The biggest challenge they faced was keeping adequate inventory in stock to meet the demand, but Ike had learned Luke's methods of tracking sales and estimating future needs. When a terrible fire in Chicago burned up a sizable portion of the city, disrupting some of their suppliers, Mr. Warner helped find other sources to fill in. Business was booming, and the ever-affable Eli was consistently their top salesman.

In early December, Jubil received a letter from Walter Trumbull, who reported that he was now living in Washington and had found a post serving under Senator Pomeroy of Kansas, as clerk for the Committee on Public Lands, of which Pomeroy was the chairman. Mr. Langford and Mr. Hayden had both come to Washington to campaign for designating Yellowstone a national park, and their combined efforts had led to the drafting of a bill that Representative Clagett of Montana would soon introduce to the House of Representatives. Congressmen would be given some time to read and amend the bill before it was brought to a vote, and Walter encouraged Jubil to come to Washington to join in the efforts of lobbying for passage. Jubil felt very drawn to Walter's proposal, but he could not leave Ike and Eli in the new store at Christmas. He wrote back explaining his situation to Walter, asking that he keep him closely informed of progress on the bill.

In mid-December, a telegram from Mr. Warner brought an unexpected surprise: he and Mrs. Warner had decided to come to Council Bluffs for Christmas. Ike and Eli were too busy with the new store to return to Bloomington for Christmas, and invited their parents to join them in Council Bluffs, but their father had declined. Jubil felt badly for Mrs. Boswell.

Jubil was pleased to see Mrs. Warner in better health, and in far better spirits, than when he had last seen her. She lit up when she saw the house full of happy people and beautiful holiday decorations that Ike had put up. On Christmas Eve, as Jubil was preparing to go down for supper, the Warners came to his room.

"Do you mind if Lily and I have a word with you?" Mr. Warner asked.

They sat in the armchairs by the window, and Jubil sat on the edge of the bed.

"As you know," Mrs. Warner began, "when we lost Sam so many years ago, I did not handle that loss well. If it had not been for Abe and Luke, I would have given up living. As Luke grew older, he never showed any interest in leaving home. We worried for him, but he insisted he was happy living with us and working in the store. Then one day you came along, hoping to find a party of adventurers you were determined to join. Luke took inspiration from your determination and drive to not let grief consume your life. When he moved to Bloomington to start a business with you, we were very proud and happy for him. He found great joy in making gear that would help you during your adventures and from vicariously sharing those adventures, and he took great pride in being your friend. In a way, you saved his life. Without you, he might have labored here faithfully with us forever, denying his own needs. We're grateful for all you did for Luke."

Jubil struggled momentarily with the feeling that came over him sometimes, that it was his own antagonism of Phineas Black that had caused Luke's death. But he would not let that feeling stop him from embracing the Warners as his family.

"Thank you," he said. "Luke was the brother I never had."

"In that spirit," Mr. Warner said, "Lily and I have a proposition for you. I am in much the same situation as you—I too have no other immediately family—other than Lily. We feel you are the brother that Luke found again. He was the primary beneficiary to our estate, and with your agreement, we'd like that to be you now."

Jubil couldn't form a coherent thought in response to this proposal.

"We aren't asking you to consider us a replacement for your parents," Mrs. Warner said, "but we don't think they would mind if we consider you our son now, under the circumstances. We are sure Luke would not. He would be thrilled."

Jubil forced himself to speak. "I'm sure my parents would be proud that you find me worthy of the proposal." He rose and embraced them both.

"Excellent," Mr. Warner said, "Now, one more thing: I think it's time you call us something other than Mr. and Mrs. Warner."

Jubil smiled. "Well, I sure can't call you Pa and Ma. I hope you don't mind my saying so, but I always thought that was a bit rustic for people of your station."

The Warners chuckled and looked at each other knowingly.

"Years ago, when I first started Warner and Company," Mr. Warner explained, "I was a plow horse, but Lily was a thoroughbred. I had always called my parents 'Pa' and 'Ma,' which Lily found more endearing than 'Father' and 'Mother,' which is what she called her parents. She taught our boys to call us 'Pa' and 'Ma,' and then over the years our 'station,' as you call it, improved. By that time, it would have felt awkward to change—so Ma and Pa it was.

"We do have Christian names," he continued. "To friends and family, we are Abe and Lily. Do you think you could manage that?"

"It will take some getting used to," Jubil admitted lightheartedly.

"We have plenty of time, I hope," Mrs. Warner said.

Jubil agreed. "Yes ma'am. Yes . . . Lily."

Mrs. Warner smiled.

CHAPTER 17

Jubil sat in Mr. Warner's office gazing out the window at the panorama, reflecting on his new circumstances. By New Year's Eve, Mr. Warner's attorney had updated their estate plan and reviewed it with Jubil and the Warners before asking for their signatures. It was an eye-opener for Jubil. What impressed him beyond their net worth, and it was an impressive number, was the complexity of their holdings—cash, real estate, stocks, bonds, business investments, partnerships, and loans. He was inheriting not only the wealth, but the responsibility of managing it, and he had a lot to learn. He would not make the same mistake he had made with Luke, allowing himself to ignore business operations because Luke was there to handle it.

The Warners had decided to keep the house in Council Bluffs as a second home and return for visits regularly. Jubil, Ike, and Eli would live there, and the Garcias would continue to operate it. In addition to beginning a review with Mr. Warner of each of his business investments, Jubil had begun a project with him of identifying and documenting each of his treasures. Mrs. Warner had begun painting again and always left her studio in whatever state her projects were in at the time. She was thrilled when Ike asked her if she would tutor him.

The Warners had returned to Nantucket the day after New Year's Day, and insisted that Jubil come visit as soon as he was ready. It was now mid-January, and he thought the boys would be fine running the store without him for a while.

"Mail call!" Ike said, walking into the office carrying an envelope. "Looks like it's from your friend Walter Trumbull."

"Thanks," Jubil said. He opened the letter and read aloud to Ike.

Dear Jubil,

I have been spending quite a bit of time working on passage of the Yellowstone bill. Senator Pomeroy of Kansas has introduced a bill in the Senate similar to the one Montana's Delegate Clagett introduced last month in the House.

As expected, there's dissention over the government infringing on the public domain for this purpose, but Senator Pomeroy believes that is a minority opinion. The senator hopes to bring the bill to a vote in the Senate later this month. I believe it would be most helpful if . . .

Jubil stopped reading aloud. He chewed his bottom lip and then looked up. "He says Langford and Hayden are there lobbying, and he thinks it would be helpful if I would come too. What would you think about that?"

"Yes," Ike said, without hesitation. "I definitely think you should go."

"You don't mind," Jubil said, "if I run off and leave you and Eli to manage the store?"

Ike looked askance at Jubil. "No offense, Jubil, but that's what you always do."

"I'm trying to do better," Jubil said, with mock seriousness.

"Luke always said your greatest contribution to the store's success was getting out of town and letting us run it," Ike said with an impish grin.

Jubil shook his head and gave Ike that round.

Two days later he set off for Washington. After attending to his business there, he would go on to see Nelly and the Warners.

A few inches of snow made Washington more attractive, covering the barren capitol grounds with a white blanket and softening the hard edges of the granite buildings.

Walter came to meet him in the dining room at the National Hotel, where Jubil was just finishing lunch.

"It's very good to see you, Jubil," Walter said as they shook hands. "Welcome to Washington. We have a busy schedule."

"It's good to see you too, Walter," Jubil said. "It's exciting that the park idea may soon become a reality. How can I help?"

"You're going to make the rounds with me of congressmen's offices, favorite watering holes, and preferred dining establishments," Walter explained. "You're going to tell them about the wonders of Yellowstone and what a travesty it would be to allow it to be despoiled. They're going to listen to you because you were there with Washburn in '70 and Hayden in '71. No one else can say that but Lieutenant Doane, and he can't help lobby—he's busy soldiering."

Walter left a copy of the bill with Jubil so he could familiarize himself with it before their meetings. It was not a lengthy document, but he felt it defined with precision what he and the members of the Washburn expedition had hoped to accomplish. The park was to be *dedicated and set apart as a public park or pleasuring ground for the benefit and enjoyment of the people*; it emphasized the *preservation from injury or spoilation of all timber, mineral deposits, natural curiosities or wonders within said park and for retention in their natural condition*; and it provided against the *wanton destruction of the fish and game* and against *their capture or destruction for the purpose of merchandise or profit.*

Walter said that no such law had ever been enacted by the US Congress, and Jubil was proud to have had a hand in it.

Over the next several days, Jubil talked more than he could ever recall having done in his life. He didn't mind, but he did tire of telling the same stories and making the same arguments over and over again. Walter, on the other hand, loved politics. It was apparent that he never tired of the game. Watching him work, Jubil gained a new admiration for him.

Jubil had mixed emotions about attending Jay Cooke's Yellowstone exhibition. He understood the benefit of bringing visitors to the park, but was concerned the railroad might despoil it in the process. The Northern Pacific Railroad had sponsored an elaborate display in the Capitol that included William Henry Jackson's photographs, Thomas Moran's watercolors, odd and beautiful geological specimens, and copies of Langford's articles and Doane's journal for every congressman. Walter led Jubil around the exhibition hall, introducing him to congressmen and delivering a quick sales pitch.

"This fellow wants to meet you," Walter said, leading Jubil by the elbow toward a tall thin man in a dark suit and tie. "It's John Carter, Jay Cooke's aide."

Carter thanked Jubil for his contributions to the Yellowstone park campaign and for coming to support the exhibition. "Mr. Cooke has asked me to extend an invitation to visit him at his home in Philadelphia," Carter said.

"I'm flattered," Jubil said without fully meaning it. He was not entirely surprised by the invitation. Langford and Cooke worked closely together, and Jubil assumed it must have been Langford who had mentioned him.

"Your Yellowstone experiences are of great interest to him, and he's aware of your plans for adventure tourism and interested in discussing them with you. You can reach Mr. Cooke's secretary at this address, at your convenience," Carter said, handing Jubil a card.

"My thanks to Mr. Cooke," Jubil said, putting the card into his pocket. "It may be a while before I have the chance to visit, as I've just recently opened a new store, but I appreciate the invitation."

"How about that?" Walter said, nudging Jubil after Carter had joined another group.

"I need to think it over," Jubil said. "I haven't decided whether Cooke is the Yellowstone's hero or villain."

"Well, if you want to guarantee the success of your adventure tourism business," Walter said with a grin, "you couldn't do better than to have Cooke for a partner." He hooked his thumb toward the exit. "Come on," he said. "That's enough of this place. I'm ready for a drink before we meet my father for supper."

Jubil gladly followed Walter out of the Capitol to the National Hotel restaurant, where they met Senator Trumbull and his fellow Republican from Illinois, Senator John Logan. When Walter mentioned Jubil's invitation from Jay Cooke, Jubil learned that in the senators' opinion, Cooke's railroad was in for a hard time. Following Jubil's return last fall, the survey team had in fact reached Fort Ellis and had gone on during the winter to extend the survey along the Yellowstone and into Sioux territory. The survey had ended badly, with the team stranded and nearly starving in four feet of snow. Though the Indians had not attacked, they were ever-present. Senator Trumbull was concerned that the consolidation of Indian resistance under Sitting Bull promised to unite the Sioux on an unprecedented scale.

As the senators spoke, Jubil arrived at something of an epiphany. As concerned as he was about the railroad despoiling Yellowstone, without it, not enough people would reach the new national park to ensure that the government would properly protect it. But the completion of the railroad might bring on an apocalyptic Indian war. He recalled General Sherman having said that if the Indians ever consolidated their resistance, it would leave the army no alternative but all-out war.

As concerned as he was about these issues, they felt far beyond his influence.

By the end of the month, Senator Pomeroy felt he had adequate support to bring the bill to the floor for a vote. Walter, as a correspondent for the *Helena Herald*, had access to the press gallery behind the Senate presiding officer's desk, so he and Jubil enjoyed the best possible seats for the event.

After the morning invocation and some other business, the Vice President read the Yellowstone bill and reported an amendment suggested by the Committee on Public Lands. The amendment added language specifying that any person locating upon any part of the protected area would be considered a trespasser, and would be removed.

"Mr. McCartney at the hot springs, and Mr. Baronett at his bridge, won't like this provision," Jubil whispered to Walter.

"But it's the right thing to do," Walter replied. Jubil nodded in agreement.

The Vice President opened the floor for debate. Senator Anthony from Rhode Island suggested that provisions for the destruction of fish or game "for gain or profit" be stricken, and made to read "for any purpose." Senator Pomeroy explained the intent was to allow parties to fish or hunt for their own subsistence, and pointed out that the Interior Department would make the final rules and should be trusted to administer the intent vigilantly.

The most forceful challenge came from Senator Cole of California, who was adamantly opposed to the government being in the park business or setting aside an asset from private use. Senator Trumbull, Walter's father, reminded the senator from California that his own state had the predecessor bill to this one, The Yosemite Grant of 1864, which Cole had supported. Then he pointedly explained the main difference—the Yellowstone bill was written to avoid the legal mess still making its way to the US Supreme Court because of the poorly drafted Yosemite bill and its resultant issues. Walter beamed at his father's deft rebuttal. Senator Trumbull's comments dampened further debate, and the Vice President asked to have the bill read one final time. A rollcall vote was taken, and it passed.

Jubil was excited by this victory and inclined to celebrate, but Walter pointed out that the job was not finished until the bill was also passed by the House of Representatives. After a few more days of lobbying, Jubil and Walter watched from the press gallery of the House as Representative Dawes of Massachusetts brought the bill to the floor. Jubil recalled Dawes's son Chester—Hayden's assistant, who he had met when Mr. Stevenson had taken him out on the little boat—the *Anna*—on Yellowstone Lake. Representative Dawes, as chairman of the powerful Ways and Means Committee, had been responsible for funding Hayden's survey and was a strong supporter of the bill. Just as in the Senate, there was some debate around the same familiar points, but Dawes skillfully rebutted each argument. When the bill finally came to a vote, it passed.

Jubil felt a sense of pride and accomplishment. Being part of the expedition had allowed him to have a hand in doing something of historical importance, and of great value to people everywhere.

"We've done it," Walter said, as he offered Jubil a handshake. "I believe we can be really proud of this. I don't think we could have pulled it off without your help."

"Thanks, Walter," Jubil said, "I think that's an exaggeration, but I'm surely proud to have played a part. Thank you for encouraging me to come to Washington."

That evening Jubil and Walter celebrated the victory with drinks and supper. The only step remaining was for President Grant to sign the bill into law, which Walter was entirely confident he would do within the next few days. Then Walter went on to explain the next political challenge, which Jubil had not even imagined existed: funding.

"Even when we have a law that says Yellowstone is a protected park, there is no money set aside to actually protect it?" Jubil asked.

"Correct," Walter agreed. "The appropriations process is another battle for another day. I'll be taking that one up next. Care to join me?"

"Sorry, Walter," Jubil said, "I have a family business to run back home."

"I understand," Walter said with a laugh. "We'll get the job done. This was the hard part. I'm sorry we didn't have much time to discuss your interest in Indian affairs and the Agency system."

"Yes, me too," Jubil said, "but there are only so many hours in a day. I'll write you again when I get home. Maybe I'll come visit again this spring."

The next day, Jubil stopped by to visit General Sherman, who congratulated him on the success of the Yellowstone bill but pointed out that, as he had predicted, its passage would increase the army's workload, since Congress had yet to appropriate any funding for the new park's protection. Jubil promised him he would ask Walter to see that oversight corrected.

By early afternoon he was on the train to Poughkeepsie. The deep blanket of snow covering the trees, houses, and streets had turned the town into a picture-book scene and silenced the hooves, wheels, and voices downtown. Jubil had telegraphed ahead, so he knew Nelly would be expecting him. Rather than deal with handling a horse and wagon, he hired a coachman to deliver him to Miss Mitchell's house and pick him up again later that evening.

He knocked on the front door, and Nelly answered. She stood looking at him for a moment then threw her arms around him.

"I am so glad you didn't get yourself killed out there," Nelly said, lightly pounding his back with her fist as she hugged him.

He held her with his eyes closed, wondering how long it had been since they had embraced this way. He must have hugged her at Luke's funeral, but he couldn't recall much of that strange day. It didn't matter, they were here now, and it felt wonderful.

"I am too," Jubil said. "I didn't exactly invite this close call though."

"I know. Come in," Nelly said, stepping back inside, "it's cold out here."

As Jubil entered the house, Miss LeVault came out of the kitchen and waved hello. Nelly led Jubil into the parlor, where a fire in the fireplace had the room cozy. They sat down across from each other, each on a velvet sofa.

"You're even prettier than I remembered," Jubil said.

"This conversation is off to a very good start," Nelly laughed. Then her expression became serious. "Does it trouble you, what happened in Bozeman?" she asked.

"No," he said. "Black was responsible for the fire that killed Luke, and he and Murphy drew on us first."

"White Dog, how did he know you were in danger?" Nelly said.

Jubil shook his head. He had wondered the same thing himself. "I don't know."

Nelly peppered him with questions about recent events. She was proud of him for his contribution to the passage of the Yellowstone bill, happy for the success he and her brothers were having with their new store, and congratulatory about his new relationship with the Warners.

"You figure in this too, you know," he said.

Nelly looked perplexed. "How so?"

"You've always been my sole beneficiary, since the first time I left home to go West. And you still are. If anything happens to me, what I own is yours."

Nelly shook her head.

"That's enough about me," Jubil said. "Will I be able to attend your graduation this spring? And your last letter didn't mention any definite plans after that. Any news?"

"Miss Mitchell has been so generous in her support," Nelly said. "Unfortunately, *The Revolution*, where I worked this summer, is suffering financial problems and will soon close, but Mr. Pillsbury, the editor, said he would recommend me heartily. Mr. Porter at *Scientific American* magazine encouraged me to contact him after I have decided which literary path I want to take."

"That sounds marvelous," Jubil said. "But I'm not sure I know exactly what you mean about your literary path."

"Well, there is a difference between the creative side and the business side," Nelly explained. "Whether I want to write the material, or work for a company that edits and publishes it. Once I know that, I need to choose between newspapers, magazines, and novels."

"That seems daunting," Jubil said, "and exciting."

Nelly nodded. "I have a confession to make," she said. "I may have to try more than one, to find out which suits me best, or to see if I'm able to do some of both."

"That makes sense," Jubil said. "How is that a confession?"

Nelly let out a slow breath. "I had the idea I would come to Vassar and find my path, and leave here sure of what I want to do. And I will, to a degree. But in a way, it's only revealed more doors that were never there before, and that has made things less simple. I thought I might be ready to settle down into a career after graduation, but now I don't think that's true. I see a lot of things I need to try and places I want to go before I decide to stay on one path or in one place . . . if I ever do."

There it is, he thought. She was easing into telling him that she would never marry—not him, not anyone. He had thought about this possibility for countless hours and come to the conclusion, over and over again, that he could not blame Nelly for refusing him if she didn't think she could be happy with him. He wanted her to be happy, even more than he wanted to marry her. It was no longer impossible to imagine being apart from her; in fact, he had become accustomed to it. Their past relationship was gone. And yet, for the first time, he did not feel crushed by that idea.

"It's all right, Nelly," Jubil said. "I'm very proud of what you're doing. I understand the need to follow your heart."

Nelly drew her eyebrows down for a moment. "Have you . . ." She looked at her lap. "Have you met someone else?"

Jubil couldn't tell if his answer would make her happy or sad. He shook his head. "I love you, Nelly. If I have to learn to love you in a sisterly way, I'll try to do that."

He tried to read Nelly's expression as she resettled herself on the sofa. He shrugged and said, "You and your family will always be a central part of my life."

"Yes, of course," Nelly said firmly. "And I suppose I could manage to love you in a brotherly way, but that would not be my preference."

Jubil felt like he had been struck by lightning. Had he heard her correctly? He stared across the space between them into her crystal blue eyes, which, if he wasn't mistaken, were aglow with passion. His impulse was to kiss her, but, as if she had read his mind, she held up her hand in a gesture that told him to stay put.

"I have a proposal for you," she said carefully.

"A proposal?" he echoed hopefully.

"I came here to find something beyond marriage and homemaking, and I've found it. As I've said, I have to follow my interests now, but I'm not sure where they will lead. I don't feel I can ask you to follow me, any more than I can follow you. And yet, I love you and long to be with you."

"Yes, I know that feeling well," he said wryly.

"How would you feel about being married," she said slowly, "but not always living together in the same place?"

"But truly married . . . and faithful to one another?" he asked, just to be sure.

"Certainly!" she said with a laugh. "The East has not liberalized me that much."

"Where do you plan to live?" he asked.

"That's part of my dilemma," she admitted. "There are opportunities at newspapers and magazines in Philadelphia, New York, and Chicago. And later, if my efforts as an author are successful, I might live almost anywhere. I also want to see the world—and I may even want to work in London or Paris for a time. I would not ask or trust anyone else to accept these selfish terms, but I feel as if you and I truly understand each other . . . and I don't want anyone else . . . I want you."

Jubil stared at her in wonderment.

"What do you think?" Nelly said finally. "Could you tolerate it if I had an apartment somewhere? You would come and live with me however often you could, and I would do the same, and we could travel together, and . . ." Nelly trailed off, her eyes searching his face.

In all of the hundreds of hours Jubil had spent longing for them to be together, it had never once occurred to him to make a proposal such as the one she had just made. But Nelly had always been the clever one.

"You are a piece of work, Nelly Boswell," Jubil said, smiling.

"Does that mean that you'll marry me, even under such unusual terms?" she asked.

"Yes . . . yes, I will," he said. "I accept your unusual terms—wholeheartedly."

They met in the middle of the parlor for a passionate kiss.

Then Nelly broke away from their embrace. "Wait right here," she said.

She left the room and returned with two glasses of wine,

one of which she handed to Jubil. She raised her glass and said, "Here's to following our hearts, wherever they may lead."

His heart soaring, Jubil tapped her glass with his.

ACKNOWLEDGEMENTS

I would like to thank my editor, Heidi Bell, for her patient coaching and insightful comments as she helped me shape the story, and Regina McCaughey-Silvia for her meticulous proofreading. Any shortcomings in the finished product are mine alone.

My daughter Lori Kaufman served as beta reader number one, and my unflagging moral support. My patient friend, Rich Teegarden, provided comments on early drafts, and suggested the expeditions would be easier follow with a map. His suggestion turned into a set of maps that his talented son, Jon Teegarden, created to grace the book. My deepest thanks go out to all of my friends and family who took the time to read and comment on the book.

For readers interested in a historical account of the expeditions described in the book, I recommend the following works: *Empire of Shadows* by George Black; *Yellowstone and the Great West: Journals, Letters, and Images from the 1871 Hayden Expedition* Edited by Marlene Deahl Merrill; *Yellowstone National Park: Through the Lens of Time* by Bradley J. Boner;

Lieutenant Doane's report: *Doane, Gustavus C., Lt. U.S. Army (February 1871). The report of Lieutenant Gustavus C. Doane upon the so-called Yellowstone Expedition of 1870 (Report). U.S. Secretary of War.*

ABOUT THE AUTHOR

Tim Piper retired from a career in information technology, and has been a lifelong hobbyist musician. He lives in Bloomington, Illinois. This is the second novel in the *Jubilee Walker* series. Book three in the series, *The Northern Pacific Railroad,* will be released early next year.

www.ingramcontent.com/pod-product-compliance
Lightning Source LLC
Chambersburg PA
CBHW070442300726

48975CB00007B/2005